Order your copy of any of Jihad's books at a 30% discount
at jihadwrites.com And family, please post a review on
amazon.com and e-mail Jihad at jihadwrites@bellsouth.net

AUTOGRAPH PAGE

· To be used exclusively to recognize that special King or
Queen for their support.

Envisions
PUBLISHING COMPANY

Envisions Publishing, LLC P.O. Box 83008
Conyers, GA 30013

ISBN: 978-0-9706102-7-0

First Printing October 2012
Printed in the United States of America

10 9 8 7 6 5 4 3 2 1

Submit Wholesale Orders to: Envisions Publishing, LLC
Envisions07@sbcglobal.net P.O. Box 83008
Attn: Shipping Department, Conyers, GA. 30013

Envisions
PUBLISHING COMPANY

APPRECIATION PAGE

There are so many wonderful Kings and Queens that helped make *WORLD WAR GANGSTER* a reality, and I may miss a few but please family, chalk it up to my tired and exhausted mind.

First and foremost I wanna thank the creator, without your inspiration and your spirit I would've given up long ago. Good looking out G.

I wrote this book for people who are tired of the Trayvon Martin's, Melissa Alexander's, Sean Bell's, Michael Bell's, Malice Greens, Mumia Abu Jamals, Mutulu Shakurs, Troy Davis's and all the non-violent drug offenders rotting away behind America's prison walls. Kings and Queens behind the walls of prisons around America, thank you for supporting me over the past 11 books. This is my coup de grace, the most important fiction book you will ever read. Thanks again to all the Kings and Queens behind bars.

Very special thanks to King Eugene Smith (Voorhees College) Queen Kizmet Knox, King Tommy Knox, (((King Marcus Wayne Hunter))) Queen Nigeria Hunter, King I-Keitz Garey, Queen La-Shl Frazier, Queen Reshonda Tate Billingsley, Queen Victoria Christopher Murray, Queen Ebony Gibson,. King Maurice Gant. King Hakim (Black & Nobel Books) King Max, King Maurice Gant and Prince Zion Uhuru, King Dr. Akinyele Umoja, Queen Dr.

Osizwe Raena Jamila Harwell, Queen Dr. Sarita Davis, King Dr. Mukungu Akinyele, and my mother Queen Arthine Frazier.

I wanna thank all the wonderful fans and bookclub members that have continued to support me on my writing journey. Queen Alisha Yvonne Monae Eddins, Queen Loray Calhoun and the Women of Distinction bookclub in Columbus, Ohio, thank you so much for pushing all of my work so hard. Queen Monique Smith and the Queens of Dialogue Divas bookclub Atlanta, Lisa Johnson and the Queens of Sisters on the Reading Edge bookclub Oakland, Queen Gloria Withers and Queen Janene Holland of Chapter 21 bookclub Philadelphia, Queen T.C. at R.A.W. Sistahs, Queen Kanika and K.O.M. bookclub Atlanta, Queen Lenda and Mo' betta views bookclub Atlanta, Queen Dr. Wright and the queens of Sisters in the Spirit 2 bookclub, Queen Tiffany
and the Queens of Distinguished Ladies and Gents bookclub Memphis, Queen Wanda Fields, Queen Alethea Hardin and the Queens of Shared Thoughts bookclub New Jersey, Queen Ella Curry of EDC creations, Queen Ellen and the Queens of Reading is What We Do bookclub Newport News, The Queens and Kings of Sugar and Spice book club, NYC, I know I've missed several Book clubs so please ad your name here.

Thanks to my family for their continued support, my son Prince Zion Uhuru, Mom, Queen Arthine Frazier, Brother King Andre Frazier, Brother King Michael Wharton and family, Sisters Queen Las-Shl Frazier, and Queen Karen Wharton, Nieces, Gu-Queitz, Luscious, Sadqua, Shami, Baby, Lameeka, and Ronni, Nephews, I-Keitz, D'Andre, and Billy.

SUPERFANS

Queen Ann Joiner of Norfolk thank you. Queen Kariymah of Philly thank you. Queen Tazzy Fletcher thank you. Queen Iliene Butler, New York thank you. Queen Martha and the queens of IPS transportation Indianapolis.

THEY SAY BLACK MEN DON'T READ. FOR ALL THE KINGS ON THE INSIDE AND OUTSIDE KEEP PROVING THAT MYTH WRONG. AND DON'T WORRY I WILL ALWAYS WRITE WITH YOU IN MY KING. I'LL ALWAYS REPRESENT.

And I'd like to give a very special thanks to President Barack Obama. If a man with the name of Barack Hussein Obama can get past the hate so can a man with the name Jihad Shaheed Uhuru.

Please log onto www.jihadwrites.com to find more about Jihad or to purchase any of his books 30% less than the store price, and if you purchase 3 books anytime on www.jihadwrites.com you get the 4th book absolutely FREE. Please tell others what you think by posting a review on www.amazon.com. Log on to www.jihadwrites.com to sign Jihad's guestbook.

Love and Life

Jihad Uhuru

Also By Jihad

Fiction
STREET LIFE
BABY GIRL
RHYTHM & BLUES
MVP
LOVE SEX & REVENGE
PREACHERMAN BLUES
WILD CHERRY
PREACHERMAN BLUES II
MVP **RELOADED**
WORLD WAR GANGSTER

Self Help
THE SURVIVAL BIBLE: 16 Life Lessons for Young
Black Men

Anthologies
Gigolos Get Lonely Too
The Soul of a Man

Please pick up any of Jihad's books at your local bookstore or you can save 30% and order Jihad's books from the secured site at jihadwrites.com If you purchase 3 books the 4th is absolutely free. Please allow 5 to 7 days for shipping.

WORLD WAR GANGSTER is dedicated to Trayvon Martin, a young king that lost his life for walking while Black.

WORLD WAR GANGSTER is dedicated Marissa Alexander, a black queen who was sentenced to 20 years in prison for shooting a warning gunshot in the air in an attempt to try to scare her attacker away.

WORLD WAR GANGSTER is dedicated to all the political prisoners being warehoused in Americas prisons.

WORLD WAR GANGSTER is dedicated to all the non-violent crack cocaine drug offenders being warehoused in American federal prison cages.

WORLD WAR
GANGSTER

WORLD WAR GANGSTER is as real as reality gets. What you are about to read is fiction but it is also very real. It's time for a book that tells the truth and provides the answer about the condition of black, Hispanic and poor peoples that are oppressed, depressed, and repressed by the illegal-legal system of government in America. I don't know about you family but something is wrong with a nation that makes up less than five percent of the worlds population, yet makes up over 25 percent of the world prison population, and the majority of America's prisoners are black, yet blacks make up less than 13% of just the American population. Now either black folks are everything the media says we are or there is a systemic problem as it regards to race in America. After you have read WORLD WAR GANGSTER I hope you see why we need a NEW constitution written by people that represent true freedom, unlike the current American Constitution that was written by 37 slave holders. You may say, well there has been amendments to the constitution. There has, but they are like putting a band aid on cancer. The problem is still there behind the colorful amended words. NO MORE MARCHING without results. We must demand change and stop asking and just marching for change. We march, the cameras go off and we go home. NO MORE. We must become WORLD WAR GANGSTERS if we ever hope to be truly FREE.

WORLD WAR GANGSTER

BOOK 1

"I don't have no fear of death. My only fear is coming back reincarnated."

-Tupac Shakur

TUPAC SHAKUR: THE PLAN:
SEPTEMBER 7, 1996

"Fam, you good?" Picasso asked.

"Hell, nah, I ain't good." Tupac walked out onto the private balcony. The Vegas lights seemed to dim as the sun began to wake up. Unlike the sun's light, its heat never slept in Vegas, especially in the summer months. This was evident by the beads of sweat forming in the worry creases of the young rap phenom's forehead.

Not ten feet away, sitting cross-legged in the suite's leather recliner, the forty-something Black-Cuban appeared to not have a worry in the world. He took a sip from the can of orange juice before uncrossing his legs and rising from his seat. "God, I been where you at. The true OG up top, tells us to fear no evil as we walk through the valley of death, and that's all good. But my lack of fear ain't gon' stop the shadow of evil from making money zombies out of our people."

The veins in Tupac's arms looked like tree branches under his skin as he gripped the patio balcony's stainless steel rails. He overlooked Sin City and as daylight peaked through the early morning darkness he said, "Fear ain't in my DNA, fam. You know that P. I knew this day would come. Just didn't expect it to be today."

"I know, none of us know when it's time until it's time," Picasso said. "At least you've been broadcasting your upcoming death to your fans through your music."

"Come on, P," Tupac said. "You already know they ain't payin' attention to the lyrics, unless I'm talkin' about layin' niggas out, gettin' money, or fuckin' bitches, and you know I only used that shit to draw 'em in. Folks just can't see the real shit I'm sayin'."

Picasso chimed in, "Maybe," he paused, "just maybe your death will make 'em open they eyes. Maybe once you're gone, our people will listen to your words for a minute instead of just bobbing their heads to the beat."

"Come on P, you know niggas are about self." Tupac spoke in a melancholy tone while still looking over the 38th floor hotel balcony.

"True dat, true dat," Picasso nodded. "But still, it's biblical, god," Picasso said, relaxing in the almond colored leather chair. "The messenger is slayed but the message lives on. But in this case, god, the messenger is gon' do the slaying."

"I hope so, fam." Tupac said. Niggas out here wil'in' and profilin', killin' over colors and money, when all they do is recycle that shit right back to the mind-rapin' mu'fuckas who control the economy. I thought this rap shit was gon' get niggas to readin' and believing, so they can be achievin' the self-mastery of getting' back to bein' kings and queens."

"It's comin', god. Just not now. The CIA, FBI, NSA, all the government's alphabet boys got an X on your head. Tonight it's definitely going down, god. Just like the feds did Malcolm, sent one of us in to pull the trigger. Just like they plan to do to you, god, just like we knew they'd do. It's time. We gon' make you bigger than life after your death."

"Then what?"

"The presidency," Picasso said. A devious smile plastered on his face.

"What's that mean?"

"Reagan and Bush have sent the nation in a downward economic spiral that is affecting over eighty-five percent of the population. We predict that within the next twelve to fifteen years, America will be thrown into a depression."

"How you figure?" Pac asked.

"America's crack like addiction to oil and world domination. Greed'll cause the nation to implode."

"And when that happens?"

"We'll have our man ready."

"What man is that? And what will he do?"

"Have you ever heard of Barack Obama?"

"No." Tupac shook his head. "Should I have?"

"No, not yet. But you will."

"Straight up?"

"No chaser, baby boy," Picasso said. "Barack Obama is the truth. Even before we began grooming him, we knew he was the answer."

"So, where he at now? Congress? The Senate?"

"Neither." Picasso shook his head. "He's teaching Constitutional Law at the University of Chicago."

"Come on P," Tupac said. "You talkin' about the presidency and playa ain't even in politics?"

"Oh, he's in politics. He just don't have a title." Picasso nodded. "And we workin' on changing that as we speak, god."

"I can't see it fam. A black president, come on now, you doin' to much."

"Never that, god. If anything we ain't doing enough. But trust and believe, we'll be doing way more when the economy is on the verge of collapse." He pointed a finger in Tupac's direction. "That's when we'll pull out all stops, spare no expense. Barak Obama will be president, you'll see."

13

"I hear you, fam. But tell me this. How you figure Caesar gon' allow a slave to rule?" Tupac asked.

"He's not," Picasso said before paraphrasing Karl Marx. "The oppressed are allowed once every few years to decide which particular representatives of the oppressing class are to represent and repress them. The US President is only a figurehead. But we need that figurehead for the next phase in the poor people's revolution."

Pac was well read, but Picasso knew he wouldn't be able to envision a black president of the US.

Tupac was quiet as he continued holding onto the balcony rail looking up at the sky. "I just can't see it. A black president?"

"Pac, the conditions in America will get so bad that the real powers that be will go on a terrorist mission, bombing oil rich countries in the name of democracy, attempting to take control of their governments, robbing them of their oil, then jacking up the prices. The world will eventually get fed up with America, and to buy time, the real powers that be will have no choice but to allow a representative from the most oppressed class to be elected to the highest office in the land, making the world think that America is really serious about spreading true democracy and not just interested in facilitating their acts of global terrorism," Picasso said.

Tupac's attention seemed to be somewhere else. But then he said, "I'm hearing everything you sayin' and it all sounds good, but right now I can't rap my mind around your vision, fam. I mean, I'm about to be ghost and I can't help but worry about my queen; how Kidada gon' handle my death and my moms, and what about my soldiers—"

"What about 'em?" Picasso asked. "I ain't gon' sit up here and tell you this shit gets easier over time. I know it hurts, but Pac, I use the memories of my sister Rhythm, my dude Moses, and my other peeps to fuel my passion for freedom.

14

Remember, god, freedom ain't never been free. It comes with a price that most ain't willin' to pay."

"Fuck it." Tupac turned from the balcony and walked back inside the suite.

Picasso extended his arm.

Tupac wrapped his hand around the golden muscled forearm of his secret mentor. "One Free."

"For life," Picasso said, pointing to the tattoo on Tupac's midsection.

The adjoining suite's doorknob silently turned.

Picasso put a finger to his lips, pushed Tupac to the side and pulled out his cannon.

Tupac did the same.

A man wearing an oversized black hoodie and some too-big matching Levi's walked into the suite. Tupac could hardly believe his eyes as he stared at the man. It was like looking into a mirror.

Tupac's trigger finger relaxed as did his gun arm, but his eyes were fixed on the man in front of him. "This mu' fucka' is me."

"Four surgeries over two years. Strict diet and exercise," the man said.

"What the fuck?" Tupac's face twisted up.

"A voice synthesizer and ten hour days for nine months," the hooded man said.

Picasso replied, "Eight years ago when I was killed, they didn't have no voice shit to make a god sound like me."

Tupac pointed his gun at the hooded man. "That nigga is me down to the tats and the small scar on my elbow." Tupac turned to Picasso. "I got that from falling on a broken bottle when I was eight."

"It's all good, fam. I got mine in a lab filled with mad genius black scientists."

"Yo," Tupac looked over at Picasso, "get the fuck outta here. Playboy sounds just like me. He got my rhythm and my flow down."

"He's supposed to. Everything's riding on us pulling this off, god. Only way Caesar can fall is if we outsmart him at his own game," Picasso explained.

"So, yo," Tupac addressed his look alike. "So, how can you... You ain't got no family?"

"Six years ago, November 8th 1990, your country bombed a school in Baghdad. My girls, Khadija and Kamari were only seven." The man trembled with rage. "Two hundred eighty-seven children. Two hundred eighty-seven." He closed his eyes. "I still hear the screams. I still smell human flesh burning. Innocent children burned to death. For what?" The man shook his head from side to side. "For what?" He paused hoping to get his emotions under control. Head down and in a calmer tone he continued, "And the US has the nerve to use the word terrorist when speaking of others who don't bow down to their economic interests." The look alike raised his head and opened his eyes. "So, yes I have a family. And I am joining them tonight in the heavens, Inshallah." He pointed to Picasso and Tupac. "I believe in what the Truth Commission is doing. I believe in the will of Allah, and I believe that there is no greater cause than to die for justice. So, I shall leave you two here in hell to fight against evil and its minions. I ask but one favor."

Picasso and Tupac nodded for the man to continue.

"Get the truth out. Let the world know what America is and what they have done."

"No doubt." Tupac balled up a fist and gave the man a pound. "On everything, fam, you got that."

Picasso stepped forward. "Fellas, here's the plan." He looked from one to the other. "As soon as the fight is over, Tupac you'll go back to Tyson's dressing room and either console or congratulate him. Let the cameras see you tonight. After you leave Tyson's dressing room, one of your entourage will get word to you that," Picasso pulled two folded eight-by-ten photos from his jeans' front pocket and handed them to the two men, "this man will be at the Grand Garden of the MGM."

The men examined the picture.

"Orlando Anderson, Southside Crips," Tupac said, recognizing the man in the gang photo.

"Once you get word, Tupac, you dash off, leaving your entourage in the hall of the MGM Grand. Right before you get to the Grand Garden, you will see a Men's restroom on your right. There will be a large yellow cleaning cart in front of the door. Run inside and – "

"I run out and proceed to the Garden to confront Mr. Anderson," the look alike interrupted.

"I'll help you into the cart and roll you out while," Picasso turned his attention to the look alike, "he's causing a scene in the Grand Garden."

*****

"We interrupt this program for this late breaking news report," the anchor's voice on Channel 11 filled the room. "We want to go straight to Wayne Hunter, reporting live from the outside of the University of Nevada Medical Center. Wayne, what's going on?"

"For six days, Tupac Shakur has been fighting for his life after suffering multiple gunshot wounds in Las Vegas." A picture of Tupac took over the television screen. "Less than an hour ago, Tupac Shakur suffered respiratory failure and went into cardiopulmonary arrest. At 4:03 pm, today September 13, 1996 Tupac Amaru Shakur was pronounced dead."

VERSE 1

Eleven Years Later

"A toast," the drug kingpin rose from his seat and looked around the club's VIP area at the thirty-something faces of his entourage, "to capitalism, the American-motha-fuckin'-dream."

Black Escobar's right hand man, Little Percy, stood up and lifted his glass, "To capitalism, and to the man we owe all our shit to," he looked at his boss, "Black Esco-"

"Sit down, li'l nigga," the three-hundred-plus pound Escobar said. "As I was saying before I was so rudely inter-motha-fuckin-rupted, this year was a good year. In two weeks we will enter into 2008," he paused, "an even greater year." He lifted his glass and waited about five seconds for the others to follow. "Tonight, the Cris and the Moscato will flow like a mighty river."

All fourteen of Escobar's street generals stood up wide-eyed as several baby-oil-shiny naked, beautiful women ascended the stairs. The charcoal colored kingpin continued. "A fleet of stallions. Young stunnas for my soldiers, all paid for. Now, let's get this pussy party crunk."

On cue, UGK's "International Players Anthem" blasted from the nightclub's high tech sound system. Escobar waved a couple naked stallions over.

While light-skinned and white-skinned slowly sauntered over to where the two men stood, Escobar said, "Before the pleasure starts, one more item of business. Find out where Bo Jack gon' be on Christmas. That li'l rappin' nigga gon' sign with us one way or anotha."

"Hi, Big Daddy," the tall hour glass shaped sistah said as she stepped up to Escobar. "Is all of this ours?" she asked using a long red fingernail to trace a circle around Escobar's massive mid section.

Escobar looked from the tall Halle Berry-looking, Queen Latifah-shaped woman to the barely five foot J-Lo shaped snow bunny beside her. "You two think you can handle three hundred and eighty seven pounds of—" Escobar's eyes were transfixed on the two women coming up the stainless steel V.I.P. stairs. "Damn!!!!"

Talking about freezing time. Hustlas and hos stopped to gawk as the two six foot Hershey's dark chocolate twins made it over to Escobar's table.

"Be gone bitches," one of the twins said.

The sista' behind Escobar dropped his fifty thousand dollar fur on the black concrete floor and stepped around in front of her benefactor. Naked as a jaybird, hands on her hips standing eye level to the woman that addressed her and her home girl, "Bitch, who the fuck you calling a bitch?"

The twin punched the sista' in the jaw. "Pop!"

"Got damn," Li'l Percy exclaimed, covering his mouth with one hand. "You put that bitch to sleep with one blow," Li'l Percy said, looking at the sista' lying on the black and white checkerboard VIP floor.

"There's about to be an encore performance," the twin turned her attention to the other female cowering beside Escobar, "if this white bitch don't get her girlfriend and get the fuck up outta my space."

"Yo' space?" Escobar spoke for the first time.

"Did I stutter, nigga?" Before he could speak, the twin continued. "Be careful. Anything you say can and will be used against you when I wrap this tight, wet, black pussy around that dick."

The white girl helped her groggy friend to her feet and they both scurried away. Violence being the norm instead of the exception in the underground world of strippers, hookers, and hustlers, the players and hos in the VIP returned to their carnal activities as if nothing had transpired.

Escobar began unbuttoning the world's largest pair of sagging Red Monkey jeans. "Bitch, you got a lotta' mothafuckin' mouth."

Slowly and carefully enunciating every syllable of every word, the twin said, "You think you got something thick enough to stop up this big mouth?" She licked her thick catcher's-mitt lips.

"Do a pig eat slop?" Escobar asked while unzipping his pants.

The other twin, the soft spoken one, spoke for the first time. "It ain't goin' down in public, big daddy. The heaven you

20

gon' experience tonight is only for you." She stepped forward, grabbed Escobar's huge meaty hand and starting at her neck line, ran his hands between the creases of her 36Ds, down her flat stomach and into her thong, where her skin was as smooth as a newborn baby's ass.

"Fuck all 'at," Escobar said, grabbing the woman's shoulders and roughly spinning her around to face the thick glass table filled with bottles of Cris and wine glasses. "This my party." Pants on the ground, he pulled out his short tree trunk, charcoal colored throbbing dick. "I paid for all you bitches and I'm 'bout to put work in."

Before the half naked kingpin could act, with cat-like quickness, the woman dropped to her knees and slid beneath his legs. She was behind him before he could turn around.

"Your money ain't long enough to pay for this big daddy." The other twin spoke as the huge kingpin waddled around to face the two Amazon chocolate twins.

"If you two bitches don't take off that shiny red lingerie shit."

One of the twins pulled out a rubber-banded, rolled up bankroll from her thong. "Big daddy, this is five stacks. Now I know you wipe your ass with small change like this, but it's a lot of money to me and my sister." She tossed the wad in the air. Li'l Percy caught it and gave it to his boss.

"What the fuck?" Escobar asked, not noticing his dick withering under his mountainous mid-section.

"Spend the night with the two of us and if we don't take you to heaven, make you cum a river, if our pussies and our lips are not the best thing you have ever had or imagined, the money is yours. But if you scared that two six-foot, one hundred eighty pound twins will turn your big ass out, then we understand."

"Scared?" Escobar looked at the women and then at his right hand man. In a couple octaves higher than his usual baritone voice, Escobar asked, "Li'l nigga, who these bitches?"

Li'l Percy shrugged. "I don't know, Esco, but hot damn, I wanna shot at the title. Shawty talkin' bout' takin' a nigga to heaven while a nigga still breathin'."

"Sweetie," one of the twins said, "we'd hurt your little ass."

"Hurt me. Please, I need some pain in my life, fuck." Li'l Percy turned to his boss. "Esco, what you gon' do, my nigga?"

The big man bent down and pulled his pants up. "What the fuck you think? I'm gon' break all nine inches of Moby off into both theses slick mouthed bitches."

"What about all this?" Li'l Percy asked, looking at the carnal scene around him.

Escobar extended his arm in the direction of the huge orgy. "Li'l nigga, look at every bitch in this mothafucka." He paused. "You lookin'?"

It was like a modern day urban Caligula. The scene was almost as freaky as one of the massive orgies thrown by the biblical King James.

"Yeah, you did your thing Esco, these stallions are puttin' in work."

"Now, look at these two slick mouth pretty mothafuckas."

"Okay." Li'l Percy turned to face the smiling beauties in front of him.

"Must I say any mothafuckin' more?" Escobar asked.

"Hell, nah. Ain't a ho' in this bitch that can touch these pretty mu'fuckas," Li'l Percy said.

"We know," the twins said in unison.

"Grab a couple hos, li'l nigga, so we can bounce."

"Uh, I was hoping you'd let me go a round with them after you finished, Esco."

"After I finish, ain't gon' be nothing left."

"I bet the nothing you gon' leave behind tastes better than everything up in this piece." Li'l Percy licked his dark, weed stained lips.

Maybe I'll put these bitches on Bo Jack, Escobar thought. But then, he changed his mind. *Nah, that li'l nigga gotta learn some respect 'fore I give him shit.*

Thinking about Bo Jack was pissing the kingpin off. He had offered that high-school nigga the keys to his kingdom, offering the rapper a deal with his record company Plead the Fifth.

But Bo Jack had turned him down and spit on his offer. Sure, Escobar had set it up so that Bo Jack would earn much less than the standard artist royalty rate, but where else was the li'l nigga gon' go? Penny-anny nickel and dime bag crack hustlin' li'l nigga.

Escobar pushed those thoughts out of his mind as he made his way from the building. He wasn't going to waste too much time thinking about Bo Jack when he had these two thoroughbred bitches in front of him. No, his thoughts were going to be all on pussy tonight. Tomorrow, he'd deal with Bo Jack.

He'll sign on with Plead the Fifth records by Christmas or it'll be his last.

VERSE 2

While most people were sleep, or getting ready for Sunday school and church, Li'l Percy was daydreaming about the previous night and his half of the twin sex superstars while cruising down Peachtree, past Lenox Mall. The sun was shining, and there wasn't a cloud in the sky. It was a lovely day. It was a rare occasion to get snow in the ATL in December, and this year was no different. The only white Christmas Atlanta residents usually witnessed were the ones they saw on TV.

Behind him, his boss sounded like a fleet of freight trains snoring in the backseat of the bullet-proof Navigator. While turning the radio even louder to block out his boss's snoring, he glanced at the outside temperature reading on the tricked out SUV's computer. Fifty-seven degrees. Last night at the Ritz Carlton, in room 1373, the temperature was hovering around hell.

Percy turned left at the light and smiled at more memories of last night. His face had been buried between the chocolate thighs of one of the twins for so long, he had lockjaw. By the time he came up for air, his tongue was so numb he couldn't speak for a good fifteen minutes.

"We fall down, but we get up," Li'l Percy sang along with the radio. "For a saint is just a sinner–"

"If you don't turn that shit down and shut up with all that blessed shit." Escobar's hands went to his forehead as he stirred from his slumber. "What time is it?"

"Almost seven-thirty."

"Fuck!" Escobar grumbled before laying back down sideways on the reclined backseats of the large SUV. "That fine-ass gymnastic mothafucka need to run a marathon before she fuck anyone. Bitch broke my damn dick, bouncin' up and down on my shit."

"Who you tellin', Esco? Mines was gooder than a mu'fucka, but them hos got to be shootin' steroids in they pussy or something. Ain't nobody got that much energy." Li'l Percy pulled into the long driveway of a large, ranch-style, older, white brick home, with black shutters. After pulling up to the garage, he turned to check out Escobar in the back. That fast, once again, his boss was sound asleep. *Good,* Lil' Percy thought as he put the truck in park, jumped out, went to the alarm pad outside the garage, and put in the code manually.

Afterward, he strolled back to the car. "Esco, wake up. We here."

Slowly, Escobar used the back of his hand to wipe the sleep from his eyes. After Li'l Percy opened the back door for his boss, Escobar asked, "Why we all the way out here?"

"Cause, this where you live."

Escobar looked down at Li'l Percy. "Don't make me fuck your li'l smart ass up." Escobar got out of the truck and walked around the other three cars in the garage. "Why didn't your dumb ass go to the high-rise? We was right around the corner at the Ritz."

"I don't know." Li'l Percy shrugged his shoulders. "I guess I thought you wanted to come home."

"Nigga, that's my home, too," Esco shook his head as he walked into the house through the garage's kitchen door. "I got to be the dumbest nigga alive for payin' a dirt-dumb, happy meal sized mothafucka to watch my back."

"That ain't why you the dumbest nigga alive," a familiar voice echoed from the living room.

Escobar pulled a glock .40 from his inside coat pocket and slid a kitchen drawer open and took out the glock's twin. Escobar waved for Li'l Percy to get in front of him.

Seconds later, a man met the two men in the hallway that separated the den from the kitchen.

"Bo Jack!" Escobar pushed Li'l Percy to the side. "Nigga, what the fuck... P, you see this shit. Nigga got his dick beaters on my Charles Bibb original, leaning his narrow ass on my painting."

"I was nappin' since I done smoked up all the cush I could find in this piece."

"What the...Nigga, how did you....?" Escobar turned to Li'l Percy. "Shoot this mothafucka. No wait!" Escobar pointed one of the glock's at the intruder's knee. "I got this one, P."

CLICK.

CLICK.

CLICK.

Nothing happened!

Escobar held up the other gun and did the same.

CLICK.

CLICK.

CLICK.

He dropped the guns, turned and grabbed Percy by his shoulder and pulled the little man in front. "Shoot that motha–"

"Calm down before your big ass has a heart attack. No one is going to shoot me, at least not this morning," the young man said as he walked back into the den.

Escobar was just about to snatch Li'l Percy's glock when another familiar voice exploded, "Put your hands down slowly, turn around, and keep walking, fat boy."

"Ain't this a bitch!" Escobar shook his head, recognizing the voice right away. He didn't have to see the woman. He'd heard her voice all last night. "Set up by two funky bitches."

"Clown, you and your little boyfriend are the only bitches in here." One of the twins walked right up on Escobar. "Now, shut the fuck up and keep it moving."

Escobar hesitated until the other twin nudged him forward with two silenced .25 magnums pressed into his back. He followed Bo Jack into the den, a huge, windowless, theatre room. The screen took up one entire wall and the other walls were painted black. There was a black leather couch and six expensive looking matching leather recliners facing the screen.

"I tell you what, young nigga," Escobar began once they stopped moving, "I'm gon' give you a pass this one time. You obviously have lost your mind coming up in my spot, thinkin' you 'bout to rob me."

Bo Jack strolled over to Escobar. He looked like a child up against a giant, as he was physically half the man Escobar was. Not in height, but in size. Bo Jack stood at five ten, like Escobar, only he weighed around one seventy.

Bo Jack took a half pack of swisher sweets out of his black jeans pocket and dropped it at Escobar's feet. "Take your pass, roll it up in a blunt and smoke it out your ass, playa. And, playa," Bo Jack raised his long slender arms in the air and arched his back to stretch. Seconds later, his arms were relaxed back at his side. Bo Jack continued, "I ain't thinkin' about robbing you."

Escobar mean mugged Bo Jack, looking him up and down. "So why the fuck you here?"

"I already robbed you."

"You just said–"

"I said I wasn't *thinking* about robbing you. Already thought about it, planned it," he held up one of Escobar's garage remotes, "got Percy in on the deal, and paid the twins very well to do their part and now," the teenager shrugged, "here we are playa."

Escobar looked over at Li'l Percy with a mixture of hurt and rage in his eyes before turning his attention back to the kid who was supposed to be his ticket into the music game.

"See, while you were plottin' on doin' some fucked up shit to me if I didn't sign, I was plottin' on takin' your money and your dope so I could put my own CD out, maybe even start my own record label. You see, the way I figure, even swap ain't no swindle."

"Nigga, ain't nothin' even about you tryin' to take my shit," Escobar barked.

"My girls here gave you my five stacks. They fucked your fat ugly ass and that pint sized Percy. You of all people know pussy ain't free, playa! I mean, what the fuck did you think? You a fat, sloppy, crispy-burnt black ugly mothafucka." Bo Jack held a hand out to the twins pointing the silenced handguns at Escobar. "Look at them. My girls ain't no crack bitches. They straight dimes. Come to think of it, I can't believe your big dumb-ass didn't question their motives for fucking with you and your mini-me flunky."

"Nigga," Escobar looked at Bo Jack from head to toe and then from toe to head. "Fuck you."

"You tried that already with that weak ass deal. Now it's my turn," Bo Jack said. "Now before you cut me off I was explaining some shit to you. Now where was I." He put a hand under his chin. "Oh, yeah, I had to pay the twins to make sure you and Percy were gone long enough for me to hit your downtown condo, and then come here and do the same. Working by myself, cleaning up the mess and my fingerprints took a while. And then I had to pay Percy for the alarm remote and the garage door opener, which I had to get from Keisha last night at the Ritz."

He looked at Li'l Percy with pure hate in his eyes. "If it's the last thing I do I'm gon' gut your pussy licking wife and them three ugly ass kids that probably ain't even yours. I swear to God," Escobar spoke through clenched teeth.

Li'l Percy took a step back.

Escobar turned his neck to one of the twins, "And you whore, I shoulda' known!" He shook his head at one of the twins. "I shoulda' known somethin' was up when your skank ass came back to the room with an empty ice bucket last night. So, the li'l bitch ass nigga Percy gave you my remotes and your skank ass left the room to give my shit to your pimp."

"I'm my own pimp, trick." Keisha blew a kiss at Escobar.

He turned to Bo Jack. "Do you really think you gon' get away with this shit?"

"I'm here, ain't I?"

"I guess you expect me to just give you my shit?" the big man asked.

"Nigga, is you deaf? Didn't I just told your fat ass, I been workin' my ass off all night to relieve you of your shit –

18 kilos of coke, $2300 in cash, and a wall safe that I gotta get busted the fuck open."

"If you got what you came here for, why you still here?"

"I didn't quite get everything I came for, I just told you that you have something I want."

"Do what you gotta do, I ain't givin' up the combination to my safe."

"That's not why I'm still here." No one, not even Escobar, saw the hunting knife until Bo Jack was twisting the eight-inch blade into the fat man's belly.

Escobar's eyes bulged.

"Now, I have everything I came for."

His mouth opened but words didn't form.

"Your first mistake was trusting a snake ass nigga like Percy, and the biggest one was tryin' to muscle me into signing with you. But no worries, you'll have eternity to regret plotting on a real nigga."

Escobar dropped to his knees. A pool of blood darkened his white T-shirt.

Bo Jack turned his attention to the female assassins. "Ladies."

Keisha walked in front of the fallen Escobar while the other walked up behind the kneeling man.

Poof! Poof!

Keisha shot the big man in the groin while the other shot Escobar in the back of the head.

Li'l Percy knew that his fate was sealed. "Please, my nigga, don't kill me." Li'l Percy slipped to the floor. "Please don't kill me. If it wasn't for me...please!"

"Percy, don't worry, playa. I'm not gon' kill you," Bo Jack said. "I wouldn't bite the hand that fed me."

Percy stumbled back up to his feet. With relief in his voice, he said, "I didn't like that fat bastard any damn way.

Fuck him." Percy hawked and spat on the man he'd worked for, for over ten years.

"That was some nasty shit." Bo Jack paused. "Ladies," Bo Jack called out. Both women raised their guns.

"You just said you weren't going to kill me," the little man cried.

"I'm not."

"God bless you. Thank you. Thank you."

"They are."

"Why?" the little man cried.

"You sold your man out for thirty stacks and some pussy. You don't deserve to share my air."

"But, but, I can help you get to Tarzan, that's who Esco—

Poof! Poof!

One of the twins shot him in the head. The little man crumbled to the floor.

Bo Jack glanced down at the two bodies before he said, "Let's roll, ladies. I got work to do and you two have a flight to catch."

Stepping over Lil Percy first, then Escobar, the three marched out, leaving the carnage behind.

VERSE 3

Atlanta was divided into several police crime zones. Zone 5 had the highest crime rate and the highest poverty rate of any section in the city. Most of the project housing apartments in Atlanta had been demolished, but inside the parameters of Zone 5, there were four project housing complexes, all located within a square mile of each other. Grant Park Village, Four Seasons, Inglewood, and the largest one, Thomasville Heights. There were nine liquor stores within that square mile. And although the police station located in Zone 5 was extremely undermanned, the cops seemed to always know what was going on in the projects.

Over the last three years, the Zone 5 officers were some of the most decorated officers in the city – largely due to one man. John 'Tarzan' O'Reilly was a linebacker-sized drug task force officer that looked like a young Hulk Hogan with a crew cut. Tarzan was known for busting heads and getting results, not necessarily in that order.

A few years ago, his fellow officers started jokingly calling him Tarzan, because he was oft times the only white face inside Zone 5. John thought of himself as Tarzan because he saw himself as the king of the concrete jungle – the sophisticate among the savages.

Last year in 2007, O'Reilly was responsible for over five million dollars in confiscated drug money and assets. Because of that, along with his outstanding arrest and conviction record, civilian complaints of brutality by O'Reilly rarely made it past the Zone 5 precinct and the few that did were overlooked.

But now it was a new year, and he vowed to unleash a new kind of hell on Zone 5. Someone had robbed and murdered Tarzan's number one informant. Black Escobar left this world owing Tarzan a hundred thousand from the six kilos of cocaine that Tarzan didn't turn in from a bust four weeks ago.

It was the first week of January. The skies were clear, and the sun was shining on everyone out in the cold except the five teenage, small time dealers that Tarzan had hemmed up on the red brick liquor store back wall.

"None of you are under arrest," Tarzan said as he paced back and forth past the wall in back of the 500 Liquor Store. "At any time, any of you homos can run."

No one moved. No one dared turn around.

"For the life of me, I cannot figure out why you punk bitches wear your trousers under your ass. You make my job way too easy." He paced back and forth, hands behind his back. "Would anyone care to tell me why you project monkeys buy and wear pants so friggin' big? You can't even run from me if you wanted to. Tell you what, I'll turn my back and count to five." He turned. "1... 2.............3. 4. 5." He turned back around and shouted, "Cowards! All of you." He started going in the young men's coats and pants pockets. "Now who can tell me why you're on my wall?" He continued putting the young men's dope trap money in his pockets.

"Why you fuckin' wit' us Tarzan?" one of the teenage boys said. "Dis some certified bullshit, man."

"I haven't even begun to fuck with you, Herbert."

The teenager sucked his teeth. "You know my name Thug," the young man said, his hands still on the wall.

Tarzan walked up, took the black Atlanta Braves baseball cap off the kids head, and dropped it on the ground before slapping the back of the kid's balled head.

The kid dropped his arms and rubbed the back of his stinging head. "Man–

"Hands back on the wall," Tarzan barked louder and more forceful than a military commander. "Turn around again, I dare you."

A tear of anger and helplessness trickled down the young man's face as he turned back to face the graffiti on the colorful brick wall.

"Thug? Maybe that's your screen name on Fuckbook or Cryspace, but from now on your name is Bitch, my bitch and you will answer to me whenever I call. Now I'll ask again," Tarzan continued his methodic pacing on the needle, glass, gravel, concrete ground. "Who knows why you are hemmed up on my wall?" Tarzan stopped and stood behind the biggest of the five boys, Herbert 'Thug' Davis. "Okay, don't every dumb fuck speak at once." He continued pacing back and forth in the forty-degree brisk January weather. "As you know, three weeks

34

ago, Carlton Webb was murdered." His voice took a softer tone, "Oh, I'm sorry, you dummies knew him as Black Escobar. Until I find out who was responsible, I am going to terrorize you every friggin', fucking day." Tarzan walked up to the back of the young man who spoke out earlier. "Bitch, tell me who killed Carlton."

When the young man didn't answer, Tarzan slapped the cuffs on the boy's wrists. "Come on Bitch, let's take a ride. I need my dick sucked and I," he slapped the back of the boy's bald head again, "choose you."

"Dude, you got me twisted. I ain't no punk," the boy said while being led to the black Dodge Charger police cruiser.

"We'll see about that soon enough." Tarzan puckered and made a loud kissing sound.

The others waited until Tarzan was pulling out of the back of the liquor store before they scattered in different directions. They all knew too well that Tarzan would often circle back around, and no one wanted to be the next bitch.

Forty-five minutes later, Tarzan drove onto a dirt road before pulling up to an old abandoned looking warehouse. "Do you know where you're at?" he asked his backseat prisoner.

The boy remained quiet.

"This is hell and I'm Satan." Tarzan pulled up to a loading dock, put the cruiser in park, got out and a minute later, dragged the young man out of the car, then threw him on the ground.

"Man, what I do to you?" the young man cried.

"For starters, you were born into my world, and your whore mammy didn't ask for my permission. Now, if you wanna keep drawing my air, you will tell me who offed Carlton."

The young man looked up from the gravel and dirt. "Man, I 'on't know who did ole boy. And if I did, I ain't no snitch."

Tarzan put a boot on the kid's neck, took out a small camera, set it to video, before unzipping his pants and pulling out his shriveled pink penis. He held the camera at a downward angle as far from his body as he could. "Who killed Carlton?" Tarzan asked again.

The young man quietly and defiantly stared right into the blue eyes of his Satan. "Ahhh, what the fuck, man." The kid turned his head as his face and hair were drenched with a steady stream of urine.

"What will everyone think when I upload this to Fagtube, Fuckbook, and Cryspace? Piss coming from a white man's dick onto your face. But, of course, if you tell me what I wanna know–"

"Man, I done told you–"

Tarzan kicked the kid in the shoulder.

"Fuck!" he screamed.

"I think your boss had something to do with Carlton's demise. A few weeks ago Bitch Jack Jones was a small time wannabe rapper, stick up kid, and now he's moving weight through the hood. So, Bitch, I'm giving you one last chance before I go to the car and upload our little home movie to my laptop." Tarzan smiled. "Of course I'm going to edit out my uniform. I can't wait till you see the finished product."

"Swear to God, I don't know nothin'," the young man cried out in desperation and disgust.

"Tell you what, tell me everything you know from A to Z about Mr. Jones and I'll give you my camera."

Ten minutes later, Tarzan still didn't know who the triggerman was, but he had no doubt that Bo Jack Jones knew something. There was no way a nineteen-year-old high school kid was moving the amount of product that Bo Jack was. And who would be dumb enough to put that much product in a kid's hand?

Not long after that, Tarzan pulled up to his backseat prisoner's home. After opening the back door, Tarzan said, "Get your pissy ass out of my car."

After removing the cuffs, the boy asked, "What about the camera?"

Tarzan pulled the camera out of the shirt pocket right below his badge. After removing the SD card, he handed the camera to the young man, "A deal is a deal."

"Come on Tarzan, what I want the camera for? That shit you did is on the SD card."

"Sue me," Tarzan said while getting back into the car. At least he had a name thanks to Herbert.

Sitting in front of the apartment Herbert shared with his mother and sisters, Tarzan pulled up the people search website on his personal laptop, put in his username and password and typed in the name Johnetta Jones. Under state he typed in Georgia and under city he typed in Atlanta. "Bingo," he said aloud. There were four Johnetta Jones's in Atlanta. Two were under twenty-five and one was seventy-five. The only one that could've been Bo Jack's mother lived at 1761 Honeycreek Drive, Conyers, Georgia 30014.

Of course he could have gotten whatever he wanted from the NCIC police and FBI database, but then there would be a record of his inquiry. And because of paper trails, he'd seen and heard about cops getting lynched by the system they swore to protect. Tarzan had always been careful. He'd never been under investigation or formally written up for dereliction of duty. He didn't drink or smoke. His mind was always clear, except for when he was lifting, sticking and licking. Steroids and young black pussy were his only weaknesses.

VERSE 4

Courtesy of Bo Jack, his baby brother, Brandon was upstairs munching on some flaming hot Cheetos, watching a bootleg version of the upcoming summer Batman movie *Dark Knight*. The upstairs TV was so loud the kid never heard the doorbell, the knocking or the back door being jimmied open. By the time Tarzan had the kid's arms and legs tied behind his back, then dumped into the upstairs tub, he heard a car pulling into the carport. After haphazardly slapping a strip of silver duct tape over the kid's mouth, he ran down the stairs, out the back door, and through the woods next door, then, back up to the street to the house he'd just left.

Johnetta Jones was removing grocery bags from the trunk of a new Silver Chrysler 300 when Tarzan walked down the driveway.

"Ma'am, excuse me."

Johnetta turned, a bit startled. "Yes, officer, can I help you?"

Tarzan couldn't believe how beautiful the dark-skinned woman was. She looked to be in her early thirties, way older than the teenie boppers he was used to. She couldn't have been bigger than a size six.

I bet she has some tight pussy, and if she doesn't, I bet that bootyhole is tight.

"Officer, can I help you," Johnetta repeated.

"Can we talk inside?"

Johnetta Jones was no dummy. The Atlanta police officer was out of his jurisdiction on foot in middle class suburbia by himself, no cruiser in sight. Something wasn't right.

"No, my boyfriend is asleep on the couch. We can talk out here."

"I'm afraid it's about Beauregard." Tarzan dropped his head and sighed. "I have some bad news. Ms. Jones."

All of a sudden her demeanor changed from one of confidence to one of worry. "What happened? Is Bo in trouble? Is he hurt?"

Tarzan shook his head from left to right before sucking his bottom lip in.

"What happened?" she asked again, her voice filled with worry.

"I really think we should go inside."

She dropped her guard and allowed Tarzan to usher her into the house, his arm around her shoulders. As they walked the few steps from the carport to the side kitchen door, Tarzan felt his nature rising. He couldn't help it. Young black pussy was his addiction. And the woman beside him had three of the four qualities he desired. Black, beautiful, and female.

After she closed the kitchen door, she turned around. Before she could act, Tarzan grabbed the small woman by her arms and lifted her off the ground.

"Your son...." was all he got out before he dropped her back to the floor and grabbed the side of his face.

Johnetta's fist had cracked a tooth in his mouth.

"Bitch," he shouted while diving for the fleeing woman. He caught ahold of one of her long, copper and black braids yanking her down to the gray-carpeted dining room floor.

She screamed as she fought until the two hundred-sixty pound man had all of his weight on top of her. He stared down to where her dress had ripped during their battle and watched her chest heave up and down.

Even though he was in the middle of a fight, his thoughts turned to all the things he wanted to do to this woman right now. *There's no way she could've breast-fed,* he thought as he stared at the perfectly round grapefruits. A mouthful. Not too big, not too small.

"Get off of me," she shouted, bringing his thoughts right back to their battle.

"Momma," her little boy called out from upstairs.

The sound of her son's voice made her pause from her struggle, but only for a moment. "Brandon," she screamed as she squirmed to get out of Tarzan's grasp. "I swear to God, if you hurt my baby."

"He'll be okay as long as you cooperate. All I wanna know is where Bo Jack lives?"

"You think I'm gon' tell your crooked ass where my baby lives, so you can plant drugs on him and lock him up?"

"Too late, I've already planted enough drugs in this house to send you away for three lifetimes," Tarzan lied.

"What do you want?" she spat.

"I just told you."

She glared at him.

He said, "Well, maybe we can work something else out." He pinned one of her arms beneath his leg and then ran his fingers gently down the side of her face. "Yeah," he grinned. "There might be another way to satisfy me." His eyes

41

went from her breasts to her flat stomach and down to her midnight-dark, silky-smooth thighs.

Johnetta had dealt with so many Tarzans in her lifetime. Most of them black, unlike the man on top of her. But each time she gave up her womanly nectar, she was either high or about to get high. Crack had been her master for over five years and she would do whatever she had to do to get her daily fix. She was one of the lucky ones, though. The drugs hadn't destroyed her looks like it had done to so many. But crack had ruined every other part of her life. She'd lost her children when Child Services had tracked them down and taken them away. She'd spent as many years getting clean as she had doing drugs.

But even though she'd worked hard and had gotten her children back, she was still filled with guilt. She hadn't been there for them, and they'd been put into the system because of her.

She'd hurt them before. She wasn't going to do anything to hurt either one of her sons now. Tarzan would never get anything out of her, no matter what he planned to do.

There was no fear in her eyes when she looked up at him. What was there to fear? Johnetta Jones had seen ten lifetimes of hell in her thirty-two years. She'd been abandoned by her mother when she was a toddler, then, she'd given birth to Bo Jack, her oldest when she was just a child herself. So, how was she supposed to be a mother when she had no example?

Because of that, her oldest son never had a childhood. Bo Jack had always watched out for his crack-addicted mother and his little brother, always hustling to make sure they ate and the lights didn't get cut off, since electricity was the only bill that welfare didn't pay in the projects. But no matter what Bo Jack did, he couldn't stop the authorities from coming and taking him and Brandon away. Once they were gone, she hadn't expected to ever have a good relationship with her children again, especially not Bo Jack since he'd been in and out of juvenile detention centers the entire time they were away from her. But surprisingly, their time apart brought her and her oldest closer. And Bo Jack had been as thrilled as Brandon when two years ago, they'd all been reunited.

But even though Bo Jack was glad to be back with his mother, he had changed. How could he not? He was grown now, hardened by the streets and the vampire-like boss hustlers who ruled them. He was a man, no longer her child, and they treated each other like adults. Johnetta was Bo Jack's best friend, confidant, and priest, confessing everything to her. He told her all that was going on in his life, every crime that he had committed. She listened, asked questions, commented, but she never judged.

Of course, she was still his mother, though neither one of them knew how to play out that relationship. The only thing she could do as his mother was love him unconditionally. And Bo Jack gave her back that same kind of love.

Since they'd been brought back together, though, Bo Jack had never rested his head on any pillow where his mother and brother slept, even though it was his money that moved them into a small, two story house in the Atlanta suburb of Conyers, forty-five minutes away from Zone 5.

Tears filled Johnetta's eyes as Tarzan ripped away what was left of her dress. But she squeezed her eyes closed, praying that Brandon wouldn't come downstairs to see what was being done to her.

As if he read her mind, Tarzan leaned over and breathed into her ear. "Don't worry about him disturbing us. Your son is a bit tied-up right now."

His words and his laughter made the tears spill from her eyes. And even though he was violating her in the worst way, it wasn't this act that was going to get him killed. No, she'd been through this before. The reason she was going to make Tarzan pay was because of what he'd done to her ten-year-old son. He had her baby tied up like some rodeo farm animal or so he had said. That was why she was going to tell Bo Jack what was happening at this very moment.

She had no doubt what her nineteen-year-old would do. And she wouldn't blame him... not one bit.

VERSE 5

"That's a wrap," the engineer spoke into the mike while looking at the future of rap music standing behind the glass.

Bo Jack wore a genuine presidential smile on his face as he took off the headphones and strolled out of the small soundproof booth.

"My dude," G-Swag, the hottest engineer in the business rushed over to Bo Jack. "You smashed that shit. Yo, that's the hottest, realest word play I done heard since Pac."

Bo Jack shrugged as he stuffed his hands deep into his sagging baggie jeans pockets. "It was a'ight."

"A'ight? My dude," the engineer shot Bo Jack a sideways look, "humility is a good quality to have, but not in this business. You the shit, my dude. And you gotta always walk like you talk. Know that shit! Do that shit! Walk that shit!

Slaves'll say shit like, 'He think he the shit.' And when the slave reflects on the shit that just left they lips, they gon' say, 'He is the shit.' Just like in the streets, my dude, you gotta wear your swag twenty-four-seven for niggas, wiggas, and sniggas–"

"Wiggas and sniggas?"

"White niggas and niggas who look like me. Only thang is I ain't from nowhere near no desert. But anywho, as I was sayin' and displayin', if your swag is thorough, my dude, a nigga gon' respect your gangsta. And when they do, they'll be lining up to eat whatever you feedin'. Understand me when I say," the engineer paused, "you know what... follow me. I'll show you how I get down."

A minute later, the two men were in a bedroom sized expensively decorated office.

Bo Jack's eyes were taking in the four walls filled with pictures and framed gold and platinum records. "Who don't you know?" Bo Jack asked admiring the picture of G-Swag and Venezuelan president Hugo Chavez making the G-Swag sign with their hands. He continued his stroll, but then stopped so suddenly, he almost fell over. "Yo'," Bo Jack turned around, "you know Barak Obama?"

G-Swag nodded as if it was no big deal. "We chopped it up a few years back when I lived in Chi-town. That picture," G-Swag pointed to a picture of him and the Junior Senator, "That's me, B-rak and our pastor, Reverend Jeremiah Wright."

"You think he gon' run for president?"

"Run," G-Swag gave Bo Jack a sideways look, "My dude, B-rak gon' win," G-Swag said as if it were a foregone conclusion.

"You smokin', my nigga. Real talk, kinfolk," Bo Jack said, "That shit ain't gon' happen in our lifetime and our grandkid's lifetime. Crackas is more fucked up than the most fucked up nigga. Ain't no way they gon' allow a nigga to be elected."

"They will if he makes them forget he's black," G-Swag said. "And whatever the turnout, B-rak is cool as a fan. Besides, he openin' doors that I might need to get into one day. My dude, I make it my business to know anyone that can help elevate my stage in life."

"That's some real shit," Bo Jack said while G-Swag sat at his desk, head down pecking away on his keyboard.

"Swag, you sound like a nigga, you even half-ass look like a nigga with them white boy dreads. You say you ain't from the Middle East. So what's your story?"

The tall, clumsy-looking, olive-skinned, hippie-looking engineer looked up. "I'm from the hood. We call them 'favelas' in Brazil. Imagine sixteen heads living in a mud hut the size of this office, no electricity, shittin' and pissin' in five gallon paint buckets. Mom-dukes is gone for days at a time, after she walked twenty miles into Sao Paulo to turn tricks with tourists so she could feed my grandma and my eight brothers and sisters."

"What about your pops?"

The producer-slash-sound engineer shrugged his shoulders. "Who knows, dude was probably one of mom-dukes tricks."

G-Swag returned to pecking away on the computers keyboard.

Bo Jack just stood there as papers began sliding out of the printer next to Swag's 42-inch computer screen. Swag removed five of the six pages before he stapled them together. He stood up, walked around the desk and handed the papers to Bo Jack. "Here."

"What's all this?"

"Our deal."

"What deal?"

"The one we about to make, my dude."

"I don't need no deal, playa. I'm a retired slave and I ain't tryin' to re-enlist. No disrespect, my nigga, but I ain't tryin' to give the lion's share of my royalties to no nigga," he said, thinking back on the deal that Escobar tried to force him into. That's why he'd had to get rid of that fat-fuck. He hoped he wasn't about to have beef with G-Swag. Bo Jack continued. "Back when my pockets was light, I might'a signed on to that dream, but not now. Real talk, you the coldest sound engineer in the game Swag, and I feel like I got what it takes to take over the rap game. That's the only reason I got my grind on for the last year, getting my weight up. So I could come break bread with you and we could put down this track. I did that. Now all I gotta do is get my single, 'Ballin' for Life' out to the public."

"Do you hear what you sayin', my dude?" Before Bo Jack could answer, G-Swag continued. "I'm the illest at what I do that's why you paid me fifty stacks to lay down that track. You may think you got your weight up, my dude, but you ain't nowhere near no heavyweight?" G-Swag got up, took a few giraffe strides around the desk, and opened the office double doors. "I got over twenty million in sound equipment out there. I done worked with everyone from the O'Jays to Outkast. Swag sat on the corner of his desk and crossed one long skinny leg over the other, "Michael Jordan, the best that ever did it on a basketball court, was one of the worst to ever do it as a coach. So, it's way more to the game than having your weight up. You have to know who to – and how to – throw that weight around. Can you do this shit without me? No doubt. But can you do it the way I promised," G-Swag pointed to the contract in Bo Jack's hands, "on line seventeen, page two."

He flipped the page and his eyes skimmed until he got to where G-Swag had just directed him. Bo Jack's lips moved but nothing came out as he read.

Bo Jack looked up from the contract. "Swag, you must think I just got off the short bus?"

"What do you mean?"

"You gon' give a nigga' a million stacks at the end of this year if the track we just laid down has not hit the top five on the Billboard R&B/hip hop charts?"

Swag's shoulder-length dark dreads danced as he shook his head. "Nah, my dude." He uncrossed his legs, reached behind him and picked up the sheet of paper he left on the printer when he removed the contract. "Here," he gave the sheet to Bo Jack, "turn it over."

Bo Jack's eyes were big as saucers as he used a finger to count out the zeros behind the one on the check he held. After counting a second time he blurted out. "A million dollars...now? Is this shit for real?"

G-Swag smiled. Proud that he'd played his poker hand just right. "As real as it gets, my dude. All yours if you sign. And if you don't crack Billboard's R&B/Hip Hops top ten by New Year's, you don't owe me Jack. All I ask is you give me one album. Thirteen tracks like the one we just laid down. Don't worry about the lyrics, I got a team of writers."

"Thirteen tracks? One album?" Bo Jack asked, thinking that if the check was legit, then Swag was the one who must've just got off the short bus. Bo Jack continued, "I don't care if a nigga clockin' like Citibank, ain't nobody gon' give an unproven nigga a mill on some future hope shit."

"Some cats bet on the ponies, some shoot craps, some bet on sports," he winked, "I bet on people."

Bo Jack didn't even have a bank account to deposit the check into. And he definitely wasn't tryin'to cash it. He wouldn't even try to stash this type of bread at his mom's house. He really wanted to do this rap thing solo, but shit, Swag was the real deal. Swag Beats Unlimited was big time, not that playground shit that Escobar had tried to force him into. And most important Swag was going to give up a mill.

"A'ight," he nodded. "My momma ain't raised no fool. Let me get somebody to make sure this contract is what you say it is and if it is we in business."

G-Swag grinned. "You got anyone in mind?"

Just like Bo Jack had hired the number one engineer to mix down and put the beat to his new track, he had to have the top-flight entertainment attorney in the business. "Joel Katz," he said.

G-Swag had him on the line within minutes. Three hours and three revisions later, Bo Jack was the newest member of Swag Beats Unlimited.

He was about to get on the elevator when G-Swag stepped out of his office. "My dude?"

Bo Jack turned around.

"I told you my story 'cause I knew you could relate. I wanted you to know, like you, I been through hell, danced with the devil, and smoked from his pipe, before escaping my destiny and making my fantasies reality. And I did all that by always finding out any and everything about the mofo's I got into bed with. I know about you: the YDC home, foster care, kiddie prison, stick-ups, your mom —"

"How you know so much about me, Swag?"

"If I tell you that, it'll even the score. And why I wanna do that? Just like you in it to win it, my dude, I am, too." The producer winked at Bo Jack before continuing. "The game is divulged in stages and wages, my dude. I paid the wage to get the 411 on you. And, it took several stages, so I ain't just gon' give it away. Always know who you sleeping with before you get into bed with them."

G-Swag nodded as Bo Jack stepped into the elevator. As the elevator descended from the thirty-second to the ground floor, Bo Jack had a million thoughts running a hundred miles a minute through his head. One million dollars. First thing in the AM he would open up an account.

Bo Jack had no regrets. He had a hundred grand in the streets, and almost a hundred grand stashed at his mom's spot. Tomorrow morning he'd have a million in his back account. This was the best of times. But then, a thought made him snap his fingers. There was something he had to do.

VERSE 6

A couple of hours later, Bo Jack was in an apartment up the street from the Zone 5 projects. He had come to meet with the four baby bosses he had put in charge of the young boys who were slangin' the dope he stole from Escobar last month. He was just about to give them the news of his decision when Thug handed him his phone.

Bo Jack frowned. "What's this?"

Thug looked down as if the answer was in his sneakers. He shook his head. "Man, you've got to look at this."

"What is it?" Bo Jack repeated.

Thug took a breath before he said, "It's a video on YouTube. Press play."

Bo Jack did that and then watched the twenty-second video. His expression did not change. He did not move as he watched the pink penis releasing urine onto his boy. When the video ended, Bo Jack looked up.

Thug's voice was full of rage when he said, "I swear ta God, big dog, I'm gon' do that nigga. I 'on't give a fuck that he five-oh. That white bitch peed on me," Thug said, before he turned and punched the wall. The paper-thin plaster crumbled beneath the force. "I'm a man," he ranted.

"Who was this?" Bo Jack asked, though he was pretty sure that he already knew.

"That bitch, Tarzan."

"He came around here?"

"Yeah, asking a whole lotta questions. But nobody told that bitch anything."

"Good," Bo Jack said calmly, even though his mind was already churning.

"Fuck that nigga!" Thug continued yelling. "Who he think he is? I ain't nobody's bitch."

"I wish we could prove—"

"Fuck proof, Bo. We don't need any proof. I was there." Thug snatched a black handgun with black tape wrapped around the handle from his pocket. He pointed it at the wall. "Next time that bitch come through the projects...."

"I know you mad as a mothafucka. I would be, too," Bo Jack said, trying to calm his young soldier down. "But, you gotta think—"

"What the fuck I gotta think about? That cop didn't think when he pissed on my head."

"I feel you, but you off him, you might as well off yourself, cause the courts gon' fry that ass."

"I 'on't give a damn," Thug said.

"You might after I tell you all the new deal." After getting everyone's attention, Bo Jack continued. "As of this minute, I'm outta this dope shit. Thug, D-Bo, Bam-Bam, H-Nic, all the money you collect from your soldiers," he smiled, "keep it."

They all stared at him with eyes as big as saucers.

"Quit bullshittin'," H-Nic, Bo Jack's number one said.

"Real talk, my nigga." Bo Jack nodded. "I just signed with G-Swag, You all know my focus always been on my music. Now a nigga payin' me to do this shit full time. I ain't got time nor the heart to keep slangin'. I'm leavin' the game to ya'll, the wolves that helped me get here."

"So you serious? You gon' let us just walk away with everything? I owe you twenty stacks," D-Bo said.

"Hell, I'm on the line for fifteen," Bam-Bam said.

"What about the Dominicans?" H-Nic asked.

Bo Jack had anticipated that question because none of his boys knew the truth. Bo Jack had told them that some Dominicans were putting him on after Escobar got burnt. That's how he explained the drugs he'd given them. It all made sense to them because Bo Jack was the most thorough young stud any of them had ever met. Bo Jack had always found ways for his dogs to eat, and none of them ever got burned by the fires he had them jump into.

"G-Swag, gave," he was about to tell his boys about the check burnin' his back pocket, but he thought back to G-Swags words, *'Don't even the score in the game if you wanna win.'* No, nobody needed to know how he got the drugs and nobody needed to know about the check burning a hole in his back pocket. He said, "You don't have to worry about the Dominicans. It's all taken care of."

After they passed a couple blunts around to celebrate, Bo Jack and H-Nic put on their bulletproof vests, guns, and coats before stepping outside into the winter-darkness.

"Big dog, I'm proud of you," H-Nic said. "It's always good when one of us crawl out the barrel."

"One less crab you gotta deal with," Bo Jack said.

"This is what you always wanted."

"What *we* always wanted, my nigga," Bo Jack corrected before bear hugging his number one.

H-Nic broke the embrace. "When you make it big, don't forget about us grunts stuck in the trap."

"Never that, kinfolk."

"You told moms yet?" Bo Jack's oldest friend asked before crossing his arms.

"I'm on my way to Conyers now."

"Dog, it's midnight. You know she in a coma."

"I know, but if I wait 'til morning, she liable to kick my ass."

"Liable to," H-Nic repeated. "Mom's gon' break her foot off in that ass. Matter of fact, take your ass over there right now. She might kick my ass if she found out I knew before she did."

The two did the brotherman hug, and then H-Nic went back inside while Bo Jack headed toward his car. Despite the uncharacteristically January Arctic cold whipping wind, Bo Jack's blood was boiling. He clenched and unclenched his fists as he moved toward his car. There was so much good news swirling around in his heart, but it was the thoughts in his head that had his heart pounding.

He couldn't get the video image of Thug being peed on out of his mind. That king of the wanna-bes, Tarzan had no right. Thug was a good nigga, and even if he wasn't, no man deserved that shit from one-time.

Bo Jack tried to shake those thoughts away, but he couldn't. It was okay, though. He knew that bitch was gon' get his. But Bo Jack was sure Thug was gon' probably get the chair behind that bullshit. Because Thug was never going to let it go.

VERSE 7

"What is wrong with these hos, Black?"

Bo Jack had his phone on speaker while he drove down the I-20 interstate with Mo-Love on the line. Mo-Love was the brotha Bo Jack called when he needed a good laugh. Mo, short for Maurice, was in his mid-twenties, built like the Michelin Tire Man, and looked like a bull dog in the face. Yet he always had a dime piece at his side.

"How you mean, Mo?"

"Okay, how 'bout this monkey mothafucka I been kickin' it with the past few days gon' tell me I gotta wait some months before she gon' let me hit it."

Bo Jack chuckled. "She one of them time keepers?"

"Hell, yeah. Talkin' 'bout I don't know what kinda' no self respectin' hos you fuck with giving it up so soon.'"

"Don't you hate that?" Bo Jack asked. "And then when they do finally give it up and a nigga step on they heart, they feel a certain type of way about all niggas. When all along, she shoulda' gave up the draws in the giddy up when a nigga was all excited." He laughed as he twisted his car off the interstate. "Mo, why you even dealing with the tramp?"

"The funky bitch got style. And she make a nigga feel good with that we-shall-overcome-kill-whitey-talk. But, what gets me is shawty think she a dime and the ho's a penny shawt from a nickel. Only reason I give her a four is for her slick tongue."

"Why don't you just cut your losses and kick her to the curb?"

"I got at least seventy dollars invested in the Twinkie eatin' bitch. I done took her to the movies and out to Red Lobster."

"Seventy dollars ain't shit to spend on a ho," Bo Jack said as he maneuvered his car through the streets. "I know you said she was a four, but is the body bangin' at least?"

"Hell, nah. Don't tell her that, though. She swear she the shit. Bo, the ho two M&M's away from shopping at Lane Bryant."

Bo Jack laughed out loud exactly the way he did every time he spoke to his boy. "Mo, you a fool, my nigga, but let me hit you up later, I'm pulling up to my destination," Bo Jack said, purposefully leaving out his exact location. He never told anyone where he was.

Mo said his goodbyes and Bo Jack turned off his headlights before he turned into the driveway. It was a little after one in the AM, and he didn't want the glare of his lights to shine into his baby brother's bedroom. The darkened house showed that everyone was already asleep.

He pulled into the carport on the other side of the new Chrysler 300 he'd bought his mother a couple weeks after doing Escobar. Unlocking the kitchen door, he slowly turned the knob, and then stepped into the black-dark house. He didn't turn on any lights, though. Just used his hands to navigate through the familiar space, from the kitchen into the dining room, then to the steps that led to the upstairs bedrooms.

"Black bird."

The voice was low and soft, but still, it startled Bo Jack. He had to catch onto the railing as he almost stumbled backward on the steps.

"Mom, you almost gave me a heart attack," he said, turning around and seeing his mother's silhouette in the moonlight that shined through the dining room window.

He reached toward the light switch, but she yelled out, "No," putting her hand against her cheek at the same time. "No lights."

But it was too late. Shock registered on his face as he took in the sight of his mother. From her blackened eye to her swollen jaw and busted lip, it was clear that she'd been attacked.

The muscles in his own jaw tightened as he stepped slowly toward her. It took him a moment to gather his words. "Ma, who did this?"

"Shhh," she put a finger to her swollen lip, "keep it down and turn out the lights." When Bo Jack just stood there, she added, "Please, son."

He did as she asked, but then he rushed right back to her side and knelt down by the chair that she sat in. Slowly, gently, he rested his head in her lap. There were so many things he wanted to know now, but he'd wait. He knew that she would speak when she was ready.

For a while, she comforted him, humming and stroking Bo Jack's short wavy black hair as she swayed. But after several minutes, she finally said, "I'm sorry, my little black bird. I'm so, so very sorry."

"For what?" he asked without lifting his head.

"For everything." She sighed. "For bringing you and your brother into this world. For getting hooked on crack. For dragging you and your brother through the streets, living under highways, sleeping in shelters, eating in soup kitchens. I just wish... I wish..."

For the first time, Bo Jack lifted his head and looked into her glassy, sad eyes. "Don't say that, Mom. You did the best you could and you were always there for us. At least when you could be." When she shook her head, he kept on, "And you always came back. You left, but you always came back. Mom, if it wasn't for you I wouldn't be me." He paused. "And you know how I love me some me," he joked.

"You wanna know why I started calling you black bird?" she asked, as if none of what he'd just said mattered.

He'd heard this story so many times, that he could recite every word with her. But he said nothing. Bo Jack just sat beside her, looking and listening as she began.

"When I was little, I saw a baby black bird that had fallen out of its nest. The cat next door must've seen the falling bird around the same time I did and it began closing in. The little, bitty baby bird, not even the size of my fist, started flapping its wings, but it couldn't fly. I watched in horror as the cat closed in. Just as the cat dove for the bird, out of nowhere it had seemed, the mother bird swooped down and scooped the bird up with her beak. I watched mother and child soar off into the sky where nothing could hurt her baby." Johnetta shook her head as if she was thinking about that day so many years ago. She continued. "When you were born, I thought back to that mother blackbird. I swore that if you were ever in danger, I would come and swoop down and take you somewhere safe where nothing or no one could hurt you."

It wasn't until Johnetta stroked the side of Bo Jack's face that she realized tears were streaming down his cheek. His voice cracked as he said, "Mom, no..."

She didn't let him finish. "I failed. I don't deserve to be a mother because I let him put his hands on my baby."

It took a moment for her words to register, but then his heart quickened. "Bran..." his brother's name stuttered out of his mouth, "is Brandon..." He jumped to his feet.

"Blackbird," she called after him.

But Bo Jack didn't stop. He dashed up the stairs two steps at a time, then ran down the hall. Opening Brandon's bedroom door, he peeked in before he stepped inside. Staring down at his brother, he whispered, "Thank God." The boy slept as if nothing had happened. He stayed for a few more seconds, just to make sure. Then, trudged back down the stairs. His mother was exactly where he'd left her.

"Take a seat, son."

He did. They sat together in the dark. Bo Jack braced himself; he knew his mother was ready to talk, ready to explain what had happened.

"O'Reilly, the Atlanta police officer–"

If Bo Jack thought his heart pounded before, it really did now. "Tarzan?" he asked as if he couldn't believe it. "Big blonde headed white dude with a military buzz cut?"

She nodded. "He came by looking for you."

Bo Jack knew everything that was on the street about that man, including the fact that he had a thing for young black women. Reaching for her hand, he held her for a moment before he asked, "Did he?"

She squeezed his hand while again nodding.

Bo Jack jerked his hand away and grabbed his head. He wanted to be strong, he needed to be. Strong was all he'd ever known. He'd had to be strong when he was beaten with an

61

aluminum bat. He had to be strong when he'd been hit by a car and left for dead. And he'd had to be strong the two times that he'd been shot. He even had to be strong when he caught his first drug charge. But how could he be strong when O'Reilly came looking for him and because he wasn't there, he beat and raped his mother?

What he felt was beyond hurt, beyond pain. His feelings for John 'Tarzan' O'Reilly were way beyond hate. His mind fought to form words. He saw himself beating Tarzan for an hour after he'd already beaten him to death with his nightstick sized Louisville Slugger baseball bat. His mind suddenly jumped from thinking of Johnetta to thinking of his little brother. "Brandon? Where was he when?" Bo Jack had to close his eyes as he asked. "If that man hurt my baby brother..."

Johnetta shook her head. "He tied his hands and his arms behind his back and placed him in the upstairs tub." It must've been the way Bo Jack looked at her that made Johnetta add, "That's all."

"No, Mom. He put tape over my mouth, too."

Their eyes snapped to the side at the same time and Bo Jack and Johnetta saw Brandon sitting at the bottom of the steps.

"Baby, how long have you been sitting there?" Johnetta asked.

The ten-year-old shrugged. "I don't know."

"Go back to bed, little man," Bo Jack said as he stood and made his way over to his brother. Brandon had been born addicted to crack and because of that, was a special needs child. He had a severe case of ADHD. The doctors said his mind probably wouldn't develop beyond a thirteen-year-old adolescent.

"The belt was really, really, really tight, Bo," Brandon said, looking up. "And my wrists and my ankles couldn't even breathe. And guess what, Bo?"

"What?"

"I didn't even cry. Did I, Mommy?"

"No, you didn't, baby."

He smiled. "I was a big boy, Bo, just like you told me. I didn't give that policeman the fatisaction."

"Satisfaction," Bo Jack corrected.

"Yeah, that too," The ten-year-old smiled. "Just like you told me, Bo. I'm the man of the house. And when I finally lickeded the tape off my mouth, guess what I didded, Bo?"

Bo Jack had to swallow the lump that formed in his throat. His rage had left him mute, so he just shrugged.

"Guess?" Brandon repeated.

The word, "What," came out of Bo's mouth in two syllables.

"I called mommy's name. I said, 'Mommmmm-meeee,' real loud."

Bo Jack couldn't take it. The thought of someone raping his mother in her own house, while his brother was tied up in the bathtub a few feet away was too much. He had moved his mother out to the suburbs so that she and his little brother would be safe, far away from the concrete jungle, but obviously not far enough away from the savage beasts that policed the concrete jungle.

"Let's go back upstairs, little man."

Brandon nodded and Bo Jack followed him back up to his bedroom. He stayed with his brother until he was tucked beneath the covers.

"Are you proud of me, Bo?" Brandon asked.

Bo Jack grabbed his brother in the tightest hug he could without hurting him. "Yeah, little man. I'm real proud of you." Then, he left Brandon alone because he didn't want his brother to feel his rage.

Back downstairs, his mother still sat where she'd been when he first came into the house and Bo Jack was glad that she hadn't turned on the lights. He didn't want her to get too good a look at him. If she could see his face, she'd see the hatred and rage plastered across it. She wouldn't allow him to leave. She'd remind him of what happened the last time he'd had that look. But what she didn't understand was that Bo Jack had no regrets about having killed her abusive boyfriend seven years ago when he was only twelve.

He leaned over and kissed his mother's cheek. "I'll give you a call tomorrow," he whispered.

"Talk to me before you make a move," she said, but she was already talking to his back.

"Okay."

"Don't okay me, Beauregard Jackson Jones."

He paused and turned. "Mom, I hear you."

Slowly, she rose from the chair and moved toward her son. She gave him a hug as she whispered, "Promise me."

"I promise," he said and he wondered if his words sounded as empty to her as they did to him.

She released her embrace and stood silent for a moment. The winter wind howled outside and made the dining room window rattle.

Once the wind calmed, she said, "Bo, maybe you should go seek out Knowledge."

He stood thoughtfully quiet for a moment, wondering why his mother would suggest this now. "It's been a long time, Ma. You think he still around?"

"Knowledge ain't goin' nowhere, son. He still in the same place he been in forever. And talking to him may help you."

He nodded, thinking that his mother just might be right. "I think I will go see him, get some understanding." He paused and added, "Good idea mom, I should've sought out Knowledge way before now."

He kissed his mother on the cheek before he slipped into the darkness.

VERSE 8

On his way downtown, Bo Jack stopped at the new twenty-four hour Super Wal-Mart off of Gresham Road in Decatur. Stepping into the store, he paused at the first register, trying to decide which way to go in the super-sized store, rather than just wandering around.

"Excuse me," he said to the cashier.

With a cell phone pressed to her ear, she signaled for him to hold on. "You think that nigga give a damn about you, just cause he told you he loves you? The nigga got you and that ugly shrimp-fried rice bitch pregnant. And I heard the Tiger Woods-lookin' bitch had herpes." She paused as the other person spoke.

Bo Jack shifted from one leg to the next.

"Girl, I ain't startin' shit. It was Tinkerbell, that dope nigga from East Atlanta with the tricked out Coca-Cola brown Impala." She paused. "Yeah, him. Nigga use to fuck her, and my girl Dreena used to fuck with him and she done had herpes since we was in middle school."

Bo Jack touched the attendant's hand.

She shot Bo Jack a nigga-if-you-don't-get-your-hand-off-me-look, then said, "Hold on girl, don't hang up." She turned to Bo Jack. "What? You ready to check out, cause I don't see nothin' in yo' hand?"

"Shawty, I'm just trynna find out where I can find some sleeping bags."

She rolled her eyes. "I have no idea where the sleeping bags are. I work the cash register. Go find somebody in that section."

"If I knew where the fuck the section was I wouldn't be asking your unprofessional ass."

She put her hands on her hips and pointed a finger in his face. "Negro, who you think you is?" She looked him up and down. "You don't know me."

"Nah, but apparently a lot of niggas do," he said pointing to all the names tattooed across her chest and down her left arm.

"Nigga, dem my kids so talk what you know."

Bo Jack shook his head. "Niggas."

"Is there a problem here, Shenika?"

Bo Jack hadn't even noticed the much older drill sergeant looking security guard as he approached. He had been too busy studying this dumb bitch in front of him.

"Nah, ain't no problem, bruh," Bo Jack said in a tone that let the guard know he needed to step back.

"I wasn't speaking to you," the big guy said as he dropped his left hand.

"I'm speaking to you." Bo Jack's eyes followed the man's gesture. "If you want it to be a problem, we can make it one, my nigga," he said as he eyed the security guard's gun. "If you pull that out, you best use it." Bo Jack death-stared the guard down until the big man took a couple of steps back.

That's what I thought, Bo Jack said inside. Cats were always testing him, just because he was young.

The security guard eased his hand away from his gun and tugged on his sagging uniform.

Shaking his head, Bo Jack stalked off. He knew he should've stopped at the Wal-Mart in Conyers. There wouldn't have been any problems there on the white side of town. He knew that was a fucked up thing to think, but shit, it was true.

Twenty minutes later, Bo Jack walked out with two sleeping bags, a kerosene heater, eight Heath candy bars, the most powerful outdoor light he could find and a Jihad book. And as he passed the first cash register, Shenika was still on the phone.

Tired, sleepy, and now even more delirious with rage, Bo Jack slung the four bags into the trunk before jumping in the car and rolling onto the I-20 interstate. It was a quarter to four when he got off the downtown exit at Capitol Avenue.

The streets were dark, silent, and just about empty, except for a couple of hard-core tranny's trying to pick up an early morning trick to feed whatever habit they had. They had to have a serious habit to be out in the cold this early in the morning. But Bo Jack understood. Heroine and crack were the coldest, hardcore pimps that ever existed. Neither of the two ever gave their whores a day off, didn't matter if you were sick and on your death bed, you were going to do whatever it took to get some H or rock. He knew from experience...his mother.

As he drove through the streets searching for a parking space, Bo Jack thought back to the last time he'd seen Knowledge. It had to be almost seven years ago when he was just twelve. It was right before Child and Family Services kidnapped him and his then three-year-old brother, days before the cops found the body of his mother's ex. Yeah, that many years had passed. Back then, Knowledge seemed to have all the answers. He didn't necessarily give up the answers but he always taught how to find them.

Bo Jack drove around the I-20 and connecting I-75/85 interstate entrances and exits before he gave up his search for a parking space. There was nothing, so he parked right in front of the Exxon gas station on University, the one right down the street from The Atlanta Braves stadium. He hadn't given any thought to the fact that this was one of the highest crime areas in the city. It was home to him. That's why Bo Jack really should have thought to go to his spot and get the Cutlass. If it was vandalized or stolen, no problem; he had full coverage insurance on it. He only had no-fault on his Benz, which was what he happened to be driving now.

That's why he parked at the gas station where there was light and activity going on. He thought maybe that would deter someone from messing with his ride.

Although the ghetto Atlanta streets seemed to be asleep, there were always open eyes hiding behind the shadow of darkness, searching for an opportunity. And Bo Jack wasn't about to let his Benz be the opportunity those eyes had been looking for.

Reclining the driver's seat all the way back, he got comfortable. It would be light in a few hours, and probably a lot warmer, he figured. So, he'd just settle in and wait. In a few hours, the streets would be lighter, warmer and friendlier as folks got up and made their way to church.

VERSE 9

"What you think, Lester?" the prostitute asked the man at her side as she peered into the black Mercedes's car window.

Lester put his dirty-gloved hands against the passenger's window and squinted as he looked inside trying to get a good view of the man behind the wheel snoring with his mouth wide open. "He ain't dead."

"Duh?" The woman stood up straight and mocked him.

"Stay here, woman, while I go across the street and get a brick," the homeless man said to the old whore.

"What your scary ass gon' do with a pipe Lester?"

"What the hell you think I'm gon' do, Mildred? I'm gon' cave his skull in if he gives us a problem. That platinum chain around his neck got to be worth a half ounce. Matter fact, we can sell half the dope and smoke the rest."

The whore peeked back into the window and took in the chain with the diamond studded crucified Jesus emblem.

"And even if it's fake," the homeless man continued, "he driving a big body 420 SEL Mercedes. He gotta have some money in his pockets."

She tested the door and then stopped for a moment, shocked that it wasn't locked. "It's open," she whispered as she gently pulled it open wider.

But then the inside light came on and before the old woman could blink, Bo Jack had a shiny silver pistol pointed at her blonde wig.

"We 'on't want no trouble, baby." The prostitute jumped back and held up her hands.

"Who's we?" Bo Jack asked.

The old woman turned her head. "Jive ass crackhead hump motherfucker," she said to the air, because there was no one else around.

He knew the old whore was on some robbing shit, but she smelled like five-day-old death. "Okay, I'mma let this go. Just please close my door."

"Can you at least loan a sistah–"

Even as he reached into his pocket, he shook his head. But there was no way he could tell the old hag no. He'd lived on these mean streets; he knew what it was like. He pulled out a couple of bills and handed them to her. "Here. Now get ghost."

With a grin that showed that she was missing half of her teeth, the old woman slammed the door shut without even saying thank you. Bo Jack glanced at the clock on the dash. 4:27. He'd only been asleep for fifteen, maybe twenty minutes.

Well, there was no way he'd be able to sleep now, and that thought gave him another idea. He jumped out of his car and jogged toward the old woman who he'd just spoken to. "Hey, you, Ms. Lady," he shouted out.

She ignored him and kept walking down the deserted street as if she hadn't heard him.

"You, with the cheerleading outfit on," he called out again.

Now, her pace quickened. As if she thought he was calling her to take back the money. Bo Jack knew exactly the way to stop her. "You wanna make a couple hundred dollars."

"Hell yeah," a voice rang out.

"I do," another voice called out.

"I'll do whatever you want done for fifty," another voice called out.

It was like Bo Jack had awakened the entire area with his words. No more than a couple of seconds passed before he had a group following him like he was the Pied Piper. Two women and four men walked, jogged and limped behind him.

"Bitches, don't make me cut you," the old woman wearing the dirty cheerleading outfit said as she finally turned to face him. "He's my trick. I found him." She swung a rusty box-cutter in the air as if she really thought she could do some damage.

"Mildew-funky whore! I'll bash your brainless head in with this brick," said one of the homeless men behind Bo Jack.

"Lester, if you even think about hitting me with that brick I will gut your skinny, white, dead-dick ass."

Bo jack interrupted. "Look, I'll give everyone fifty dollars if I come back and no one has touched my car." He pointed to where he'd left his Benz.

"Give it here," a homeless brotha, no older than fifteen or sixteen said, holding out his gloved hand.

"After I get back."

"Nah, you need to give me mines now," the kid wolfed.

"Me too," another voice said.

Bo Jack reached into his Mark Buchannan leather coat and came out with his chrome Sig Sauer P226 .380 caliber handgun. "Okay Billy-bad-ass," Bo Jack said to the kid about his age that just barked at him, "come take it."

They all took a few steps back, though none of them seemed willing to turn away completely.

"Fuck all 'dem, homeboy," the scrawny old Willie Nelson looking white man said. "I'll wash your windows and put some shine on them tires while you gone. You can give me a hundred and I gare-rone-tee, that no one will touch your ride but me."

"I wish you would," the old cheerleading outfit wearing whore screamed. "I promise I wish you would. Please give Lester a hundred dollars after you get back. Please," the woman begged Bo Jack. "Watch how quick it'll be in my hands."

As the white man and the old black fake cheerleader bickered, Bo Jack shook his head and wondered what he'd gotten into.

As if he could read Bo Jack's mind, one of the other homeless men said, "They do this every day. Mildred and Lester been together way too long."

"They're a couple?" Bo Jack asked, wondering why he was getting all caught up in this drama.

The white man turned to Bo Jack. "Yeah, I'm married to the stank whore."

"Suck my dick, Lester. If it wasn't for me, your white ass would've been dead a long time ago." The woman turned to the other homeless faces. "And you bitches. How y'all gon' let this Uncle Sam looking white boy disrespect a black queen."

"You meant crack fiend, didn't you?" Lester said. ""Cause I know you didn't say black queen, funky heffa."

Bo Jack held his hands up in the air before he tucked his gun away in his front pocket and headed back to his car.

"Hey yo, what about the money?" one of the night watchers called out.

Without turning around, Bo Jack hollered out, "There's six of you and if my car is untouched when I get back, all of you get fifty dollars." He paused and turned around. "I said untouched, meaning don't touch my windows, my tires, don't touch nothing."

"When you coming back?"

"Later," he replied before popping the trunk, and removing the four Wal-Mart bags. Then, he hit the alarm remote and carried two bags in each arm as he crossed the street.

VERSE 10

It was freezing outside, but Bo Jack's thoughts had him sweating. Thoughts of his mother, his brother, and Tarzan. His rage had him heated.

Bo Jack looked up, surprised that he'd already arrived at his destination. Gallons of memories flooded his consciousness as his eyes surveyed his surroundings. The highway underpass hadn't changed much. This was the very spot that he, his mom, and little brother once called home. He remembered how the first night had been hard, but after a couple days, he'd gotten use to the car horns, engine noise, and even the exhaust fumes from the highway above this homeless community.

G-Swag spoke of using the bathroom in paint buckets when he was growing up, but a paint bucket to sit on would've been a luxury when he was on the streets. G-Swag had also talked about how his mother had sold ass to keep food in the mouths of his eight brothers and sisters.

Well, Knowledge fed ten, twelve kids and grown ass people every day without lifting a finger. Knowledge knew everything and he gave game and wisdom away to anyone who sought him out. And every day, his students repaid him by bringing food and other necessities into the small homeless community. Everyone played a part in the survival of each community member. Knowledge got everyone to understand how they were responsible for their fellow man in the community more than they were responsible for themselves. Under that underpass was the only place that Bo Jack ever experienced group unconditional love. That's where Bo Jack began to learn the value of extended family.

As Bo Jack stood there reminiscing he realized that his happiest childhood experiences were had while living under this highway. Back then, he had no worries, because he and his mother and brother were part of a much larger family who worked together so that everyone was cared for.

So the hardship of struggle wasn't so hard because of the love everyone showed each other. There were no fights over material shit. Nobody sweated anyone else for what they had, cause what one had, they all had. There was no crime and no major fights within the community. Knowledge had created a utopic model of community cohabitation.

Even back then, no one knew how old Knowledge was. Whenever anyone broached the subject of age, he'd say he had been born before time began.

Bo Jack didn't understand what he had meant back then, and he certainly didn't understand it now. All he knew was that Knowledge was full of wisdom and that's what he needed right now. A little game and guidance.

As Bo Jack carefully stepped through the community of people cocooned inside sheets, blankets, quilts and even newspapers, Bo Jack knew exactly where he was heading. There were several cardboard structures beneath this highway, but none were as big as Knowledge's.

It only took him a minute to find the huge cardboard structure whose sides flapped in the wind. Four old car tires prevented the five foot high, five by eight foot structure from blowing away.

Bo Jack stood outside for a moment, before a deep voice resonated from inside, "Come into my palace, King. It's been a while son."

Knowledge sounded as if he knew Bo Jack was the one outside. There was no way he could no that under the cover of a cardboard box.

Bo Jack stepped into Knowledge's home and took in the man sitting yoga-style in the corner with a book on his lap. He looked the same - exactly the way he looked seven years before. The only thing that was different was his salt and pepper dreads were longer, past his shoulders.

"Did you know it was me outside?"

He nodded. "I did."

"How?" Bo Jack asked.

"Your scent, Black man. No matter how old you get, how much cologne you wear, your bodies natural scent doesn't change. It's unique to only you, King."

Bo Jack pulled out the two sleeping bags, handing one to Knowledge. "But, I ain't - haven't seen you in years."

"Only because you haven't looked," the man said. "But, I've been watching you, King."

Even though it didn't feel as cold as Bo Jack had expected, he still unboxed the heater, placed it between them and turned it on. Once he sat down, he handed Knowledge the Heath bars.

"For me?" Knowledge asked while reaching for all eight. "You shouldn't have."

Bo Jack started pulling his arm back. "Okay, I'll take 'em home with me."

With the speed of a striking viper, Knowledge lurched forward grabbing the bars from Bo Jack's hand. "But, since you already did, who am I to turn down such generosity?"

Bo Jack smiled, but his mind was on the words that Knowledge had spoken. *I've been watching you, king.* This was the second time in 24 hours that someone had said they'd been watching him. G-Swag had said that earlier and now Knowledge. As careful as Bo Jack was, he hadn't had a clue that he was being watched. But if G-Swag and Knowledge had those kind of street eyes, maybe Tarzan was watching him, too.

Of course, he's watching me, Bo Jack thought. *That was why he knew where Momma lived. Then again if he was really watching me, he'd know where I rested my head every night....*

"So, Black man," Knowledge said, drawing Bo Jack's attention back to the present. When Bo Jack turned toward him, Knowledge placed an advanced copy of the upcoming book, *The Survival Bible, 16 Life Lessons for Young Black Men* in his hands. "I want you to read this. It has the questions and the answers inside. Now you wanna tell ole Knowledge what has your heart so troubled?"

"What makes you think I'm troubled?" Bo Jack asked, knowing good and well that Knowledge knew all things. Trying to turn away from the turmoil that was inside of him, Bo Jack added, "Matter of fact, yesterday, I signed a million dollar recording deal with the hottest producer on the planet."

The old man stared at him for a moment as if he was waiting for Bo Jack to add something more. Then, he said, "Son, I'm happy that you've finally got the big break you've been hoping for, but you didn't come here to tell me about your million dollar record deal. You came to me because there's something bothering you. The only time people come back for Knowledge is when they have problems that they can't solve.

Now if it's agreeable with you, I'd like for you to share what bothers you."

Bo Jack sat in silence trying to think of where to start and what to say. He knew he could speak freely. Knowledge was safer than a priest when it came to telling and keeping secrets.

"Begin with the last twenty-four hours. And I say this, because that is when your problems eclipsed enough for you to be sitting in front of me now."

Bo Jack was quiet for several moments, letting the words he was about to say settle inside of his head. "I have to kill a man." He stopped again, but this time it was to let his words settle in Knowledge's mind. When Knowledge said nothing, Bo Jack continued, "A white cop broke into my mother's home, tied Brandon up and he...and he..."

"Take your time, son."

Bo Jack inhaled trying to suck all the wind out of the air. As he released the air from his lungs the words, "He forced himself on my mother," spewed forth from his mouth.

Knowledge nodded, though his expression gave no indication of surprise. "So, now you feel as if you must get revenge?"

Bo Jack nodded.

"With his death?" Knowledge asked.

Another nod.

"All right," Knowledge said. "So after this man is dead, how will that even the score?"

"It doesn't," Bo Jack said right away. "The score will never be settled in my book, but at least that animal won't be able to hurt anyone else."

"That makes sense," Knowledge said as if he agreed. But then, he added, "King, have you ever had relations with a woman under false pretenses?"

"What do you mean?"

Knowledge stayed silent for a moment as he loosely tied his long dreads into a knot.

"Have you ever lied to a female in order to have relations with her?"

Bo Jack shrugged. "Hasn't everybody?"

Knowledge smiled. "I don't know. I haven't asked everybody. I asked you, King."

"Yeah. Of course."

"How many times have you done that?"

Bo Jack frowned. "I don't know."

"Would you say one, two, ten, twenty, a hundred times?"

"I don't keep count, but most times when I get it in, it's because I sold a female a dream."

"I see," Knowledge said. "Do you see, King?"

The lines in Bo Jack's forehead deepened. "See what?"

"The similarities."

"What similarities?" Bo Jack asked, sitting back a bit as if he'd been insulted. "I know you're not comparing what I've done to what that monster did to my mother."

"That's exactly what I'm doing. A man takes a woman by force. A man takes a woman by trickery. Without the force, without the trickery, the woman would have said no. Son, Karma is the balance between the positive and the negative. The energy you put out is the energy that will come back to you."

"Karma ain't got nothing to do with what that man did to my mother." Bo Jack shook his head as if he wasn't about to accept Knowledge's words.

"Oh, yes it does," Knowledge said, his voice still as soft and as calm as when he began. "Karma has everything to do with what happened, King. I don't know why it happened, but, son, there are no accidents in this world, only purposes. If a baby gets shot down as a result of a drive-by, there is a reason for it. For every action, there is a reaction. Nothing on this earth is new. Everything goes back to where it came from. Everything that has happened, repeats itself." He stopped and stared at Bo Jack for a moment, as if he wanted to make sure that Bo Jack had heard everything. After some moments, Knowledge said, "Now, I want you to close your eyes." He reached out. "Take my hands and think."

He reached for his hands, but he still asked, "What do you want me to think about?"

"Use the end to find the beginning. Ask yourself what happened to bring this evil into your mother's home?"

Bo Jack closed his eyes and the image immediately popped into his mind.

Escobar.

He had murdered Escobar. And stolen his money. And taken his dope. But...but...but....All kinds of excuses floated through Bo Jack's mind. *Escobar was the devil! But did I have a right to take his life?* Now, as he meditated, Bo Jack thought about the fact that Escobar had never really done any kind of harm to him or his family. And truly there were mothers, wives, daughters, and sons who probably thought that Bo Jack was the devil. He was the one who had sold crack to their family members. People were hooked on drugs because of him. People were dead because of him. Women had sold their bodies, their children, and their souls to get what he used to sell.

His mind gave him reasons for what he was doing, though. Bo Jack told himself that he was providing jobs for niggas who otherwise couldn't get work. But then, on the other hand, now his nigga Thug was in a situation. *Thug coulda died 'cause of me.* Thoughts of Thug getting pissed on and those pictures all over the internet reminded Bo Jack that Tarzan really was the enemy. And now, he was on that blue-eyed devil's radar and Tarzan was on a mission to get him. But why him? Why now? Tarzan had never had any concerns about Bo Jack, but all of a sudden, he was pissin' on one of his soldiers, tying up his brother, and raping his mother.

Bo Jack sat in the silence, tossing and turning the thoughts over in his mind like Knowledge had told him to do.

And then, it hit him. There was only one reason why Tarzan was after him now. It had to be Escobar. Tarzan and Escobar must've been connected somehow.

Now he remembered...the words that Li'l Percy had been trying to say right before one of the twins put a bullet in his head. He hadn't cared about what Percy was trying to say two seconds before his life was over, but now, he wished that he'd listened.

Them niggas was probably in bed together.

Tarzan was probably pimpin' Escobar. It all made sense now. Bo Jack had been in the streets his whole life and he had never heard of Escobar doing a bid. He'd been popped a couple of times, but as far as Bo Jack knew, Escobar had never done any real time.

That was it. Escobar was Tarzan's bitch and Bo Jack had taken him out.

Not only that, he'd made money off the dead man's dope and yesterday he'd signed a million dollar deal..... Bo Jack opened his eyes.

"Do you see now, Black man?"

"I see." Bo Jack nodded. "You were right, Knowledge."

"Knowledge is always right. But without understanding even knowledge is useless. Do you understand, King?"

"Yeah," Bo Jack nodded. "I think I do."

"So, what are you going to do?"

Bo Jack shrugged a little, nodded his head a bit. "I'm not sure, but at least I'll make my move with a little more information than I had before."

The older man smiled just a little. "You'll be making your move with a little more knowledge and more important," he pointed a finger in the air, "you'll be making your move with understanding of that knowledge."

He hated lying to Knowledge. He had no reason to lie and didn't know why he said he wasn't sure what his next move was. Bo Jack knew exactly what he was going to do. He just had to face karma when it came back to bite him in the ass. He could live with that. But, what he couldn't live with was knowing Tarzan was still drawing air.

VERSE 11

Bo Jack's frustration mounted as the days turned into weeks and the weeks turned into months. This was his last semester at Washington High School and despite his fair grades he wasn't going to graduate as he'd promised his mother. Bo Jack hated going back on his word, especially to his mom, but sometimes things just couldn't be helped. The last two months he'd been way too busy. Way too busy watching, planning, tracking O'Reilly's every movement to even think about school.

Last month, he'd even broken into O'Reilly's home while the cop was in his bedroom banging his neighbor's wife. In five minutes, Bo Jack was in and out, gathering all that he needed. It had been more difficult gaining access to the cop's gated community than it was breaking into Tarzan's half million-dollar home where Bo Jack had removed the alarm pad by the door, took the bubble gum out of his mouth and jammed it between two connectors before replacing the pad. Now, when O'Reilly armed and disarmed the alarm it still beeped, but the signal would never reach the alarm's brain.

If O'Reilly wasn't a cop, and if he hadn't raped his mother, Bo Jack would've just flown the twins back in from Ocho Rios to off him. Escobar was all business, well almost. Escobar had tried to strong-arm him into signing a shady record deal. O'Reilly, on the other hand, was purely personal. No one knew what Bo Jack was planning, not even his mother, who he'd always kept in the loop in the past. But this was a different day.

*****

Kids all over Georgia were on Spring Break. The Atlanta April showers had begin a week early. The rain was falling in buckets as O'Reilly drove home after his weekly Thursday night poker game with the fellas.

His phone began singing, "The devil bowed his head because he knew that he'd been beat. He laid that golden fiddle on the ground at Johnny's feet."

O'Reilly hit the ignore button, silencing the Charlie Daniel's band classic, "The Devil Went Down to Georgia."

He didn't even check to see who was calling, since he was pretty sure that it was probably Mike just wanting to gloat. *You can tell the sorry bastard has never won shit,* O'Reilly thought, still pissed that he'd lost a thousand dollars to the poor schmuck in just one hand. He still couldn't believe it. *I guess that's why the game is called Blind Man's Bluff. He called mine.*

O'Reilly shook his head. It had been dumb of him to bluff that way, but Mike truly was a schmuck. He never brought his balls to work; the joke was that Mike's wife had taken his balls away from him long ago. That fucker had busted his ass for twenty years on the force and he didn't have shit to show for it. Nothing, except for a bleeding ulcer and an unfuckably, ugly wife. But tonight, he'd shown some balls and had taken O'Reilly for a grand, even though O'Reilly was sure that Mike was never more than two seconds away from eating his own service revolver. At least, that's what O'Reilly believed, because that's what he would've done if he'd been living Mike's miserable life.

"Fuck," O'Reilly banged his hand on the wheel.

He didn't care about the thousand dollars. That was chump change compared to the money he took off Zone 5's project kingpins and freelance street level dealers. Losing to a loser who didn't know how to win was what had him royally pissed off.

His Charlie Daniel's band ringtone interrupted his mental evaluation of the night and O'Reilly shifted his souped-up midnight blue '72 Camaro Super sport before tapping the button on his earpiece. "Yeah."

"Yeah?" the soft voice whispered. "What kind of way is that to answer the phone?"

He reached for his phone and glanced at the screen. 'RESTRICTED' flashed across the caller ID.

"John, can you hear me?" the woman raised her voice just slightly.

Who is this? he asked himself. He had no idea, but whoever it was, she sounded like the perfect person to cheer him up. Actually anything with a wet tunnel between her legs would've sounded good to him on a rainy, late Thursday night.

The best way to get over being pissed off is to be pissed on.

"John, are you there?" the woman purred.

"Yeah, I'm here," he said, refusing to ask who was on the other end.

"Ms. Meow is cooing for Slippery Sam."

O'Reilly grinned. Slippery Sam was the name he'd given to his tongue. Now he knew exactly who was on the other end of the call.

"Where's Gene?"

"In the bedroom reading and marking up papers. District attorney stuff."

"Where are you?"

"In the basement."

"So, why are you whispering?"

"Because, I'm sitting on the basement stairs with a bucket of ice and some Halls cough drops. Oh, did I say I was completely naked?"

He kept his left hand on the wheel, while he shoved his right hand down into his pants. "No, you didn't mention that."

"I can only play with myself for… for... ...oh...." She paused, "so long...shit."

He had no idea what she was talking about, but it was the way she sounded that had him stroking his hardness while he drove.

"I'm sorry, babe," she gasped softly. "My lips are barley touching the cough drops that are stuck to the ice."

"Your lips?"

"Uhm-hmm," she cooed. "The ones between my thighs."

His hand and his car sped up. "You wish that ice cube was my tongue running across those thick… pink… throbbing… lips, don't you?"

"Uhm-hmmm."

"You want me to stick my finger in your ass while my tongue is twirling and vibrating on your clit."

"Uhm-hmmm. Fuck, yes. Yes," she said louder, no longer whispering. "I want you to stick Sammy Sausage in my ass, John."

"I'll be home in fifteen minutes," O'Reilly said.

"You know I can't come over there."

O'Reilly shook his head. This was exactly why he would free fuck for the rest of his life. Women were friggin' basket cases. All of them. Playing games with a man's nature was just not fucking cool. This was exactly why men just wanted to fuck. Too many mind games.

"John?"

"Fuck Sandra, you call me at midnight, masturbating on the fucking phone. What did you think I would say? Especially after the time we had this morning?"

"Okay," she said, giving in right away. "Just leave your front door unlocked and I'll try to come over for a few minutes after Gene's asleep."

O'Reilly pulled up to the security gate and swiped his card before driving through the black gates of his subdivision. "I'm not leaving my door open, Sandra. When your husband falls asleep, call me."

"But suppose...."

"Don't worry. I'm a light sleeper. I'll hear the phone."

"Sandra!" O'Reilly heard what must've been her husband call out to his lover.

"Okay, gotta go," she whispered before disconnecting.

He clicked off his phone right as he pulled into his driveway. He didn't know if she would call him tonight or not. It didn't matter to him since she didn't mean anything to him. All Sandra was was a good lay. And he had lots of those on speed dial if he needed a quick fix.

By the time he stepped into his home, he'd forgotten all about his next door neighbor, the district attorney's wife.

VERSE 12

Earlier in the day, Bo Jack had disguised himself as a caddy to get onto the country club grounds located right behind Tarzans secured East Lake Shores subdivision. There was no way Bo Jack could've walked through the upscale golf course without being seen if it weren't for the cover of darkness and rain. It took him almost two hours to walk through the three-mile dark, cold, wet golf grounds. It was hard to see five feet in front of him the way the rain was coming down, and the cover of night made it even more difficult to see.

After arriving at the rear of the two story custom brick house he used the duffel bag he'd carried to break a pane out of one of the double French back doors that led into O'Reilly's home. He waited a few seconds, listening for any movement. Satisfied, he stepped over the broken glass and into the house.

Once inside, he peeled off his wet clothes and changed

into the dry ones he'd brought. After putting on the black jeans and black hoodie, he removed his nigga-be-cool stick and slid it through the front pocket of his hoodie. Next, he removed his chrome Sig Sauer P238 .380, screwed the silencer on, and pulled the stock back, loading a bullet in the chamber.

He'd already taken care of the alarm's horns and the signal to the alarm service command center last month, but he didn't do anything about the alarm's flashing red warning lights that appeared whenever the alarms perimeter was breached. So, he walked over to the front door, put on his rubber gloves and pressed in 1-8-7-7, O'Reilly's code. After deactivating it, he reactivated the alarm, solving the flashing red light problem.

Ten minutes later, Bo Jack was on edge. He'd pulled his gun at the sound of thunder and he almost shot at a streak of lightning he saw through the window he just happened to be standing next to. His hands trembled with rage and anticipation as he waited.

He'd been there for just over an hour when he heard a car pulling into the garage.

The scene that he'd been planning for these last two months played over and over in his mind. How Tarzan's bitch ass would walk through the door from the garage and he'd be standing there, waiting.

Bo Jack imagined Tarzan closing the door and when he turned around, the barrel of his .380 would be staring at the middle of O'Reilly's forehead. *Nice house,* were the words that Bo Jack imagined that he would say.

Next, Bo Jack would bust him over the head with his mini-baseball bat. He was sure that O'Reilly would look up at him with hate in his eyes. But Bo Jack didn't care about O'Reilly's hate because he'd have ten times as much in his own eyes. They'd have a stare-down before Bo Jack would lift his P238 and *bang, bang, bang*! He'd blast him until all six bullets exploded in his face. Not even his own mother would recognize him.

The twisting of the doorknob brought Bo Jack back to reality and the door was barely open before Bo Jack charged. Tarzan blocked the first swing, but the second time, the miniature baseball bat hit its target. Bo Jack's prize was O'Reilly's broken nose and an endless supply of spurting blood.

"Heard you been looking for me, bitch." Bo Jack pummeled the big man with the miniature bat. "Hit me like you did my mother, pig." Bo Jack swung. "Piss on me, like you did my man." He flung the miniature Louisville slugger like a mad man. Blood was coming from Bo Jack's own mouth where he'd bitten his tongue by accident while trying to drop Tarzan.

Tarzan took the brunt of most of the blows and he was hurt. But instead of trying to cover up, the big man slowly bulldozed forward in an attempt to grab hold of the wild man-child.

It only took Bo Jack two seconds to pull the Sig Sauer from his jeans' pocket. Just as he came out with the silenced handgun, Tarzan did some type of Jackie Chan spin-kick, sending the gun flying across the hardwood kitchen floor.

The pain in Bo Jack's hand was intense, but his adrenaline blocked the pain as he charged for the knife rack on the kitchen's island.

"Come here asshole," Tarzan shouted as he clamped his left hand on the back of Bo Jack's neck. A second later, Bo Jack went flying over the granite bar top. Glass shattered on and around him as several wine glasses that had hung above the bar crashed to the floor.

As Bo Jack struggled to his feet, Tarzan grabbed him in a bear hug. "You my bitch now," he said, as he tried to squeeze the air and the life out of Bo Jack.

Using the only weapon he had, Bo Jack clamped his jaws onto the policeman's already broken and bleeding nose. Tarzan screamed as he stumbled backward, never letting go of Bo Jack. The two men crashed to the floor in front of the Sub zero stainless steel refrigerator.

Fighting off his pain, Tarzan rolled over until he straddled the nearly unconscious young man. His right arm was in the air, about to crash down onto Bo Jack's face when he heard the unmistakable poofing sound of a discharged silenced handgun.

His eyes were wide as he stared down at what looked like Bo Jack's lifeless body. Even in the dark, he could see the blood that was everywhere. The only problem was, Tarzan had no idea it was his blood. Furthermore, he had no idea that he was the one that had been shot.

But then, he definitely felt the next nine shots to the back of his head. At least for a couple of seconds.

*****

Johnetta dropped the gun in the small black Coach bag draped across her shoulder. She knelt down and pulled two hundred and sixty pounds of dead weight off of her son as if O'Reilly was a bag of feathers. She allowed only one tear to escape from the corner of her eye as she lightly touched her unconscious son's swollen jaw. She got onto her knees and lifted his back up off the hardwood kitchen floor. His limp body dangled in her arms.

"Momma gon' handle everything my little black bird," she said as she rocked her son back and forth the way she used to do when he was a child. "You'll be all right, Blackbird." Against her will, another tear escaped. "I love you so much, Beauregard Jackson Jones. I abandoned you once." She stroked his brow. "Never again."

She dried her eyes with the back of her black leather-gloved hand, then glanced around the darkened kitchen. She'd bought cleaning supplies and her plan was that in a couple of hours, she'd have the place so spotless, not even the ultraviolet light used in forensics would be able to detect her son's blood.

But now, as she glanced back down at her son's unconscious, beaten, bruised and swollen face, she knew she had to take different action. She couldn't risk her son dying.

Grabbing Bo Jack under his arms, she dragged him through the kitchen to the front door. "Momma's gon' get you out of here, Blackbird." At the door, she took a final look around the room. It was still black-dark, but the streetlights lit the room just enough for Johnetta to see that blood was splattered everywhere and some of the blood had to belong to her son.

She had to move quickly. She only had 72 hours before forensics would have the results from the two sets of blood samples that they would take from the scene and send to their police crime lab.

VERSE 13

Johnetta moved with strength that she didn't even know that she had. But within a few minutes, she had Bo Jack laid out on the back seat of the latest rental that she'd used to follow her son around. Only this time, the car wasn't rented. Having a spare key to a significant amount of Avis rental cars made it so much easier to steal one. A different car every week. It had cost average two hundred to duplicate each key, twenty-four hundred dollars in all. She had to do it this way, to almost ensure that a car would be available for her to steal at the spur of a moment.

She'd done it this way because she knew that her son was going to try and kill O'Reilly. She wasn't sure when. She wasn't sure how. But she knew that Bo Jack was going to try. And when he did, she'd promised herself that she would have her son's back, even if he didn't want her to. He may have considered himself a man, but to her, he would always be her baby, her responsibility. And like every good mother, she knew her baby and knew what he was going to do. From the moment she'd told him how O'Reilly had raped her, she knew her son's plans. She just didn't know the specifics of what he was going to do. But she knew he would do something, because he'd done it before - seven years ago when he was only twelve, two months before Child Services took him and his brother away...

Johnetta's boyfriend—and part-time pimp, had one hand snaked around her neck and the other in mid swing when Bo Jack walked through the sliding glass patio door of the Section 8 project apartment where they had lived.

Tank had turned to the skinny twelve-year-old. "Why you home so early boy?" he'd asked, surprised that Bo Jack was home from school.

"Take your hands off of my mother," Bo Jack had said in a voice that was so low, so calm that it had even scared Johnetta.

"Take your little ass back outside, boy. This don't concern you."

But neither the man's size, nor his words moved Bo Jack. He continued standing there, glaring at the man that had his hand around his mother's neck.

"I'm not gon' tell your li'l bad ass again," Tank said, giving his own glare to the skinny preteen.

Bo Jack balled and unballed his fists.

"Nigga, you deaf?" Tank asked.

Bo Jack still didn't move.

Tank's hand was still wrapped around Johnetta's small neck. "My momma used to say a hard head makes for a soft ass. Now get your narrow behind up out this apartment 'fore I give you some of what I'm 'bout to give your momma. Now git."

Bo Jack's lips barely moved when he said, "Take your hands off my momma."

"Or what. What the fuck your li'l ass gon' do if I don't." And when Bo Jack didn't immediately respond, Tank went on, "That's what the fuck I thought."

Tank, baby please," Johnetta had pleaded.

Tank had turned back to Johnetta, "Bitch, shut the fuck up. Talk to damn much."

"I will kill you," Bo Jack had said.

The man laughed, "Your li'l punk ass gon' do what," Tank said. A second later, he punched Johnetta dead in the center of her face.

She screamed and Tank laughed right before he punched her again.

Another scream.

Another laugh.

Tank said, "Say again, li'l nigga, what you gon' do?" Another strike. "To who, li'l nigga?"

Bo Jack ran and jumped on Tank's back, but the huge man swatted Bo off like a fly. "Fuck you, bitch," Tank said, spitting out the words as he glared at Johnetta, who had fallen to the small kitchen floor.

"'Cause you can beat up a woman and a kid, that makes you a man?" Bo Jack had cried, as he pushed himself up.

"Nah, li'l nigga," he grabbed his crotch, "these make me a man. One day you might grow some." He laughed.

"If you not careful, somebody might take yours."

"Your momma tried, she almost choked." With another laugh, he grabbed his jacket and then Tank slithered out through the patio door.

But then three days later, Tank was found dead in a boarded-up home behind the Thomasville Heights housing

97

projects where they were living at the time. Someone had cut his penis off and when the body was discovered, his severed penis was stuffed into his mouth.

An abused dog received more attention from the authorities than a black male murder victim, so Johnetta never worried about the truth being discovered.

But even though the police didn't know, she did. She knew her son had done the deed, even before he told her that Tank had been found dead. He never said anything else, but he didn't have to. Bo Jack was a planner and a thinker, like she was.

It was because of his thinking and planning and the fact that Escobar was a black man that Johnetta never worried about Bo Jack being picked up in connection with Escobar's murder.

But offing a white cop? That was like offing Jesus. APD would pull out all stops, exhaust every resource to find the responsible party.

Well, if she had anything to do with it, they'd never find out that her son, had anything to do with the cop's murder.

*****

Fifteen minutes after driving through the exclusive subdivision's gates, Johnetta pulled the stolen rental up to Northside Hospital's Emergency Room entrance doors. She ran inside, screaming like a madwoman. "A man is fucking bleeding to death right outside these fucking emergency doors."

For a moment, the hospital staff and patrons just stood, staring at her.

"I'm not kidding," she screamed. "There's a man out there," she pointed to the glass doors behind her, "bleeding to death."

Medical staff scrambled to the doors and followed Johnetta to the car. Two attendants and a nurse transferred Bo

Jack to a stretcher, then they rushed inside, taking Bo Jack to waiting doctors. Johnetta stayed behind, giving her information to the nurse who asked so many questions.

Four hours, fifty-three minutes and twenty-seven seconds after Bo Jack had been wheeled away, a doctor dressed in full scrubs, walked slowly through the Emergency waiting room door. His blue eyes were sad, but they shot daggers into Johnetta's. "Ms. Herscovitz," the man said softly.

She stood. "Yes," she said, responding to the fake name that she'd given them that matched the fake Georgia driver's licenses and Social Security card that she'd acquired just days after she told Bo Jack what O'Reilly had done to her. She had prayed that she'd never have to use the false identification, but she'd been prepared.

The doctor gently reached out for Johnetta's hand. "Beauregard had already lost so much blood by the time he was brought in."

Johnetta's heart pounded even harder if that was even possible.

"He was already in toxic shock and his blood pressure was extremely low. So were his sugar levels. So low, that we couldn't operate until we got his pressure and sugar levels to stabilize."

Why was he telling her all of this? Johnetta wanted to know only one thing – when would she be able to take her baby home.

But the doctor kept on. "Nothing we did was working and then, your son...he died on the operating table."

Time stopped, for a moment and then, Johnetta howled, "Nooo!!!!! My baby!" How had this happened? This was not the way it was supposed to be. "Nooo! You're lying!" she screamed.

"Mrs. Herscovitz." The doctor tried to calm her with his tone, but there was nothing that he could do to stop her from screaming. She swung her arms in the air, her fists flying, aimed at nothing and everything.

"Mrs. Herscovitz," the doctor called out to her again. "Please, please let me explain."

This time, she looked up at him and wondered why his face was fuzzy. Then, her legs weakened. And then...nothing.

It was hours before she woke up, laying flat on her back in a hospital bed. It took her a moment to collect herself. "Where am I," she asked aloud. She tried to blink the fuzziness away. She turned her head right and then left, finally realizing that she was in a hospital room. And then, she remembered.

The hospital room's brown wooden door opened. She couldn't see the face, but she heard footsteps.

"Mrs. Herscovitz."

It was the same doctor that had told her that her oldest was gone. She shook her head. "No, don't say it again," she groaned.

"But, Mrs. Herscovitz, your son is alive!"

Silence and then, "What? What did you say?"

"Your son is alive and actually it looks as if he will be able to make a full recovery."

"But you told me...."

"You didn't let me finish. You didn't let me explain that your son did die. He flatlined for over two minutes before he came back to us."

"How?" she asked in a slow drug-induced drawl.

The doctor shook his head. "We have no earthly idea."

Tears of joy rolled down her face. She pushed herself up and looked toward the ceiling. She wasn't a praying woman, but she wanted to send up a prayer of gratitude now. "How long...how long before I can take him home?"

"Your son is still very weak and there are lots of tests that we still need to do. But barring any setbacks, he should be able to check out in four, maybe five days."

Thank God, thank God! "Thank...you," she said to the doctor. "My sons are my everything...." *My sons!* She'd forgotten all about Brandon.

She tried to jump from the bed, but her mind started to spin and she fell right back into bed. Frowning, she turned to the left and that was when she noticed the plastic bag, and the tube that led to her arm. She studied the single drops that dripped from the bag into the tube that was inserted into one of her veins.

Seven years. It had been seven years since Johnetta had shot up. Seven years without a needle, without a glass dick. But now, it had come to this.

Were they serious? Had she lost her mind that much? So much that she had to be drugged? How was she supposed to stay clean?

A tear dripped from her eye and rolled down her nose before it fell onto the white hospital bed sheet. "How long have I been...." She didn't finish the sentence. Her eyes stayed on the needle in her arm.

"Six-hours. We had no choice but to sedate you. You were a danger to yourself."

As carefully as she could, she slid the needle from her arm. "I have to go." Now, she could stand, but when she did, she stumbled. The room was spinning.

"Wa, wa , wa," was what she heard from the doctor before she fell back onto the hospital bed.

She blinked rapidly. "What did you give me?"

"Wa, wa wa.......Wa, wa, wa, wa."

She closed her eyes and tried her best to push them open, but hours passed before she was conscious again. This time, she shot up in the bed like a cannon.

"Brandon!" she screamed her son's name.

Her words echoed around the four walls of the hospital room, but no one came. She took a deep breath and pushed herself up slowly. At least the room wasn't spinning this time. She took a step. No, not spinning. The room was rocking now. Rocking, she could handle.

Slowly she moved toward the edge of the room, then braced her back against the wall. She took baby steps, sideways toward the chair where her clothes had been neatly folded. She had to stop, and close her eyes before she reached for her pants and blood-soaked top and sweater.

But even though her clothes reminded her of what she'd been through, she had to put them on. She had to get out of the hospital.

She took her time getting dressed, steadying herself each time the room rocked. By the time she was fully clothed, the rocking had smoothed out enough for her to walk out the door. She had to get home. Brandon had been home all night by himself.

VERSE 14

An hour later, Johnetta stood outside the Office Depot that was right up the street from her house. She got out of the stolen car, removed the cardboard temporary dealership tag and put the Avis tag back on before she wiped it down. Satisfied, she turned away from the car, leaving it just a couple of spaces away from where she'd stolen it yesterday. The April sun was shining today; Johnetta didn't have the cloud and rain cover that she'd had yesterday, but still she walked to the corner and jumped into the waiting cab that she'd called before she pulled into the parking lot that Avis shared with Office Depot.

It just took a few minutes for Johnetta to arrive home and she could hear the television before she stepped through the side kitchen door. Glancing down at her watch, she saw that it was 2:30. Brandon obviously hadn't gone to school. The special education bus didn't drop him off at the top of the driveway until 3:45.

"Brandon!" she shouted. "Brandon!"

She ran through her house and up the stairs. She released the breath she'd been holding when she saw Brandon standing in the hall outside her bedroom still wearing his Batman pajamas.

"Momma, where you been?"

She wrapped her youngest son in her arms.

"Momma, you hurtin' me," he said as she squeezed.

She relaxed her grip and for the first time in hours she smiled. "Baby, are you all right?"

"Yeah, momma. I was just worrieded about you. I didn't go to school 'cause I didn't know where you was. And you didn't answer your phone. And Bo Jack didn't answer his phone."

"I'm so sorry, baby. I didn't mean to scare you."

"I wasn't scared, mom. I was worrieded. What kind of example are you and Bo setting for me?"

She was so caught off guard. She didn't know what to say. She would've laughed if the situation weren't so serious.

She grabbed his shoulders and looked him in the eye. "Son, you know momma loves you, don't you?"

He nodded.

"More than anything in this world. Anything, Brandon. You and your brother are everything to me and I will do anything to protect you."

"I know, mom."

"Baby, can you do momma a favor?"

He nodded.

"Never forget that, okay?"

"Okay," he said, even though Johnetta knew that Brandon didn't have any idea what he was agreeing to. She could tell that he just wanted to appease her.

"Family, Brandon," she continued with her lecture that she knew was too much for her ten-year-old. But she had to say these things to him. "Never forsake or forget family. Family is more important than money, fame, anything and everything combined."

"Okay."

A tear cascaded down her cheek and Johnetta thought about how much she'd cried in the last hours. "I need you to understand that. Do you, Brandon?"

"Yes." He nodded. "Family first."

"Whatever happens to us, no matter what distance, what walls that separate us, I will always, always," she put her fist over her son's heart, "be right here. And," she grabbed his hand and placed it over her heart, "you will always be here."

"Okay."

"Come on, let's pack." She pushed herself up and moved toward Brandon's bedroom.

The little boy followed her. "Where we goin'?"

"You'll see when we get there, baby. Now, come on, help momma."

Johnetta didn't talk to her son anymore as she packed a bag for Brandon first, then went into her bedroom to gather up a few essentials for herself.

It was all happening so fast, but Johnetta had it under control. Especially since she'd been told that Leon Herscovitz, the name she'd admitted Bo Jack under, was making steady progress. She'd wanted so badly to go into his room and see for herself, but she knew that Bo Jack was safe. She'd been gone overnight, and with Brandon having a learning disability there was no telling what was going on his world. Her worries had been transferred from one son to the other.

In less than an hour, Johnetta had Brandon strapped into her Chrysler. Two hours later, she'd dropped Brandon off with Knowledge after briefly explaining what had gone down. A half hour later she'd walked to her car and was back on the interstate, in the standstill Friday afternoon rush hour traffic.

She pressed the numbers on her cell and made the call she had to make. "Hello, Kimani?"

"Yes, this is she?"

Johnetta was relieved when Kimani picked up. Johnetta was afraid that after all these years; she would've changed her cell number. "This is Johnetta Jones."

"Girl, how are you doing?" Haven't heard from you since..."

"I'm in trouble," she interrupted. "Big trouble."

"I was just leaving the office. You wanna come in Monday?"

"It can't wait till Monday. I can be there in ten minutes." When Kimani paused, Johnetta added, "It's a matter of life and death."

Sensing the urgency, Kimani said, "Okay, I'll be here."

"Thank you," Johnetta said, once again grateful that she'd met this woman eight years before.

*****

Kimani Knox had been fresh out of law school and was determined to change the system from within when she'd met Johnetta. She was going to be a champion of the poor and the underrepresented and that's why she'd turned down higher-paying positions for an entry-level position with Atlanta Legal Aid.

The first week Kimani had been in her office, she'd met Johnetta. Johnetta had come in one day and had impatiently waited for three hours to speak with someone. Despite the building being a little chilly, sweat was dripping from Johnetta when she was finally called into the small cubicle assigned to the caramel-colored baby-faced, barely five-foot tall attorney.

With much attitude, Johnetta had that rotating neck-wandering eyeball thing going on. The bags under her red eyes had looked like folded curtains. Those were all signs that Kimani had been all too familiar with since she'd grown up with two drug-addicted parents.

Kimani might have been small in stature but her walk, her talk, everything about her, radiated confidence and self-love. Johnetta knew that the young attorney was a winner, even after Kimani had sent her home without an interview that first day.

"I can't help you until you help yourself," Kimani had told Johnetta.

And even though she was pissed, Johnetta knew the girl was right. The next week, Johnetta had checked herself into the ninety-day program that Kimani had gotten her into. And as soon as Johnetta completed the program, she returned to Legal Aid and Kimani, determined to get her boys back.

But to Johnetta's dismay, Kimani still didn't begin working on her case.

"You need to be stable," Kimani had told her. "In order for a judge to even consider the notion of you having custody of your sons again, you're going to have to be gainfully employed for at least a year, and you have to have a decent home."

Once again, Johnetta had been pissed. But once again, she knew Kimani had been right.

The next week, Johnetta had gotten a job as a cook at a Waffle House and that's when Kimani had gone to work. She'd found Johnetta an apartment, then helped her move out of the drug transition home. Over the next five years, Kimani helped

Johnetta cross all the T's and dot all the I's. She'd done everything the courts had asked and required. During that time, the two women worked closely together, and became more than attorney and client; they became friends.

And after a five and a half year uphill battle, mother and sons had been reunited.

Well, Johnetta needed her again and her prayer now was that Kimani could come through for her once again. The way she had before.

*****

Over the past eighteen months since closing Johnetta Jones' case, Kimani had often thought about her. Johnetta was her biggest success and her biggest failure. Johnetta had done everything she had to do to get her sons back, but at the same time, she hadn't done anything to find herself. Kimani had wanted Johnetta to care about herself as much as she cared about her sons. That was the only way she'd make it long term, Kimani was sure of that.

Kimani had tried to get Johnetta to read. She'd given her books about black women who had walked in similar shoes and how they'd come to know and love themselves and how they'd turned sand into sugar. But Johnetta wasn't interested. If it didn't pertain to her boys, she didn't want to know anything about it.

Kimani knew that was a mistake and she knew Johnetta's sons would suffer too. Kimani knew this from experience. She herself was still suffering. Her father had always been strong, before the drugs. And having recovered, he was strong once again. But her mother...she was a different story. Her mother had never truly gotten it. She'd never found herself. And now she was gone.

Kimani was a realist. She knew that once Johnetta got her boys back, she would be of no use to Johnetta and truthfully, she never thought she'd hear from her again. But in the minutes since she'd hung up the phone, Kimani was still caught off guard.

What does she want? Kimani wondered. Her instincts...and Johnetta's words told her that it wasn't good.

As promised, only ten minutes passed before Johnetta walked into her office. The two women hugged, but then, Johnetta sat down and began to tell her story.

Kimani listened, shaking her head in one place, taking notes at another point. The entire time she listened to Johnetta, she thought about her own background. She'd gone to school to be a defense attorney – that's what she'd always wanted to be.

But then, when she was an undergrad at Georgia State, she interned at Northside Woman's Day shelter on the Westside, near downtown. There, she counseled and worked with women who truly needed her. These women had no one to fight their causes and the law damn-sure wasn't going to protect them. So it was a natural progression for her to gravitate over to Legal Aid once she'd passed the bar.

In the years since she'd graduated, she'd only worked at Legal Aid. She didn't have one day of any defense experience.

But after hearing Johnetta's story there was only one thing she could do. She had to help her.

It was after-hours, but luck and blessings were on her side because Kimani was able to talk to the DA and two judges. And before the clock struck nine, she and Johnetta Jones left her office to meet up with the DA at the main DeKalb County precinct on Memorial Drive.

A deal had been struck – a deal that would cost Johnetta at least twenty-five years of her life.

WORLD WAR

GANGSTA

<u>BOOK 2</u>

They say we N-I double G-E-R, we are
Much more, but still we choose to ignore
the obvious, we are the slave and the master
What you lookin' for? You the question and the answer.

-Nas
The Slave and The Master

VERSE 1

Despite America's systematic bombing of five oil rich countries; despite America's mass media propaganda to sway public opinion of world leaders of oil rich countries; despite America's sanctioned assassination of two world leaders in hopes of controlling the Middle East's oil reserves, America was on the brink of financial collapse. The economy had been unstable since the housing market crash of 2007. For the last five years, the American middle class had been systematically downsized so much that economists predicted that by the year 2020, there would virtually be no middle class. Unemployment was at an all-time high and race relations were at a low that the country hadn't seen since the Jim Crow era.

The Tea Party Movement began very similar to the way

the Ku Klux Klan had been founded in 1866. Now, one hundred and forty three years after the Klan's inception, the Tea Party Movement rose in America, similar to the way the Klan had. Disguised as a political party against big government, the Tea Party has proven to be nothing more than a modern day non-violent Ku Klux Klan.

Barack Hussein Obama, America's first black president was the real reason the Tea Party Movement was formed, and his presidency is what has fueled the movement since its creation in 2009. Over the last four years, even white billionaires such as Donald Trump had publicly expressed racist sentiment toward the president. Major media publications such as *The New York Times* and *The Washington Post* had published racist caricatures of the president and they'd printed racist sentiments shared by many whites and blacks.

Before Mitt Romney was elected to run on the Republican ballot, the nation and the world got a chance to see the true ignorance of American politicians. The first six months of 2012 leading up to the Republican nomination was like an ongoing segment of *Saturday Night Live*. Republicans all over America cringed in embarrassment at some of the statements that came out of the nominees' mouths. Every week, there seemed to be a different front runner until Mitt Romney, captured the nomination in June.

And on the 17th anniversary of the Million Man March, President Obama shocked the world with his last major television address before the election. It was all over the news the next morning. President Obama had vowed to push through the Reparations Bill before the election in a few weeks: free education and healthcare for African-Americans for the next one hundred years. Major and minor news networks showcased their pundits analyzing every angle of the bill. The Commission knew that once the president rolled out the bill, the real powers behind government would be forced into immediate action.

The members of the Truth Commission were actually

surprised that the government hadn't already moved on the president. The day after President Obama proposed the bill, one of the Truth Commission's moles sent Bill Gates a message. THEY ARE MOVING ON THE ANSWER. HELICOPTER CRASH. WILL GIVE DETAILS ON WHEN AND WHERE LATER TODAY.

Upon receiving the message, the computer software magnate sent a message to Picasso who was already in Chicago. Based on America's past, the Truth Commission was reasonably sure that the real powers that be would strike fast after President Obama rolled out the Reparations Bill to the public. No way the real powers that be could allow him to be elected again if it meant reparations, and the president was so far ahead in the polls, he was sure to win unless....

Everything down to the second had been planned. The Truth Commission had become experts at counterintelligence, studying and accurately predicting the actions of those who influenced and controlled government, foreign and domestic. That's why Picasso, President Obama's double, and the preparation crew was in Chicago, hoping and waiting.

The University of Chicago, where the president taught Constitutional Law back in the mid '90's was the perfect place for the president's last major television speech for the sole reason of Soldier Field having an air and heating duct system that was just large enough for the president to fit inside. For security reasons, when leaving out of Chicago the president sometimes took a chopper from Soldier Field to O'Hare International, where Air Force One would be waiting.

While people all over the world were still picking their mouths up from the ground the morning after President Obama's historic speech, Michelle Obama was standing in one of three bathrooms inside Oprah's private suite at Harpo Studios.

The Secret Service team assigned to the First Lady wasn't as detail oriented, as the team assigned to the president, which was why the Truth Commission used her to relay all communications to her husband.

A few months before his assassination in 1965, Malcolm X, Mao Tse Tsung, Fidel Castro, historian John Henrik Clarke, and a young Muammar Qadafi formed the Truth Commission to end America's and Western Europe's terroristic reign of all peoples of color throughout the world. Although all the original founders (with the exception of Fidel Castro) were now deceased, their legacy lived on through the seven hundred and seventy-seven men and women who made up the top secret organization. A few of the Truth Commission's members were thought to be deceased by the general public. For example, Picasso, he was standing with Michelle Obama in the suite's small bathroom.

In the early 90's, the Truth Commission began watching Michelle Obama (then Michelle Robinson) during her time at Princeton, where she studied Sociology and African-American Studies. With her passion for freedom and exceptional intelligence, they knew she would be an asset in helping to emancipate the minds of the American people.

Barack didn't come to the attention of the Commission until he and Michelle met at Harvard. Over the next few years, the commission watched and secretly aided the couple's cause of uplifting the poor. In 1996, Michelle carried the title and the responsibility as Associate Dean of Student Services at the University of Chicago, while her husband was a part-time lecturer at the University's law school. By then, the couple had been under the Truth Commission's surveillance for five years. From 1991 to 1996, the Commission gathered intelligence and secretly helped pave the way for what was about to happen today. Being elected the first black president was only part of the plan. If everything went according to the Commission's plans, then President Obama would become bigger in death than he was in life as the first black United States president.

Picasso had stepped to Michelle first, in the winter of

'96 and she introduced Picasso to her husband days later. However, Picasso knew the Obama's wouldn't fully believe in what the Commission had spent over thirty years trying to do, until Picasso told them how and when Tupac was going to die, just a day before Shakur was shot in Las Vegas. And one month after Tupac's death, the Obamas rededicated their lives to the Commission's mission – right after they met the very-much-alive Tupac Shakur.

This morning, like always, no words were exchanged between Michelle and Picasso. He handed over the first note.

THE CIA IS MOVING ON THE ANSWER. HELICOPTER CRASH ON SOLDIER FIELD. TOMORROW.

The Answer was the codename that the Truth Commission used when referring to the president. Michelle read the note, nodded, and then handed it back to Picasso. He opened his mouth, stuffed the paper inside, chewed, and then swallowed before he handed her another.

THE ANSWER NEEDS TO WEAR HIS BLACK ARMANI SUIT JACKET, SLACKS, RED SILK DIOR TIE AND STARCHED WHITE SHIRT WHEN HE LEAVES TO CATCH HIS FLIGHT AT SOLDIER FIELD.

Once again, Michelle read, and Picasso took the strawberry-flavored three-by-five sticky note from her before he chewed and swallowed. Then, he gave her the final note.

THE ANSWER IS TO GO INTO THE NEAREST RESTROOM AS SOON AS HE WALKS INTO SOLDIER FIELD. THAT IS WHERE HE WILL EXCHANGE PLACES WITH A LOOK ALIKE.

6:00 PM THE SAME DAY

"Twenty-two minutes ago, President Obama," the reporter paused to collect herself. She pressed the tips of her fingers against the earpiece. A steady stream of tears flowed from her eyes and down her face.

Her professional, un-biased mask disintegrated, violating the unwritten code of non-emotional journalism. Even before she spoke her next words, the world that was tuned into CNN knew before Chin Li gathered herself that something had happened to the President.

"Along with the pilot and four Secret Service agents, the 44th president of the United States of America, Barack Hussein Obama, was killed in an accidental helicopter crash while en route to Chicago's O' Hare International Airport. Michelle Obama, Secretary of State Hilary Clinton and several aides and Secret Service agents were awaiting him on Air Force One."

President Obama's face was bigger than it was in life as it flashed across TV screens all over the world. Under the picture, the caption read, "President Barack Hussein Obama, August 4, 1961- October 17, 2012.

VERSE 2

A year ago Johnetta Jones was transferred to Pulaski State Women's Prison in Gainesville, about thirty miles outside of Atlanta. Her previous location was Metro State Maximum Security Prison for women, which used to be home to some of the nation's most dangerous and violent women. Pulaski had been a low and medium security prison, before Metro's maximum security inmates were moved there after Metro closed down. Now, Pulaski was extremely overcrowded and there was much more con-on-con violence than Metro had ever had.

Johnetta had never for one minute regretted the spur of the moment decision she had made over four years ago. She would have died for either of her children without giving it a second thought. So, the plea bargain Kimani had negotiated was a no brainer. She would have agreed to anything as long as Bo Jack wouldn't be implicated in O'Reilly's murder. To this very day she nor Kimani had no idea that O'Reilly had been messing around with the District Attorney's wife. Just like his wife didn't know that her District Attorney husband knew she had screwed O'Reilly the morning before the cop was killed.

Gene Shockey realized that Johnetta had done what he didn't have the balls to do. And for this, instead of the electric chair, or life in prison Shockey offered Johnetta twenty-five to life on second degree manslaughter. She had signed the deal later that night after the DA included that Bo Jack would never be charged as a co-conspirator.

This deal had eventually cost the DA his job and he was almost disbarred after evidence clearly proved that O'Reilly's murder was premeditated and that Bo Jack Jones was also a perpetrator in the act – a perpetrator that could never be charged now that the deal was signed by both parties.

Over the four years she'd been in prison, Johnetta had done a one hundred and eighty degree turnaround. Thanks to Knowledge she'd become an avid reader of history and culture. Bo Jack had become the biggest star breathing; Brandon had overcome his ADHD and Johnetta was one of the most respected inmates at Pulaski. She was also making a difference, especially since her Knowledge Be Free Society was working toward freeing the minds of the inmates and stopping the con-on-con violence.

Johnetta now loved herself, something she had never known how to do on the streets. Just today, she'd received the court papers making her name change official. "Johnetta was a slave," she told everyone who asked why she had chosen to change her name. "Isis represents the mother of truth and Uhuru represents freedom."

Thanks to all the books Knowledge had her reading the past few years, Isis genuinely loved her blackness, her struggle, and the struggle of her sisters and brothers. Any other inmate would be crazy to confront the leader of the largest gang in Pulaski. But Isis was far from being any other inmate. Isis was fearless. Big Mac's reputation and propensity for violence didn't frighten her. Not confronting Big Mac is what scared her. The gang leader had too much potential to be wasting her life destroying her sisters with the drugs she sold instead of building them up.

Isis shook her head as she stood in front of the prison gang leader's cell, holding onto the stainless steel railing, which looked over the second tier down to the first. *Who would've thought?* she wondered as she stared down at the common area where women were playing cards, reading books, talking shit, or waiting in line for the next available phone.

Isis's thoughts trailed off as the squishy sound of wet shower shoes on the gray concrete prison flooring approached.

"You got something on your mind, Isis?"

Isis turned and faced Big Mac. She took in the sight of her prison mate, holding the black shower bag in one hand and her dirty clothes in the other. The woman looked like a poster child for female bodybuilding.

Isis began with what was now her most pressing sadness. "*They* killed another one of our kings."

"Who did what?" The tall woman asked, stood with only a bone-colored towel wrapped around her muscular chest and small waist.

"President Obama."

"Ain't nobody killed that man," Big Mac said walking toward Isis. "He died in a helicopter accident with four white agents and a white pilot. Ain't nothin' more accidental than that. You think they would kill their own?"

"First, the white agents and pilot was not one of *them*. Oppression is not about black or white. That's just a disguise, Queen. Oppression is about green. Money and the people who oppress only make up about one percent of the American population and the Secret Service and a pilot don't have the money to oppress, Queen." Isis smiled. "Second, what happened to President Obama was on purpose, not an accident. Less than twenty-four hours after he does a George Bush and announces the Reparations Bill, he's dead." Isis paused, hoping Big Mac would understand the weight of these statements. "Come on, Queen. The agents and the pilot were just collateral damage. That helicopter was rigged."

"Coincidence," was Big Mac's one-word reply as she pushed past Isis, walking into her small cell.

"No such thing. There are no coincidences, or accidents, only reasons and purposes. And *their* purpose in killing the president was because that bill made him a threat. *They* must protect their power structure."

Big Mac said, "*They*. Everybody talk about *They*, when speaking of government conspiracy shit. I need to know who the hell *They* is, because a bitch need *They* ass to help a bitch get up out this cage. I'd marathon-suck all *They* dicks if I knew who the hell *They* was."

There was no way Isis could begin to speak of who *They* were, when Big Mac didn't even know who *she* was. She'd began calling herself Isis three years ago after reading books by Fanon, Akbar, and Diop. "Can we talk inside?" Isis asked.

Brenda "Big Mac" Cutter was serving a life sentence for stabbing her ex-boyfriend to death. "Enter at your own risk. You never know, I might eat you up. Me being the big bad wolf and all," Big Mac said, referring to the name some inmates called her behind her back. Big Mac propped a leg up on the small metal desk adjacent to the metal bunk beds.

Isis stepped inside the cell and walked up to the naked six foot tall, muscled, bald headed peanut butter colored woman. She put a hand on her shoulder, looked her in the eye and said, "Queen, it's time."

Big Mac removed her leg from the desk and jerked away from Isis's touch. "Bitch, if you don't get your feelers off of me. I ain't buying into that self-love bullshit you selling."

"Time you start buying into what I'm giving away. It's time for you to take your proper place in society among your sista's who need your strength, Queen."

Big Mac pointed a finger in Isis's face. "Let me tell you something, bitch. I ain't nobody's queen, so don't call me that shit. My name is Big fucking Mac."

"No, it's not." The little women stepped forward. "Your name represents the type of woman you are, your character. Big Mac doesn't even begin to describe the God in you, Queen."
The heavily muscled woman looked Isis up and down, sizing up the fit, five-five, one hundred and thirty-pound woman in her mid-to-late thirties. The twenty-something-year-old Big Mac didn't say a word as she slipped into some gym shorts and an oversized wife beater T-shirt. Once she was dressed, she said, "Bitch, you can't be playin' with a full fifty-two, coming up in my cell with that black love queen shit." The convicted killer took a step closer, her 36 C cups were close enough to kiss Isis' nose. "Give me one reason why I shouldn't knock you the fuck out?"

"Because you're scared," Isis responded as calmly as if she were telling her the temperature.

"Scared?" Big Mac shouted. "Bitch, I'm Satan in this hell, the boss bitch of Pulaski. What the fuck I gotta be scared of?"

"The truth."

They were silent for a moment as Big Mac's cellie walked in and strolled toward the stainless steel toilet. Her pants were halfway down her legs when Big Mac growled, "Li'l bit, I know that ass ain't about to sit on that toilet while I'm talkin'."

"I gotta pee," she whined.

"If you don't get your young, dumb, disrespectful ass down the hall to the community bathroom, I'm gon' put my size twelves so far up your li'l ass that..."

The young girl wiggled back into her pants, then scurried out of the cell before Big Mac could finish.

Big Mac turned back to Isis. "Now, what was that shit you were saying?"

"I was saying that you're afraid to hurt me because you're not sure if what I'm teaching these sista's is really the truth. You perpetuate the ignorance that you do because you don't understand any better."

Big Mac squinted and balled, then unballed her fists. "You calling me stupid?"

"No." Isis shook her head. "Stupid is what stupid does. Ignorance is acting without understanding the knowledge presented or misrepresented."

Big Mac dropped her arms. "What the fuck you trying to say, Isis? Why don't you just speak English?"

"I'm saying, you are strong. You are a leader. People follow you. You run the biggest gang in Pulaski. The queens in your clique…"

Big Mac corrected, "My Boss Bitches."

"Yes, them. They think you the end all to be all. It's just too bad that you don't think of yourself the way they do."

"Oh, I get it." Big Mac crossed her arms and tilted her head. "If I had knowledge of self, if I knew who I was, where I came from, then I wouldn't have my girls running dope, selling ass, and taking bets." The scar on Big Mac's jaw widened as she smiled. "Bitch, you got me fucked up with one of them lonely, homely Thorazine-medicated bitches in the psych ward. I love the fuck outta me. Look at me." The statuesque woman spread her arms and turned in a full circle. "I'm six-foot, one hundred and seventy-five pounds of muscle. I cum several times a day unaided and sometimes aided by damn near any bitch I desire. I got almost one hundred money-making boss bitches who will die for me," she snapped her fingers, "just like that.

Isis said, "I do not question your esteem. I can see that it's very high, extremely high. What I question is the respect you have for yourself," she paused to let the words sink in. "Queen, these little boys out there wearing the sagging pants think they look good. And you can't tell them otherwise. They think we like to watch them waddling around like human penguins. And how about Clarence Thomas? He thinks he's everything with his white wife and white life. Looking into his life, it appears that his self-esteem is in the clouds, but his self-respect is non-existent." Changing gears Isis added, "Tell you what. Give me one month, Queen, just me and you, two hours a day, three times a week. And if you're not convinced of everything I say, I will disband the Knowledge Be Free Society."

"What I care about your Knowledge Be Free Society? That shit don't have no effect on my money."

"Okay, if we don't see eye to eye in a month, I'll have twenty thousand sent to anyone you want."

"Now, you talkin' my talk, bitch."

"Talk ain't nothing but letters put together to make words if the walk doesn't support the talk, Queen."

"I hear that hot shit," Big Mac said.

"No, you don't not. At least not yet. But I promise," Isis nodded, "you will."

"Isis, I like you, but please believe if you don't make good on that money in a month, the CO's, your Free Be Knowledge bitches, not even that fine-ass superstar rapper son of yours will be able to save that ass."

"Understood." Isis nodded.

"What you gettin' out of all this?" Big Mac asked. "Why you putting so much on the line?"

"I'll be getting one of God's queens back to black. And with your ability to inspire and lead," she whistled, "we'll be closer to freeing the queens in here."

"Bitch, is you talkin' about," Big Mac's voice dropped two octaves, "escape?"

Isis nodded. "That's exactly what I'm talking about." Isis meant mental freedom, but of course she would let the woman in front of her think she meant physically escaping.

"I'm gon' fuck with you, Isis." She pointed a long finger in Isis' face. "You got one month, Bitch. And after that, you better have my money!"

VERSE 3

Muslims in Indonesia, Christians in Ethiopia, Buddhists in China, Hindus in India, images of individuals and groups from across the globe were shown grieving the loss of one of the world's greatest orators and humanitarians. News about the President's passing dominated the airwaves twenty-four hours a day, all over the world.

But Sarita Davis from ABC News was covering another story as she sat in a leather lawn chair on the gazebo overlooking the manmade lake on Bo Jack's multi-million dollar mansion.

"Mr. Jones," the journalist crossed her almond-colored legs, "in three years, you have become a living legend, an icon in music. Each one of your three albums have gone multi-platinum. You have crossed genres with your melodic rapping style. Can you tell our viewers the secret to your success?"

125

Brandon sat in the corner on a barstool while Bo Jack sat in a leather chair facing the forty-something beauty in front of him. As he took in all of her fineness, Bo Jack's thoughts were on the fact that a couple of years ago, Sarita Davis would have been prey. But after reading the autobiographies *Assata* and *Part of My Soul Went With Him,* he couldn't even use the B word to describe black women, let alone look at them or treat them like a piece of meat.

"Real talk. That's my secret," Bo Jack said, finally answering her question. "My music is a reflection of black life in hoods all over this country. I don't," he paused, "I don't sugar coat... I don't sugarcoat anything." He paused to glance over at his fourteen-year-old brother.

Brandon shook his head from left to right.

"Mr. Jones." She placed a hand on Bo Jack's knee. Her infectious smile was replaced by the serious look she now wore. "Three days ago we lost President Obama. Can you share some of your thoughts and feelings about his passing?"

Bo Jack suddenly became uncharacteristically somber. He turned to his left. Behind the three-man camera crew over in the corner, at least ten feet away, his brother sat in the same place. He couldn't see the look on his little brother's face, but he could imagine the disappointment that his brother would feel if he didn't stand up. Malcolm X, once said take the word freedom out of your vocabulary if you weren't willing to die for it. The young rap phenom took off his Gaultier shades and leaned forward.

"Real talk, Ms. Davis. I thought the president was a sellout until I met him personally last year after performing at the Super Bowl. But let me tell you something, President Obama was a real man, a free man who lived for the day he could help repair the mentality of forty million descendants of slaves." Bo Jack stood up. "You wanna know how I feel? I'm mad as hell. I'm fucked up on several levels. This was a man who risked his life to run for the highest office in this nation – a man who tricked the nation and the world. That's why they killed him."

"What do you mean, tricked?" she asked.

"President Obama, taught Constitutional Law at the University of Chicago. He was a Harvard scholar. He married a woman who got a degree in sociology and African-American studies. Obama new the game. He taught it. I mean he knew the racist constitution inside and out. His wife gets a degree in blackness and being sociable, so you know Michelle broke down blackness and sociology to him, if he already didn't fully understand. President Obama made the world and even black folks think he was a go along to get along president with an agenda that didn't include black folks. But when he rolled out that Reparations Bill and said he was passing it into law, he messed white folk up everywhere. Imagine free education and healthcare for black folks for the next 100 years. As soon as he made the speech, I knew he was done."

"I'm sorry," Sarita said, shaking her head as if she didn't understand. "What are you trying to say?"

"I'm not trying to say anything. I'm saying that the president didn't die as a result of an accident. Let's keep it one hundred: President Obama dies in a freak helicopter accident the day after he announces reparations, three weeks before he was a done deal to be elected for a second term. Go into any poor black community in America, the people will tell you. The powers behind government sanctioned a hit on President Obama. Just like they did Dr. King after he came out against the Vietnam War. Just like they did Malcolm after he came back from his pilgrimage in Mecca."

"Who are the powers that you are speaking of, Mr. Jones?"

Bo Jack's little brother interjected as he approached. "The Illuminati. Not the fake *Hidden Secrets* video circulating across the Internet. I'm talking about the secret sect of international bankers, oil company heads, Haliburton and warlords who have controlled economies and wars since the Rothchilds and Adam Weishaupt started the international banking system in the late 1700s."

The cameras turned their focus to the skinny teenager as he slowly walked toward Bo Jack, then stopped when he stood at his brother's side.

Bo Jack waved for Brandon to chill before he patted his chest. "My whole life," Bo Jack began, "I've been running to or from something. I done robbed, sold dope. I done did all types of dysfunctional shit in my life, including the type of music I've been recording. Music I just defended. Music that ain't gon' benefit no one but me, and my producer. I don't even write the lyrics on my tracks. I'm out here rapping about the streets, the dope game, all types of material meaningless shit, when I need to be rapping about the mind raping mothafuckas who control the economy. I need to be rapping about the brothas and sistas fighting overseas for a government that never meant for them to be free. It's time for us to wake up and fight the real enemy. From this moment forward, I'm standing up. I am not going to let the president's death be in vain." He stopped suddenly, leaned back, and slipped his shades over his eyes. "I'm sorry Ms. Davis, interview over. I can't do this anymore. I have to tell the truth." The young superstar's voice trembled and tears slid from under his sunglasses.

It didn't take long for Sarita Davis and the cameras to pack up and leave, breaking down much faster than the time they'd taken to set up. Now alone, Bo Jack and Brandon sat silently on the gazebo, both gazing out at the world, both silently reminiscing on how they had arrived at this place in their lives.

"Smoke Til You Choke," and "A Hundred Grand Draped Around My Neck," were two tracks from Bo Jack's first album *Ballin' for Life*. Both tracks had been in the top twenty on the Billboard charts for a record one hundred sixty-four consecutive weeks and his last album *Saggin and Swaggin* had broken Michael Jackson's *Thriller* album sales record.

G-Swag had been right about Bo Jack. The former drug dealer was bigger than Tupac and Biggie combined. He was so popular that a handful of celebrities rushed the stage at the Grammy's earlier this year when Bo Jack performed his sensual mega hit, "Three Tongue Motion."

Bo Jack was surrounded by the people that he knew. He employed his old crew, every one of them who was alive and not in the pen. They were his bodyguards, his back-up rhythm section, and whatever else he needed them to be. Although he and Brandon were the only ones hooked on history and black culture, some of his and his brother's words and newfound ideologies spread to Bo Jack's thirteen-man entourage, the Goon Squad. His closest seven lived in the twelve bedroom, sixteen bath, twelve thousand square foot mansion that G-Swag helped him custom build after receiving his first multi-million dollar royalty check.

Brandon's eyes were glued to Bo Jack's new UH-1 Huey helicopter parked in front of the tennis court on the new helipad. It was the same type of helicopter that the president was killed in.

"Bay bruh." Bo Jack put an arm around his brother.

"It's just hard for me to keep my mouth closed," Brandon said with tears in his eyes. "I'm fourteen and I can see that the president's death wasn't no accident. Our people are just scared, afraid to die." He shook his head. "The sad part is our people don't even realize that they slaves to the economy, and death is more inviting than being a slave. If they knew about the black heroes and sheroes who died trying to free America's 17th, 18th, 19th, 20th and 21st century slaves..." He turned to his big brother. "I'm sorry."

"Don't be. What you said was real. A little too real, but it is what it is,"

"I'm tired, big bruh. We believe any ole shit the media put out there. People know Obama was killed. That's common sense," Brandon said as he looked up at the sky.

"As Knowledge says, common sense isn't common" Bo Jack said.

"Knowledge ain't never lied."

Bo Jack nodded. "That's why I'm about to change the game."

Brandon looked up at his brother with hope in his eyes. "What can I do?" he asked.

"Help me write. I ain't about to spit another lyric that G-Swag's team writes for me. And since G-Swag's writers don't know the truth, they can't write it. We have to give it to 'em raw and uncut, bay bruh. We 'bout to give the slaves the game we been getting the four years Momma been on lock."

Brandon smiled. "If you're... I mean if *we* are going to change the game, you need to begin with changing your image."
"How you mean?"

"Bo Jack Jones and the Goon Squad don't fit who you are now and what you're going to be doing. You need to become King Black and H-Nic, Porkchop, Bam-Bam and the others need to be the God Squad."

"King Black and the God Squad." Bo Jack paused for a moment, then nodded. "I like that. Momma is gon' be mad proud. King Black," he repeated before getting back to where he left off. "All the work mom and Knowledge been puttin' in trying to get me to start rapping about reality and freedom – "

"I'm really proud of you, too."

Bo Jack put his arm around his little brother. "You're my inspiration li'l bruh. After the way you were born. Doctors saying that you would never develop beyond the eighth grade. I believed them all.

"But then when Momma went away and Knowledge took you – " Bo Jack paused and shook his head. "After just four years of home schooling, look at you." Bo Jack extended an arm toward the lanky, six-foot tall teenager.

"I owe it all to the creator and the ancestors whose spirits dwell inside of me," Brandon said, sounding much older than his fourteen years. "If it weren't for Knowledge's teachings and readings, I would still be in someone's special education class."

"I wish Knowledge would let me take him off the streets," Bo Jack said more to himself than to Brandon.

"He allowed you to buy tents for the community. That's a start. A lot of homeless folks won't be sleeping in cardboard boxes."

"That was nothing, bay bruh. And it wasn't enough. I just don't understand it. Why would Knowledge or anyone want to continue living that way? Outside in all the elements, with no running water, no bathroom. I just don't get it. Nobody in their right mind would choose to live on the streets," Bo Jack repeated, "I just don't get it."

Brandon turned to his brother. "I get it."

Bo Jack looked at Brandon with his question in his eyes.

Brandon said, "But, I'm not going to try to explain it to you. You need to talk to Knowledge and let him break it down for you. Who knows, you might sit down with Knowledge and he might help you write the next album."

Bo Jack stared at his little brother for a moment and marveled at the wisdom he possessed. "Maybe," Bo Jack said. Changing gears, he blurted out, "Bay bruh, I think you should move in with me. Helping to write my next album is going to require a lot of me and you time."

"You know I can't do that, Bo. I mean King Black." He smiled. "Knowledge has gotten me this far in my understanding and I'm loving it. Don't get me wrong. You my big brother and I love you, but I need all the Knowledge I can get and I'm getting it, living beneath the bridge."

The smile faded from Bo Jack's face.

"But don't worry," Brandon continued. "I will be wherever you need me to be at whatever time you need me to be there. But, I can't leave."

Bo Jack was proud of his little brother. If the shoe were on the other foot, if his brother were offering him a home, there was no way Bo Jack would not take him up on his offer. He would give up living under an expressway bridge in a New York minute. The only reason Bo Jack allowed Brandon to live that way was because he was with Knowledge.

Ever since Bo Jack had read his first book *Visions for Black Men* a couple years ago, he wanted to rap about his vision for black men, but G-Swag had explained that black consciousness don't make dollars and if it don't make dollars it don't make sense. He also explained that Jay-Z had once wanted to rap about black consciousness, spit like Common.

But then, Jay-Z sold a million records and after that, he hadn't once thought about rapping like Common, since.

G-Swag was right in a sense. Common, Mos Def, Jada Kiss, Rakim, and his favorite, Nas; if you take all their sales and roll them up into one, they wouldn't add up to half of what Bo Jack had sold with his first album. But still, Bo Jack had mad love and admired the group of conscious rappers for foregoing the big paydays and speaking truth in their lyrics.

It was just now becoming clear to him. He was just beginning to understand what his mother had explained to him about money. When he'd gotten his first royalty check from G-Swag three years ago, he'd made a copy of the 4.2 million dollar check and sent the copy to Johnetta. A few days later, she had sent him a letter.

*****

King,

I am happy for you and at the same time I am scared for you. Money has made slaves out of its masters time and time again. I need you to remember that money cannot buy the things that really matter in life. And what really matters is the relationships you develop with others while you're here on this earth. That is a person's true and meaningful legacy. You were born into this world to help the next man or woman. Just think, what kind of world would this be if everyone did unto others as they wanted done unto them?

Loving me, loving you,

Queen Isis

VERSE 4

At the insistence of their leader, H-Nic and the other twelve members of the Goon Squad had recently put down their big Tees and starter jackets for dark blazers and button-down shirts. They'd discarded their True Religion sagging jeans and Air Force One sneakers for Armani slacks and Forzieri dress shoes. No neck ties though, because they all agreed with Bo Jack. Neckties felt too much like nooses. Not all of them agreed on the new dress code, but King Black was the boss and they all were loyal to him.

H-Nic and D-Bo were wearing their new outfits when they got out of the front seat of their boss's half-million dollar, bulletproof Maybach and together they scanned the gloomy grounds that the Pulaski Women's Prison was built on. After being convinced that the grounds and visiting parking lot was clear of any reporters, fans, or haters, H-Nic opened the back door.

Bo Jack sat in the back of the car with his cell phone pressed to his ear. He glanced at D-Bo, held up his finger and mouthed, "In a minute," and then returned to his phone conversation with Kimani Knox.

"Sarita was pissed. I could tell the way she enunciated her words whenever she referred to her bosses at ABC." These were the same bosses that accused Bo Jack of making anti-patriotic statements during the interview. "So, what do you want me to tell her, King?" Kimani asked.

Bo Jack had fired his personal assistant and had hired his mother's defense attorney a couple of years before. She cost ten times what he'd paid his first assistant, but Kimani earned and was worth every dime. Besides, Bo Jack didn't mind shelling out the cash for Kimani. She was a highly sought after criminal defense attorney moonlighting as his personal assistant and media go-between. She wasn't a kiss-ass, didn't care a bit about his money, could care less about his fame, and totally and completely had his back. Bo Jack knew that he could trust her.

"Why you askin' me, when I already know you told her something?" he said.

"You think you know me, Beauregard Jackson Jones?"
"I do know you, Kimani Amina Knox, but obviously you don't know me."

"If you know so much, Mr. Jones, then what did I tell ABC's top black interviewer?"

Half-stepping out of the black luxury vehicle, Bo Jack answered, "You probably said something like, 'My client isn't interested in having his and his brother's comments edited completely out.' And then, you probably said that I wouldn't be interested in answering other questions to replace the ones they wanted to take out."

"Wrong!" she said.

"Hold up, Queen, I'm not finished. You probably ended up telling Sarita that I would do an interview with ASPIRE as long as their interviewer asked the same questions and they, like ABC, let us approve the final product before it aired."

"Wrong!" She chuckled. "So are you ready to let me tell you what I said?"

Even though she couldn't see him, Bo Jack grinned. "Okay. Go ahead."

"Well, first, I told Sarita that you would not be interested in having ABC air the edited interview. And second, I told her that you would allow Magic Johnson and his camera crew to come out to the house and do a thirty-minute close up as long as he asked the same or similar questions that she had asked *and* I already warned Sarita that you would answer the same way *and* she said that's what Magic Johnson wanted."

"Isn't that what I just said?" Bo Jack asked.

The two laughed together.

But thirty minutes later, all of Bo Jack's laughter was gone as he sat in the small, cold room waiting for his mother. He reared back in the black, leather chair, pushing himself away from the table. Whenever he came to the prison, his thoughts were on his mother and how his life had changed. He had a lot of money now and he'd learned just how to use it. There was so much that money could buy – like the twenty-five thousand dollars that it cost him every year to be able to visit his mother in the attorney-client visitation room. This wasn't anywhere near luxurious, but at least he could visit with his mother alone. They could touch and hug and have a private conversation. A luxury not afforded to the other inmates.

Yes, money got him a lot of things...and a lot of people. Especially women. He hadn't met a woman – single or married – that he couldn't buy. Well, there was one exception – Kimani, though she wasn't his type. Bo Jack liked a woman who was similar to a small fast sports car. He wanted his women young, fast, fine, and petite. She could look like a pit bull in the face, but she had to have hips, ass, and thighs. And she had to have a tight stomach.

Kimani, on the other hand, was more like a three series BMW: luxurious, but with a little girth, not at all built for speed or the life that Bo Jack led. She was definitely cute in the face, but not thin in the waist and that was a must of all musts. The twisting of the key in the steel visiting room door interrupted Bo Jack's thoughts.

"Queen, you are so much better than the way he treats you," Isis's voice came into the room just a few seconds before she did. "Have you looked at yourself lately? I mean, you shine, girl. You're beautiful."

Isis walked in followed by a box shaped, butter-colored female guard. As the guard used a key to remove her handcuffs, she asked Isis, "You really think so, Isis?"

Wow, Momma even has the COs calling her Isis.

"I know so," Isis said as she rubbed her wrists where the cuffs had been. "But none of that makes any difference if you don't feel beautiful."

The guard lowered her head until her chin rested on her chest.

"Queen," Isis used the tips of her fingers to make the guard look her in the eye, "on your next day off, go get your hair, nails and toes done. Buy yourself a brand new outfit, nothing cheap. Spend some money on yourself and buy something that shows off those beautiful curves, girl. And after you find the perfect outfit, then buy yourself some sexy lingerie."

"Lingerie?" The guard frowned.

"Sexy lingerie," Isis repeated.

"And then what?"

Isis tilted the guard's chin up just a little bit higher. "First, hold your head up girl. The only time you should be looking down is if you're looking for something. Now after you buy that outfit, you put it on and go to that man. If he really loves you, he will show you. And I don't mean by what he says. Watch the way he looks at you, the way he speaks to you. Pay attention to the way he says what he says. Words can lie, but body language usually tells the truth."

As Bo Jack watched the interaction between his mother and the guard, for the first time, he saw a smile cross the heavy-set Hispanic woman's face.

"I'm going to do it, Isis," she said with excitement. "And if Jorge doesn't recognize what he has, then I'm going to go right on down to the Latin Quarter and find me a man who can and will appreciate the gift of me." She nodded her head like she was determined, then strutted out of the room with a confidence that she didn't have when she walked in.

Isis smiled as if she was pleased. Turning to her son, she said, "I need to spend a little more time with Officer Ramirez, but not right now. I haven't seen you in over a month." She held open her arms and Bo Jack fell into her embrace.

"I love you, Mom."

"I love you, too, Son," she said as she took the chair right across from him.

Bo Jack sighed as he unbuttoned his suit jacket. "I have the number one album in the country. I'm on billboards and buildings across the country. I'm in three commercials. I'm starring in the next *Transformers* movie. I've got more money than some small countries, but I can't even get my mother out from behind these walls."

Isis leaned across the table and stared into the eyes of her first born. He was a mega star to the world, but he was her little boy – and would always be her baby. The smile on her face couldn't be mistaken for anything other than pride.

"Son, these walls do not confine me. I travel every day, sometime as far as the Orient, and often to a different time." She cupped Bo Jack's face in the palm of her hands. "Books are my preferred mode of travel, and your momma has an unlimited amount of frequent flyer miles."

"I know, Mom. But, I need you. Everything I've done, all of my accomplishments–"

"For which all praises are due to the creator," she interrupted.

"I know, and I'm grateful for everything that He's blessed me with. But none of that fills the void in my life. I would trade it all, give it all back for you to be at my side."

"But, I am–"

"No, Momma" he said, shaking his head before she could even finish. "You are not free. And you're not by my side. So, please don't say you are. You're not. I don't care how many books you read or how many people you help. You've been in here for four years. Four years, Mom! So much has happened and you've missed it all."

"Yet, so many things have stayed the same, Son. We are still who we were yesterday. Our love is just as strong today as it was yesterday. Our determination to win is just as strong as it was yesterday. And I know you don't want to hear this, but I am closer to freedom than I have ever been. I've found purpose in my life. I'm doing something good with these women in here.

These sistas come into this prison already locked up. They come in here addicted, abused, confused, and lost and I'm helping them. I'm helping to build their character. I'm teaching them the importance of understanding. I'm setting women free and sending queens back to their families and communities. I'm giving these queens what no women ever gave me, understanding of self and unconditional ride or die love. And with that, these women can leave here understanding how to grow their sons into kings, how to grow their daughter into queens, how to be a good wife and a good woman."

He lowered his head and his eyes. "I'm sorry, Mom. I don't mean to belittle anything that you're doing. You're doing your thing, making a difference. It's just that, I want you with me and Brandon." His voice was softer when he said, "I guess I'm just being selfish."

She used her index finger to lift his chin up. "Not selfish. You're being my son."

He nodded and was silent for just a moment. "Mom, you know I understand how you feel about life and community. I used to feel the same way, but my mind is all twisted up right now. I've been messed up the last few days since President Obama died. It seems like black people don't even care about what happens to our leaders. We crying all over the place and praying in every house. Memorial services are being held all over the country for President Obama. Every congregation in every black church is singin' 'Lift Every Voice and Sing.'

"But no one is talking about or addressing the real issue. You don't have to be no brain surgeon to see that President Obama was assassinated. When are we going to stop praying and hymn singing and start lifting every fist and swinging? This country is f'ed up," he said, careful not to curse. "Our people don't have any direction. We still letting the media choose our leaders."

Isis smiled as if she was unmoved by her son's outrage. She didn't say a word, at first.

Bo Jack continued, "We allow the media to put any ole nonsense in our heads. We see it. We hear it. We believe it." Her smile was still wide, but soft. "So, Son, what are you going to do about the direction and leadership that *we* don't have? What are you, Beauregard Jackson Jones, going to do about the media propaganda that *we* blindly feed into?"

Bo Jack leaned toward his mother and planted the palms of his hands flat on the table. "First thing I'm going to do," he said as if he'd already thought about this, "is legally change my name to King Black Horus Uhuru Jones."

Now, Isis's smile widened.

"I think that's the perfect complement to you, Mom. I love your name, Isis Uhuru Jones and I want to be connected to you that way."

Her expression was filled with pride. "That's a strong name to live up to."

Her tone was so serious that Bo Jack leaned back a little. "You think I'm doing too much, Mom?"

She shook her head "Not at all. Not at all, Son. You're going to wear that name well."

"Thanks, Mom." He nodded. "But I'm moving in the right direction all because of you and Bran. I would've never understood if you and Brandon hadn't inspired me to read. If I would've read Fanon, Akbar, Dr. Ben, Diop, Ani, Clarke, Windsor, Massey, Rodney – I could go on and on, but if I would have been introduced to any one of them when we were on the streets–"

"You wouldn't have been ready to receive them then," she interrupted before he could finish.

"But if I had started reading before," Bo Jack said, shaking his head.

"Don't be so hard on yourself, Son. It took me a while, too. I wasn't ready to find myself until I realized that I was lost. And Knowledge was like my flashlight. First, he turned on the light so that I could see that I was living in darkness, and then he helped me to see with clarity. It took me losing everything that I could touch before I realized that the only reality is what can't be felt by touch or seen with the human eye. Am I diving to deep, Son?"

"Nah, Mom, not at all. You're talking about levels of consciousness." Bo Jack nodded. "Nefer Amen breaks it down in *Meter Neter*."

"I haven't introduced you to metaphysics yet," Isis said.

"Brandon did."

Her eyes widened. "Your little brother is reading *Meter Neter*?"

"Reading it? Mom, Brandon has read it and dissected *Meter Neter*. He can teach it. Brandon is just a young version of Knowledge. I'm telling you, Ma, your baby boy is the truth. He's so much like Knowledge that he'd rather live with him in a tent under the expressway rather than to leave Knowledge and live with me."

Isis leaned away from her son, though she was still smiling. "Are you hearing yourself? You've been talking all of this wisdom and knowledge, but now you're allowing your lower self to dictate to your higher self. Knowledge is the greatest luxury of all. Knowledge is invaluable. How one uses knowledge determines your inner and outer struggle. The disseminator of knowledge is the one who controls his or her surroundings."

Bo Jack sat silently for a moment and lowered his head just a bit. Standing up, he said, "You're right, Mom. I've got the vehicle and the avenue to take control. We've sat by and let them take Martin, Malcolm, Lewis, and Qadafi." He banged his fist on the table and said, "I'll be damned if I let them get away with taking Obama."

Isis stood and slowly circled around the table until she stood in front of her son. Looking up and into his eyes, she once again took his face into her hands. "This is your purpose. Walk in your destiny, Son. Do what you were meant to do and be who you were meant to be."

Her lips felt soft against his cheek as she kissed him. It was time for their meeting to end. They both turned toward the door.

VERSE 5

G-Swag leaned back in the brown leather high back chair and puffed on a blunt. "My dude." Reaching forward, he offered Bo-Jack the weed-filled cigar.
G-Swag always smoked the best, Bo Jack thought as the weed-scented air swirled around his nostrils.

"My dude?" G-Swag said with his hand still in the air. He pushed forward just a bit more, extending the blunt even further toward Bo Jack.

Bo Jack stared at the blunt like it was a piece of candy. It was hard to turn down, but Bo Jack was trying to cleanse himself. How could he cleanse his mind of all the toxins if he wasn't willing to cleanse his body first? He'd read a lot. He knew what marijuana did to brain cells and remembering that made him shake his head. "No, thanks. I'm good."

"Damn, B," G-Swag began as he leaned away from him. "Now you can't even blow trees with your dude?" He sounded hurt. "My dude, you blowin' my high with all that negativity you radiating." G-Swag took another pull on the cigar filled with the sweet smelling, crumbled up leaves.

"How you mean?" Bo Jack asked.

It took a moment before G-Swag could speak. With smoke billowing through his nostrils, he said, "You blowin' my high with all this fundamentalist shit. Knowing your history is where it's at, my dude; I get that. But you can't let that make you obsessed. You have to use your understanding of history and cultures to control your audience. And when you control your audience, they will feed you. Them Flintstones done enslaved the world with their manipulation of history. Well, we do the same shit with our music, but we can make the choice to give back to the slaves or build bigger castles."

"That's what I'm planning to do with my music."

G-Swag shook his head. "Nah, my dude, you tryin' to get yourself blackballed, blacklisted, and quite possibly blacked out. You need to read Paul Robeson's biography. He was a lot like you, but the CIA shut him all the way down because of his black militancy and he was the most popular male opera singer and actor in the world during the 1940's and 50's, before them Flintstones did him in. Look what they did to your man, Obama. They made him look incompetent. They turned black leaders, pastors, and black historians against him before they laid him down. So, if they could do it to him, trust, they will do it to you. It won't be hard, given your background. They'll be able to silence you easy, my dude."

"I already know they'll come, but by the time they get at me, if they get at me, shit, I will have awakened an army of kings and queens ready to take up where I left off."

G-Swag laughed. "My dude." G-Swag was still chuckling as he shook his head and put out the blunt inside an Evian water bottle cap. "That's some of the craziest, insane, retarded rationalization I done ever heard." G-Swag coughed before taking a swig from the Evian water bottle. "My dude, niggas make up twelve percent of the American population, and half the people are too young or too old to wake up. And the ones who you will wake up, half of them'll be in jail or running from the law. You have a better chance of taking a hundred dollars into a Vegas casino and walking out owning the joint, than you do at waking up black people."

G-Swag chuckled, but Bo-Jack did not. "I disagree, Swag. David killed Goliath. So don't tell me about odds, Swag. The odds been against me since birth, but I've managed to bet on black and win. So, I'm gon' keep betting on black and bet that there will be others who'll agree with me. What they did to President Obama, that shit can't go unpunished."

"My dude, I'm with you. Obama was my nigga. I applaud the hell out of what he tried to do, but at the end of the day, he failed. Now, Obama been dead a week. We drawin' air, he ain't. And there ain't nothing we can do to bring the man back. All we can do is go on and be successful. So come on, my dude, you gotta move on. Let's get back in the studio and do what we do best." G-Swag stood up, hoping that Bo Jack got the message that the meeting was about over. "What you need to do is relax," G-Swag said, looking down at Bo Jack. "Get you some pussy and stop acting like a bitch over a nigga in the ground."

Bo Jack sat still for a moment, glaring at G-Swag. Then, with his eyes still on him, Bo Jack slowly stood up. "Swag," he almost whispered, "the only reason you ain't pickin' your teeth up off this white marble floor is because I respect your gangsta." Bo Jack leaned across the desk that was separating the two men and finger-jabbed the mega producer in the chest. "But, if you ever, ever in this life or the next refer to me as a bitch, a dog or any animal, you will be picking your teeth up." He paused, with his glare still hard on G-Swag. "And with or without you, I am going to wake up my people."

G-Swag didn't back down. "Do what you have to do, my dude," he said, clearly not afraid of what Bo Jack had just laid down. "But do it, after you fulfill your contract with G-Swag Unlimited."

Bo Jack shrugged. "I ain't got no problem with that. I just need a little time to write for my next album."

"Write?" G-Swag asked. "That's not your job. We already have some hot shit written for you to spit on your next album."

Bo Jack frowned. "So, you saying, I can't write for my next album?"

"Read your contract," he said, shaking his head.

He could hardly believe his ears. "Read my contract? Swag, I thought we were better than that."

"We are as long as your interests serve my best interests. When I first met you, I told you I was an opportunist and you were opportunity. You so hell bent on history. My dude, it was my understanding of history that led me to invest in you."

The expression on Bo Jack's face was one of shock. "I thought we was like kindred spirits or some shit. I mean you grew up like me, Swag. You even read. We share a similar fucked up upbringing. I thought you felt my pain."

G-Swag shrugged a little. "My dude, the only thing we share is the music and the money we make. I ain't trying to feel nobody's pain, only pleasure. That story about my mother being a whore and me being homeless, that was game. I didn't grow up in any ghetto."

Bo Jack's eyes widened. "So, none of that stuff you told me was true?"

G-Swag didn't say a word, just shrugged.

"So you been using me?"

"We've been using each other, my dude. This was a two-way street. You had something I needed. I had something you needed. It's a wonderful partnership."

"Not anymore," Bo Jack said, shaking his head. He stood up straight and looked at G-Swag like he'd never seen him before. "I'm out!"

"Why you gotta be like that?" G-Swag said calmly. "I just came clean, kept it real with you. And you know what I'm saying is some real shit. Right now we have a great thing going. You're king. I'm the kingmaker. Let's just do this last album together, get this money, and then you can move on and do whatever you feel you have to do."

"Well just like you kept it real with me, Swag, I'm gon' keep it real with you, *my dude*. Like I said, I'm out. I can't be a part of this any longer. I can't fuck with nobody I can't trust to be real with me. I woulda' signed with you without you making up that story about how you came up." He shook his head, "Nah, I can't fuck with you on this rap shit no more. As of this minute, we're done."

G-Swag sat back down. "If you do this, I'll take you to court. And if I take you to court, you'll lose in more ways than you realize."

Bo Jack shrugged. "I'm doing what I have to do. Peace, *my dude*." He stepped toward the door and never looked back. A couple hours after walking out of G-Swag's office, Bo Jack was on his way to DeKalb Peachtree Airport where his pilot was waiting to fly him out to LA. He'd promised Diddy that he would perform at half-time of UCLA's homecoming game this year. It was Diddy's son, Justin's first year playing football for the University.

The Maybach's computerized voice interrupted Sade's melodic one. "Mr. Jones, the law offices of Spencer, Taylor and Knox are trying to reach you. Would you like me to take a message or send a text?"

"No, Maya, just put the call through to me." Bo Jack pressed the privacy window button and held it until the glass was completely closed. Then, he pressed his phone to his ear. "Mr. Jones."

That was a signal to Bo Jack that there were others in the room with Kimani. That was the only time she addressed him by his last name. It was a signal that they'd set up a long time ago.

"Hey, you sexy little motha'–"

"Mr. Jones," Kimani tried to interrupt and speak over Bo Jack's words. "This is–"

"Baby, I know that voice, that mouth," he said, putting extra emphasis on his words. "After last night when you had it wrapped around my…"

The limo's computerized voice began, "The caller has disconnected the call. Mr. Jones, would you like me to…" Before she could finish the phone rang again. "Mr. Jones, Kimani Knox is calling in."

"Patch her through to the rear speakers, Maya."

"I'm gon' fuck you up, Beauregard Jackson Jones," Kimani hissed into the phone.

"What?" Bo Jack asked innocently.

"You know what. I'm standing outside in the hall because I didn't know what you were gonna say next. I had you on speaker, fool. My partners and three paralegals heard everything you said."

"Really?" he asked, trying to keep his voice steady from the laughter that rose inside of him.

"Yes, really! And, I am so, embarrassed."

"I'm sorry, Queen. I didn't know." Bo Jack's voice quivered just a little as a chuckle tried to sneak through his lips.

"I find that hard, if not impossible to believe," she said. "Calling me, saying all that made up stuff – "

"Are you saying that you believe that I intentionally made up a story to purposely embarrass you?"

"That's exactly what I'm saying."

"I'm hurt that you would even think such a thing." Bo Jack said

"Not as hurt as you're gon' be when I see you. You play too much. Big ole twenty-four-year-old, playing on the damn phone. Now I'm going back in the conference room and I am going to call you to discuss your contract with G-Swag Unlimited. So act your age and not your shoe size."

She may have been a little upset, but it was all worth it to Bo Jack. And besides, last week she'd met him at Sambucas restaurant in Buckhead to get a copy of his two contract with G-Swag and she had played the ghetto babymomma on him while he was trying to woo Megan Good who was only in town to promote her new movie. He just wished that he could've been there to see the look on everyone's faces – especially Kimani's. Maya, the computer voice came through once again.

"Patch the call in to the rear speakers, Maya."

"Baby momma, this you? I need you to stop by the crack house on the way home. Get me a fifty dollar slab, and get yourself one, too. I just added another whore to our stable, so we can really celebrate," he said, barely holding back his laughter this time.

"Are you finished acting the fool and embarrassing yourself, Mr. Jones?" Kimani sounded like she was speaking through her teeth.

"For now, I think so, Ms. Knox," he said imitating her slow, deliberate speech.

"Thank you. Now, the reason for my call, Mr. Jones. About your contract – "

"Yes," Bo Jack said, now fully in business-mode.

"We've gone over your contracts and they're pretty straight forward," a voice Bo Jack didn't recognize, said.

"What does that mean?" Bo Jack asked.

"You can break the contract, but if you do, there are quite a few limitations. For example, you cannot release another single, album or perform at a free or paid event within twelve months prior to or after the projected release of the next album."

Bo Jack paused for a moment before he said, "I guess I can live with that."

"Not so fast, Mr. Jones," Kimani said. "There are major penalties as well. But here's the big one." Bo Jack braced himself. He could tell from the tone of Kimani's voice that this was serious. "You also forfeit any future royalties from the previous albums."

"What?"

"You forfeit – "

"No, I heard you. That's not what I meant. I mean, how can he do that? How can he take my money? Take money that I'm making off of some shit I've already done?"

"Mr. Jones, this is Chris Spencer, one of the senior partners. Let me explain; the last contract you signed was for a three album deal. The last recording was a part of this contract, which if you breach, gives G-Swag Unlimited all the rights to

151

any and all projects included in the said contract. It will also cost you upwards of two million dollars in penalties."

"That's some real bullshit," Bo Jack said under his breath, though he was sure everyone at the law offices had heard him.

The senior partner continued, "It would be in your best interest to do this last album, promote it and then you can walk away."

"Damn!" he whispered again. "As quick as G-Swag had gotten Katz the biggest entertainment attorney in the biz on the phone when I signed my first deal, I shoulda' known something wasn't right, but I had a million dollar check in my hand. Damn, G-Swag had Katz in his pocket," he said more to himself than to the others listening in." He took a minute to think. *Fuck it. I ain't never played the bitch role and I ain't about to start now. G-Swag had me all the way fucked up in the game. It would be dumb for me not to do one more album with the slug ass nigga, but just like I made it to the top with G-Swag, I can stay on top without him. I could even go over to Diddy's camp. Nah, shit I had paper, I know the game. I can do this shit solo. But, if I did that slug ass G-Swag would make so many millions off my first three albums and I wouldn't see shit.* Bo Jack made a decision. "Kimani... I mean, Ms. Knox, are you still there?"

"Yes, Mr. Jones."

"I need you to call my bank and have them prepare a cashier's check for one million nine hundred and ninety-nine thousand dollars and ninety-nine cents. Have them make G-Swag Unlimited the recipient, and in the memo section of the check, have the bank type in the words – For the purchase of King Black Horus Uhuru Jones's freedom." That wasn't his legal name yet, but for this purpose it was perfect, he thought.

"And why do I need to do this now." Kimani asked.

"1,999,999.99 was what I was advanced on my last deal which is lunch money compared to the royalties I'm pullin' in." Then, Bo Jack hung up the phone without saying goodbye. *I'm on pace to break two hundred million in royalties for this year which I won't get paid on until next year. Oh, hell no. Fuck Swag. I wish that motha fucka would try and not pay me. I swear ta God.* His thoughts trailed off as the car pulled through the gates of the private Peachtree-DeKalb airport. A minute later D-Bo was pulling up next to Bo Jack's latest toy: a four-year-old customized, eighteen million dollar challenger 300. The whirring of the jet's turbo engines caused H-Nic and D-Bo's suit jackets to flap back and forth as they surveyed their surroundings before opening the back door for their boss.

"Is Bam-Bam and Dre Dove on the plane?" Bo Jack shouted over the engine noise.

H-Nic nodded.

As Bo Jack trotted up the metal steps to enter the plane, he made a mental note of what he would say when he called Kimani from the air. He planned to write a letter and then email it over to Kimani. He'd have her send it over to *The Atlanta Journal and Constitution*, *The New York Times*, *LA Times*, and *The Washington Post*.

G-Swag wasn't going to be the winner all by himself. Matter of fact G-Swag wasn't about to win a damn thing.

VERSE 6

Bo Jack hadn't blown any trees since the President's passing and in that time, his mind had been much sharper, more focused. But after leaving G-Swag's spot, all he could think about was laying back with a tight body, big booty freak, puffing on some icky sticky to relax his mind and his nerves. Yeah, some icky sticky, the best indo weed on the market.

At seven stacks a pound, it should be the bomb, Bo Jack thought while Simone pulled, rubbed, and kneaded the muscles in his shoulders and back.

"This plane is so bitching," The high pitched valley girl's voice definitely didn't match her Gabrielle Union looks. "How am I doing, Mr. Jones?"

Bo Jack was naked with the exception of the white towel that was wrapped around his waist. He was face down on the massage table he'd had specially built for his jet. There was no greater way to relax while soaring through the clouds, than to have these magic fingers on his body.

"Just keep doing what you do, Babygirl," Bo Jack said without lifting his head. "Damn, this feels good!"

She smiled at his words, still not believing that she was on a plane massaging Bo Jack Jones. She couldn't wait to tell her friends, though she had a feeling that no one would ever believe her. Her friends would go ballistic if they knew that right at this moment, she had her hands on Bo Jack Jones's beautiful, tight muscles.

She wished she had her phone. She wished she could take a picture of her and Bo Jack together. But the only way she got this gig was by signing a confidentiality agreement. She couldn't say anything. She couldn't take any pictures. She wasn't even allowed to bring a phone with her. When she got to the plane, she'd had to give up her cell phone to that gorilla looking H-Nic. Just thinking about him made her shiver – and not with delight. She wasn't a whore, but the opportunity to meet Bo Jack Jones was a once in a lifetime thing. Letting H-Nic jump up and down inside of her for five minutes was a small price to pay for soaring through the clouds with a god.

As Simone fantasized about Bo Jack, he was doing the same about her. With his face down and his eyes staring at the Berber carpet through the face-hole on the massage table, Bo Jack imagined the Kennesaw State University chiropractic student taking her massage beyond his back. He could almost feel her massaging his johnson with her mouth, and after he was spent, they'd lay up and puff on some trees.

That sounded like the play of the day, but Bo Jack had to stay focused. He had a lot to do and he had to do it now. He had never been a procrastinator and he wasn't going to start being one now.

Still glancing down, he asked, "What time is it, Queen?"

She giggled before answering, "Seven twenty-five." There was still two and half hours before they would land.

"Simone, can you hand me my phone?" He pointed to the bed where he had put his clothes after getting out of the private jet's dual shower.

"You can get reception at this altitude?" she asked as she passed him the phone.

"This is a satellite cell. I can get reception on Mars with this thing."

"Oh, that is so asymmetrically radical. Wow."

As fine as this girl was, she wasn't fine enough. Her mother should have named her Squeaky. That would have been much more appropriate. Listening to her speak had the same effect on Bo Jack as if she stood in front of him scraping her fingernails down a wall. Right now, though, her voice was a welcomed dick deterrent because Bo Jack was on a mission.

"Turn over, Mr. Jones, so I can get to your traps better. You're just like most of my athletic clients. You guys have to drink more water. Don't you know that your muscles are water and protein? You need water to build them. Water is more important than all that weight you guys lift. I mean the world is made up of three-fourths water. Your body is made up of two-thirds or three-fourths water, I can't remember. But anyway, it's all about H2O, you have to drink way more when you are working out. Before, during and–"

"Simone!" Bo Jack shouted out as he rolled over onto his back.

"Oh!" She giggled. "I'm talking too much, huh? My mother always says–"

"Simone." Bo Jack smiled, though inside he cringed. "I have to make an important call."

"Oh, okay," She took her hands off him. "Just call me when you're finished. I'll go and–"

He grabbed her wrist, stopping her from stepping away. "No, I want you to keep doing what you're doing. I just need you to do it quietly. I need to concentrate."

A moment later, Simone was massaging his feet when he called Brandon. "What's crackin' wit' you, bay bruh?"

"Tryin' to save the day from the night big bruh."

"How's that workin' out for you?"

"Look outside, you'll see for yourself," Brandon said.

"I can't see nothing but clouds from my viewpoint."

"That's right, you on your way out to Cali to do your thing at UCLA's homecoming," Brandon said referring to P. Diddy's son. "Ask Justin if he ever got a chance to read *Last Man Standing.*"

"You talkin' about the Geronimo Pratt biography?" Bo Jack asked.

"Yeah, I sent it to him a couple months ago. He was asking me some stuff about the Panther movement. He was real high on Huey, so I decided to send him the story of the hardest Panther that ever lived."

Bo Jack lost all concentration when Simone slipped the towel away from him. And just like he'd been imagining a few minutes before, she proceeded to give him a different kind of massage. "Oh, shit. Ooooh, shit," Bo Jack blurted out as Simone filled her mouth with his manhood.

"What's wrong?" Brandon asked.

"Nothing." Bo Jack's answer was short and quick, making him sound a lot like Kermit the frog. Simone's voice was irritating as hell, but her mouth was heaven.

"So?" Brandon asked.

"So, so what?" Bo Jack asked, trying to figure out what his brother was asking him. But, it was hard for him to concentrate. Damn, her head was moving like a jackhammer. He grabbed her head, making sure she didn't move so he could speak.

"We were talking about Geronimo Pratt."

"Uhm-hmm." It still took a moment to think with his brain again. Then he finally remembered the main reason for the phone call. "Bran, I need you to ask Knowledge to compile a list of fifteen of the world's top English-speaking black psychologists, historians, African Studies and African-American Studies scholars."

"Okay. How soon you need the info?"

"Yesterday," Bo Jack replied. "Just get me the names. I'll have H-Nic and Kimani handle getting the contact information and find the people."

"Okay, I'll get on it. But tell me, what you cookin' in that brain, Black?"

"A feast, like nothing the world has ever seen."

On the other end of the phone, Bo Jack was sure that his brother wanted to ask more questions. But he wouldn't. Brandon knew not to pry.

"Bran. I gotta go," Bo Jack said, releasing his hands from her head. She immediately went to bobbing her head up and down and this time making slurping noises. He used all of his power to sound coherent. "Call you…. back… after… I…" He pressed 'End' on his cell.

Simone's head was still bobbing up and down at speeds he'd never experienced. She made humming sounds like a Formula One Indianapolis 500 race car.

Bo Jack was supposed to be in his office suite composing an e-mail for Kimani to send to the four major newspapers in the country. But, right now the only thing on his mind was the Hershey's dark chocolate head bobbing up and down between his thighs.

Bo Jack wrapped a band of Simone's Hawaiian silk weave around his hand and pulled her head up.

"What's wrong?"

"Nothing." He slid from beneath her, spun her around, pulled up her cheerleader's skirt, and pushed her over the massage table. No Panties. Good! Just two perfect identical chocolate half moons staring back at him. He spread her moons with his hands and was about to drive his petrified redwood hard pole into her earth, when she said five magic words.

"I'm not on the pill."

He backed up, not believing he was about to go up in this chick raw. It wouldn't have been the first time, but after reading so much about diseases, parasites, and all types of shit, he hadn't run up in a female butt naked in a couple years.

"You can stick it in, Mr. Jones," she moaned. "Just don't cum in me."

"Hell nah, Babygirl. You ain't 'bout to have me on Maury waiting on a paternity test." He reached down, picked up his FUBU slacks and retrieved his wallet. In no time, he was rolling a Magnum down the shaft of his johnson. He playfully slapped one of the half moons staring up at him.

"Stick it in," she moaned. "Oooh, come on."

His Johnson was harder than Chinese arithmetic, but then an image came to his mind. An image of Kimani. And suddenly, he felt guilty.

What the fuck? Kimani could be his mother. She was pushing forty and he'd not too long ago turned twenty-four. She wasn't his type. He hadn't even as much as sniffed the pussy and he hadn't even known until that moment that he wanted to. Why the hell was he feeling this way?

"Mr. Jones!" Simone clapped her half-moons together, breaking his thoughts. "What are you waiting for?"

"Nothing," he said as he watched his hard-on fade away. "Uh...I just remembered. I have some work to do." He grabbed his pants, then went into the back room, leaving Simone still bent over the massage table wondering what the hell had just happened.

VERSE 7

It had been a good weekend. The UCLA marching band had gotten down while Bo Jack had rocked the mike on Saturday night at UCLA's homecoming game. P. Diddy's son Justin had caught the winning touchdown against Stanford and Bo Jack had dedicated his smash hit "Holla Back" to Justin that night. It didn't matter how many times he had performed over the last three plus years since his first album dropped, Bo Jack was still amazed at how many people would pay to hear him drag. Three years ago at the Grammy's, G-Swag described Bo Jack's music as Southern Drag, because of the way Bo Jack dragged his words, sort of like a slurring drunk with rhythm. Others called his music hypnotic. Whatever the case, Bo Jack was already becoming a legend. And folks were loving and hating as they always did and always would.

"Diggety, does the pressure of being you ever get to you?" Bo Jack asked Diddy.

It was close to one in the morning and Simone, the pilots, and his boys were already on the plane ready to take off. Bo Jack was in the back of a Hummer stretch on the way to the Van Nuys private airport in Cali.

"I think it gets to everybody, Black," Diddy said.

"That's real talk," Bo Jack said. "I just hate the way this life is sometimes. I mean, you have no privacy. The media lies and has people believing all types of bogus shit. Like you, it's so much bullshit out there about you. And now with your son out here in Tinsel Town playing ball, the media is even up in his."

"Justin can handle his own. He's been dealing with the paparazzi his entire life. It's all he knows," Diddy said.

"That don't make it no better."

"That's the price we pay."

Bo Jack shrugged. "It is what it is Diggety."

"Only you, Black," Diddy said.

"Only me what?"

"No one would dare call me Diggety. But you my man and fifty grand. Who knows, I might use P. Diggety for something one day."

"Just make sure I get my royalties on the name," Bo Jack said.

"Straight up." The entertainment mogul got serious for a moment. "I know this was last minute, and I know you had other shit to do but you came through for me. You're my son's favorite artist. And you and your little brother have been a great influence on him—and me. I was trying to think of a way to repay you but how can you repay a man who has everything?"

"Diggety, your friendship is worth more to me than a mountain of gold. Money I can make, but true friendship is one thing I can't buy."

An hour later, Bo Jack was soaring through the clouds. Bam-Bam, Dre Dove, and Simone were asleep as Bo Jack sat at his desk in his office suite in the jet. He glanced to the bottom right hand corner of the thirty-two inch computer screen. It wasn't even midnight back at home.

The only sound in the suite was the quiet whirring of the jet's twin engines, Bo Jack's fingers tapping against the computer keys, and Natalie Cole remembering her father through song. He leaned back for a moment, listening to Natalie's words. He could relate. Unlike Natalie's father, his mother was still here, but he still missed her. Isis was Bo Jack's unforgettable.

Tears welled in his eyes as he sang along with Natalie. *"Unforgettable, though near or far. Like a song of love clings to me. How the thought of you does things to me. Never before has someone been more. Unforgettable in every way. And furthermore, that's how you'll stay."*

Even though his life was filled with good things happening, he still felt incomplete. And he would feel that way as long as his mother was locked up. He'd trade everything, even his own life for his mother's freedom.

"Why God?" he said aloud. "Why?" He shook his head, thinking of what his mother would say if she heard his cries right now. "Because it is meant to be, son," she would say in the serene tone she always spoke in.

But that answer wasn't enough for Bo Jack. Since he'd become rich and famous, everyone talked about how blessed he was and how thankful he should be. People were always telling him how other people had it so hard.

But no one could feel or understand his pain. No one understood how bad he really had it. No one knew what his mother being in prison was doing to him.

It wasn't that he was ungrateful. He knew he had so much to be thankful for, but his mother was sitting in prison. Doing time for something he should have done. If Bo Jack had his way, he'd turn back the hands of time.

But then, other thoughts came into his mind. If his mother hadn't gone to prison, would she be the woman she is now? Would she be at peace? Would she have the understanding that she had gained from reading and speaking with Knowledge every week? Would Brandon have gained so much knowledge and wisdom?

And if his mother hadn't gone to prison, where would Bo Jack be? Would he have ever picked up a book? And more importantly, would he have ever come into contact with that damn Kimani?

That last thought took him back to the email he'd been working on. Kimani had sent him three texts. The last one was the reason he was up jabbing on his keyboard while everyone else was asleep.

Kimani had written some mess about Bo Jack not doing what he said he was going to do. That pissed him off. She knew he was a man of his word. Who did she think she was? She worked for him, not the other way around.

True enough, Kimani handled business, but it was mostly his business. How was she gon' check him? Fuck her!

He thought about Simone. What he needed was to be inside that massage student right now. He got up from his chair, tempted to wake her up, but Kimani popped right back into his mind. And he sat back down and wrote the letter he wanted sent to four major newspapers.

Two days later, Bo Jack was front page news. But this time, it wasn't for his music. He'd handled his business and Kimani had handled hers. His letter first ran in *The Atlanta*

Journal and Constitution, The New York Times, LA Times, and *The Washington Post* before two hundred and ninety seven national and foreign syndicated newspapers picked up the story.

*****

G-Swag was vacationing at his beach house on Tenerife, the largest of the Canary Islands located off the coast of the Mediterranean. The sun was smiling. A gentle late October sea breeze made the palm trees outside of G-Swag's beach home dance. The light wind wafted into the room where G-Swag was lounging. He had cucumber slices over his eyes and a beautiful woman was caking a mud-thick substance onto his olive skin when his executive assistant burst into the rental beach house.

"Have you seen this?"

"Amber, I can't see anything with food over my eyes."

His assistant turned toward the half naked woman with the mud cake plate in one hand. "Can you excuse us a moment, please?"

The exotic beauty looked at the fiery assistant and smiled.

"Pode nos dar um momento," G-Swag said to the half naked woman.

The woman put the mud plate on the cabinet behind the stylist's chair. "Tomar o seu tempo, me ligue quando você estiver pronto para continuar."

Before Amber could ask, G-Swag said, "She's Portuguese."

The woman turned to Amber, gave the assistant the once-over, and smiled before turning to G-Swag, "Você deve ensinar a seu cão algumas maneiras."

"What did that bitch say?" Amber asked as the woman left the room. She had to play her role, even though she wanted to slap the shit out of the woman that had just told G-Swag that

165

he should teach his dog some manners. If she only knew. If G-Swag only knew. But Amber had to keep her emotions in check. G-Swag didn't know she could speak eight languages. Hell, G-Swag had no idea who she was, and she'd been working for him for eight years.

"She said that you were beautiful." G-Swag smiled.

"Bullshit, Swag. That bitch didn't say that. But I ain't got time to play with these trick-ass island hos."

"Okay, so why have you interrupted my facial with your negative energy, Amber?" he asked, taking the cucumber slices off his eyes.

She held her iPad in the air. "Your boy is all over the papers."

"Who?"

"Blow Jack, that fake ass gay rapper that got everybody fooled but me."

"Amber, why must you be so negative? And please quit calling him Blow Jack. He is not gay."

"Whatever," she said, blowing him off. "Let me read you what he said in the Times this morning."

"I'm listening."

"He titled this shit 'My Obituary.''"

"Okay, go on. Keep reading."

She held her iPad up and started, "What's crackin', kinfolk. This is Bo Jack Jones. First, let me show love to the Creator and to all the peeps responsible for my rise. I had to get at you before the story got twisted. You see I'm committing artist *suicide*. My ex-producer, G-Swag refuses to let me flow from the heart. He says I can't write my own lyrics. He says I have to continue using his team of writers. Only thing is, those lyrics aren't reflective of who I am and the way I feel. We had a good run, however short it may have been. I apologize for my producer's actions and my actions, but I refuse to be a slave to anyone. The money is not worth my dignity. So as of this moment, Bo Jack Jones is dead. Real talk, I don't have no beef with G-Swag. He taught me how to fly, but now I'm ready to soar through the clouds with some real talk. Don't trip, fam, I'll be resurrected in a couple years after my contract with G-Swag Unlimited expires. As of right now, October 25, 2012—yours truly is *dead*. Peace out, Kinfolk. P.S. I'll rise again. We will rise again. Loving me, loving you." She paused for a moment. "And it's signed, King Black Horus Uhuru Jones, the artist formerly known as Bo Jack Jones." She stopped and glared at him. When G-Swag stayed quiet, she asked, "So, you're not going to say anything?"

"What is there to say?" He shrugged. "Sounds like Bo Jack is dead to G-Swag Unlimited."

"Huh?" His assistant of eight years wore a bewildered look on her face. "You made that clown. He was a sagging-pants punk ass drug dealer when you signed him."

"Amber," G-Swag began in a tone that showed he was not at all affected, "this is a business. You can't take anything personal. At the end of the day, I'm still going to get mine. Getting upset is only going to cause undo stress."

Although he was calm on the outside, it was a whole different story on the inside. G-Swag was a master at hiding his true feelings. If Amber only knew. And if Bo Jack only knew, he wouldn't have written that article.

G-Swag shook his head. Bo Jack was just a child trying to play a grown man's game. *I'd warned him about fundamentalism. He should've heeded my words about Malcolm, Martin, and Obama's demise.*

But he didn't, and now he was going to pay.

VERSE 8

Bo Jack had his hands inside his Miami Heat Starter jacket. It was unseasonably cold for late October, even at four in the morning as Bo Jack made his way to Knowledge's tent. Bo Jack couldn't control his thoughts and spoke out loud. "Real talk, I ain't tryin' to act brand new, like I'm above regular shit, but walking down the emergency lane on the I/75-85 interstate at four in the A.M. isn't no regular shit. Matter fact, it is some straight up bullshit. The bloodsuckin' paparazzi would have a field day if they saw me now."

Bo Jack shook his head at the thought of what he was doing. He always had to go to Knowledge since he could never get Knowledge to come to him.

As usual, at this time of the night – or morning – it was quiet, except for the car noise above and to the left of the bridge. Pretty soon, they would be asked to move if this homeless community got any bigger.

Outside of Knowledge's tent, Bo Jack stood for a moment. And then, he heard his voice.

"Come in whenever you're ready, King."

Bo Jack took a close look at the red, black and green dome-like tent, before cupping his hands over the red part and peeking inside. He couldn't see anything.

Bo Jack unzipped the tent's door before kneeling and crawling through the opening. He was half-way in before he saw Knowledge sitting up in the corner.

"How did you know I was outside?"

"I felt you this time." Knowledge was sitting cross-legged with his back against pillows propped up against a tent support pole. A kerosene lamp provided the light he was using to read the book he had in his hands.

"Real talk?" Bo Jack asked.

"Real talk, King Black Horus Uhuru Jones." The old man smiled before putting a finger to his heart. "You are a part of me. I am a part of you. When you are truly in tune with yourself and nature, you will feel other's energy before you physically see them. Energy is the most powerful force in creation. It cannot be created. It cannot be destroyed. Everything that you see, do, and feel requires it."

All that and I still don't know how he knows whenever I'm outside, last time he said it was my scent, Bo Jack thought.

"How did you know I was changing my name?" But before he gave Knowledge a chance to answer, he answered himself. "Brandon told you."

Knowledge shook his head. "Isis did."

"So what do you think about it?"

"I like the name..."

He stopped, though Bo Jack could tell that Knowledge had much more to say. "But?"

"As your career describes what you do, your name should describe who you are, your origin or the type of person your parents envisioned that you would be." Knowledge held his index finger in the air. "Your pride is going to be your downfall, King Black Horus Uhuru Jones."

This was the time when Bo Jack would usually speak

up and defend himself. But he was trying to learn. He wanted to learn. So instead, he just sat and listened.

"Your obituary," Knowledge said.

"What about it?"

Knowledge held the book up he was reading. "In *The Art of War*, Sun Tzu writes, 'Move not unless you see an advantage; use not your troops unless there is something to be gained; fight not unless the position is critical. If it is to your advantage, make a forward move; if not, stay where you are.'"

As Knowledge had taught him to do, he sat there a few minutes until he was able to dissect Sun Tzu's words—understand them as they pertained to him and the letter he'd written that was now headlining papers throughout the country. And, it hit him. "I messed up," Bo Jack said softly.

"Your first blow should be your last blow. When it's not, you allow your enemy the opportunity to strike."

"Sun Tzu?" Bo Jack asked.

"No King, that's just plain ole Knowledge."

"Well, I'll take that knowledge and next time learn from it." He paused, giving Knowledge a moment since he wanted to change the subject. "Did you get a chance to compile that list?"

He nodded. "I did." He flipped through the pages of the book he'd just quoted from, found a folded piece of notebook paper, and handed it over to Bo Jack.

It took Bo Jack a few minutes to study the paper. He glanced over the names, saying each one out loud. "Dr. Akinyele Umoja, I've never read anything by him." Bo Jack looked up. "I wanted the best of the best, Knowledge."

"Do you think the media propaganda machine will give voice or recognition to the best of the people that they oppress?" Without waiting for Bo Jack's answer, Knowledge continued, "Dr. Umoja is a free black man, unafraid but always aware. He helped outline President's Obama's Reparations Bill. Dr. Umoja has been fighting for reparations and for the emancipation of Tupac's father, Mutulu Shakur, and other political prisoners for as long as I've known him. The brotha' is not the most knowledgeable, but his understanding of what he knows is what you need most. Remember, King Black Horus Uhuru Jones, many have knowledge but most don't understand what they know, Dr. Umoja does."

"What about Osiz – heck I can't even pronounce half these names."

"Raena," Knowledge nodded. He wore the look of a proud father on his face. "Dr. Osizwe Raena Jamila Harwell." He turned his attention away from his thoughts and back to Bo Jack. "You've read *Assata*?" he asked.

"A couple years ago," Bo Jack said.

"Raena has the heart, ambition, and fight of a young Assata Shakur. She's a recent graduate of Temple and she walks what she talks and King Black Horus Uhuru Jones, she might just be the strongest in the chain of scholars on that piece of paper."

He nodded, satisfied that he'd received what he came for. "You wanna know why I asked you to put together this list?"

"Do I need to know?"

Bo Jack shook his head. "No, not yet." He wanted to tell Knowledge but he really wanted to do this. He had to do this, and if he told Knowledge his plans, there was a good chance that Knowledge would enlighten him on why not to do what he was planning. He was pretty sure that Knowledge would approve, but then again, he'd thought Knowledge would have approved of his obituary. Knowledge was right. He should have never written the thing.

The machine was the enemy and Bo Jack had used it to strike the first blow against G-Swag. Looking back, Bo Jack didn't know why he'd thought G-Swag would bow to the pressure that the public was sure to put on him after reading the letter. All Bo Jack wanted was to write his own lyrics and give the people the knowledge that he was getting. But now, he knew there was no way that G-Swag would bend.

"I messed up a lot of stuff in my twenty-four years on this earth, Knowledge. The obit was a huge mistake. But it is what it is."

"That's true." Knowledge nodded in agreement. "Just as long as you understand that you still also have to live with the consequences, and oh yeah, drop the Horus from your new name. It's beautiful but King Black Uhuru Jones embodies who you are, just a suggestion."

VERSE 9

Bo Jack didn't realize he was working backward until now. All he wanted to do was give his boys the freedom that he had begun to receive upon learning about his history and other's true history. A couple million was nothing when it came to freeing his thirteen homies who were captives of their limited understanding. King Black was lonely and had only his moms, Brandon and Knowledge to speak to. He wanted so bad for all of black people to wake up, but his boys, they had been down with him since ninth grade or earlier and H-Nic had been down with him since kindergarten.

He just wanted them to see the world as he saw it. He wanted them to feel his passion, so he set on a journey to hire the best scholars to educate him and the others, and he didn't want any distractions. That's why he chose Dubai. No paparazzi. His boys couldn't go off and get with one of their shorties or one of the groupies. The condo in Dubai was secluded and he felt that Dubai would be conducive to focusing on learning and at the same time, they'd all be mad comfortable in the Middle Eastern man-made paradise. He never thought his boys would turn down the offer. They'd always went with whatever he said. He'd just assumed everything would be all good.

Why didn't I meet with my boys before I had Kimani fly all around the country meeting, propositioning and getting seven of fifteen of America's most gifted scholars, professors, and historians to commit.

Bo Jack, Brandon, and the thirteen members of Bo Jack's Goon Squad entourage were sitting at the twenty-thousand dollar hand-carved table in Bo Jack's formal dining room.

Thug stood up and backed away a bit from the table. "Big dog, we go way back to Juvey." He licked his fingers. "I been ride or die ever since I been in yo' car, but I can't ride this one out."

D-Bo interrupted. "Nigga, ain't your momma ever told you not to talk with food in your mouth."

"She probably did, but I was so busy servin' your momma, I must've forgot," Thug replied before returning his glance to Bo Jack. "Sorry 'bout that B, I was sayin' – " The blunt he and D-Bo had just smoked made him forget what he was just saying, so he changed the subject. "Damn, nigga, these wings are gooder than a mu' fucka," Thug said, pointing to the plate in front of him that was filled with chicken bones. "And I don't usually fuck wit' no lemon pepper wings."

"You gon' hog the floor, Thug, or you gon' get to it and sit your fat ass down," D-Bo said.

Thug looked at his boy, D-Bo. "Nigga, why is you ridin' my nuts so hard? Damn, a nigga just sayin'—"

D-Bo guzzled down his bottle of Heineken. "What the fuck is you sayin', nigga? That's what we all tryin' to figure the fuck out?"

"I'm sayin', I ain't good at school, never liked school, and I can't leave my kids for no eighteen months."

Those were just words. Thug half-ass saw his three

boys now. The only reason he dropped down twenty stacks to his baby momma was to catch his child support up so he could stay out of jail and keep rolling with Bo Jack and the Goon Squad.

Thug sat back in the high-backed, throne-like chair.

Pork Chop was the next one to rise. He guzzled a Corona before he spoke. "King Black, my nigga, you just can't expect a nigga to just up and leave the country for a year and a half. How I'm gon' get wit' one of them Dubai hos if I can't even speak Dubai. You been mad good to a nigga," he waved his arm around, "to all of us. We done made a grip in the traps and a triple grip times ten body guardin' and representin' for you. But I can't go to no damn Dubai. Dubai too close to them crazy Iraqi and Pakistani niggas. Them mu'fucka's don't care 'bout shit. I be done went down to the Ali Baba Mickey Dees and some cat be done walked in that bitch with a bomb strapped to his back." Pork Chop shook his head. "Hell double nah, dog. I like the way I'm livin'. No hard feelings, you still my nigga, but uh, I gotta sit this one out."

Bam-Bam pushed his chair back and stood, ready to say his piece. "I damn sure could use ninety-stacks, but eighteen months of intense reading and studying," Bam-Bam put a hand to his chest. "I know you ain't know, my nigga, but I can't read too well and like Thug, I hate school with the passion of the Christ. And if it ain't on TV, or if a nigga don't tell it to me, a nigga ain't gon' know about it."

H-Nic jumped up before Bam-Bam sat back in his seat. "I can't believe this shit. Y'all some ungrateful ass niggas. I mean for real." He extended his arm toward Bo Jack who sat at the head of the table quietly absorbing it all. "Black coulda' left us in the trap. He ain't had to bring us up with him. All of us been eatin' off my nigga's plate ever since he signed with that snake ass G-Slug. Bo Jack done shown us shit, took us places that we would've never seen." H-Nic looked over at Bam-Bam. "And ain't none of us here no scholars. Don't none of us like school. Shit, Bo Jack didn't even graduate. I didn't graduate, and most of y'all didn't either." Bo Jack's closest friend paused to collect himself as H-Nic felt himself getting heated. So he took a few deep breaths, exactly the way his doctor told him to do to control his high blood pressure.

H-Nic continued, "But my nigga done rented a spot in the most luxurious country in the world. You know how Black do it. You know that shit is gon' be laid the fuck out. And Chop," he looked over at Pork Chop, "can't none of us speak no damn Dubai, but you know good and got damn well Black gon' make sure a nigga don't get blue balls over in the desert. With the five stacks a month Black gon' set out for each of us, you can buy you some Dubai pussy, Chop, and I promise, you won't have a problem communicating. Money is an international language." H-Nic turned back to the others. "Black gon' give us five stacks a month for eighteen months for listening, reading, and learning our history and you ungrateful mothafucka's wanna bail? Where the fuck you gon' make ninety stacks over a year and a half?" H-Nic shook his head before sitting down. "Ungrateful ass niggas."

For seconds, there was nothing but quiet. And then, Brandon stood up. For a fleeting moment, he thought about telling the fellas that Dubai wasn't a language and that the people primarily spoke Arabic and English, but that would only lead to questions that would cause his fifteen-year-old head to hurt even worse than it did now.

Brandon began, "Right after 'the man' freed the slaves, a white slave master said to his slave, 'Charles, you is a free man they say, but ah tells you now, you is still a slave and if you lives to be a hundred, you'll still be a slave, cause you got no education, and education is what makes a man free.'" Brandon paused to give those words a chance to hopefully sink into their thick skulls. He took the time to glance at each face in the huge dining room. It seemed like his words had connected with some; he could see the shame on their faces. But still others wore a look of indifference. But it was the ones whose faces shined with determination that pleased him. Those were the ones who would follow King Black, no matter where he led them.

Brandon continued, "We've all heard the saying that the easiest way to keep a secret from a black man is to put it in a book. And yet we allow that saying to be true. We don't read and the ones who do, read what the white man tells him to read." He looked over at his brother. "King Black is willing to spend close to three million to arm all of you with the greatest and most powerful weapon ever imagined or created."

"Next time a nigga cross me, I'm gon' throw a book at his ass," Man-Man loudly whispered to Bam-Bam.

The two men snickered, but that didn't deter Brandon. "Ignorant comments like that is one of the reasons why black people all over this country continue to suffer from mental illness. The most powerful weapon," the teenager pointed a finger at his head, "is your mind. The human mind is what makes people into followers—slaves to what they don't understand. Knowledge makes a man free, and the lack of knowledge is what keeps a man enslaved. The mind's manipulation of knowledge has started revolutions and ended them. The mind's manipulation of knowledge has been used to turn little girls into little boys—little boys into little girls."

Thug interrupted. "That's exactly why a nigga ain't tryin' to get with no knowledge. Some shit a nigga just don't need to know. Niggas fucked up now cause they tryin' to be hos and hos tryin to be niggas. Besides, ain't none of us gon' go away for eighteen months and come back no brain scientists."

D-Bo jumped up. "Thug, you 'bout as smart as a bag of bricks."

"D-Bo," Brandon nodded. "I got this." He turned his attention to Thug. "Man, I was born addicted to crack. The doctors told my mom that I had a learning disability and that my mind would never develop beyond the eighth grade level. I just turned fifteen, my I.Q. is one hundred and seventy-five. By America's standards, I'm a genius. A genius who spent kindergarten through fifth grade struggling in special education classes. It took me five minutes to read one page of the kindergarten book, *See Spot Run*. But, after my mom went to prison, Knowledge homeschooled me. He taught me how to read and now I can't stop. I read about everything. Books about the streets, culture, the black experience, European history, sociology, African history, everything and you tell me," Brandon said before he paused, making sure he had everyone's attention. "Do I sound like a fifteen-year-old special ed student?"

No one said anything. But their silence spoke volumes. They were thinking about what he had just said.

Once Brandon took his seat, it was time for Bo Jack to speak. Slowly he stood, and glanced around the table making sure that he made eye contact with each one of them. "I respect everyone's gangsta. Thug, Bam-Bam, Pork Chop, Nardo, Cootie Man, Charlie, Man-Man," he looked at the fellas, "I owe you an apology. I never should have taken for granted that you all would be down for leaving the country. No hard feelings, y'all still my folks." Bo Jack changed gears, talking to the six soldiers who'd agreed to go to Dubai and be schooled by the dream team Knowledge had put together. "Anyway, we outta here next month in December, Bo Jack said, the Monday after the *BET Hip-Hop Awards*."

"What about passports?" D-Bo asked. "I don't know if I can get one with my record."

"I got that covered. I'll have all the passports, the flights, everything in a couple weeks. I'll tell you what I need from those that are coming later. And since the Awards are going down in our city, we gon' represent the A, like never before. I'm gon' rent Club Compound for the night and we gon' throw the livest afterparty the ATL has ever seen."

"You still want the rest of us who ain't goin' to Dubai

to help you rock that shit at the BET awards?" Thug asked.

"Nigga, are you serious? Did you just ask me that dumb shit?" Bo Jack smiled. "We've been puttin' in work for months rehearsin' for the performance and Swag done already had our space ship built. Just cause y'all crack babies ain't coming to Dubai, don't mean y'all ain't my niggas. We began this chapter together. We gon' end it together."

"Dig that, Big Pimpin'," Bam-Bam shot back.

"Saturday, December first, it's on. BET is about to see me," Pork Chop said.

"And on that note," Bo Jack said, "This meeting is adjourned.

VERSE 10

"Blow Jack be nimble. Blow Jack be quick. Blow Jack ain't nothin' but a motha fuckin' trick. Like the little old lady that lived in a shoe, nigga got so much bitch in him he don't know what to do. Don't worry, don't fret. Homicide is your best bet. Back down, ass up that's the way he like to get fucked. Blow Jack, low Jack, ho Jack, nut sack."

G-Swag's shoulder-length black 'white boy' dreads danced with the rhythm of the bassline behind Homicide's lyrics. "Hell, yeah, my dude, you killed that shit." G-Swag pressed the power on the remote, cutting the music off.

G-Swag sat on the corner of his desk, smoking a blunt. The man standing by the door didn't have to tell anyone that he'd done time. The six-foot-something, solid built man leaning up against G-Swag's office wall looked like the stereotypical image of a black convict. He'd never be a superstar in the rap game—too angry, too hard, and way too ugly, yet G-Swag had just signed him.

Pretty Ricky 'Homicide' Rasul had a I-don't-give-a-fuck-attitud about life. Homicide had spent half of his thirty years behind bars—ten years as an adult and five years as a juvenile. Pretty Ricky truly lived up to his nickname, Homicide. He was a fearless fool with no morals—loyal only to the hand that fed him at the moment.

G-Swag had done his research. Homicide could flow. His voice reminded you of a deeper version of Rick Ross. He knew everything there was to know about his new artist. G-swag had no plans on developing the monster that stood near his door. Homicide was the perfect villain. If Bo Jack wanted to leave, he could go. But he knew how to still make millions off of the young rap phenom. And Homicide was the perfect puppet to ignite the rivalry between him and Bo Jack that would financially benefit G-Swag Unlimited. And if everything went according to plans, then Bo Jack eventually would be dead and Homicide would be doing life for Bo Jack's murder. In a nutshell, G-Swag was about to make all the money off of the two idiots.

G-Swag said, "You don't even understand what's about to happen, my dude."

"Explain it to me again." The thirty year-old newly signed rapper growled as he leaned against the wall with his huge tatted up arms crossed.

Shatima Rasul actually named her son Pretty Ricky. He was rattlesnake mean, pit bull ugly, and he had had to fight his entire life. So, he was good at it. Knocking his boyfriend out thirteen years ago is what had landed him in the county jail on his eighteenth birthday.

Back then, Pretty didn't wear his shoulder length hair in cornrows like he did today. He wore it straight down his back. The six-two, two-hundred and forty pound man had walked into the prison dorm strutting as if he was the warden. And when he had walked through the jail's common area, he switched harder than a two dollar crack ho' on truck driver payday.

Despite his unattractive face, two inmates ran into Pretty Ricky's cell that first night in jail. The two had come in swinging socks loaded with bars of soap. "Bitch, we gon' tap that big ass tonight," they had said between blows to Pretty's body, head and arms.

Pretty covered up best he could while using his powerful legs and arms to get up out of his bottom bunk. The biggest of the two would-be-rapists didn't see the razor blade until after Pretty had sliced a straight line across his neck. The other attacker made the mistake of trying to help his already dead cohort, when Pretty palmed the back of the man's head and rammed it against the cell's concrete wall, causing the attacker to suffer a concussion.

Unfortunately, Pretty couldn't prove to the jury that the men had tried to rape him. As a result of what had happened that night, Pretty had done ten years in the penitentiary. While serving time, he began rhyming and calling himself Homicide as a reminder of what he had done to the men who had tried him back in the county jail. In prison and for the almost three years he'd been out, he strived to be the hardest gangsta rapper in the industry. What motivated him to be so hard and so ruthless was his gayness. He wasn't ashamed of being gay. What he was ashamed of was the frilly, soft, girly image associated with gay males. He wanted to show the world that gay men were men—that there was nothing soft about being gay.

Finally, now Pretty was getting his break. But though he was pleased, he didn't change his stance. He stayed by the door, leaning against the wall, with his muscled, tatted-up arms crossed while he listened to G-Swag.

"What's about to happen, my dude, is you about to be bigger than life. To be the king, you have to defeat the king, and with your new track "Blow Jack Blows," game over. You 'bout to dethrone dude. Ole boy is history and even if he comes at you sideways, we'll write lyrics that will crush his heart."

"If he come at me, I can handle mine." Pretty flexed his biceps while making the muscles in his chest jump.

"Nah, my dude. No violence. That shit don't make money unless you in a ring or bettin' on a dude who's fighting in a ring. And if it don't make money, it don't make sense." He could hardly keep a straight face after the bullshit that just came out of his mouth. Hell, he knew that after Bo Jack comes back on Homicide, his track will be ten times as hard as Blow Jack Blows and given Homicides I-don't-give-a-fuck attitude and history of violence, put the two in the same room and one of the two killers would kill the other and G-Swag had his money on Homicide and G Swag had never lost a bet. "Here," he feigned a cough while offering the blunt to Homicide.

Homicide reached out and took the weed. "Good lookin', big baby."

G-Swag continued, "I'm talking about some Dirty South, East Coast rap beef. Billions were made off the Tupac-Biggie drama. The bigger and more personal the beef is, the more media attention, which means people attention, which calculates into sales."

Homicide exhaled, making the smoke from the blunt come out in circles. "I can get with that."

"And then you got an advantage comin' into the game, that Bo Jack doesn't have. "

"What dat is?"

"The gay community."

"Psst." Homicide sucked his teeth. "Them pussies don't embrace me. They say I'm a thug. Pussies don't realize I'm changing the gay image from fabulous to ferocious. When people think of punks, they think of hopscotching, jump roping sissy shit. Half the butt busters out here are Timberland boot wearing, sagging and bagging, tatted-up cats like yours truly."

"You preachin' to the choir, my dude," G-Swag said in almost a whisper.

When he wouldn't look Homicide in the eye, the big man asked, "Whachu mean, dog? Don't tell me you swing to the left." The gay rapper's eyes lit up.

G-Swag slowly lifted his head and his eyes were filled with water. He put a hand over his face and exhaled before dropping his arm away. "I was eight the first time my uncle came into my bedroom."

"What did you just say?"

G-Swag repeated it louder and much clearer this time.

Homicide shook his head. "Man, that's fucked up."

"It was." G-Swag squeezed his eyes together, pretending to shake away a painful memory. "It went on for two years before I had the courage to tell my moms."

There was pity and understanding in his eyes when Homicide uncrossed his arms and silently listened. He too had been molested but it was by an aunt. Betty Jean was the biggest, ugliest woman that ever lived, Homicide thought back to His forty-year-old six foot tall three hundred and fifty pound aunt. He was a five foot tall ninety pound ten year old flag pole when she first strapped his arms behind his back while sitting on his face.

"I don't know if moms didn't believe me or if she just didn't want to believe that her little brother was a pedophile."

"She was in denial," Homicide said. "Most mothers are. Most of them choose the man they fucking over their own seed. I bet she still in denial." Homicide took a step toward G-Swag.

The producer nodded his head yes. "I bet you're right."

"I bet your uncle never served any time for that fuck shit he did to you."

"Not a day."

"They hardly ever do," Homicide said with a far away look on his angry face. "Where he at now?"

G-Swag smiled. "Six feet under."

"Good."

Swag was hoping Homicide asked how his uncle had died, but when he didn't, G-Swag decided to tell him, "They found him in an alley beaten to death. They never found his dick though."

Homicide was silent for a moment, then smiled, "Me and you got way more in common than you think, Swag," Homicide said, thinking of how he wished his Aunt hadn't died from diabetes before he got out of juvey half a lifetime ago. "You all right with me, big baby."

"That's good to hear, my dude, but like you said, we built alike so, I'm gon' give it to you uncut. Bo Jack is the king, but not for long. Dude forgot who made him. See, like you, money don't make me, I make money, and with or without Blow Jack, G-Swag Unlimited is going to flourish.

"Next week, the day before the BET Awards, billboards in LA, New York, DC, Atlanta, Chicago, and Detroit are going up. You, my dude are going to be the new face of G-Swag Unlimited. Next Friday, November 30, you're doing BET's *106 & Park* and then Wendy Williams. Tomorrow morning, 'Blow Jack Blows' will premiere on black radio stations all over the nation."

"That's love, big baby." The rapper put an arm around G-Swag. "You's a good nigga, Swag. If you ever want ole boy to come up missing – "

"Nah." G-Swag shook his head before Homicide could even finish. "We need Bo Jack for now. He'll likely come out in the media against me again. He'll put a single out dissing us. We'll just come back out against him and we'll keep riding the wave until the waters calm. But, I would like you to step to him at the BET awards show."

"You ain't said nothin' but a word, big baby."

G-Swag continued, "Blow him a kiss. Piss him off in person and in public. But be careful 'cause Bo Jack travels with some mean-looking characters."

"Psst." He sucked his teeth. "Them Goon Squad pussies. I'll pull out my dick and pee on them bitches and them pussies won't do shit. They ain't no thugs. They punk ass former nickel and dime crack dealers. I used to rob and rape pussies like them in the pen."

G-Swag's office phone rang. He pressed the speaker button.

"The speech writers are here for Mr. Homicide."

"Thank you Amber, I'm sending him right out. Do me a favor and set them up in Conference Room B, then come to my office after you're done," he said before clicking off the line.

"Speech writers?"

"They're here to go over the questions and your answers for the *106 and Park* and Wendy Williams interviews next week."

"I don't need nobody to tell me what to say, big baby. I know how to handle myself in an interview," the rapper said, crossing his arms once again.

"I'm sure you do, but if I don't know how to do anything else, I know how to play to the public, and trust me, if you wanna be king of the rap jungle, then do everything I say. Remember, Homicide, I made the king and if I made one, I can make another. Besides, the men you are about to be schooled by cost me twenty-five grand. They're good. They know what they're doing."

"Damn, big baby, next time you wanna throw money away, throw it my way. Twenty-five stacks, and all they gon' do is tell a nigga how to answer some dumb ass questions?"

"Nah, I'm paying twenty-five grand to make sure you to say the right thing with the right attitude to get people to purchase and download 'Blow Jack Blows.'"

Homicide paused for a moment, thinking. Then, he asked, "Why me, Swag? You got all this talent in the South, and you come to D.C. to give me a play." Homicide held his hand, passing the blunt back to G-Swag.

"Kill it. I'm good, my dude." G-Swag remained propped up on the corner of his desk. He crossed one leg over the other. "It ain't nothing personal. It ain't even our shared upbringing. I can't explain it, but you got *it*, and I want *it*. I'm an opportunist, my dude. And you," G-Swag pointed, "are opportunity. I want to exploit your *it*, get paid off your *it*. I'm a wolf with a bottomless pit. And your voice and your swag are going to make us a lot of money."

"That's what the fuck I'm talking about. I ain't mad at all. Pimp my voice out, nigga. Do whatever you gotta do for me to take over this rap shit."

Even smiling, Homicide still looked angry, mean... and ugly.

"And that fifty-thousand I gave you to sign and relocate to the A was lunch money compared to the cheddar we gon' make off that gravelly voice of yours, my dude."

"I'm ready, big baby. You just lead the way."

G-Swag smiled. That was exactly what he was going to do.

VERSE 11

Bo Jack, the Goon Squad, and the dancers had just finished rehearsing the routine they were going to perform that night on the *BET Hip-Hop Awards*. They'd been at it all night, making sure the routine was beyond perfect. It was hard for the Goon Squad to focus on anything besides fuckin' Homicide up, and fuckin' the fine ass half naked females that they were performing with. Homicide's dis of Bo Jack was a dis to all of them. For a week now, the media was going crazy about the new song that was getting more airplay than Bo Jack's number one hit "Trick Ass Niggas."

The fifteen professional female dancers' frustration was evident by the look on their faces. They'd all been rehearsing for three months for this night, and had gotten the routine down a month ago. But last night until just now, they couldn't make it through the seven-minute dance routine without one of the Goons messing up.

"Thank God." The little man choreographing the dance routine threw his arms in the air. "Finally," he said, as they'd made it through the routine twice without error. "We are going to do it one more time, but for now, take fifteen. Go pee, drink some Red Bull, whatever, but be back here at," the little man looked at his watch, "six thirty-five."

Half of the dancers and the goons didn't go anywhere. They just dropped to the indoor tennis court green top where they were rehearsing in the basement of Bo Jack's home.

Bo Jack reached for his cell, even though he already knew he didn't have a signal. This was one of the only things he hated about his house – he couldn't get cell phone reception in his mall sized basement, and his satellite phone was upstairs in his bedroom. It was just six-twenty, the sun wasn't even up yet, but he needed to get in touch with Percy Neil, one of his homies from back in his dope-boy days.

Percy's Paint & Body Shop was the place to go in the hood if you had the bread and you wanted your ride tricked out to the fullest—airbrush, hydraulics, suicide doors, and now helicopters. Percy was supposed to have the helicopter/spaceship airbrushed by nine this morning. His crew had worked throughout the night for Bo Jack's last minute airbrush paint job.

"I'll be right back," Bo Jack said to no one in particular as he walked through the Plexiglas door to the elevator. He was bent over, drenched in sweat, and was about to get on the elevator when H-Nic walked up.

"Black, we need to talk."

The elevator opened.

"Come on," Bo Jack said, motioning for H-Nic to follow him.

Neither man spoke until they got off the elevator on the fourth floor. Bo Jack had owned the mansion for going on three years now, and he still couldn't get over having an entire floor, dedicated to being a huge master bedroom suite.

"Fuck the dumb shit, Black, we gotta do something. That nigga G-swag and his homo thug got us looking like Grade A bitches," H-Nic said.

"I feel ya, big dog," Bo Jack said, though his voice was much calmer than H-Nic's. "I wanna flatline both them niggas, but this ain't the hood."

"Hell if it ain't. I'm the hood. We the hood." H-Nic banged his fist against his chest. "We need to bring it to them G-Slug niggas. That fake ass Ossama Bin Laden lookin' nigga got his homo thug on billboards everywhere. And G-Slug got a nigga in a dress on the billboards—a nigga that supposed to be you dog. And the caption above the depiction reads, 'Blow Jack Blows.' Hell nah!" H-Nic said as he paced back and forth in front of Bo Jack. "And that nigga got that whack ass 'Blow Jack Blows' shit playin' on the radio more than yo' shit. I can't believe them niggas went there."

"I can't either."

"Black, what's the deal, my nigga? Back in the day, you woulda' been plottin' on bodyin' that nigga by now. You ain't even got worry lines on your forehead."

"Cause I ain't goin' off on some cowboy shit. But don't get it twisted; you think I ain't fucked up about a nigga scandalizin' my name and calling my manhood into question? Am I pissed? Fuck, yeah! But, I already made the mistake of startin' shit with Swag in the media. I been studying the book *The Art of War* and—"

"My nigga," H-Nic frowned up, "you readin' books while this Harold & Kumar lookin' nigga bringin' it to us?"

"What better way to understand war than to get the game from the master?" Bo Jack asked.

"Master, I ain't never heard of no *Art of War*. What kind of shit is that? Ain't nothing artistic about no damn war. War ain't about no nigga writin' no book. War is all blood and guts, conquer and control my nigga."

"You right, but the nigga with the best strategy is most times the one left standing. Don't worry about them clowns, H-Nic, I ain't tryin' to have my number one nigga rottin' in a jail cell behind bodying one or both of them clown ass niggas." Bo

Jack smiled. "When I step to 'em," he put his arm around H-Nics shoulder, "when we step to G-Slug and Homothug, the media won't be televising or makin' money off that shit."

For the first time, the frown left H-Nic's face. "You got a plan, don't you, Black? That's why you reading that book."

"You know how I get down. Now, let's go back downstairs. Tonight is our night to shine one last time before we jet the country."

Bo Jack rode back down in the elevator with H-Nic. He hadn't forgotten about the call he had to make, but that could wait. He had to make sure that H-Nic and the others understood that he had a plan. And he didn't need any of them being hotheads and going off on their own. He was going to take care of G-Swag very soon.

VERSE 12

For the first time, the *BET Hip-Hop Awards* were held outside. On this beautiful, unseasonably warm December night, the Georgia Dome's new retractable roof was open. The who's who of the entertainment industry were on hand for the night's huge award show. G-Swag and Bo Jack's feud was the biggest story in entertainment. Comedians Kevin Hart and Katt Williams had the star-studded Georgia Dome crowd rolling.

"Katt," Kevin Hart addressed his co-host. "Where did this homo side cat come from?"

"I don't know, but he need to go back, before he put the horror movie industry out of business," Katt replied. "He so ugly, he'd scare a ghost."

The audience roared with laughter.

Kevin Hart said, "Tie ten pork chops around his neck, the dog gon' take one look at his face and say, 'Damn! I done lost my appetite.'"

"Ain't there some kind of gay code or something? I mean big homey too ugly to be gay. Plastic surgery, gloomzilla need plastic urgency surgery. He need to buy ten facelifts, get one free or some shit," Katt said.

"And how he gon' dis Bo Jack Jones?" Kevin Hart asked.

The crowd roared at the sound of Bo Jack's name.

"The coolest cat on the planet," Kevin Hart continued. "Bo Jack's so cool, time waits on him. Bo Jack has to be somewhere at nine. He looks over at his clock. It's eight fifty-nine. He says, 'Clock, I need you to stay put for about an hour. An hour later, I be damned if it ain't 8:59."

The Georgia dome suddenly went dark. An instant tornado gust of wind from above blew, and sent programs, empty food wrappers, and other debris swirling through the air. The sound of propellers—huge, wind-stirring propellers—drowned out the gasps of shock and fear from the crowd.

Everyone was on their feet looking up, trying to focus, trying to figure out what was going on. But all anyone could see was light—bright lights. Lights so bright that no one could see the source. Then the bass line from "Superfly" began to vibrate and resonate throughout the dome. The same bass line that G-Swag had sampled for Bo Jack's "Trick Ass Niggas."

Then, the lights began to dim as the source of the light slowly descended into the open dome.

"Trick ass niggas can get it for free. You got the right one, fuckin' with me."

Thousands stood on their feet, screaming, singing the hook to the triple platinum hit song. *"Trick ass niggas can get it for free. You got the right one, fuckin' with me."*

The lights became dimmer as the silver spaceship descended from above. Thousands pointed, sang, and screamed. Not one of them had ever seen a flying saucer before.

G-Swag had paid an aeronautical engineering design firm in Vegas a couple hundred thousand a few months ago to make Bo Jack's helicopter resemble a spaceship.

A week ago, as soon as he heard the song "Blow Jack Blows," Bo Jack went into action. He was mad, and at first, all he could see was red. He wanted blood, but he settled for paint.

The image of G-Swag on his knees sucking Homicide's dick was very clear, very vivid for the thousands in the Dome and the millions who were watching the live taping in their homes. Of course, the viewers wouldn't see the graphics on the space ship – FCC regulations, but thanks to the Internet, the world will know about it within minutes. Percy Neil, the guy who'd airbrushed the visual art on the aircraft had put it all the way down. And just so no one could misinterpret what they were seeing, the caption above G-Swag and Homicide's image left no doubt in their minds.

Big as life, in rainbow, raised lettering it read, *G-Swag Unlimited Uninhibited.*

When the spaceship doors opened, a cloud of smoke emerged covering the flying machine and it's twenty-eight inhabitants.

The bass line was still vibrating through the arena and the crowd was still screaming, only now, many of them were in shock. A few still sang along, *Trick ass niggas can get it for free, you got the right one, fuckin' with me,* but most stood with their eyes and mouths wide open.

A minute later, the spaceship-like helicopter lifted back off, and left the way it had come.

The crowd's roars were even louder when Bo Jack stepped out of the smoke and into the light for all to see.

"Trick ass niggas can get it for free. You got the right one, fuckin' with me," Bo Jack sang.

He wore black throw-back shark suit pants, no shirt, a long throw-back black Cab Calloway zoot suit jacket, dark Ray Bans, and a black mob boss Stetson hat—no feather. He tapped his black and white patent leather shoes on the white stage floor.

"Trick ass niggas can get it for free. You got the right one, fuckin' with me!"

Bo Jack was sandwiched between two of the finest

vanilla-wafer-colored twins this side of heaven. They wore military boots and black daisy duke shorts. A camouflage half baby tee hugged their C-cup sized chests, leaving their flat stomachs exposed. Seconds later, the stage lights came on, revealing Bo Jack's thirteen goons dressed in zoot suits and penguin patent leather shoes. All of the dancers were dressed like the two beauties dancing next to Bo Jack.

The seven minute mini concert was electric. And when Bo Jack and his goons and dancers were finished, the stage went completely black.

The applause and cheers bounced off the walls like thunder.

All evening, Katt Williams, Kevin Hart, the presenters, and the award recipients couldn't stop talking about Bo Jack's flying saucer and his amazing performance.

Half the goons were inside the special dressing room with Bo Jack, while the other half lounged outside the room, playing the dozens and one upping the next, when Homicide made his presence known backstage.

Homicide threw his hands up in surrender as he approached the two mountain-sized security guards who were blocking Bo Jack's area. "Big Baby, I don't want no trouble. Just tryin' to congratulate my label mate." Homicide held out a G-Swag Unlimited press pass as he tried to push past the guards, but at the same time, both men grabbed his arms.

Homicide glanced to where the men held him, then he looked up at the guards. "I come in peace," he continued, "but if you niggas don't get your paws off me, you'll be leaving this bitch in pieces."

The grossly overweight men looked at each other before they released him and stepped back. ":You know that pass still don't get you backstage access to Bo Jack and the Goon Squad.

Homicide pulled two envelopes out of his True Religion jeans pocket. "I got a stack for each of you," he said slowly. "All I wanna do is congratulate my motha fuckin' label mate."

The Rick Ross-looking bodyguard turned to his Ruben Studdard sized partner.

"What you think?" Rick Ross whispered to Ruben.

"If some drama jumps off we won't get another gig with Bart," Ruben said referring to the temp to permanent employment agency that had given them the job working security on the east hall of the makeshift Georgia Dome back stage area. The two guards were just two of two hundred security guards covering the awards show. The only reason Bart had called them was that they ran out of qualified men and women that were registered with the temporary employment agency.

"It's December and this ain't nothing but the third job Bart done sent us on this year," Rick Ross said. "Hell, I hope some drama does jump off."

"Why?" Ruben asked.

Without answering, Rick Ross turned to Homicide and held out his hand. "You say anything about this transaction, partna– " Rick Ross pulled up his dark blue uniform pants, sucked his stomach in and puffed his chest out. "I'm gon' put my boot so far up that ass you gon' taste the leather."

Homicide gave the guard both envelopes before responding. "Really?" He looked Rick Ross in his eyes. "Hold that thought, big baby. I'll be back to get a taste of that boot leather." Homicide eased between the two men.

Homicide was a few steps past them when the quieter Ruben Studdard size guard spoke up. "I told you 'bout writin' checks yo fat ass can't cash," he said to his big-mouthed Rick Ross look alike partner.

"Fuck that punk," Ross said, waving his hand in the direction of Homicide. "I ain't scared of him," big mouth said, patting the stun gun holster on his belt. "Come on, before we lose him."

"Now you trying to get me killed," Ruben said while following Rick's orders.

"My baby momma's little cousin's girlfriend used to fuck with one of them Goon Squad niggas," Reuben Studdard said. "She said them studs ain't nothin' to fuck with. And don't forget, Bo Jack momma the one that merked that cop back in the day."

"What cop?"

"That ain't important. What is, is that if ole boy momma gangsta like that, then you know Bo Jack gotta be a beast." He pointed up ahead at Homicide. "Ole boy popped that hot shit on the radio, callin' out Bo Jack with that song. Homicide might be comittin' suicide walkin' up on them Goon Squad studs. In any case we gotta get that action on video." Rick Ross held up his phone.

"For what?" the other asked while speeding up.

"Fool, we 'bout to blow up. We gon' pimp that video out to the TV, sell that shit to Media Take Out and to one of them *Enquirer* or *People* magazines."

The two men turned the corner just as Brandon walked into the hallway restroom. When they noticed Homicide pick up his pace, the guards did the same.

"Oh shit," both men said at the same time. They knew there were in trouble if anything happened to Brandon.

"Hey, hey," the more laid back Reuben Studdard sized guard called out. "Homicide."

But the big rapper did not turn around. Instead, he dodged straight into the restroom. "Oh, shit!" the bigger guard said. Then, to his partner, he said, "Go in there and make sure nothing jumps off while I run and get help."

"I ain't gettin' involved in that." Rick Ross shook his head. "That ain't my business."

He took one look at his boy and shook his head, before he took off running down the hall.

VERSE 13

Some of the fellas were outside of the dressing room shootin' the shit while Bo Jack and the others changed clothes inside. The entire crew was told to stay backstage for a minute since it would be easier when they called Bo Jack's name. He was nominated in 7 categories.

"The way some of them good dancin' broads was sweatin' me, hell if I don't go up in one of 'em," Thug said.

"Them females got business about themselves, Thug. Your pockets ain't long enough to pull any of dem," D-Bo said.

"Nigga, I ain't like you. I got more game than Milton Bradley and Parker Brothers. I wish a ho' would ask me for some money." Thug turned his head to the side. "Nigga, bitches pay me."

"To leave them the fuck alone," D-Bo said before he cracked up.

"You the most hatin' ass nigga." Thug looked at D-Bo sideways. "Got damn," Thug said.

"You got hatin' mixed up with realness baby boy. Ain't

nothin' wrong with payin' for pussy. Everybody pays one way or the other."

"I ain't everybody," Thug said.

"D-Bo right," Bam-Bam said.

"Got damn," Thug shook his head, "Can a nigga give Bam-Bam some pom poms and a fuckin' skirt, ole cheerleadin' ass nigga."

The others laughed.

"Fuck all that hee-hee shit. I'm being real," D-Bo said. "You may not give the money up front, but every hard leg in this bitch done took a female to the movies, out to dinner, or to the park. That shit cost money. And even if you just went to the park, you spent time with a female and time is money. So, if all you wanna do is run up in a female, why not give the money up front that you gon' spend on them in the long run or the short run any damn way?"

"Take a look at this nigga," one of the fellas pointed to the security guard running toward them. "How in the hell did that heart attack waiting to happen get a job in security.

"Nah, how did they find a uniform to fit his wide ass?" Bam-Bam asked.

"Go get Bo Jack. Go Get Bo Jack!" The security guard shouted.

The desperation in the big man's voice made D-Bo's heart speed up enough to take action. He pushed open the door to the dressing room. "Black, come quick," D-Bo yelled.

Not even a full five seconds passed before Bo Jack dashed through the door with H-Nic right behind him.

The guard was bent over, and out of breath from his running. He grabbed an inhaler from his pocket, put it inside his mouth and took a deep breath. "The bathroom," he pointed down the long hall. "Your brother and Homicide—"

There was no need for Bo Jack to hear the rest. He took off in an all out mad sprint.

VERSE 14

Homicide pushed the door open, then stepped inside. The tall, lanky kid, pissing in one of three urinals turned his head in Homicide's direction.

Damn, he just a kid, Homicide thought. Well, it was too bad. He was going to scare the shit out of him anyway. Standing at the door, he mean-mugged the kid as he looked him up and down. Homicide made a sucking sound with his teeth before he spoke. "You must be Blow Jack's little brother, Blow Job? huh," he grunted.

Brandon continued pissing, though he kept his eyes on Homicide.

When Brandon didn't say a word, Homicide added, "One of them quiet types, huh?" He grabbed his crotch. "You like boxing, Blow Job? I like boxing. Matter of fact, my record is better than the great Floyd Mayweather Jr.'s. After fuckin' Cotto up, a few months ago, he forty-three and oh. Twenty something knock outs." Finally moving, Homicide walked over to one of the three fancy metal sinks. "I'm forty nine and oh." He shadow boxed, admiring himself in one of the three oval shaped mirrors. "Forty-three knock outs, all of my fights in Rikers and Attica."

Brandon looked away for only a moment to zip up his pants. Then, he turned around and faced Homicide. In his eyes, he saw nothing but evil. But Brandon didn't flinch.

"You see in the pen," Homicide said, "we got a rule. If you get picked, you got three choices." Homicide cracked his neck to the left and then to the right before using his fingers to count off the options. "You can fuck, fight, or check in." With his eyes still on Brandon, once again, Homicide grabbed the crotch of his suit pants. "I'm sure I don't have to explain the fuck or the fight, but let me explain what checking in is, youngster." He smiled. "Checking in is when a con runs to a CO and tells him he's afraid for his life and he needs to be placed in protective custody. The guard then proceeds to take the pussy to the hole until he's transferred to another prison. Just like I'm blockin' the door now is the way I blocked the prison cell door. Whoever my victim was had to go through me to get out. Guess what?" Homicide smiled while flexing his chest muscles. Forty-three tried to get past me and I knocked forty three the fuck out before I fucked 'em. The other six voluntarily laid down on their stomachs."

"Am I supposed to be scared now?" Brandon asked in a condescending tone.

"Pussy, I don't give a fuck what you feel. The only thing I care about is the way you about to make me feel."

Brandon stepped back, turned around, then charged into Homicide's mid-section. Caught off guard, Homicide's back hit the door before both of them fell to the Italian marble floor. Homicide landed on top and his huge hand was around the fifteen-year-old's neck, when Bo Jack exploded through the bathroom door.

"Bitch ass nigga! Get the fuck off him." He kicked Homicide in the head.

Brandon wiggled from underneath the huge man, then

crawled to the corner. He sat up, trying to catch his breath.

Bo Jack reared back for another chance to knock Homicide out with his foot. But the big rapper grabbed Bo Jack's leg just as it was coming toward his face. Homicide flipped Bo Jack, making his head crash into the sink, decorating the porcelain with his blood right before his body crashed to the marble floor.

Footsteps. A lot of them came closer to the door.

Blood was all over Homicide's face and head. He was weak, but his adrenaline pushed him to his feet just as the bathroom door swung open. Homicide slammed the door on H-Nic's arm causing the .32 caliber handgun to fall to the floor Homicide was bending down to retrieve it when the door again swung open hitting Homicide in the butt, making him lose his balance.

H-Nic stepped in and grabbed Homicide's left arm, while Homicide's right came around and shattered the bones in H-Nic's nose.

"Hey!" Bo Jack barely said. He just wanted to close his eyes. The pain he felt from hitting his head on the sink was beyond excruciating. .

Homicide looked down. Bo Jack was lying on the floor with H-Nic's .32 pointed right between Homicide's black beady eyes.

"What the – "

But then the shots rang out. Four of them. Blood and brain matter flew everywhere. Homicide crumbled to the white marble bathroom floor. The gun fell from Bo Jack's hand as he slipped out of consciousness and into a coma.

BOOK 3

VERSE 14

Thirteen Months Later: January 2014

Mitt Romney had only been president for a year and the American people were calling for his resignation. It was January 2014, gas was six dollars a gallon and the national unemployment rate was at an all-time high of fifteen percent. Corporations across the country were downsizing and even dismantling as a result of the depression-like turn in the economy.

Despite the country's financial woes, America was still the biggest consumer in the world. And to continue its consumption, the government continued to borrow more and more, raising the debt ceiling to unheard of heights.

America's war machine was especially in trouble. There was no way America could afford to continue its public and secret bombing campaign against Afghanistan, Yemen, Syria, Iraq, and Palestine – countries refusing to bow or bend to America's economic oil interests. But, while the secret military budgets were being depleted, the country couldn't stop or even slow down their missions against these countries. The stakes were too high. Victory meant oil and oil meant the eventual stabilization of the American economy. For this reason, the Truth Commission leaders were meeting at the farmhouse located fifty-five kilometers outside of Basel, Switzerland.

The farmhouse and the three barns had been owned by the commission since 1969, four years after the Truth Commission was founded. When purchased, it was a heavily wooded, secluded forty-acre sheep farm, as it still was today.

The temperature outside was ten below, and the falling January snow made it almost impossible to see anything further than five feet ahead.

Nine average looking, heavy duty SUVs and four-wheel drive vehicles were parked inside the newly renovated second barn. Under the barn was an elaborate control and state-of-the-art half billion dollar command center.

The net worth of the sixteen men sitting at the United Nation's-like round table under the barn was well into the billions. Although the sixteen men and the one woman were from different nations, religions and cultures, they all shared a united Afrocentric worldview influenced by several Eastern philosophies for peaceful cohabitation of mankind. It was clear – the Truth Commission was a peace seeking body. But, they fully realized that the international bankers and corporate heads of the world were anything but peace seeking people. So, for the last three decades the commission had spent upward of ten billion dollars developing an undetectable and virtually invisible rocket powered nuclear missile.

"Lady and Gentlemen, it is an honor for me to present to you the MX-65," Chinese Nuclear physicist, Xin Yiu said, extending an arm toward the two-hundred-inch projector screen.

The seventeen Commission leaders looked on in awe, taking in the scene in front of them. The missile was a grayish black and it looked like a jet sized cigar with wings. The flying bomb was made of a metal-like substance that was as durable as tempered steel.

Bill Gates was the first to speak. "How long before it's ready for production?"

"We project that the MX-65 will be ready for action in six to nine months."

"Fascinating." Gates said.

Yiu continued, "As you all know, the aircraft is made from graphite and nitrogen hardened carbon. The agent used in bonding the two materials has to be strengthened ten-fold in order to carry the planes nuclear cargo overseas. We also have to do more testing on the covalent bonding of the nuclear material in the missile's reactors. We have to find a way to keep the temperature inside the reactors below thirty-two degrees while in the air."

Venezuelan president Hugo Chavez turned his attention to one of the elders of the Commission. "Where are we at on Jones's progress?"

Knowledge stood. "The medical staff at DeKalb Medical Center are still saying any day now."

"He's been in a coma for over a year now. Is he at least stable enough to be transported to one of our facilities? St. Augustine's Trauma Center in Havana, Cuba is only a three hour flight from Atlanta," Assata Shakur, the American-exiled freedom fighter said.

"His disappearance from DeKalb Medical Center would bring too much attention. That, he doesn't need. The good news is that his brain activity is slowly increasing as the brain swelling slowly decreases," Knowledge explained.

"And what if he doesn't come out? Or what if he has brain damage?" Tupac asked.

"He will be fine," Knowledge said.

"How can you be so sure?" Hong Kong billionaire, business magnate, Li Ka-Shing asked. Shing was the oldest and second richest member of the secret commission. He and Knowledge were the only living founding members of the secret organization. Shing had only recruited one person in the forty-seven year Commission history. But his recruit, Bill Gates, had more resources and money than the other seven hundred seventy-seven Truth Commission members combined. People outside of the Commission would never believe that Bill Gates, the richest man in the world, would be a part of a secret society that if successful, would redistribute the wealth in the country. If economists knew of their plans, many would say that Gates was committing financial suicide. But Gates would simply say, "Wealth is meant to be shared not hoarded."

Knowledge looked into the eyes of every man and the one woman in the conference room. "I am sure that King Black will be fine, because what we are doing has already happened before. You just have to open your eyes and minds to the lessons of the past. I have never lead any of you wrong, have I?"

"He's right," Gates said. "We have to believe. All of us, we've come too far to question any part of the plan. When King Black emerges from his coma we have to put all of our collective efforts on getting him ready to use his lyrical skills to get the youth behind the revolution. He and Tupac will record an album together. The public will hear Tupac's voice and will wanna see if it's really him. The tracks on the duo's album will be all about Tupac's disappearance, the revolution, and us—the Commission."

"Thanks to you," Picasso nodded in Gates' direction, "The world will see and hear it live via the internet."

"Gates smiled before continuing, "After the album's release, I mean right after the release, King Black does Madison Square Garden or Giants Stadium. And when Tupac comes on stage, the world will know that the lyrics on the album are true. Lyrics that will expose the lies and atrocities perpetuated by the real powers that be. Atrocities such as the CIA's murder attempt on Tupac. People around the world will then begin to believe and support the poor people's revolution that Dr. King so adequately called the fight for freedom."

"I think we all believe or otherwise we wouldn't be here," Chavez said. "I think we would all be more comfortable if King Black were in one of our facilities. You all are well aware of what the American judicial system can and will do to a young black male. When he wakes up, remember he will be waking up with a felony drug charge that he knows nothing about. I think we should move on liberating his mother and his brother, and then we go get King Black. When he does wake up, his mother and brother will be at his side. They are the glue that drives him."

Dr. Akinyele Umoja and King Black Uhuru Jones had never been introduced, but the African-American Studies professor felt a strong kinship to the young rap star. Two, three days a week, four, sometimes for six hours, Dr. Umoja would read essays, books and material related to black culture, psychology, sociology, and world history to the comatose rapper.

King Black had been in a coma for thirteen months. He was even more famous after falling into a coma after hitting his head on a bathroom sink before killing Homicide. His last album *Saggin' and Swaggin,* had gone quadruple platinum. Six of the thirteen tracks were currently on Billboards R&B/Hip Hop top twenty and the album had been out for over a year and a half now.

Kimani had control over King Black's finances and was paying a small king's ransom for extra security on top of what DeKalb County was already providing to keep people away from the hip-hop icon's hospital room. Kimani, Dr. Umoja, and Henry "H-Nic" Nicholas were the only civilians authorized to visit the private intensive care unit that had been set up for DeKalb Medical Center's famous patient.

Dr. Umoja wearing jeans, a black Free Mutulu Shakur T-shirt and a black leather motorcycle jacket looked more like a middle-aged student than he did the chair of the African-American Studies Department at Georgia State University. And that was fine with him. Dr. Umoja was a humble man.

He stepped into the room and as he always did, he surveyed his surroundings quickly. A consistent beep pattern came from the machine monitoring King Black's vital signs. The sheet that covered him, slightly rose and fell between his slow, yet steady breaths.

King Black looked so peaceful, Dr. Umoja thought as he took his book bag from around his shoulders. As he'd done for the last year, he sat down in a chair next to the hospital bed, ready to impart knowledge and wisdom to the young man's unconscious mind.

Just as he began his lesson, H-Nic barreled into the room. "Sorry I'm late."

"I'm just getting started," the professor said. "I figured you'd be late. Pulaski Women's Prison is a hump from here."

H-Nic nodded as he took a seat on the other side of the bed. This hospital room was his classroom, as it had been just about every day since Bo Jack had gotten hurt in his altercation with Homicide. It was by accident that he began listening to the knowledge that Dr. Umoja was imparting on Bo Jack. H-Nic had been in the room one day, and Dr. Umoja just began speaking to Bo Jack like he could hear him. At first, it seemed crazy to H-Nic, but then, he was mesmerized by the man's words and he'd wanted to know more. Plus, he'd seen the effect that education and the knowledge of history had had on Bo Jack and his folks. H-Nic figured that if he kept ear-hustling, he'd be able to get down with this knowledge thing without having to read because Dr. Umoja had done enough reading for everyone, and his lessons came from what he'd read.

At first, H-Nic had been fine just listening to the

professor's passionate orations. Later, he began reading just a little and now, he seemed to always have a book in one hand and his cell phone in the other.

"So how is Isis holding up?" Dr. Umoja asked H-Nic.

"That woman is a rock, Doc. If you knew her back in the day, there's no way you would believe she's who she is today."

"So, I've heard," Dr. Umoja said.

"Nah, Doc, you had to have known her when she was getting high. Back then, her mind didn't have the range of a windshield wiper," H-Nic paused. "And now, Doc, she's the female version of Ghandi and Malcolm rolled into one.

"H-Nic reading?"

At first, the sound of those words froze both men. And then, Dr. Umoja and H-Nic turned their heads slowly toward the sound.

"When you... learn... to read?" King Black's words came out choppy and barely above a whisper.

Dr. Umoja jumped up from his chair and dashed from the room while H-Nic sat on the edge of his chair with his mouth wide open as if he was waiting for King Black to speak again.

Although his next words were much more coherent, they still came out a couple octaves above a whisper. "My nigga, stop starin' at me like I'm food and help me get up." He tried to sit up, but fell back on the bed. "Do the cops know... That I did... That I did that bitch nigga..." he paused and closed his eyes for a few seconds. His memory was coming and going. "Homicide last night?" he asked, his voice louder but scratchy.

Before H-Nic could answer, a nurse and a doctor rushed into the room.

"Would you mind waiting outside?" the doctor asked H-Nic, though he didn't wait for an answer. He went immediately to work, checking out King Black.

Outside the room, H-Nic and Dr. Umoja paced as if that would help the time to pass faster. Twenty minutes went by with no word, then suddenly medical staff began trickling out of the room followed by King Black's bed. Dr. Bridges, King Black's primary physician walked over to where Dr. Umoja and H-Nic were pacing. "Dr. Umoja, I don't know what to say. I've been practicing medicine for over twenty years and I've never seen anyone come out of a coma after so long with this little memory loss."

"Where are you taking him," Dr. Umoja asked.

"We're taking him for a cat scan, and we're going to run some more tests. But, it seems that your nephew will be alright."

Six hours later – King Black was back in his room and Dr. Umoja and H-Nic were told they could go in.

Both men smiled as they looked at King Black's opened eyes. "King Black," Dr. Umoja extended his arm, and took the young man's weak grip into his. "I am Akinyele Umoja."

"Okay…."

"You hired me to –"

"Oh, yeah," King Black interrupted, "My, uncle right?"

"That's the only way I could get him in," H-Nic said.

"It's all good," King Black said. "So, Unc," King Black addressed Dr. Umoja, I don't wanna be rude, but can you give me and my guy a minute?" he asked, looking over the professor's shoulders to H-Nic.

"Sure, no problem, I'll be down the hall at the snack area," he replied.

After the door closed behind the professor, King Black said, "My nigga, what the fuck? The doctors kept telling me that today is January 8, 2014."

"It is," H-Nic said.

"2014?"

H-Nic nodded.

"They say I've been in a coma since the BET awards."

Again, H-Nic nodded as if he was too choked up to speak.

"Yo, what's wrong with you?"

It took a moment for H-Nic to push his words through the lump in his throat. "I was beginning to lose hope. If you passed… Shit been real crazy while you been asleep."

H-Nic shook his head as he thought of how half of the old crew was locked up, or on drugs, and Bam-Bam had been killed by some young kid trying to rob him back in June. When King Black went down, it seemed that the Goon Squad did as well. They'd never had the chance of becoming the God Squad. And the saddest part was when King Black went down, they all had paper. They didn't have to go back to the streets.

Bo Jack made a futile attempt at sitting up, but his body felt too heavy. The doctors had already told him that he still had a long way to go. His muscles had atrophied from being in bed for so long and it would be a while before he would walk again they had said.

Bo Jack reached for the button on the side of the bed and slowly, the top half of his bed began to rise. But the movement was too much and he blinked rapidly as the room began to spin. He closed his eyes, but even the dark behind his closed eyelids was spinning.

Then, relief came when H-Nic pressed the button, making the head of the bed descend to its original flat position.

"Black, you tryin' to do way too much way too soon. The doctors said it'll be a minute before you get your equilibrium back."

So many thoughts were going through King Black's mind. He knew prison was looming in his near future for bodying Homicide. How much time would he do? And what about his family – Isis, Brandon?

"How's mom? I know she's worried sick about me."

"Isis is good, Black. You'd be surprised. She ain't worried one bit. She has always said that you had too much to do. She kept saying that it wasn't your time to pass on. She's always said that God wouldn't have brought you through the belly of the beast just to end the journey before you were able to complete it, whatever that means."

King Black smiled. "She is something else, dog. I love that woman."

H-Nic nodded, though he kept his eyes lowered and away from his boy. He held his breath waiting for the next question.

But King Black only asked, "Damn, what about the fellas? All that loot I shelled out for our trip to Dubai. I guess I lost all of my deposits."

"The fellas are doin' what they do, you know," he said as he released a long breath, so glad that Bo-Jack hadn't yet asked about Brandon. He had no idea of the sacrifice that Brandon had made for him. H-Nic said, "Dr. Umoja been checkin' on you two, three times a week. He would've been here more often but he's been helping his wife open up another private school."

"He's been checking on me? For what?"

"You paid him a nice size deposit to do a job. And since he'd already taken a leave of absence from Georgia State, he asked me and Kimani if he could come check on you from time to time. We okayed it. I made sure I stayed the first few days he came just to be sure. But, I'm telling you, I sat here listening to that brother and he was dropping science for like six, seven hours on black history. The way he broke things down had me thinking. I started thinking about stuff you had said about the white man and the economy. I started thinking about your little br –"

"Brandon, how's – "

Shit, he thought, realizing too late that he'd slipped up. He didn't mean to bring up Brandon. King Black loved to talk about elevating black folks. Maybe if he stayed on the subject of his elevation Black would hold off on questions about his brother, so H-Nic went on as if he hadn't heard his boy. "Things began to make sense about life, oppression, and the reasons that so many black people are in jail and living in the hood – why blacks with money often separate themselves from the poor. I started thinking about all type of things I had never thought about. I thought about the names we call each other: Dog, Big dog, cool cat, foxy momma, bitch. And then that word 'nigga.'" H-Nic paused and shook his head. "I don't even use it anymore. I can't identify with a term created by the oppressive class to denigrate and further dehumanize our people. Chinese are descendants from China. The French are descendants from France. Americans are descendants from America. Niggas are descendants from where, Niggaland?"

As H-Nic talked, tears streamed from King Black's eyes.

"What's wrong, King?"

"That's what the fuck I'm talking about. You get it. My nigga! You get it."

H-Nic nodded. "Like the desert sun in the Sahara."

"Dog, I mean," King Black paused. "Yo, I feel you like a toothache on the word nigga and all that, but it's gon' take me a minute to eliminate them from my vocab, shit just come out my mouth natural. I don't even think before I use the words nigga and dog."

H-Nic shook his head. "Most of us don't realize what we're saying. It comes out as if it were natural to address each other as animals and less than human."

"Damn, I just can't believe you done got all philosophic and shit." He reached for the button on the bed, but changed his mind and kept the bed flat. "I don't know how we gon' work it, but they say I'm gon' have to do physical and occupational therapy for at least six months. They say I have to slowly build my muscles back up and then I have to re-learn how to walk."

"It may sound like a lot," H-Nic said, "but I know you

can do it, King."

"I know I can too, ain't no trip, my nigga. I'm actually going to try and drag my rehab out for a year. Maybe that'll put my murder trial off and in the meantime, me and Bran, can write our asses off. And somehow we gon' record my next album from here, too. I wanna move on as much as I can before they lock me up.

"Black," H-Nic interrupted.

King Black ignored him and continued, "I don't care what it costs. If C-Murder can record an album from prison, hell I know I can make it do what it do and record from in the hospital. Matter of fact, call Kimani and tell her I'm back. I need her to get at me ASAP. We got shit to do and I don't know how long we have before they indict me for burnin' Homicide. Hell they might have already. But, I figure as long as I'm under a doctor's care and can't walk, the state won't arrest me. But, then again –

"Black!" H-Nic shouted.

King Black looked at his boy.

Now that he had Black's attention H-Nic said, "I got some news for you." He took a two-second pause. "Brandon's been locked up in the Psych ward at Central State Hospital."

"What?!!"

"He took the fall for killing Homicide."

Central State Hospital, formerly known as the Georgia Lunatic Asylum, the State Asylum for the Insane, and the Georgia State Sanitarium, is the oldest and largest psychiatric facility in the state. Located on a sprawling 1750 acre campus in Milledgeville, GA, it was one of the largest psychiatric facilities in the world.

When Brandon arrived almost a year ago, the hospital was underfunded, overcrowded and its inmate patients were way over-medicated as they still were today. Brandon Malachai Jones was the exception to the over-medicated. Just days after arriving, he'd learned to tuck his medication under his tongue while drinking from the four-ounce paper cup that the nurse dministered four times each day. He didn't know what they would try to do to get the drugs into his system if they ever found out that he wasn't drugged up. So, since he didn't want them to find out, he acted like he was in a constant drug haze whenever he left his padded, one-man cell.

Thirteen months ago, in that bathroom with Homicide, Brandon just knew he was about to die before his big brother came through the door and saved his life. It had all happened so fast. He was on the ground. Black had gotten H-Nic's gun and he had slipped into a coma as a result of him hitting his head on a bathroom sink a few seconds before he shot and killed Homicide.

As his brother laid there unconscious, Brandon knew that he had to act. Black was a felon. He would be going away for life on a gun charge because of Georgia's three strike law. Self-defense wouldn't have been an option because a convicted felon wasn't allowed to carry a gun, not even to defend himself.

So Brandon had done what he had to do – he'd crawled over to his brother, picked up the gun just as the police had barged in.

"Drop the gun," the first cop had barked.

He dropped it, then rolled back on his heels and stuck his thumb in his mouth. "I had to. He wa. He wa. He-he-he-" Brandon had kept stuttering, hoping that the police would buy the fact that he was not stable and then the law would send him to a mental institution. This scenario that had come to him quickly was much better than going to juvey or worse, being tried for murder as an adult.

The scenario had come to him so fast that H-Nic almost didn't catch on to what Brandon was doing. But then, on the sly, Brandon had winked and H-Nic took over. H-Nic explained to the cops that Brandon was Black's mentally challenged little brother. And since Brandon's school records had confirmed that, Kimani had used an insanity defense.

At first, Kimani didn't want to go that route, but Brandon had already played the role of a mentally unstable kid in front of the cops and if all of a sudden he appeared normal and tried to instead use the self-defense angle, a jury wouldn't believe them. Plus, self-defense was too risky, being that Homicide was unarmed.

Local mental institutions were so overcrowded that the state had remanded the then fifteen-year-old teen to Central

State until his seventeenth birthday, pending he pass a psychological evaluation.

Now, he'd just turned sixteen and he only had a year to go. He'd be able to handle just another year. At least there were parts of the day that he did enjoy. Like mail call. Every day he received a letter from his mother, and H-Nic and Knowledge wrote to him twice, sometimes three times a week. With him having no immediate family that was eligible to come and visit, the letters were his only keys to the outside world, except for Kimani. As his attorney, she was the only one allowed to see him. She came to check on him from time to time.

There were good things coming out of his stay with the state. Like the fact that he and his mother communicated more now than they ever had in the past. Even though they'd always been close, now they both had the time to share their thoughts and ideas. They talked about books they'd read and new authors they discovered. They talked about everything from slavery to freedom, sex to salvation.

After she had read them, Isis forwarded all the books that Knowledge was sending her. Some, Brandon had already read, but he still read them again – always gaining more understanding the second time around.

Brandon enjoyed his interaction with H-Nic, too. His brother's friend was Brandon's only connection to King Black and he lived for the weekly updates. For the first few months, H-Nic's letters just spoke of his brother's unchanged condition and the old times that H-Nic and Black had shared. But in the last eight months, H-Nic had begun doing his own reading, and now when he wrote, his letters were filled with questions, questions that required more thought from Brandon as H-Nic continued reading.

But Brandon loved the challenge. It was a wonderful way to pass the time as he got closer and closer to his release date. Brandon continued to read, continued to study, continued to be challenged. Because when his brother came out of his coma, he was going to be ready to write for his next album.

G-Swag sat in the District Attorney's office with his legs crossed, studying Gene Shockey's facial expressions as he spoke.

"It's Thursday afternoon. There is absolutely no way that I can convene a grand jury by Monday. And even if I could, I wouldn't. For Christ's sake, the man just came out of a coma only hours ago."

G-Swag uncrossed his legs and leaned forward. He looked the State of Georgia's District Attorney in his eyes. "You can and you will convene a grand jury by Monday, Gene."

The only noise in the DA's office for the next thirty seconds was the sounds of the heavy January rain pelting the state building's windows.

Slowly, the DA stood up and walked around his desk. Gene Shockey was an imposing figure at six-five, two-hundred fifty pounds, towering over the seated five-foot-ten inch, rail-thin entertainment mogul.

"Who in the God friggin' hell do you think you are?" The DA asked, glaring down at G-Swag. "Consider yourself lucky if you leave the way you came in." He paused and pointed to his office window, eight floors up from the ground. "I have a mind to throw your scrawny ass out that window, you and all that damn hair." He pointed to the door. "Now get the fuck out!"

In a nonchalant tone he asked, "Are you finished?" Then, he leaned back and crossed his legs once again, as if he had no intention of leaving.

"You're pushing it." The DA pointed his index finger in G-Swag's face.

"Look, I don't know why we have to go through this. You huff and puff, try and intimidate me with idle threats when we both know that I have a copy of your wife, Sandra riding O'Reilly's dick the morning before he was killed. And I have great shots of you standing outside in the rain with a gun in your hand looking directly at O'Reilly's house when several flashes of light, that I presume to be gunshots, were fired. And then think about the fact that Officer O'Reilly's body wasn't found until nine hours later after an anonymous caller phoned the police. Now putting all of that together, I wonder who that anonymous caller was?" G-Swag pointed a finger in the air. "And don't forget, without my money and my influence you wouldn't have gotten your job back."

"Without you money and influence I wouldn't have offered the Jones woman that deal."

"Nobody forced you to take the fifty grand."

"The DA's face was beet red as he stood behind his desk fuming. Shockey pressed his lips together and breathed hard through his nose.

"My dude," G-Swag stood. "You need to go out and get you a bag of cush. Smoke a blunt. It'll take the edge off. Or either go buy you some pussy, 'cause we both know your wife ain't giving you none; she too busy fucking everybody else."

"Get out!" the DA growled.

"Okay, okay, my dude. I'm out." He turned as if he was leaving, but then suddenly, stopped. "But it's either your ass or Bo Jack's. You have one week. Convene a grand jury and make them supersede the drug indictment and charge the little shit with racketeering," G-Swag said before he moved toward the office door.

"I went along on the questionable drug bust last year at Bo Jack's mansion, but now you are asking for too much."

"His mansion? My dude, did you forget I'm on the deed. I built the damn house for him." G-Swag had his hand on the doorknob when he turned around. "Besides, I'm not asking anything. I'm telling you."

"You think your money makes you untouchable?" the DA asked.

G-Swag shook his head. "Nah, my dude," he pointed to his forehead, "my mind makes me untouchable. Now in one week or less, somebody is going to get fucked. It's up to you to decide who it's gon' be."

VERSE 18

"Gimme fourteen hookers and a pimp to run them hos," the toothless old female con said, counting fifteen while slapping the domino down on the table.

Brenda "Big Mac" Cutter stood up, domino in hand. "Twenty century fox, big-legged hoes and cocaine rocks," she shouted, counting twenty points and slapping the double five domino on the card table in the game room of the women's prison.

Isis looked over at Brenda. "I'd like to place an order," she laid down the blank five, "quarter pounder with cheese, please, hold the mayo." She counted twenty-five before continuing, "and queens, I believe that is the game."

"Girl, to be so edumacated, you can talk shit with the best of us," Brenda said to Isis.

"How do you think I learned? Dr. King got out of lots of fights growing up because of his smack talk. And before Malcolm Little became Malcolm X, he'd used his word-hustling skills to get a job as a porter on a train."

"Uhm-hmm, and he used those same word-hustling skills to get between a nasty white ho's thighs and that's what really landed him in prison."

"Go head, girl," Isis said admiring Brenda's quick wit before standing up from the table. "You queens can have it. I need to write my son."

"Ladies, I'm out, too. I'm tired of teaching y'all how to play for free, shit," Brenda said as she also stood.

"Last year this time, you was the Boss Bitch of Pulaski, Big Mac," Jablonski shouted from across the room. Lisa Jablonski was a snow white, untanned mixed martial arts professional fighter and compound prison officer at Pulaski. "Now you Isis's bitch, following her around like a lonely puppy dog."

"Come on, girl, don't even feed into that," Isis said, putting her arm around Brenda's now tense shoulders.

The officer threw an almost empty pack of Camel's across the room, hitting Brenda square in the forehead.

"There's one cigarette in the pack. Have your bitch come over and lick my clit, and it's yours, Isis."

Brenda shrugged Isis's arm off of her as she turned to Jablonski. "It's your world for now *Officer* Jablonski. You got the badge. I got the inmate number. But please don't get it twisted. I ain't nobody's bitch."

The officer took off her badge and put it on one of the card tables.

"Jablonski, I'm just trying to do my time, so please leave me the fuck alone," Brenda said as she followed Isis to the open door.

The officer's lips spread into a slow smile. She loved messing with the sistas, and ever since Big Mac stepped down from the Boss Bitches, Officer Jablonski rode her hard.

Back when Big Mac was running crack and meth in the prison, she and Jablonski were close. Jablonski profited close to three grand a week off the meth she brought in for Brenda to distribute. And that was three thousand even after she paid off the other officers who turned their heads when she brought in the drugs.

There was a rumor going around the prison that Jablonski had been recently suspended from the MMA professional fighting circuit due to failing her last two pre-fight drug tests.

"Bitch, don't walk away from me," Jablonski said. "I will spit in your face and you won't do a damn thing about it. Just tuck your tail between your Chicken of the Sea funky legs and run off like the dumb follow-the-leader bitch that you are."

Those words made Brenda stop right in her tracks. She tensed up and closed her eyes. "Lord, give me strength." She silently prayed, something she'd been doing a lot of since becoming close to Isis. Brenda knew Jablonski was fucking with her because Brenda's mother had just died and the former queen pen of Pulaski's illegal drug trade had been granted a furlough to go to the funeral tomorrow. Nothing was going to stop her from saying good-bye to the woman that gave her life. The woman who had loved her unconditionally the thirty-four years she had been on this earth.

When she opened her eyes, Jablonski was right there, standing in front of her, having shoved Isis out of the way. The six-foot-tall manly-built officer hawked and spit in Brenda's face.

It was only instinct that made Big Mac raise her fist and smash Jablonski's nose, dropping the mixed martial arts fighter to the floor.

"I'll kill you, you fucking bitch," the guard screamed.

Might as well finish whipping Jablonski's ass, Brenda thought. There was no way she was leaving the prison to go to her mother's funeral now.

Jablonski struggled to get to her feet, but she went right back down after Brenda stomped her in the face, this time, fracturing the officer's jaw. She only had the chance to kick her twice more before a sea of blue and white uniforms swarmed onto the scene. In less than two minutes, it was Brenda who was laid out on the ground, unconscious. And five minutes after that, Brenda was dead, beaten to death by male and female officers sworn to protect and maintain order inside the women's prison.

The other prisoners were returned to their cells, in shock because one of their friends was dead, but not surprised because this harassment and these beatings went down all the time, just not as severe. Isis was the only one who shed tears, crying through the night at the senseless loss of life. Brenda Cutter was her friend.

A week later, life was seemingly back to normal—at least as normal as it could be in an overcrowded women's state prison. Isis was still very much affected by what had happened, though the visits from Knowledge helped. He'd come to see Isis twice in the last week and it was the plan that he had that helped her to keep moving on.

On Dr. King's birthday, the prison always had a celebration for the inmates – a special dinner and a movie in the auditorium afterward. But for this dinner, Isis volunteered to help serve the fried chicken, collard greens, and watermelon.

"Make sure you put on that cap," one of the kitchen guards barked.

Isis hated bottling her dreads up under the plastic hair cap, but it was regulation. Anyone with hair working around food had to wear one.

For the first hour, Isis served food and made jokes as the women passed through the chow line. Then, she went into the back into the cooler to get another tray of sliced watermelon. As she was filling the tray, another inmate came into the cooler.

"Isis."

She acknowledged the inmate with a simple nod.

Without another word, the inmate handed Isis a small

pile of folded clothes. Then, the inmate made an X with her arms across her chest, the sign for freedom and liberation that Isis's Knowledge Be Free prison society used. The inmate hugged Isis before she whispered The Knowledge Be Free motto, "Knowledge be free. Just us for justice." And then left the cooler.

For a moment, Isis closed her eyes and meditated on what was about to go down. Then, with a deep breath, she stuffed the clothes down her baggy pants. Her oversized green prison-issued button-down shirt hid the bulge the clothes made. After a final check, Isis grabbed the tray with the watermelon and went back to her station.

After dinner, the inmates filed into the prison auditorium for the rest of the evening's celebration: last year's blockbuster movie *Transformers Reloaded*, starring Bo Jack Jones.

As the prisoners filed in, Jablonski, with her wired-jaw, eyed the Black-Asian petite beauty that had been giving her the eye for the last few days. When the woman smiled at her, Jablonski's already muscled-up-on-steroids body swelled. She paced back and forth and kept her eyes on the Blasian woman.

Just as the lights began to dim, the prisoner stood up and with slow steps moved toward the back of the auditorium. The whole time, she kept her eyes and her smile centered on the prison guard. The prisoner kept walking toward the restroom at the rear left, the one that had been out of order for a few weeks. She was inside for less than a minute before Jablonski followed her in.

She was standing at the sink when the guard entered and Jablonski grinned when she took in the prisoner standing there.

"Well...."

But, she never got another word out. The guard glanced down and saw the blood gushing from her neck to her uniform. She'd barely felt the razor that had just slid across her neck. As the guard gripped her neck trying to stop the blood, Isis stepped from behind the door. She stood next to the guard as her knees folded and she crumbled to the ground. The guard's hands were still in place, trying to act as a Band-Aid.

"Queen, make sure Monae put the Out of Order sign on the door," Isis said to the young woman.

Just like the one who'd brought Isis the clothes earlier, this inmate nodded before crossing her arms across her chest before mouthing the words, "Knowledge be free. Just us for justice."

As soon as the inmate walked out of the bathroom, Isis jammed a knife-like object in the door jam, just in case anyone tried to enter the out of order restroom. Afterward, she knelt down in front of the officer who was just two minutes away from death. She said, "Surely you didn't think you would live after taking out a black queen."

She was still crouched over Jablonski when someone tried the door. A second later they were gone and Isis turned her attention back to Jablonski. She used the razor and a pair of homemade scissors to cut off Jablonski's left thumb. Then, she rinsed the bloody appendage off and stuck it inside the plastic hair cover she'd worn earlier while serving food in the chow hall. Next, she went to one of the four sinks, tore off a handful of brown paper towels and wiped and rinsed the dead guard's blood off her hands before removing her prison greens and slipping into the guard's uniform that one of her girls had given her earlier.

As she dressed, Isis thought about the plan. She'd told Knowledge that even with the phony credentials and the compound officer uniform, it was still going to be impossible for her to get past the four guard stations. She wouldn't have even agreed to Knowledge's plan if Jablonski hadn't been the reason for Brenda's demise. But, after watching her friend be beaten to death, there was absolutely no way Jablonski could go on breathing.

"Everyone knows me," she'd told Knowledge after he explained the plan.

"Trust me. All you need to do is get from the auditorium to the visitation building. You only need the officer's uniform to get across the yard."

That made sense to Isis. If she was wearing a guard's uniform, no one in the guard towers would be suspicious of her moving around the grounds unattended. But what didn't make sense was how she was going to get from the visiting room past three other guard stations to the civilian prison entrance.

Dressed, she took one final look at the guard who was the reason her friend had been murdered, then she pulled the shank out of the door and slipped out of the bathroom. She held her head down, as she walked with purpose, not too fast, not too slow. It seemed like it had taken forever and a day to get to the visitation building located a football field away from the auditorium where the movie with her son in the starring role was playing.

At the brown metal door, Isis reached into her pants pocket and removed Jablonski's thumb from the hair wrap. She pressed the thumb against the print scan and followed that with the four-digit code on the number pad.

Nothing happened.

She took a deep breath before she tried it again. She pressed the thumb against the black glass-looking pad and slowly punched in the numbers 5,3,2,8. A second later, a buzzing sound followed, a click, and then Isis was in.

She walked inside and stopped right in front of Officer Ramirez. She sighed, resigning to her fate. The gig was up. Officer Ramirez knew who she was. They'd had extensive conversations on men and self-love.

Ramirez stared at her before she said, "Turner," reading the nametag under the silver badge that was on Isis's shirt.

She frowned, but nodded at the same time. Officer Lana Ramirez knew her name wasn't Turner. Now, she didn't know what to say or expect.

"Officer's restroom, last stall, behind the vent. Use your nails to take out the four screws," Ramirez instructed. "And follow the instructions. Especially the one concerning your hair."

The surprise almost made Isis want to stop and hug the chubby Hispanic female guard, but she rushed to the restroom.

Eight minutes later, Isis was in a short line to exit the visiting room. She had done as Ramirez instructed and had retrieved and changed into a wig, a pants suit, dark shades, and some two inch heels. Her head was stinging from having cut her shoulder length dreads off so quickly with the homemade scissors that were dulled from cutting off Jablonski's thumb. Cutting off her dreads was the only way the black wig would work.

The line moved slowly, taking way too long. Isis took several concentrated breaths trying to stay calm as she got closer and closer to the front.

Most inmates had despised the sadistic Jablonski, but every prison had its share of dry snitches – inmates who told on others for nothing more than a few extra privileges. A few days off a work detail or food from the officer's dining room could get some inmates to give up their peers. Isis couldn't help but wonder how soon someone would dry snitch about the dead officer laid out on the restroom floor. Although there were two other restrooms in the auditorium, someone had to have ignored the OUT OF ORDER sign on the restroom door by now, Isis thought.

Finally, it was her turn. She made it out of the visiting room and past two more guard stations. She could see the civilian prison entrance. The two guards manning the last station didn't seem to be paying any attention to her. And, then the sirens went off.

She was less than five feet from freedom, but no matter how close she was, she wasn't going anywhere now. She knew the drill. When the sirens went off, the entire prison was locked down. No one came in and no one went out, including civilians.

She looked at the two armed guards standing in the way of her physical freedom.

They looked at her, then slowly moved their hands toward their holsters as if they sensed something.

Five feet to freedom.

The officer's eyes darkened.

Five feet from freedom.

"Don't worry, Isis," Knowledge had said. "You will make it out. I promise you, you will make it out alive."

Knowledge had never led her wrong.

So, she ran.

VERSE 19

Kimani Knox seemed to have aged ten years in the last thirteen months. Overseeing King Black's estate was more than a full time job. On top of that, she was in love. In love with a man fifteen years her junior.

She didn't admit it to herself until she received the news of his condition late Saturday night on the first of December, back in 2012. She'd been devastated to hear about King Black. She'd cried for three days straight, and after that, there were no more tears. She had gorged on Ben & Jerry's Cookies and Cream ice cream while having her own marathon of her favorite movie *Love Jones*. She watched the movie seven times, back to back to back.

She and King Black were from two different times, two different worlds. When Bo Jack had barged into her office demanding that she do this and that for his mother six years ago, she had thought that he was a pompous asshole, a pompous *rich* asshole. But as she came to understand him, she saw that he actually cared more for others than he did himself. She saw that he was a lion amongst men, unafraid to be different, unafraid to risk all for what he believed. All of these qualities made him a leader that others wanted to follow. Including her. But she had failed him miserably.

Kimani had just gotten word that King Black was awake and that he wanted to see her. But how could she face him after everything that had transpired over the last year? If Isis wasn't King Black's mother, she would have confided in her. She'd heard so much about this man named Knowledge, but she'd never met him and even if she had, he was still a stranger. She couldn't confide in someone that she didn't know.

But she had to have an outlet; she needed someone. And so, she turned to the man who had caused her a lifetime of pain and gave her a lifetime of understanding.

Kimani's father, Tommy Knox lived in a small apartment in the drug-infested Cleveland Avenue area of town.

"Shawtayyyyy?" a young man called out as Kimani got out of her small SUV. "I got that killa, killa and it's Bo Jack Jones certified," the young man said waddling his way toward Kimani.

"Killer, Killer?" Her eyebrows furrowed.

"Yeah, Shawty."

The young man looked to be about the same age as Brandon. The teenage boy pulled up his Coogi black jeans, reached in his front pocket, and took out a plastic baggie before his pants dropped right back under his behind. "This that Loud, Shawty." He held out several quarter sized green transparent plastic bags filled with marijuana.

"I'm good," she said.

"They usually go for twenty-five a bag Shawty, but a nigga gon' give you the new customer discount, two for one." He held out two bags of the pungent smelling weed.

"I don't smoke."

"No problem, Shawty, a nigga got them swaggin' and swervin' pills that'll make you feel like you flying on a pink elephant." He dug into another pocket.

She held up her hand. "Don't. I said I'm good." She shook her head, still wondering about his last analogy. Why would anyone want to feel like they were riding on a flying pink elephant?

The young man hiked up his pants before turning around.

"Hold on," she said.

He was smiling when he turned back to face her. As if he knew that she would change her mind. Surely, she was gonna buy something from him.

"How do you know I'm not five-oh?" she asked.

He waved his hand in the air as if that was impossible. "You don't look like the poh-poh," he said. Then, he added, "Are you?"

"Too late to ask that now, don't you think?" As she reached in her purse, in one quick fluid motion, the young man raised the t-Shirt he wore under his Atlanta Falcons bomber Starter coat, put a finger in one of the empty belt loops on his pants, hiked them up, and took off running.

She laughed. She was just going into her purse to give the young brother a business card. At the rate he was going, he was going to need her legal services one day for sure.

But her thoughts returned to why she'd come to her dad's rundown apartment complex. But before she could step onto the front steps, Tommy Knox opened the door. "Well, you handled that well, Sunshine."

"How long were you there listening, daddy?"

"Long enough to see that the young buck is a statistic waiting to happen," he said. "Come on in, let's get out of the cold."

"Can we just sit in the car and talk there? I'll turn on the heat," she said shivering outside in the cold.

The sixty-two-year old father of three knew what his daughter's request was about. If she could help it, she would never be near the apartment that he shared with his two women. He understood how his oldest couldn't understand how he could be in love with both women. So, he agreed and nodded as he followed his daughter to her small champagne colored, ten year old Chevrolet Tracker SUV. After she unlocked the door, they both slipped into the front seat. He tenderly wrapped his huge, calloused fingers around his daughter's cold hand.

"So what's this dilemma you're struggling with, Sunshine?"

"King Black is out of his coma." Her sigh was heavy.

Not even a beat passed when he said, "And the problem with that is?" He paused. "I would think this would make you happy."

Kimani looked out the window and shook her head. "Well, Daddy, a few months after King Black went into his coma, I received a subpoena to testify at a hearing concerning King Black's estate. His former manager, G-Swag, contested King Black's rights to any future royalties."

"Can he do that?" The slender man with dark chiseled facial features asked.

"Well, according to a morality clause in his contract, if King Black was charged and convicted of a drug related crime, he would forfeit any future royalties from G-Swag Unlimited."

Her father shook his head. "That doesn't make sense," he said. "What does his recording contract have to do with his behavior outside of the studio?"

"G-Swag's attorneys argued that King Black was a reflection of the company he represented. They said that all of his actions—inside and outside of the company—affected endorsements, sponsorships, and reflected on other artists. The whole company is impacted—at least, that's what the attorney's argued."

"I can't believe you let him sign a contract so shady."

"He signed that before I came into the picture. Back then he was represented by Joel Katz's entertainment law firm."

"So, King Black has done something to violate this morality clause?"

"I don't think so," she said. "It feels like a set-up to me. A set-up by G-Swag. It happened right after King Black fell into a coma. It wasn't even a week before G-Swag pushed the Atlanta drug task force to search his estate."

"Huh? How did he get that kind of power?" her father asked. "It's King Black's estate, right?"

"Yeah, but G-Swag is on the deed."

"What the hell?"

"I know," Kimani said, shaking her head. "I have no idea why."

"Okay, so I take it that they found something."

Kimani nodded. "Drugs."

He was silent for a moment. "You know none of this makes sense."

"I know Daddy."

"That boy has more money than God, why would he be involved with drugs?"

"Same thing I said. But, that's what they found. I was there when they found fifty pounds of marijuana beneath his bed."

"Oh, yeah. This is a set-up for sure," Tommy said matter-of-factly.

"I know, and all this time, King Black hasn't been able to defend himself."

"Defend himself? What? Don't tell me there's been a trial?"

"No, no, no, though that kind of thing has been done before. But in this case, King Black hasn't been tried and hasn't been convicted. But, the charge against him started a firestorm that no kind of insurance could cover," Kimani said.

"How do you mean?"

"The judge has frozen all of King Black's assets, at least the ones that the IRS hadn't already taken."

"But he'll get that stuff back after he goes to court, right?"

"If he beats the case, he will. But that's not all, Daddy. Remember what happened to his little brother?"

"Now, don't blame yourself for that, Sunshine."

"I know it wasn't my fault. I just wish life would deal me some aces when dealing with the Jones family sometimes."

"Look at me." His face became serious. He glared into his daughter's eyes. "You know I love you and your sisters more than anything in creation? Don't you, Sunshine?" He squeezed her hand.

"Yes, Daddy, I do." She smiled. Her father could always make her smile no matter how bad things were.

"Lord knows I hate what I took you and your sisters through when you all were kids. I can't change that. But when I kicked my habit, I did everything in my power to be the best father that I could be. So, you see life dealt me some losing hands, but," he reached over and hugged his daughter, "I ended up winning the game. Look at you. A big time lawyer in Buckhead, when I look at you and your sisters, I know that I did something right."

"You did, Daddy. You did. You were my superhero growing up and you're my superhero now. When you were using, you still spent time with us. You still helped raise us and even in all of that, you showed us the definition of a man."

The way he blinked, Kimani knew that her words had brought her father to the brink of tears. He was always this way whenever they had these kinds of talks. He'd told her many times that while he was their reason for being. They were his reason for continuing. He never would've made it back from the insanity of crack addiction without the love he received from his three baby girls. "So, look Sunshine, you just go on down to that hospital and tell that man the truth. And while you're at it, tell him how you feel about him, too."

"Huh?"

"Don't huh me, that's my line," he said. "I'm your daddy. I know you better than you know yourself. You can't hide nothing from me, little girl." He opened the door and got out of the SUV. Then, he peeked back in the window. "You just drive on down to that hospital and tell that man that you love him. You hear me, Sunshine. You tell him the truth about everything – business and personal."

VERSE 20

"So, Dr. U, are you saying that there is not a conspiracy to eliminate the black man?" H-Nic asked.

It had not even been twenty-four hours since King Black came out of his coma, yet the professor was giving a lesson to H-Nic and King Black.

"King Black, do you think that's what I'm saying?" Dr. Umoja asked.

He thought a minute before answering. "Based on some of the things Claude Anderson asserts in his books, *Powernomics* and *Black Labor, White Wealth*, it would be detrimental to white wealth to kill off black labor. America is a huge plantation. This country makes up a quarter of the world's prison population and black males make up most of that, and prison is America's biggest industry. And now with so many private prisons, the privileged class have found a new way to legally re-institute slavery. So, I don't think you meant killing off the black man."

H-Nic and Dr. Umoja could hardly believe that King Black's mind was so sharp less than 24 hours from emerging from a yearlong coma.

King Black had no idea where what he'd just said had come from. He had never read or heard of Claude Anderson. Then he thought about Dr. Umoja and the last thirteen momths he'd been coming to see him and teach him.

The sound of the squeaking door stopped all talk and their eyes turned.

"Excuse me?" Kimani peeked in the room, a mile-wide smile on her face.

"Bout time," King Black said acknowledging Kimani while raising his bed just a little. "Glad I wasn't dying."

"Glad you wasn't either," she laughed. "I don't have any life insurance on you," she said, walking into the room. She held a hand out toward Dr. Umoja. She smiled, "Hi, I'm Kimani Knox."

"You don't remember me?" he asked. "Akinyele Umoja."

"Oh yes, Dr. Umoja. You look different without the African garb you had on when I met you. What? About eighteen months ago at your office."

"Dr. U, H-Nic," King Black addressed them, "you think we can continue tomorrow. I really need to speak with Kimani."

Dr. Umoja looked at his watch. "Just after four. I might make it home before rush hour begins."

"Doc, it's Friday and it's raining," H-Nic said. "Now you know…"

"I can always hope." The doctor laughed.

"You see where *hope* got Jesse," King Black said.

The professor said his goodbyes and H-Nic followed him out. When he closed the door behind him, Kimani turned to King Black.

"Well, I hear we have a lot to talk about," he said to her. With his head, he nodded toward the chair. "Pull that up and let's get started."

She nodded and for the next thirty minutes, Kimani recounted the last fourteen months. His face stretched with surprise. His mouth opened with shock. His eyes teared with emotion when she spoke about his brother. He still couldn't believe Brandon had taken the fall for what he had done. First it was his mother and now his little brother.

When she finished, he shook his head. "You know, I feel like I slept through a tornado that destroyed my life and now, I'm just left with the broken pieces of yesterday."

"If what I told you wasn't so sad and wasn't so true, I'd say those words were beautiful. But...."

He tried to keep his voice calm, steady, when he asked, "So you let the state put my baby brother in a nut house?"

She shook her head. "There was nothing I could do. Brandon had already convinced the arresting officers that he was mentally ill before I got down to the station. I thought that with Brandon's documented record of having severe ADHD—"

"You thought?" King Black cut her off. "He was fifteen. Kimani, my baby brother was fif-fucking-teen. They would've tried him in kiddie court."

"Not necessarily," she said, shaking her head. "Especially knowing that he was your brother...I just didn't want to take that kind of chance with him."

King Black's eyes were filled with water. "Homicide was a felon twice his size and twice his age. Even I could have figured out a way to make it so that Brandon could have easily walked on self-defense."

"It wouldn't have been easy to prove," Kimani said, trying to keep her voice calm even as King Black ranted. "Homicide was shot four times at point blank range. Have you forgotten what happened to that woman in Florida a few months after Trayvon Martin was killed?"

"What woman?"

"Marissa Alexander, the woman who was sentenced to twenty years for firing a warning shot in her own garage to scare her husband who was going to jump on her and her daughter. She had a master's degree and had never been in any trouble with the law and the Stand Your Ground law didn't work for her. Her only crime was being black. I wasn't going to take that chance with Brandon's life."

"And?"

"And what?" She really was trying, but now, she was getting pissed off. He was blaming her? It was true that she didn't like the outcome, and yes, she felt like in some ways she'd failed him. But it wasn't on purpose. She'd busted her ass trying to do right by the Jones family. She even hired security to protect his ungrateful ass while he was in a coma. Twenty-four hours, seven days a week, two guards were posted up outside his hospital room, to make sure media, fans, G-Swag, no one could get in that wasn't on the list she gave the men protecting him.

King Black closed his eyes and reclined the hospital bed back to its prostrate position. His head was pounding with all of the thoughts that were inside. How could Kimani have allowed his little brother to be sentenced to a nut house?

"I'm the biggest star in the country, maybe the world. I've made countless millions and not only is my brother locked up, but my house, my cars and my bank accounts have been frozen." He paused as if he was waiting for her to say that everything she'd just told him was part of a bad April Fool's joke. But when she said nothing, he added. "And on top of all of that, G-Swag hasn't paid me and doesn't have to according to some bullshit clause?" When she stayed silent, he finished with, "Tell me that I've interpreted what you've said the wrong way. Please tell me that."

"No, you've got it right, but I want you to understand that right now, everything is in limbo. Now that you are out of the coma –"

"Fuck that. Kimani," he said, interrupting her. "I trusted you." He shook his head and lowered his voice a bit when he repeated, "I trusted you."

"I…" She stopped, not knowing what else she could say.

"My mom, and now my brother. Fuck G-Swag. Fuck the money, the fame, fuck everything!" He reached for the phone on the stand to his left, but then, his arm fell and hit the metal bed railing. He was too weak to hold it up. He looked at Kimani with dead eyes. "Can you please hand me the phone?"

She got up, lifted the phone and placed it on the bed. "You want me to dial a number for you?" she asked as King Black slowly raised the head of the hospital bed again.

"You can dial 911, and then you can leave. I never want to see you in this life or any other. You are dead to me, Kimani Knox." Tears spilled down his face. "Dead, do you understand?"

Without a word, she nodded before picking up the phone, dialing the three numbers, and putting the phone to his ear. Next, she turned and walked to the door. After closing the door behind her, she stood up against the outside of it in the hallway, numb. The hulking security guards Kimani had hired over a year ago didn't say anything, just stood outside the door looking like secret service men. As much as she hated to admit it, King Black was right. She had fucked up his life. She really couldn't blame him.

Inside the hospital room, King Black had the ancient 1980's phone receiver to his ear.

"911. What is your emergency?" the operator asked.

"I'd like to report a murder." He decided to use his former government name as this was what the world knew him as. "My name is King Black, I mean Beauregard Jackson Jones. I'm at Dekalb Medical, and I need to tell the truth. An innocent man is in Central State's Psychiatric Ward," he said before hanging up the phone.

She had not moved and Kimani heard what King Black had said to the 911 operator. There was no way she was going to let him do this. No way she could let him incriminate himself. But how was she supposed to stop him? He'd made it very clear that he never wanted to see her again.

Taking one last look at the door, she stepped away and walked toward the sixth floor elevator. The elevator's down arrow lit up just as she was about to press the button. Kimani waited for the two men to get off before she got on, but still she eyed them. They were detectives for sure, but how did they get there so fast? He'd just gotten off the phone.

Before the elevator doors closed, she jumped off and followed the two men to King Black's room.

"FBI," one of the two men said, before they both showed the guards their credentials. Then, one of the security guards nodded and stepped aside so that they could go in.

Kimani walked in right behind the two G men. "Gentlemen, my name is Kimani Knox. I am Mr. Jones's attorney," she said, hoping that King Black didn't start screaming for her to get out of the room.

But, he said nothing as both men turned and looked down at the barely five foot tall attorney.

"Good, we can kill two birds with one stone. We went to your offices earlier, Ms. Knox," one of the G men said.

"What do you want with me?"

"We just have some routine questions to ask you."

Routine questions were never routine to the person being questioned. Kimani knew this from experience. "What is this concerning?"

One of the G Men looked down at his notes before asking, "Ms. Knox, where were you at the start of the week, Monday January 20th, between the hours of 5:00 PM and 9:00 PM?"

She crossed her arms. "What is this concerning?" She ignored his question and repeated hers.

The other G man said, "We'll ask the questions, ma'am."

"And I wanna know why do you feel the need to question me? I am an officer of the courts."

"We understand that, ma'am. We're just doing our jobs."

"What does questioning me have to do with your job?"

The two men exchanged glances as if they were each looking for the other to take over and take control of this woman. After a moment, the taller man spoke.

"Look, Ms. Knox, we can do this here or we can go downtown to the Richard Russell building. It's your choice."

She thought for a moment. Did she really want to deal with these men downtown? Not to mention that it was cold and raining. And after what King Black had said to her, all she wanted to do was go home, take a hot bath, and cry.

So to get this over with, she answered his question. "I was at the gym. L.A. Fitness in Buckhead."

"From when to when, and do you have an address for the gym?" One of the G men asked while his iPad 5 recorded Kimani's statements.

"I don't know the address, but it's at Peachtree and Piedmont in the Towers Place Pavilion. I was there at 5 PM. I was in the Monday night aerobics Funk Dance class until six. After that I took the 6:45 spin class that ended at 7:30, then I sat in the steam room, before showering and changing. I must've left between 8:30 and 9."

"Where did you go from there?"

"Home."

"Is that the address," the G man looked down at the iPad, "841 Pine Ridge, Stone Mountain Georgia 30088?"

"Yes, it is."

The G men turned their attention to King Black. With almost as much personality as a rock, one of the men asked, "Mr. Jones, when is the last time you had any contact with Isis Jones."

"What? Are you serious? I just came out of a coma."

"Thirty-two hours ago," one of the agents said, looking down at some notes. "Can you please just answer the question?"

Ignoring the agent, King Black asked, "Is my mother okay?"

"We don't know."

"What the fuck do you mean you don't know? What happened?"

The men ignore him as if he hadn't spoken. "Mr. Jones, have you had any contact with Isis Jones since you've been awake."

"No, my mother is incarcerated. And I don't think she has my number here at the hospital."

"No need to be facetious, we're just doing our jobs." The G man looked from King Black to Kimani and then back to King Black. "Have either of you had any contact with Brandon Jones in the last twenty-four hours?"

"No," they both said.

"Okay we've said enough. Now what is this about?" Kimani asked.

"Approximately forty-eight hours ago Monday evening, Isis Jones killed a prison officer at Pulaski State Women's Prison before escaping. Two accomplices at the prison entrance opened fire on two other prison officers, but no one was seriously injured."

VERSE 21

Dr. Na'im Akbar is to African-American Psychology what Albert Einstein was to Physics. Now retired, Dr. Akbar was still one of the most sought-after lecturers in Black Psychology. About three months after Brandon had been a resident inmate in the youth section of Central State Hospital, the psychiatric department had just gotten word and was ecstatic upon hearing that Dr. Akbar would soon be working with the youth patient inmates.

Some of his peers in academia and at the hospital must've thought Dr. Akbar needed to be a resident at the hospital instead of a doctor residing over the residents. Dr. Akbar coming out of a comfortable retirement to work at Doom & Gloom—as the residents and many of the staff referred to the colossal mental institution—was a little crazy. Moving from sunny south Florida to the nothing town of Milledgeville, Georgia was a lot crazy, even if it was only a one year assignment. At least that's the way it looked to the outside world. But it was a move that was well thought out by all the members of the Truth Commission. Dr. Na'im Akbar and Brandon Jones had grown very close, especially since Brandon knew the truth behind the doctor being there.

It was early afternoon, though it looked more like the night. The thick clouds that released the pounding January rain, blocked out the sun's light.

Dr. Akbar sat at his desk studying the coded instructions in a text message late night the night before. It was about time, he thought to himself. Forty years of intelligence gathering, planning, and recruiting had come to this. Dr. Akbar felt a surge of adrenaline as he began to visualize freedom. Real freedom for America and its forty million black stepchildren. Freedom for Hispanic Americans, Asian Americans, Native Americans and even poor white Americans. It was coming. The psychologist knew it. He could feel it, just like he had known that the Truth Commission was going to be successful in steering Barack right on into the White House. And they did.

The White House—Dr. Akbar had another dream. He hoped that in twenty years, Brandon Jones would occupy the oval office. That young man would be perfect for America. Really, he would make a great President now, except for the fact that he was only sixteen. His mind though, was far greater. It was as if he'd been here before. His fellow Truth Commission member Knowledge had been correct, Brandon had reached a higher consciousness that was unheard of for someone so physically young.

It amazed Dr. Akbar that when he was with Brandon at times it was hard to tell who was the therapist and who was the patient. For the last several months, the two of them had flip-flopped their respective roles as therapist and patient as Brandon grew into understanding and was able to conceptualize principles and schools of thought in Afrocentric Psychology. They'd spent hours, days, weeks, and months breaking down principles and concepts that were in many of the books that Dr. Akbar had written.

But his thoughts returned to the message he'd decoded this morning before coming to work and then, he looked up at the sound of keys clanging on the steel office door.

He knew the time before he even glanced at the clock: three o'clock.

"Come in," he called out, knowing who was on the other side of the door.

Moments later, the guard was removing the cuffs from the six-foot-three inch, linebacker-sized teenager. "I'll be back for the boy a little early, doc, around five-fifteen," the tobacco chewing guard told him.

"Boy?" Dr. Na'im Akbar frowned. "I think you mean, young man," he said, correcting the leather-skinned officer.

"Say again?"

"You referred to this young man as a boy. I merely corrected you."

"Huh?" The guard was still confused.

Dr. Akbar didn't have the time to explain racial etiquette to a white man who probably didn't even realize that he was a racist.

"Why are you coming back for Mr. Jones so early?" Dr. Akbar inquired, deciding to change the subject.

"They talkin' 'bout closing 44 and Route 29 cause of floodin'. I'm tryin' ta leave early as possible. My eyes – can't see so good in the rain no more."

So because he didn't want to be inconvenienced, he was shortening Brandon's visit. Dr. Akbar shook his head, then led Brandon over to the sofa once the officer left them alone. He checked the door once more before he sat next to Brandon and handed him a three-by-five card.

Brandon read the message: ISIS IS SAFE AND IN OUR CARE. WE LIBERATED HER FROM PRISON LAST NIGHT AND BECAUSE OF THE CIRCUMSTANCES BEHIND GAINING HER FREEDOM, WE HAVE TO COME GET YOU THIS EVENING.

Just in case the walls had ears, Dr. Akbar spoke, as if he was continuing yesterday's lecture session. Brandon continued reading, card after card, memorizing the instructions, then eating the cards.

"There has never been a period in our experience in North America where we haven't been trying to somehow gain liberation to get freedom, to get away from the oppressive restrictions on our humanity that this culture has enforced. What has happened over the years is that there has been stages of freedom," Dr. Akbar lectured.

Dr. Akbar handed over another card.

"Brandon, you see when you deprive people of their fundamental humanity, they tend to lose sight of what true freedom is. When you begin to rob people of their basic contact with reality, then they are not very clear on what is real. Under those circumstances they know something is wrong, but they aren't exactly sure what it is that is wrong. Because of the uncertainty about what's wrong, people begin to engage in whatever frantic and frustrating effort they can to break free. So they look at the immediate restraints, the shackles, manacles, and rings around their necks... the dogs used to restrain them, the cages they are locked behind... being subjected to these conditions is the most effective way that the people can understand and see to define what slavery and what freedom is."

As the doctor lectured, Brandon read, memorized, then ate the cards. This continued for ninety minutes because the guard came to the door fifteen minutes before he had said.

It was fine, though. Brandon was ready.

*****

At seven-fifteen that evening, Brandon was in the day room watching ReShonda Tate Billingsley's latest TV1 movie *Preacherman Blues*. Twenty minutes into the movie, he reached inside his khaki institution pants and removed the one-inch needle that Dr. Akbar had taped to his groin area. He took a breath and plunged the needle into his arm. Seconds later, Brandon toppled from his seat. His eyes bulged to the size of tea saucers and a thick, green-foam bubbled from his mouth. His body convulsed as he laid on the heavily padded gray carpet.

"What the hell?" one kid said.

"What's wrong with him?" another asked.

"Help!" another shouted.

All kinds of screams rang out from twenty different kids in the dayroom. They were frantic with confusion and fear as an older white woman, wearing a lab coat rushed into the large open room. She was followed by two guards.

"Lois, Lois," one of the teenagers pulled on the gray-haired woman's lab coat, "Lex Luther got to Superman!" The inmate pointed to Brandon still convulsing on the floor. "Kryptonite!" But then, he turned away. "Hold on, I have to take this call." The Drew Carey looking white kid removed the stained Fruit of the Loom underwear he wore on his head and put the drawers to his ear.

By the time the physician assistant knelt down next to Brandon, he was as still as a corpse. "Get the stretcher," she shouted to the guards as she placed a spoon into Brandon's mouth to prevent him from choking on his own tongue.

Once she had the spoon in place, the guards took over.

"One, two, three, lift," one guard said to the other and they lifted the teenager onto the stretcher.

"Hurry," the old nurse shouted. She wiped the foam from Brandon's mouth before pressing a button and shouting into the radio she held to her mouth. "This is Garett. Gotta code blue over in Juvenile Psych lock-up. I need a bus ASAP."

She didn't give the guards time to question why they didn't go through the four buildings to the main hospital ER, instead of going outside in the pouring rain. "Come on," she shouted. She may have been middle-aged, on the cusp of being a senior citizen, but she moved at the speed of a woman half her age.

"Code blue!" She flashed her I.D. at the guard station camera.

"Hold on," the guard behind the window said.

"Hold on for what?" she shouted. "We got a dying boy here."

"Protocol," the guard behind the window started to explain.

"Screw protocol." She pointed to the unmoving teenager on the metal stretcher behind her. "You wanna be responsible for this kid dying?"

A second later, a buzzing noise followed by two clicks sounded, and then the metal sliding door opened. The nurse and the two guards rushed the stretcher through and hurried to the second station.

This time, the guards who were manning the station were so caught up with watching LeBron James beat up on the Oklahoma City Thunder that they barely turned their heads before pressing the button to open the steel door.

"The outside double doors," the physician's assistant barked at the basketball-watching guards.

One of the officers behind the window waved without looking up from the cell phone where they watched the game. He pressed the red button, causing the steel double doors to slide open.

The revolving red and blue lights on the ambulance lit up the rainy night. The furious rain pelted the guards, Brandon, the physician assistant and the two paramedics who helped load the stretcher in the back of the bus.

Once Brandon was safely inside the back of the ambulance, the nurse called out, "Fellas!"

The two guards turned and looked up at the gray-haired, white nurse, who now had a tranquilizer gun in her hand.

"Sleep tight, don't let the bed bugs bite," she said as she pulled the trigger twice, tranquilizing the two institution guards with wild animal tranquilizer darts. She couldn't allow them to get into the back of the ambulance as protocol had called for.

Minutes later, after they had cleared the institution grounds, Brandon watched through eyes that were half-open as the nurse peeled off skin like material from her face, hands, and legs. She was actually a black woman – the most beautiful black woman the sixteen year old had ever laid eyes on.

The Atlanta streets were deserted because there was no one fool enough to be out in this storm at two in the morning—no one except for the inhabitants of the small U-Haul truck pulling up to the security gates at the People's Storage facility near the Atlanta Braves stadium. The fake nurse and the two men that had been up front had ditched the stolen ambulance in a Wal-Mart parking lot in Milledgeville near the U-Haul truck they had rented earlier in the day – the same U-Haul truck they drove over eighty miles in a violent storm back to Atlanta.

It was a little after one in the morning when they pulled up to the large U-Store-It facility. The driver stuck his arm out the window and pressed in the five-digit code. The eight-foot chain linked gate opened. After backing the truck up to the last storage unit, the driver and his partner jumped out. While the driver used his key to open up the orange and white metal storage garage door, his partner unlocked and lifted the gate door to the small U-haul.

Brandon stood around watching as the others worked in the small cramped storage unit. The drug he'd injected in his arm a few hours ago had just about completely worn off. Brandon tried not to stare at the woman known simply as Raena, but it was difficult. He was a young man who'd been locked up in a loony bin for months and this woman in front of him was cute in the face, thin in the waist, and she had just the right amount of luggage in her trunk. Plus, she had Michelle Obama class.

"Help me move this couch," the driver said, pointing to the older beige leather couch propped up against the concrete storage wall.

After the couch and the rug under it were moved, one of the fake paramedics got on his knees and removed a rough looking 80's manila keyboard from under a propped up, used queen sized mattress. After pressing a few keys, a well-concealed concrete and metal trap door electronically rose up where the couch was, revealing black metal spiral stairs.

Everyone but the driver descended the stairs. After all three were down, the driver picked up the keyboard and pressed the proper keys before the trap door closed.

Brandon was in awe as he looked around. The bunker looked like the inside of Star Trek's U.S.S. Enterprise spaceship. There had to be a hundred TV monitors hanging on the walls. Buttons, computer keys, switches and joysticks jutted out of one long wall. And the huge, white and gray bunker was hospital clean.

A metal door opened to the rear of where Brandon stood.

"My baby!"

Brandon turned around, not believing the voice that called out to him. "Mom," he shouted as they both ran across the concrete floor.

"Are you all right?" she asked, as she studied her youngest between hugging him. "Did anyone hurt you in that place?"

"No, mom. I'm good." He was so glad to see his mother that he wanted to cry. But he wasn't about to do that. Not in front of Raena. (He'd learned her name in the ambulance.) He didn't want Raena to think he was soft.

"Look at you. My baby has grown up big and tall." Isis wrapped her son into her arms again. "I missed you so very much."

The longer Brandon was locked inside his mother's embrace, the harder it was for him to not break down. He was ten when his mother went to prison. And for six years, Knowledge had reassured him many times that this day would come. Over the years, he'd grown more impatient for this day, but he'd never lost faith.

"Isis. Brandon."

Mother and son broke their embrace as Knowledge walked through a door in the underground bunker.

"Come," Knowledge waved, "sit down." He led them to a small table surrounded by four beige leather office chairs.

"Raena," Knowledge said, addressing the beautiful Georgia State University African-American Studies professor that had led both rescue teams. She was one of the professors that Knowledge had referred to King Black a couple years ago. "Can you take the team into the strategy room? I need a little time," he said.

She nodded. "Gentlemen," she said before leading the fake paramedics out of the room.

When they were alone, Knowledge grabbed hold of one of Isis's hands. "You cannot even begin to know how proud I am of you. Your growth over the last six years since being incarcerated is amazing. Your growth over the last fifteen years is even more amazing, Queen."

He used his free hand to grab Brandon's hand. "And you, young man, young king, you have surpassed all of my expectations for you." He squeezed both of their hands. "I love you both so much."

The three embraced.

"We love you too, Knowledge," Brandon said.

"Without you, I'd be still lost," Isis said. "Without you, we all would be lost. Without you, the world would be completely dark," she said.

"Both of you are beyond extraordinary." Knowledge said. "Your understanding of history and culture has allowed you both to reach your higher self. And with your gift of discernment you can better identify the signs that God gives us to overcome oppression, repression, and suppression. You both understand what is real and what is not. Am I correct?"

They both nodded.

"This place," he looked around, "these machines, computers even me, my physical presence is not real. Five hundred years ago, was this place here? Were these walls here? Were these monitors here? Was my physical body here? No, but knowledge was here. Knowledge and understanding have always been here. But unfortunately, most of the world is inhibited by the blind trying to navigate this world with their eyes and ears instead of their minds."

Isis and Brandon sat on the edge of their chairs, holding onto every word that Knowledge spoke.

Knowledge turned his attention to Isis. "Queen, Brandon has been viewing the world and society with his mind instead of his eyes and ears for a few years now." Knowledge turned to his star student. "Brandon, you wanna explain the rest to your mother?"

He nodded, then jumped right in. "Mom, Knowledge, a few others and I have been manipulating the media to create the conditions that will spark unrest that we believe will lead to revolution."

Isis shook her head. "Violence is not ..."

"Not a physical war, Mom. No one wins when mass life is lost. But how do you fight a system designed, created, and maintained through violence? You fight that system with the same seeds used to create it. You fight it with fear. We have to create something that will cause a greater fear in the system administrators than they can create."

"I'm a little lost, son," Isis confessed.

"Okay, let me start at the beginning." He took a deep breath. "Mom, in the early 60's the Truth Commission was formed by Knowledge, Malcolm X, Mao Tse Tsung, Fidel Castro, John Henrik Clarke, Li Ka Shing, and Muammar Gaddafi to study and find ways to stop the colonialism and imperialism that America and Western Europe had imposed and on weaker nations. The Truth Commission has indirectly been involved with several wars since Vietnam, and what they've concluded is that America is the head of the snake. And that head has used the media to manipulate and control mass opinion. It has taken almost half a century, but our time is nearly here."

"What time is that?" Isis asked.

"Nation time, Mom. The conditions have to be right for revolution and America's greed has created the right conditions. The national debt is astronomical. China has emerged as the strongest nation on the planet and America is deeply in debt to China. China has never forgotten the Opium Wars and they are poised to take action when the Truth Commission is ready to act."

"The Opium Wars?" Isis questioned. "Western Europe was responsible for them."

"I know. But again, the head of the snake is America, chop that head off and Western Europe will fall."

"When will all of this happen?"

"Soon. But for now, we continue planning and waiting as America continues spending billions in unauthorized funds to finance their bombing campaign against Middle Eastern nations for oil. And Mom, America is losing that battle. Right here at home, the Truth Commission created the conditions that put their man, their black man in the White House."

"Yeah, and we see how that turned out," Isis said.

"Exactly as the Commission planned."

"They planned for the president's assassination?"

Brandon smiled. "Yep, planned it every step of the way. Just like they gave millions to Romney's presidential campaign."

"Huh?"

He paused a moment because he wanted her to really get the full effect of what he was about to say. "President Obama is alive and well, Mom. That was a double who was killed."

His words had the effect that he'd expected. Isis fell back in her chair with her mouth wide open.

"And we got behind Romney because he was the best candidate to send the nation further spiraling out of control."

She shook her head. "I still don't see how all of this will spark a revolution."

"Mom, 'revolutions are created by the conditions that people are caste into and revolutionaries aren't born,' as Che said, 'They are created by their conditions.'" He continued, "Just look at American society today, Mom. The middle class has been all but eliminated. Seventy-four percent of Americans are living below the poverty line. The national unemployment rate is at fifteen percent and rising. Crime is out of control. And since Trayvon Martin's murder a couple years ago, the Commission has been able to bring right wing whites to the fight of racial injustice. The American people are poor, hungry, and upset. They feel dejected, let down by their country. They want change like never before."

"So, I don't understand. What do we have to do with this? Why you? Why me? Why were we chosen as part of this?"

"That part is simple. Tupac was supposed to be the Truth Commission's messiah to sway the youth in the nation, but the government put an X on his head when they saw the positive influence he was having over the young people."

"I get it." She nodded as if no further explanation was necessary. "They want your brother to take Tupac's place. They want him to use his music to create revolutionaries."

"Nah, mom, he can't. Tupac...." He stopped. He was about to tell his mom about Tupac, but she would see soon enough. "I mean, nah, Black can't make a man a revolutionary, but he can open eyes so folks can see who they really pledging allegiance and paying taxes to, and then that realization can cause others to become revolutionary."

"But, what part do we play in this picture?" she asked.

Knowledge answered, "Isis, you and Brandon have also been groomed to help lead this nation into a new day. Your understanding of history is the key to a cohesive future."

"So, what's our next move?" Isis asked.

"It's time we go and wake your other son up," Knowledge said, "He's out of the coma."

VERSE 23

G-Swag was in one of the five studio mix down booths. He was sampling beats from the old Tupac blockbuster "I Wonder If Heaven Got a Ghetto," when his cell phone vibrated on the soundboard. He looked at the caller ID before answering. "What's good, lieutenant?"

"Somebody just broke the kid out."

"What kid?"

"Brandon Jones, Bo Jack's little brother."

G-Swag's momentum caused his seat to roll back against the wall after he jumped up out of it. "What did you just say to me?"

"I said someone just –"

"I heard what you said. How? Who?"

"We don't have much. We just got word ourselves."

"What do you have?"

As the lieutenant explained about the breakout from the women's prison and then from the mental facility, G-Swag felt his blood pressure rising. When the lieutenant finished, the music producer put the phone down on the soundboard because he needed a moment. He closed his eyes and took three deep breaths. He paid way too much money to entirely too many incompetent people. Then, he picked up the phone and once again pressed it to his ear.

"Hello? Hello?" the lieutenant said.

"I'm going to ask you again?" G-Swag spoke slow and clear. "What information do you have?"

"Well, as I said, we don't have much."

"I heard you the first two times."

"I didn't think you did, asking me the same question twice."

"Look, I don't wanna get into a pissing match with –"

The cop interrupted, "You'll lose if you do."

"My dude, can you please just tell me exactly what information you do have?"

"Well actually, all we know is that Brandon Jones is not in the psych ward and he is nowhere on the hospital grounds."

G-Swag took another deep breath. "My dude, what kind of operation y'all running down there?"

"You should be glad I called you at all. We are the Dekalb County Police Department, not the Milledgeville PD," the lieutenant said. "The perp disappeared from an institution in Milledgeville, Georgia. Milledgeville is about seventy-five miles outside of Dekalb County's jurisdiction. Are you beginning to see where I'm going with this?"

"Calm down, my dude."

"Do not tell me to calm down. I got all hell breaking loose around me because of that damn storm last night, and the chief tells me to take time out that I don't have to speak with you about something I could care less about. The boy escaped, got broken out, I don't know and frankly, I don't care."

"You need a hug, my dude."

"I am not *your dude*, Gregory Reagan," the lieutenant shouted, addressing G-Swag by his government name.

"It's all good, my dude. So, I guess you gon' beef up security at DeKalb Medical. The hospital *is* located in DeKalb County. That *is* your jurisdiction, right?"

"I don't care what the chief says. One more sarcastic remark..."

"So, what about more security?" G-Swag interrupted, ignoring the lieutenant's attitude. "It makes sense. Think about it. After thirteen months, Bo Jack comes out of a coma and that same night his mother kills a guard and breaks out of prison. The next night, his little brother breaks out of the nut factory. Don't you see the pattern here? Somebody's going to break Bo Jack out of the hospital."

"Mr. Jones is not being held against his will, so he cannot break out, or be broken out."

G-Swag said, "He should be. The man— "

The lieutenant interrupted, "Has not been convicted. We are well aware that he has charges pending against him, but until a grand jury hands down an indictment—"

"I know that, what I meant was, don't you think someone may come and take him out of the hospital?" G-Swag asked.

"You're reaching," the lieutenant said. "Gregory, this is real life, not TV."

"So, you don't see the connection with the two escapes?" G-Swag asked. "And if his mother and brother are missing, you can bet that soon, he will be missing, too. And then, he'll never be indicted."

"Even if I wanted to put a couple of men in the hospital, I couldn't," the lieutenant said. "Half the city's traffic lights are out because of last night's storm. My men are out doing traffic duty while the city is dragging their asses on repairing the damn lights."

"Excuse after excuse. I pay top dollar for firsthand news and I get third class clowns giving me useless information."

Two seconds after he said that, the line went dead.

G-Swag looked at his cell phone. *No he didn't just hang up on me.* He grabbed a piece of paper and pressed so hard as he wrote down the name of the lieutenant, that his pen burst. "Damn it."

He looked for something to wipe the ink off his fingers. After finding nothing, he pressed a button on the office phone. "Amber, please bring two or three wet paper towels into Studio Sound Room B."

Amber Way was so much more than an executive assistant for the hottest producer in the business. She went way above the call of duty for her boss and was paid very well to do everything from foreplay to gunplay. For these reasons, she travelled the world with G-Swag, knew more about him than anyone. Amber Way had worked for G-Swag for over ten years, but really, he still didn't know much about her. At least, she didn't think so.

Amber walked into the soundproof room and took a seat behind a million dollars of sound equipment, next to G-Swag.

"Amber, I need security over at DeKalb Medical today."

"Now you're protectin' him?" she asked with nothing but disdain in her voice.

He gave her a disapproving look. "Now, Amber you know better than that. If I'm protecting him it's because it'll benefit me in the long run, and furthermore, I'm not protecting him, I'm doing everything that I can to ruin him. Before I'm finished with him, he'll wish he were dead. And by then, he will take his life or we'll kill him and make it appear as if he'd taken his own life."

"So then, why security at the hospital?" she asked. "I don't get it?"

"His mother escaped from prison two nights ago and his brother escaped from that nut house last night. *Someone* big is behind the jailbreaks and it seems likely that this *someone* will come and get Bo Jack next."

"How do you know someone's coming for him? Blow Jack is in no condition to be moved."

He smiled at her purposeful mispronunciation of his name. "I study history. The FBI calls it trends. The only family Bo Jack has escapes from jail less than forty-eight hours after he's come out of a thirteen-month coma."

"No one could have known he was going to come out of the coma when he did. Swag, you're overreaching. Isis and Brandon's escape was just a coincidence that just coincided with Blow Jack's recovery," Amber said as she stood in front of G-Swag with her arms crossed.

"Amber, do not talk to me as if I'm stupid. I told you long ago there was no such thing as coincidences; there's a plan for everything." He paused to regain his composure. He didn't want to give her any reason to suspect that he knew who she really was. He smiled, thinking about his favorite saying, keep your friends close but keep your enemies closer.

Two people couldn't get much closer than he and Amber Way.

He continued, "Better yet scrap the security, grab Henry Douglas, Bo Jack's best friend. He'll know where Isis and Brandon are hiding."

"And after he talks?" Amber crossed her long well-defined runner's legs.

"Do I really have to tell you what to do with him?" G-Swag asked, his dark orbs staring inter Amber's cold hazel-brown eyes.

"And after I take care of him?"

G-Swag thought for a moment. "I want mother and son found naked in a sexually compromising position. If the deaths of his mother and little brother don't send him to suicide, the media coverage of how they're found, will. Bo Jack will be bombarded with questions about his mother and brother's sexual relationship."

"And you expect all of this to happen over the next few days?"

"No." He shook his head before raising his left index finger in the air, "I expect this to happen now." He clicked a couple of keys on the keyboard in front of him, then turned back to his executive assistant. "As of two seconds ago, you became a half million dollars richer."

"What?" she asked.

"I just wired five hundred thousand into your Swiss account. This needs to happen now, you understand?" he asked wondering if her bosses at the CIA knew she had a Swiss account.

Amber stood up. The winter white wool dress she wore hugged her pear shaped waist, hips, and ass like a second skin. She knew she should just stay quiet and take the money, but she had to ask. She could care less about Bo Jack Jones. G-Swag was her priority and she'd helped make him the megastar that he was today. "Swag, why are you spending so much time and money on that nobody?"

He responded as if the answer was on the tip of his tongue. "Tupac sold ten times as many records after his death. And Bo Jack has already surpassed Tupac in sells and he's still breathing. And because Bo Jack broke our last contract," G-Swag locked his hands behind his head while leaning back in his chair thinking that if the government ever came after him for whatever reason, proof of the people that Amber exterminated would be his get out of jail free ticket. He continued, "Guess who gets all the royalties from his sales in the event that he dies?"

Amber smiled. Now, she got it. Bo Jack's demise would only make G-Swag larger than he already was. Her handler at the CIA would be pleased.

VERSE 24

It was a beautiful, sunny late January, Friday afternoon. The temperature was approaching sixty and if you hadn't lived through it, you wouldn't have believed that thirteen violent tornadoes had swept through Georgia and Tennessee the night before. Sixty-four people were dead and over 200 more were hospitalized throughout the two states. President Romney had already declared several counties in Georgia and Tennessee disaster areas. He pledged the government's full support to the families who had been affected by the weather. Damage, as a result of the storm, was estimated to be in the billions.

The storm may have been the biggest news in the nation, but King Black's recovery and family drama was a close second and in some markets, King Black was the number one story. News trucks from all over had battled the storm coming into Georgia to try and get interviews about King

Black's recovery and his mother and brother's escapes. The Chief of Police and Atlanta Mayor Kasim Reed were able to keep Isis's escape out of the media at first. But after her sixteen year old son escaped the next night, all hell had broken loose after G-Swag leaked both escapes and the attempted police cover-ups to the local media.

The grounds and surroundings areas outside of DeKalb Medical Hospital looked like the Million Man March of journalists and fans. Everyone was jockeying for position. The fans held out hope that they would see King Black, hear his voice, or something...anything. The journalists were fighting to interview anyone who was permitted to see the superstar rap phenom. Word of King Black's awakening had gone viral over the web within hours of his waking up. Even with King Black's private secret service-like security team, it had gotten so crazy during the almost seventy-two hours he'd been out of the coma, that the hospital had to move King Black and his security to different private rooms each day. And somehow the media still found out what room he was in, although no outsiders had been successful in getting in to see the recovering king of hip-hop.

At a quarter of six in the evening, a Fox News helicopter landed on DeKalb Medical's rooftop helipad. Long silky black hair blew in the wind as the female ran to a rooftop door. She was followed by two men carrying cameras and production equipment. Before the woman turned the doorknob, she took the gun out of the black satchel that was draped around her shoulders. She pulled the stock back, loading a bullet into the chamber.

"We got one shot. And we have to make it quick. Everyone below saw the helicopter land up here." The woman spoke over the helicopter noise to her cameramen. "You got your guns ready?" she shouted. "Safeties off?"

The two men nodded.

"Let's make it do what it do," she said before using a pen-sized laser to cut the lock out of the rooftop metal door.

A blonde, six-year-old white kid pulled away from his mother and took his thumb out of his mouth. "H-Nic," he said pointing a stubby finger in the direction of where a casually dressed young black man made his way through the crowd of onlookers and media representatives.

With all the commotion no one had heard the kid. H-Nic hadn't hear a thing. He was too focused on getting to the hospital doors, but that focus was disturbed when someone else recognized him.

"H-Nic," one of the fans yelled out.

Then others started to look his way, and they all began screaming. "H-Nic. Ahhhhhhhh. The Goon Squad."

Fans and the media broke out running toward him, H-Nic took off toward the glass revolving hospital doors.

Behind him, he heard questions.

"Did you help Bo Jack's family escape?" "Where are they now?" "Is Bo Jack really inside the hospital?" "Was Bo Jack ever really in a coma or is he recovering from a sex change procedure?"

That last question almost made him stop. But he just shook his head and kept running. He burst through the hospital doors and ran right into the chest of a huge white man with dirty blonde hair.

The blind lady working the hospital information desk said, "He's okay, Frank. That's Henry Nicholas, Bo Jack Jones's best friend. He's on the list," she said to the DeKalb County police officer.

H-Nic didn't even ask. He never did. He really didn't care how the matronly-looking, older blind woman knew it was him whenever H-Nic passed her station.

H-Nic rushed to the elevator and was surprised to see a hospital security guard manning the elevators.

"Floor?" the Justin Timberlake-looking security guard asked.

H-Nic noticed the slight bulge under the Ackerman security uniform. There were three others on the elevator who probably didn't notice, an older black couple and a middle aged sickly looking white man. None of them looked like groupies. "Nine," he said.

"Oncology?" the security guard/elevator attendant stated as a question.

H-Nic nodded. "Yes, sir," he answered. But questions swirled in his head: Why did the guy have his gun down the small of his back instead of in a holster? And what was hospital security doing wearing a ten thousand dollar Presidential Rolex?

The white guy got off on three and the older black couple got off on five.

The elevator was probably passing the sixth floor when the security guard pressed the emergency stop button. Both men inside stumbled from the sudden stop. No siren.

In one motion, the hospital security guard pulled the gun from the small of his back and turned toward H-Nic. But H-Nic was ready. His fist connected with the man's mouth and the next blow put the Justin Timberlake look-a-like to sleep.

"Shit. What the fuck?" H-Nic said to himself before pulling the emergency stop button out so the elevator would resume its climb. He couldn't worry about the clown he'd just laid out because he had to get to King Black. Something clearly was going on.

The elevator stopped. H-Nic prepared to run out, but he looked up and noticed that the elevator had stopped on eight. King Black was on nine. The door opened before he had a chance to think.

H-Nic's last vision was of the exotic beauty who shot him full of electricity with a taser. In seconds, he'd collapsed to the elevator floor.

Stepping over him, Amber got onto the elevator. Once the doors closed, she pressed the emergency stop button, before speaking into a mic secured to the collar of her hospital security uniform shirt. "Open the hatch."

A trap door in the ceiling of the elevator car opened, and a harness attached to a metal rope was lowered into the elevator. Amber secured the harness around H-Nic before she said, "Pull him up."

Five minutes later, both men had been pulled up through the elevator trap door. Amber had even cleaned up the blood and any other evidence that an altercation had ever happened on the elevator.

The heavy duty electric winch used to pull Amber and the two men up through the elevator roof's trap door was also used to lower them ten stories to the basement elevator shaft were the rest of the team she had hired awaited. The basement elevator shaft was actually a huge area surrounding the elevator car with cables, voltage boxes and other elevator supplies. It was also were one of Amber's crew disconnected the elevator emergency stop siren. The four dry cleaned and plastic wrapped black suits looked out of place on top of one of the dusty voltage boxes.

The leader of the team pointed before opening his mouth. "Amber, the suit on the end of the box is yours, John, yours is next to hers, then Brian's." He shook his head at Gino and then he turned to H-Nics unconscious form. "Damn shame, kid brought his fists to a gunfight and whipped your tail, Gino."

A minute later, they were changing from their security uniforms into the black and white suits.

"What the fuck y'all looking at? You dicks act like you ain't never seen a woman's body," Amber said stripping off the security uniform. "So, what? There are plenty of women who don't wear panties. I wouldn't even be down here if fuckface," she pointed to the guy that she'd had to rescue, "hadn't got knocked the fuck out."

"You saw the feed. The fucking guy caught me as I turned. He knew."

"He didn't know shit. He saw the bulge of your gun, asshole. Why the fuck would you have the gun down your back instead of down the front of your pants?" Amber said. "You are just fucking lucky I saw your dumb ass before you got on the elevator."

"If you saw me why didn't say something?" Gino asked.

"I tried to signal you but your idiot ass wouldn't look my way and then the elevator door closed."

"If –"

Amber cut Gino off. "Let's just get the fuck outta here." She was putting her shoes on when she looked over to the leader. "Mike, go get the death bed while we wait here."

The death bed was the rolling bed that was used to take bodies out to the hearse after the hospital morgue released them to the funeral home. The suits they changed into were supposed to make them look like they were funeral directors coming to get a body from the hospital.

Amber and the others waited in the basement elevator shaft. Surprisingly things weren't going too bad for this to be a last minute snatch and grab job. The Gino thing could've been disastrous, but Amber was prepared as she was one of the best precautionary intelligence agents that the CIA had.

Actually, the drama outside the hospital worked to the team's advantage. Although the hit team she'd hired wasn't CIA, they were private contractors that the CIA had used in the past. The cops and real security guards were too busy with crowd control to have noticed anything that was going on.

An idea popped into Amber's head. The job was costing her one hundred and eighty grand. She still had three hundred and twenty left that her handler at CIA did not know about. G-Swag had paid a half mil to take out Blow Jack's mom and brother, when what he really wanted was Blow Jack out of the picture. He wanted the rapping fuck to commit suicide, which was some soap opera drama bitch nigga bullshit.

G-Swag's feelings were all caught up in this shit. The bottom line was he wanted all of Blow Jack's royalty rights and if Blow Jack was dead he'd get them. The Brass at CIA headquarters would be pleased and G-Swag would be happy. It didn't make a difference if he died by suicide or homicide. Bo Jack Jones just needed to be dead.

"Hey, you three," Amber looked over to the elevator shaft trap door where the others were moving H-Nic's unconscious body. "I'll pay a hundred grand to the man who goes back up the shaft and kills Bo Jack Jones."

The three men paused. "A hundred stacks for Bo Jack's head?" one of the men asked.

"You must think we just got off the short bus?" Gino, the man who got knocked out, said. "Bo Jack Jones's head is worth at least five times that much."

"What? Are you serious? You geniuses are taking out three on this job for pennies compared to what I'm offering you to body one motherfucker."

"Bo Jack is more popular than God," one of the other's said.

"What does Blow Jack's popularity have to do with one of you dicks going back up that elevator shaft and burning that rapping mother fucker?"

"What about security?"

"Fuck it." She shook her head. "That's what I get for hiring second rate killers."

The wall panel was being removed. "Come on let's get out of here," the leader of the team said as he helped pull H-Nic's body through the three foot by four foot elevator shaft opening.

After they had H-Nic secured to the bed with the sheet over his head, Amber spoke to the leader. "Change of plans, Mike. You four go on without me. I'll touch base with you in," she looked at her watch, "say twenty minutes, at six-thirty and if for some reason you don't hear from me, kill him."

He shook his head. "You know how I work, Amber. You not leaving with us was not the plan.

"As long as I'm the one paying, the plan is whatever I say it is."

"She's going to go back and take out Bo Jack," Gino said.

She looked at the man who'd just spoken. "Don't push your luck, white boy. You already got knocked the fuck out once today."

"Eat a dick, bitch," the Justin Timberlake look-a-like said while he grabbed his crotch.

"Pull it out sissy," she said. "That's what I thought," she smiled, "little boy.

Mike knew better than to say anything else. When Amber had her mind made up, there was no changing it.

Ten minutes later, Amber was back in her security get up. The wig and glasses made her almost unrecognizable to anyone who'd seen her before. After running up ten stories of fire exit stairs she stopped and bent down to catch her breath at the ninth floor fire stair exit door. A moment later she went over the new plan in her head while screwing the silencer on her .25 Baretta. It would take her three seconds to shoot both of Bo Jacks security guards in the head, three seconds to reach Bo Jack's bedside, one second to put a bullet in the middle of his forehead and ten seconds to get back to the stairs. It would then take six seconds to get down to the eighth floor, where she could enter the elevator shaft and use the winch to lower her to the basement floor. She pulled the stock back on the gun, tucked it in her front pocket, took a deep breath, blew it out, and opened the ninth floor stairwell door.

"Flannigan." The doctor posted up at the nurses' station read the name tag pinned to Amber's chest as she approached the nurses' station. He was leaning against the station desk twirling his stethoscope. "You must be new."

"Dr. Daniels," an older nurse playfully hit him with her clipboard, "let the woman do her job, you horny toad." The nurse turned her attention to Amber. "Honey, don't pay him no mind. He'll flirt with an AIDS patient with brain cancer if she's young and beautiful."

The doctor smiled before taking a bow. "My lady, I am a gentleman. Broom Hilda here is just angry because her time has passed." He took Amber's hand, raised it, and was about to plant a kiss on the back of her hand when she pulled away.

"I'm sorry, I'm kinda in a rush," she said before hurrying away.

She stopped and stared down the hall. Where were the security guards? Had the hospital moved Bo Jack again? Those were her questions as she moved quickly. Just as she got to Bo Jack's room at the end of the corridor, two security guards came out of the room.

"Good evening, fellas."

Before they could respond, Amber had shot them both in the head, before opening the door.

Amber took one step into the room.

"Pop! Pop!"

She dropped her gun and crumbled to the floor. "Move," the woman who'd came in on the helicopter said to the two fake cameramen.

While she dragged Amber's body further into the room, the two fake cameramen dragged the dead bodies of the two security guards into the room.

"Anybody see you?" she asked.

"No," one of the fake cameramen responded before going into the small bathroom inside the private hospital room.

"What are you doing?" the woman asked the fake cameraman in the bathroom.

"Getting some paper towels to clean up the blood outside. A single bullet to the forehead, small caliber handgun. Not very messy."

"What?" the woman that had just shot Amber asked.

"The two security guards manning the room," the fake cameraman looked down at Ambers still body, "shot 'em in the head at point blank range."

Raena turned to King Black. Before Amber walked into the room, Raena had explained who she was and why she was there. "Looks like we got here just in time," she said.

He was leaning over the side of the bed while Dr. Harwell stood over the woman who had just tried to take his life. Dr. Raena Harwell was holding the woman's black wig and her gun.

"You know this woman?" Raena asked as she grabbed the woman's legs.

"Her name is Amber Way, she's G-Swag's number two," King Black explained. "Is she dead?"

"No, but she'll wish she was when she wakes up in a few hours with a headache from hell. The cartridge I shot her with has enough Ketamine in it to stop an elephant."

"I can't believe this shit," King Black said. "G-Swag done stole everything from me and now he makes an attempt on my life? I ain't done nothin' to playa, but make him an ass load of money."

"So, what do you think he's after?"

"I don't even know. But, the nigga got my attention. I'm wide the fuck awake now. Now, it don't even matter what he after." King Black nodded his head as if he were plotting on G-Swag.

"Money," she said. "G-Swag's going after all of your future royalties and rights to remaster and resell any of your music. He knows that you will make way more money in death than in life. But don't worry, the Commission has a mole on the inside that will make sure none of this will happen."

"How do you know this?"

"It's our jobs to know the questions and the answers."

King Black interjected, "Well then you know that we have to take her with us." He pointed to the woman Raena was dragging to the bathroom.

She smiled, glad King Black had suggested bringing Amber along but not wanting him to know why. The Commission knew that Amber was CIA, but King Black didn't have a clue. "Wishful thinking, but there's no way we can get her out of here and onto the roof without attracting attention." She looked at her watch. "We're already running two minutes behind schedule. It's only a matter of time before the authorities figure out that the helicopter on the roof doesn't belong to FOX News."

"I have an idea," Black said with a smile on his face.

Three minutes later, King Black was Queen Black. He had on his own clothes, which were falling off of him due to the forty pounds he had lost lying in bed for thirteen months, but he also wore a black wig, sunglasses, and face makeup. He looked more like an ugly, high-yellow tranny instead of a woman, but he definitely didn't look like the hip-hop icon whose photo was plastered all over the television. One of the fake cameramen had taken a wheelchair from the hallway. By the time he got back with the chair Amber was dressed in King Black's hospital gown. In no time, both chairs where being wheeled down the hall toward the fire exit stairs.

VERSE 27

Evening had made way for night and then, night had made way for the morning. Amber had been out for almost forty eight hours when the pitter patter of rain pouncing on nature and a window seal awoke her. She slowly opened her eyes. She blinked, and tried to focus. When, suddenly, she sat up in the bed. Her eyes roamed around the room.

Where am I? She searched her mind for answers.

Well, she definitely wasn't in any kind of dungeon. Looked more like a hotel room – a nice one at that. Then, she looked down, and was surprised that she was naked. But that wasn't her worry right now. The pounding in her head was made worse with every move she made, but she flexed her muscles anyway. She needed to see if she had her strength, and she did.

She looked down at her private parts, before touching herself. There was no pain, no bruising. She didn't think she was raped, but then again why was she on top of a queen sized bed naked? Maybe they were waiting for her to awake so they could rape her. Whoever had done this to her had no idea of who they had taken. She looked at the sheets she laid on top of. Expensive. The dark blue satin had to be at least one thousand thread. The sheets would do if she needed them to make a noose to strangle her captors.

Her head shot up when a sliding door across the room opened. A man who looked like Father Time entered.

Her eyes widened and it was because of her shock that she didn't even bother to cover up. She wanted to speak, but couldn't. The man that had just walked into the room had been on the CIA's top ten enemy list since before she was born.

"Do you know who I am, Amber Way?" the man spoke with a strong Hispanic accent.

"Fidel Castro," she mumbled at the white-haired, former Cuban ruler. Whatever the hell was going on, this had to be major league if Castro was involved.

"Si." He nodded. "And now, it is up to you whether you live or die. I would prefer you live and so would the others, but again, that is strictly up to you." The eighty-seven-year old former Cuban leader looked into the two-way mirror behind the bed. The two-way mirror where Barack Obama, Isis, Picasso, and King Black watched and listened.

"You think she'll talk?" Isis whispered to Picasso and Barack.

"We'll see," Picasso said, though his tone revealed that he doubted that she would cooperate. He, Fidel, Raul, and Barack were the only ones in Cuba who knew that Amber was with the CIA.

The former U.S. President interjected, "Amber Way could prove to be a valuable asset to our cause. We just have to show the Afro-Cuban sista' the error of her ways."

Minutes later, Fidel pulled down the projector screen and then, G-Swag appeared on it. A Truth Commission tech had used re-imaging and sound match software to create the conversation that played out in front of Amber.

"Yeah," G-Swag said as he leaned forward on his desk to talk into the speaker phone. "She's expendable." He leaned back, then, stretched his feet out on his desk. "Tell you what. After she handles that piece of business for me later this evening, you can have her."

From the speakerphone, Amber heard a laugh. "Thank you! There is nothing that I would enjoy more than having that Afro-Cuban whore with my seed in her ass, mouth, and snatch. You say she's a feisty one in the sack?" the voice asked.

"Feisty," G-Swag said. "She's wild, tight, and wet and she likes it hard and rough. And that tramp can suck a basketball through a straw, my dude."

"Okay, enough. I'll get you your grand jury first thing next week, and we'll get an indictment, but after I finish with her, you have to be the one to get rid of her body."

Amber sucked her bottom lip in and nodded as she watched the video feed. "I'm a tramp now," she said, playing the role she hoped her captors wanted her to. G-Swag was a snake, but he needed her and there was no way that he would sell her out that easy.

G-Swag smiled and threw a fist in the air. "I wouldn't have it no other way, Lieutenant."

The picture on the screen then jumped to the hospital room last evening where Amber was being stuffed into a wheelchair by the almost-bald black woman who had shot her. The camera moved to the private hospital room bathroom.

"That is Lieutenant Royce, the one you heard on the phone," Fidel explained, "and that's Detective Armstrong on the floor lying beside him." The former Cuban leader studied Ambers facial expression. He was looking for a twitch a smirk, anything that alerted him that she wasn't falling for the act that the Truth Commission was putting on. They hoped that Amber was as good as their intelligence said. If so she would see right through the farce. Would she give up G-Swag and how much would she tell the Commission was the question?

"G-Swag had sold me out for an indictment after all I'd done for him." She pointed at the screen. "That old cop must've followed us to the hospital. He was going to arrest me there and take me somewhere to have his way with me," she said, hoping she wasn't being too dramatic. "The cop with him was probably going to take a turn, too," she said, trying to sound sincerely forlorn. Amber was sure that Fidel had no idea that she had no allegiance to G-Swag. She'd gladly give him up to earn the former leader's trust. She didn't quite know what was going on, but again she had a feeling it was big if Fidel Castro was involved. Her handler at the agency would be pleased...if she lived to report back.

"What is the American saying?" The former Cuban leader snapped his fingers. "It is what it is."

"Nah, it is what I make it. It's probably too late to save them, but Blow Jack, I mean Bo Jack Jones's mother and brother are most likely dead by now," she said with no emotion in her voice.

"No, both of them are very much alive. They're here with us."

"Where is here?" Her heart skipped a beat as she waited to see if he was going to tell her.

"Cuba. You are in Cabo, Cuba."

"Well," she dropped her head, "you are definitely too late to save Henry Nicholas," she said thinking how easy she could take Castro. But she was no fool. She knew there was a two-way mirror behind her. She hadn't noticed it until Fidel kept looking behind her. She would have to play the dumb woman scorned until she could figure out something else.

"Nooooo not H-Nic," King Black shouted in the room behind the two-way mirror. He fell over in his wheelchair trying to stand. "If G-Swag had H-Nic killed," Black busted his hand hitting it against the marble floor. "I swear ta God..." He winced in pain and anger.

VERSE 28

Two months later: Langley, Virginia; CIA headquarters

The nine men sitting around the table in the strategy room had been responsible for more loss of life over the last thirty-five years than Al-Qaeda, the Taliban, and every terrorist sect in the world combined. These men had been responsible for training, arming, and using over fifty percent of the world's leading terrorist sects – to help topple lesser nations governments so America could instill her own leader of those defeated nations.

Oil is the world's number one source of energy and like everything else of value, America had to control it. Six Middle Eastern nations and one African nation controlled the vast majority of the world's mined oil. Over the last four decades millions of innocent Middle Eastern and African people had died in America's quest to control the governments of these oil rich nations.

The nine men sitting comfortably at the round table, drinking hundred-year-old wine decided which Middle Eastern foreign leader to kill and how they were going to get the American people behind them.

These nine men made the decision to bomb and kill Muammar Qadafi's baby girl after the bombing of Pan Am flight 103 in the early 90's. These men blamed Libya for the passenger jet bombing although they had planned the bombing from inside this very room.

These men used media propaganda to instill fear in the American people, making them believe that Iraq had weapons of mass destruction when they knew if Iraq had nuclear weapons then they would have used them.

The Civil War in Iraq began because of decisions these men had made. The war torn Middle Eastern populations had been decimated over the last four decades and America was still losing the underground "Oil War" and thanks to Amber Way, the CIA's and NSA's top nine had just uncovered intelligence as to why the CIA and NSA hadn't been able to bring the Middle Eastern countries under America's control.

Bernie Shwartz, or BS, as the bald man was affectionately called, was slight of build and of average height. But, he was a giant in the spy world. He looked more like a librarian than America's top economist and political strategist. Together, the nine men in the room wielded their power to control American public perception and America's war machine.

The man held a glass in the air. "A toast to tomorrow."

"To tomorrow," the other eight men sitting in the underground strategy room toasted before drinking the Bordeaux.

A short, portly man with liver spots on his pasty seventy-five-year-old skin looked at the others with disgust. His was the only glass that hadn't been touched. He bounced his wide frame out of the leather chair. "We've planned and

orchestrated civil upheaval in the Philippines. We've found
and killed world leaders hiding out in deserts five thousand
miles away from our shores. We've started wars between other
countries. We've used the media to make America believe
whatever propaganda we wanted, but you mean to tell me that
we are just finding out about an international intelligence
organization created to stop us

BS pointed at the man who had just spoken out of turn,
"Thomas, before we even planned Tupac Shakur's death, I told
everyone at this table that we needed to assign more agents at
the executive levels of rap music, and if memory serves me
correct, it was you, Thomas, who said we needed to leave the
domestic problems to the FBI and focus all of our energy and
attention on the Middle East."

"Yeah, but –"

"But what? After the Senate committee hearings led to
the disbanding of COINTELPRO in the early '70's we didn't
think minorities in America would ever successfully organize
against the system."

BS looked into the time-weathered faces of the CIA's
and NSA's top brass before he continued, "The reason we
didn't see this coming was because it's not an American
organization. The Truth Commission is an international
organization controlled by those who understand the value of
freedom. And now that we know a little about this Truth
Commission, we can begin to formulate a plan to eliminate any
evidence that they have ever existed, but we have to move
fast."

Another man stood up. "How do you propose we
handle the media?"

"We don't," BS said. "For right now, we continue
gathering information. Anywhere Agent Way goes, we will
have her coordinates. She has the GPS chip in her right
shoulder, just like all of our field agents. In a few hours, Agent
Way will have multiple ways of relaying intelligence to us."

To be the world's top economist and political strategist, you had to have the world's best poker face and BS, Amber's handler, had exactly that. No one, not even a polygraph machine, could read his fear.

Agent Way had told him that Barack Obama was alive and well. She hadn't seen him for herself, but the others spoke of him being there, she'd said. Her GPS chip had her in a rural town in Cuba, near the Sierra Maestra Mountains. That meant that the Castros were definitely a part of this Truth Commission. Fidel and Barack allies – that could prove to be very scary. That's if Barack Obama was really alive.

The body would be exhumed soon. BS had already hired a black ops security team to get a DNA sample from the corpse buried in President Obama's plot.

If DNA confirmed BS's worst fear, he'd be dead before another team went in and killed the real Barack Obama. The CIA were unforgiving when it came to mishaps like this.

It was Bernie Shwartz's team that allegedly took out the former president two years ago, a few weeks before the eight men successfully ushered Romney into office.

"Gentlemen, this is a happy day," BS said. "We have one of our best agents on the inside and soon we will know everything and we'll be that much closer to completely leveling Iran, Iraq, and Afghanistan." He raised an arm and pointed a finger in the air. "I vote 'I' to multiple nuclear strikes the day after we close the chapter on this Truth Commission. Now, who besides me is tired of all these Middle East war games? I say we do this and ask the U.N. for forgiveness later, like we did with Iraq. Hundreds of millions of people will die and the land will be unlivable for fifty to one hundred years, but we'll have control of the world's largest mined oil reserves."

It seemed like yesterday, when King Black couldn't lift his arms above his shoulders and could only move his legs from side to side. The doctors at DeKalb Medical called it severe muscle atrophy. They'd said that it would take a year of intense occupational and physical therapy before he'd walk again.

Wow, that was just three months ago, King Black thought as he sat on the stump waiting for his trainer to complete the obstacle course.

Over the last three and half months, King Black had been relentless in his efforts to regain his athletic conditioning. Thanks to Cuban medicine, Cuban doctors, and G-Swag's former executive assistant, he'd done what he had set out to do. And that was to get back in shape in just a quarter of the time his former American doctors had said.

The world labeled Cuba a third world country, yet their citizens had free health care, a low incarceration rate, and free education. King Black was living proof that Cuba provided some of the most advanced and best medical treatment in the world. He was not as strong as he was before hitting his head on the bathroom sink at the BET awards a couple years ago, but he was in much better cardio conditioning.

As he stood at a cliff on top of the mountain, he wondered why Cuba wasn't one of the world's top tourist attractions. The beauty of the island was simply breathtaking.

There were no words to describe the majestic view of Cuba from where he now stood at the edge of a cliff atop the Sierra Maestra – the mountain range located at the south part of the island.

He'd been waiting awhile now and he began to wonder where Amber was? He surveyed the trees, the short grass and the colorful flowers around him. This was only the second time he'd beaten her around the mountains grueling seven-mile obstacle course. He looked up at the clear blue April sky before peeling off his sweat soaked T- shirt. The world was so peaceful on top of the heavily wooded and green mountain, but even in the middle of this peace, he felt such sadness.

H-Nic had been to King Black what Che Guerva had been to Fidel Castro and the Cuban Revolution. He and H-Nic had been through so much together. They caught their first case together. They'd fought together. They even got their first piece together. Yes, Big Tammy Turner. She was 16, H-Nic was 13, and King Black was 12 when she initiated both boys into manhood, one right after the other.

King Black remembered telling H-Nic that he needed to wash his johnson ASAP, because he had accidentally peed inside big Tammy. Both boys laughed when H-Nic explained that Bo Jack hadn't peed, but nutted in the girl.

"What you need to be worried about is becoming a daddy," H-Nic had said.

They'd even caught the clap around the same time. After H-Nic had told him about the metal toothpick that the doctor stuck up his pee hole, he knew that he'd die from an STD before he let anyone do anything like that to him. He remembered talking H-Nic into going back to the free clinic and telling them that he'd lost his penicillin pills.

We'd gone from being broke to balling in no time. First it had been Momma, then Brandon, and now H-Nic – the people in this world I loved the most had suffered the worst because of decisions I had made. And now H-Nic was dead because he chose to follow me. He looked up toward the sun, "Why God?"

Amber Way had arranged H-Nic's death, but King Black knew she was just doing a job and that G-Swag had ordered the hit. Still, he wanted to strangle her whenever he saw her face. But, that urge only lasted until she smiled.

At first he'd suspected that something wasn't right with Amber. It was like she was doing too much to gain everyone's approval. She'd given up the men that G-Swag had hired to kill H-Nic. She'd also told all she knew about G-Swag. But over the last four months that she'd been in the mountains with them, she'd grown on him. She was still an enigma, but one he enjoyed. And she had been pivotal in his speedy rehabilitation. But, King Black could care less about the so called thugs G-Swag had hired. They were just doing a job. G-Swag was the real killer. Picasso and Barack had promised him that the killers that Amber had given up were his to take care of.

The killers had wrapped H-Nics body in a landscaper's tarp and thrown him into a dumpster like ordinary trash. Fucking trash. The funeral was a closed casket service because of the way the killers had mutilated H-Nic's body.

Looking down the road, he saw Amber heading his way.

VERSE 30

You could say Amber Way had inherited the art of deception, her cold heart, and her above genius IQ from her CIA operative parents. In the Fall of 1996, Amber was only twelve when her parents were instantly killed by three young thugs in a random drive-by. The three black teens, high off ecstasy and weed claimed that Snoop Dog's rap song "Murder Was the Case" had influenced them to shoot up the convertible white Jaguar that evening. Amber believed the boys. She didn't hold them responsible. She held the rap movement responsible for the death of her parents.

Amber's father's best friend Bernie Shwartz, also a CIA operative took the twelve-year-old into his home and before the agency buried her parents, Amber went to Bernie, and demanded that he begin training her immediately. She told him that he could either train her or be responsible for whatever happened to her because with or without him she was going to do whatever it took to kill the rap movement and kill whoever got in her way.

The hip-hop movement was generally a young people's movement, so almost immediately, Bernie and the CIA spared no expense over the next seven years in educating and preparing Amber to infiltrate and be a force in the hip-hop music community.

The reason the FBI wasn't involved with the prevention of a Black Messiah's rise in rap music was because the mission wasn't sanctioned by any of the three branches of government. Tupac Shakur was the last hip-hop artist to emerge as a potential threat. There had always been conscious hip-hop artists and there would always be, but there could never be another like Tupac Shakur—a young black man with the knowledge, charisma, and a voice to organize the most dangerous faction of American society—its young.

By the age of nineteen, Amber Way's knowledge of hip-hop music, its origins, and its history was equivalent to someone who'd earned their PhD.

In 2003, at the age of twenty, she began screwing Gregory "G-Swag" Reagan. Over the next eleven years she'd lied, screwed, and killed to further hers and the CIA's aims. And at the same time she helped make G-Swag the second biggest name in hip-hop.

Because of his extreme capitalist mentality and his high hip-hop music IQ, G-Swag had been specifically targeted by the agency. He was the perfect vehicle to promote self-hate in America's urban community. G-Swag had no love for people, his loyalties rested only with the numbers in his bank accounts. This lack of consciousness made him easy to manipulate and control.

And after almost thirteen years of infiltrating the hip-hop industry, Amber Way accidentally stumbled onto possibly the greatest threat to the American way of life. She'd only known about the Truth Commission for the three and a half months she'd been in Cuba. She first arrived as a prisoner of the Truth Commission and now she was trying to slowly become a part of the organization.

She'd only been able to communicate information to Bernie eight times over the last three and a half months, largely due to her isolated wooded location and the time it took for the CIA to get a solar powered Satellite phone into the mountains of Cabo, Cuba without detection.

So now, after filling Bernie in on what she had learned since their last communication, she faked a sprained ankle as soon as she was close to being in King Black's eyesight. It was her excuse for falling so far behind.

"Babygirl, you hurt yourself," King Black said running toward Amber.

"It's nothing, just a slight sprain," she said taking a seat in a field of mountain top low grass and red, white and pink Spring flowers.

King Black took a seat beside her.

Shit, she thought. The last thing she wanted was this glorified thug sitting next to her in a secluded area. *If he tried to touch her...*

"Here." He reached out.

She glanced at him sideways. "I'm fine." She smiled. "For real."

Before she realized what he was doing, he had her bad ankle in his hands. She tensed up and was about to pull her leg back, but she didn't want to give him any reason to further distrust her. It had taken her three and a half months to get this close to him.

He had her left sock and Nike cross-trainer off. "Doesn't look swollen, but let's see if we can minimize any future swelling," he said tenderly massaging her foot.

Damn, that feels good, she wanted to say, but then again she didn't want him to think that she had any interest in him. "So, I understand the Truth Commission's objectives, but

King, do you really think that they can overturn 'a two thousand year old system of divide, conquer, control and enslave' as you put it last week?"

"I wouldn't still be here if I didn't believe," he said, with her ankle still in his hands.

"King, what gets me is that everyone I've met and that's only been you, Isis, Picasso, and Fidel, you guys are well read and you know how much military might America has. You understand how technologically advanced and how much support America has among the world's nations, and you all really believe that this is going to happen – that you can really usurp America's power structure. You guys must have a helluva plan?"

He was silent for a moment. "Amber, do you believe in the creator?"

"God?" she asked. Her forehead creased with confusion.

"Allah, God, Jehovah, Yahweh, Rickey Bobby, don't matter what you call him, do you believe in Him?"

"Wow, I didn't take you for being one of those."

"One of those what," he asked.

"Religious people."

"I'm not." He shook his head. "There's been more division, more wars throughout history because of religion. I just don't think God promotes confusion and strife and if we are God's creation, I'm sure He doesn't want us to kill each other, destroying what He created. Just like that name thing." He put the hurt foot down and took her other leg into his hands.

"What name thing?"

"You know, every religious culture has their own name for God and they swear it's His name, but how can that be when God is not human and He is not of this world. He sees, hears, and knows everything, so I'm sure God knows who is speaking to Him no matter what name they use. People are religious. God isn't. And I'm not either."

"Hmph," she said, thinking that what King Black was saying made a lot of sense.

"Anyway," he continued, "my faith is what keeps me going. It's what keeps all of us going at the end of the day. Faith is our secret weapon."

"You had me for a minute, but now you lost me with that faith as a secret weapon," she said.

He smiled. "I know."

"And what is it that you think you know, Mr. Jones?"

"That I had you. And if I had you for a minute then I can have you for an hour, a month, a year, a lifetime."

"What are you talking about?"

"You just said that I had you for a minute, until –

"You know what I meant."

"I know what you said."

She pulled her leg back, realizing she had gotten way too comfortable, something she had never done. She had never even had an honest relationship with a man. She had never been in love or even believed in the love between man and woman. Even her parents had a marriage of convenience – both were lonely government spies, living a life of lies and deceit. Their time together was the only time they could be themselves without all the lies. That was the only thing that had drawn them together.

"So when am I going to get the chance to meet Obama?" she asked, back in spy mode.

"Soon, babygirl. Soon."

"Hmph." She shook her head from side to side.

"And what does that hmph mean?" he asked.

"It means you people need to expand your vocabulary."

"Huh?"

"'Soon' is the most frequently used term whenever I ask 'when,'" she explained.

He chuckled, but then became serious. "The Commission has been around this long because of its evasiveness and limited vocabulary."

"But, doesn't the information I gave up about G-Swag count for anything?"

"It does," he said.

She got to her feet and stretched. "And what about the fact that I haven't asked or tried to leave Cabo in the three and a half months I've been here?"

He nodded, still sitting in the low mountain grass. He watched the sun's eye shine on Amber's flawless golden bronze skin.

"And haven't I read everything that Picasso has put in front of me?" She crossed her arms right under her red sports bra.

Her dimples danced to the rhythm of her words when she spoke. And the way she was standing with her legs spread and arms crossed, made King Black think of the black female action figure superhero Storm from X-Men. The biggest difference between the two was that Storm had straight silver hair and Amber had reddish brown locks.

"So?" she asked. "What do I have to do to earn the Commission's trust – to be included in the mission?"

Let me bend you over pull down your shorts and grudge fuck you – blow your back all the way out, was what he desperately wanted to say.

He stood up with Amber's red footies and her Air Max running shoes in his hands. "Babygirl, you are included. You just don't know the role the Commission is planning for you to play. You have to understand that right now you're being tested."

"I know that," she said, frustration clearly in her tone.

"Tell you what," he said, "I'm going away for a little while, but if you want me to, I'll find you when I get back and we can finish this."

"Finish what? There's nothing to finish, King. I don't know what you think there is between us, but...." She stopped. Her words had come out before she had a chance to think about it. Shit. This had never happened before. She had to stay focused on her mission.

"There it is, babygirl," he said with a little smile. "There's so much unfinished business between us," he said thinking of the hand she played in the death of H-Nic.

"What about Obama?" she asked, wanting and needing to change the subject. "I wanna meet him now, this evening."

He hesitated as if he wasn't sure if he was going to let her get away with changing the subject. But then, he said, "He's gone."

"Gone where?"

Instead of smiling, now he frowned just a little. "That's privileged information that I don't even know."

"So, where are you going?" she asked. "And when will you be back?"

He smiled.

"No, I didn't mean to sound like that. I mean," she playfully punched him in the chest. "I just wanted to know when I'd get the chance of beating you on this silly mountain obstacle course again."

She played it off, but still she wondered what was wrong? Amber had always been in control of every situation. She'd been that way since she went to work for G-Swag over ten years ago, but it felt like now, she was allowing her emotions to get in the way.

"You still never answered my question," he said.

"What question?"

"God, do you believe in Him?"

She thought for a moment, wondering if she should tell him the truth. But if she did, he might ask for more, which would lead to more lies. Still for some reason, she wanted to tell him the truth. "No, I don't believe in anything I cannot see or understand."

"Maybe you're not looking hard enough."
King Black snaked his arms around her small waist and pulled her to him. He hesitated for a minute as he looked into her eyes. He waited, wondering if she would move away like she always did. But when she didn't, he gently lowered his lips onto hers.

She was reluctant, but something deep within made her part her lips and welcome him in.

Their kiss was soft and sweet.

VERSE 31

"Yo, what it do, P. Diggety?" King Black asked after the hip-hop mogul answered his cell phone.

P.Diddy instantly knew who it was, because no one else even dared call him P. Diggety. And King Black only did it in private. "Hold on," the entertainment mogul said. A minute later Diddy was back on the line. "Call me back at 718-640-9710."

King Black hung up, keyed in the numbers, and pressed Send on the satellite phone.

"You all right? The media are going crazy over your mom's and your brother's..." he stopped as he searched for the right words, "their disappearance." That was the way he chose to say it. "Son, my artists can't get any airplay because of your missing in action ass. The rock stations are even playing your shit, son. What's the deal?"

"How secure is this line?" King Black asked.

"Come on, Black, I know you in some shit, that's why I gave you another number. This phone is a dollar store burner – it's untraceable," P. Diddy explained.

"I'll explain everything in time," King Black said, "but I need a huge favor quick, fast, and in a hurry."

"Talk to me," P. Diddy said.

"There is a Jane McCarthy buried in a plot at Crown Hill Cemetery in Indianapolis, Indiana, lot number 1234. I need someone to climb the fence and meet me at the plot with a shovel, a bag of leeches, and six to eight alley or sewer rats at 11:00 PM tomorrow."

"Leeches and rats? What the hell? You know what," P. Diddy said, "don't even tell me."

"So, you got me?" King Black asked.

"Come on, Black. You know how I carry it." He paused for a moment. "Sewer rats and leeches. I don't know how I'm gon' do it, but I gave you my word."

"Tomorrow night at eleven," King Black said before pressing the End button and stepping onto the plane. He'd been there for two hours and no one had recognized him at Havana's Jose Marti International Airport. The Truth Commission had the best plastic surgeons and make up artists in the world. Isis didn't even recognize him after the make-up artists had finished with his disguise.

He had actually looked forward to this trip back into the concrete jungle. If his tracks were getting airplay like P. Diggety said, then gospel stations would be airing his music after what he was about to do to G-Swag.

*****

Every year since Amber had worked for G-Swag, she had told King Black that he spent the night before Mother's Day the same way. It didn't matter if it was pouring down raining outside or whatever...between the hours of 2 AM and 4 AM, he visited his mother's six foot by six foot tomb. And during that visit was the only time he was without his security team.

Amber had no idea that giving up this information actually saved her life. But she had shared this with King Black a couple months before he'd gotten to know her. She was also the only one who knew of his plan to do G-Swag.

There was not a moment after hearing of his boy's demise that King Black didn't salivate at the thought of killing G-Swag. He hated to have the others thinking that he wanted to go after the people that actually did the deed. Just like Amber was a pawn, so were the hitters who took out H-Nic. Murder was just a job to them.

G-Swag could get a pass for Brandon being sentenced to a mental hospital. He could get a pass for stealing King Black's fortune and causing him to be in a coma for over a year, but having H-Nic killed... he had to answer for that. King Black knew nothing he did would bring his man back, but ain't no way the nigga who had him murked was gon' keep sucking air.

H-Nic's death motivated King Black to bust his ass, in his physical, occupational, and muscle memory rehab therapy sessions. He knew that Mother's Day was his only shot.

It was eighty-five degrees on the warm clear night in Indianapolis, Indiana. A average looking white guy who called himself Calvin Klein had met King Black at the tombstone just like he and P. Diddy had agreed. Calvin hadn't asked any questions. He just handed over a small black suitcase and a plastic grocery bag with a clear plastic baggie full of creek water and black blood sucking worms.

Less than an hour after Calvin's arrival, he and King Black had dug a two foot hole on top of the dirt where Jane McCarthy was buried. King Black hated bugs, rats, and anything squirmy, but he hated G-Swag a hundred times more than anything in creation.

At a little before one AM he crawled into the hole and after Calvin put the carry on bag filled with rats scrambling around and the water filled plastic bag beside him, the man started piling dirt on top of him. After Calvin had finished, no one could see the two straws sticking up through the ground – one for the rats, and the one that King Black breathed through.

His heart was pounding at a speed that he couldn't believe. All he wanted to do was jump out of the grave, when he felt the furry, disease-carrying scavengers rub up against him from inside the small suitcase.

"Please God," he prayed from inside the grave, "please don't let them chew their way out of the suitcase."
King Black hadn't even considered that when he planned this. He was terrified at the thought of the rats getting out and crawling all over him, feasting on his flesh. And the blood-sucking leeches....

Now, it was hard for him to breathe. It was hard enough breathing through the straw, but his anxiety made it worse.
It seemed like he'd been buried forever. In actuality he'd only been in the ground for twenty-seven minutes when he heard the faint sound of approaching footsteps crunching on the manicured dry cemetery grass.

G-Swag looked left, then right before looking down to the grave. King Black wasn't worried—the breathing straw sticking out of the fresh dirt mound two plots in front of G-Swag's mother's tomb was almost invisible.

"We'll just be over here boss-man," King Black heard the voice.

Although he was buried beneath two feet of dirt on top of someone name Jane McCarthy, he could hear every word. He'd been told that G-Swag was going to be alone and he wasn't prepared to take out more than one man. The only weapon he had was an eight inch rusty ice pick, and a Taser gun that was only good for one shot of electricity. But maybe the element of surprise and the cover of night would give him a chance to take out two if he had to. He hoped that two was all he had to contend with.

"Nah, ain't nobody out here but crickets and dead niggas. You two go on back to the car," G-Swag said. "I'll call you in a couple hours when I'm ready."

King Black's smile was cut short as he felt something crawling on his arm. He had no idea what it was but it felt like all kinds of shit was crawling all over him as he lay under the dirt.

But then, he calmed down as he heard G-Swag's voice.

"Mom, it became official last month. I made *Forbes'* Top 100 Richest in the World. I came in at number eighty-nine." G-Swag spoke to the wall outside of the tomb. "I raked in over two-hundred million last year off of Bo Jack Jones alone, and all of my artists are blowing up because of what I've done with Bo Jack. The world couldn't be better Mom, I'm telling you."

Behind G-Swag, the dirt moved and King Black slowly rose. But the producer didn't notice.

"Oh, yeah, ma, I'm afraid something happened to Amber. She never made it back from her assignment. I'm a little worried because I know she's CIA. She just doesn't know that I know. I guess they pulled her back in. Hell, for all I know, she might've gotten the CIA to kill H-Nic."

King Black paused, thinking that she had lied about who had killed his boy. He could've gone after the wrong folks. And C.I.A? He wanted to think that G-Swag was mistaken, but if King Black didn't know anything else about the slimy mega producer, he knew that the man was paranoid as shit and very thorough.

G-Swag continued, "Mom, you know I send her on dirty missions, so I can have shit on her and the CIA when they come for me. For what, I don't know, but I do know they are coming. Why else would Amber be with me this long?"

Suddenly, things began to make sense to Bo Jack. That's why she kept asking about getting more involved, about a secret weapon, about Obama. That's why she hasn't tried to leave. The CIA knows about us. They know about the compound in Cabo. *Shit, she was the only one that knew I was coming for G-Swag.*

Instinctively, King Black did a three sixty with his head and eyes. He couldn't see ten feet in front of him, but the CIA had night vision gear. Fuck it. He'd come this far and there was no way he was turning back now.

"My fault, I'm rambling, but so much has transpired since last year, I forgot you didn't know about me sending Amber to get a line on where Bo Jack's mother and little brother were. How about somebody helped them escape from prison a few months ago? If I track them down and have them killed, Bo Jack will most likely kill himself and if he doesn't, I'll make sure his death looks like suicide. I don't even know why I'm telling you this, mom. Hell, I couldn't move on Bo Jack, his mother or his brother until I find out what's up with Amber. Damn! You just don't know. I mean, I can't even imagine how far Bo Jack's record sales will go through the roof after his death. I already have his next album ready. *From the Depths of Hell.* It's going to be hot. But of course, I can't release it until after his death. Whenever that will be. I'm telling you, Mom. It's hot."

"Not as hot as you're about to be bitch," King Black said.

G-Swag swung around to face the voice behind him. "Who are you?" he asked.

King Black had forgotten he was disguised. "Trick ass niggas can get it for free. You got the right one, fuckin' with me," King Black rhymed.

Cool as a cucumber G-Swag said, "My dude, what's crackin'?"

"Your ribs." King Black hit him in the midsection, making the slender man bend right over.

It took him a moment, but when G-Swag rose up, he held a gun in his hand. But only for a moment; King Black stabbed him in the arm making G-Swag drop it.

King Black kicked the small handgun up against the tombs wall – out of both man's reach.

"What the fuck?" The super producer grabbed his injured arm while King Black stabbed him in the midsection several times with the ice pick. Blood was oozing out of his midsection, but none of the wounds were immediately life threatening. King Black just wanted to break the skin initially, cause him pain that would not yet kill him.

"My dude?" G-Swag dropped to one knee. He used the tombs wall to keep himself from falling all the way to the dry ground.

King Black pulled out his Taser gun and shot G-Swag. The producer made a jerking motion before passing out beside his mothers tomb.

He stood over the body for a moment, then began to move. He had to do this quickly. He only had about three minutes before G-Swag woke up. And it was going to be tough doing this all in the dark.

Again, King Black did a three-sixty with his eyes, looking for the U.S. government's hit squad. He sort of expected them to run up on him any minute.

When he saw that he was still alone, he grabbed G-Swag's arms and dragged him about five feet to the closest flat tombstone with a stone flowerpot protruding from it. There he secured G-Swag's arms with handcuffs to the pot. Next, he stripped G-Swag naked before spreading his legs and tying some rope around his ankles. He pulled the rope tight to cut down on G-Swag's ability to move. He secured the rope to two tombstones in opposite directions. When King Black finished, G-Swag looked like a human slingshot, his legs were wishboned while his arms were straightened and stretched out above his head.

He was beginning to stir from his electric nap. King Black watched as his eyes fluttered open and then focused.

"What the fuck, my dude?" G-Swag said, after realizing he was naked. "What kind of homo shit are you on?"

King Black responded by unzipping the gallon sized Ziploc bag and pouring leeches and creek water over Swag's bloody midsection.

G-Swag's eyes bugged as the black worms attached themselves to his wounds.

"What the fuck?" G-Swag screamed. "What's this shit you put on me?"

"Leeches, motha' fucka'."

"Help, somebody help me, ahhhhhhhh!!!" G-Swag hollered.

King Black wanted to hear G-Swag's agonizing screams, but there was no telling how far away his security clowns were. He wasn't worried about the CIA, because they would have already stepped in if that had been their plan. Still, he needed to stop G-Swag's screams. He wrapped duct tape around his head and mouth. Next, he took the ice pick and stabbed small slits in G-Swags groin. His screams were muffled, but King Black knew that his enemy was in pain.

As he retrieved the small suitcase, he could hear the rats moving inside. From his pocket, he pulled out a few honey packets from Church's Chicken. After using his teeth to tear the plastic packets open he squeezed the honey out over G-Swag's groin and balls.

"This is for plotting on my momma and my little brother, bitch."

He spit in G-Swag's face before setting the black carry-on suitcase on its side. He unzipped the bag, then dashed over to the tomb. It was only six feet high, so he climbed on top where he watched.

First, one brown rat peaked out of the suitcase before ducking back inside. Then another peaked out and began climbing out. The rat stood next to G-Swag for a moment, sniffing.

"G-Swag looked like he was possessed the way he was jerking. Once the rodent saw that the body could only move so much, the rat charged toward G-Swag's groin. The others followed. And in minutes the rats were eating away at G-Swags dick and balls.

King Black had seen enough. He jumped down and ran, leaving the leeches and rats to feast on the biggest leech and rat of them all.

VERSE 32

King Black should have been exhausted, having travelled to five cities on two continents in three days, but he wasn't. He didn't have time to be exhausted or tired.

He hadn't seen Brandon in eighteen months, not since the night of the shooting. While Isis was sent to Cuba to support King Black during his rehabilitation Brandon was sent to the Truth Commissions underground central headquarters in Sweden to work on Bo Jack's and Tupac's upcoming album.

And then there was Tupac. The greatest voice and one of the greatest lyricists to ever spit on a microphone. Was he really alive? What did he look like after eighteen years? Was he as real as his lyrics? Where was his mind at after all these years?

Basil, Switzerland different from hot and sunny Cuba. It was cold and rainy.

He had wanted to call the emergency number Picasso had given him long before he went back to the States, but he didn't want to take a chance on the CIA somehow finding a way to listen in on a satellite call. On the drive, he kept looking out the side and back windows. Every car that got behind them, he suspected until they disappeared. He still couldn't believe Amber – if that was really her name – had played him, had played all of them. CIA. *Fuck!* he screamed in his mind.

After driving through mountain country for a couple hours, the Mercedes Benz pulled alongside a six-foot barbed wire fence. King Black wondered if the CIA were already there waiting—or worse, what if the U.S. Government sent a hit team? No. Lord, please no.

King Black hadn't said a word on the two and half hour drive and the Middle Eastern looking driver hadn't spoken either. Behind the fence in the near distance, there had to be over a hundred sheep grazing in the pasture. The car pulled up to a long metal red gate. After a few seconds, the gate electronically opened.

As the car pulled through the gate and into the driveway, King Black saw a blinking red light high up in some trees to the left. He slid down in the back seat. He didn't know if the red light was from a snipers infrared scope or if it was a surveillance camera movement detection light.

A couple minutes later the black Mercedes pulled up to a two story reddish brown barn door.

"Out," the bald, fat driver grunted after coming to a stop.

King Black didn't ask questions. He just opened the back door and reluctantly got out. The driver turned the large sedan around on the gray concrete barn floor before pulling out. As soon as the metal barn door electronically closed, King Black turned in time to see some stainless steel looking elevator doors open. He got on and right as the doors closed, he almost pissed himself upon seeing a blinking red light up in a ceiling corner of the huge hospital sterile looking empty barn. He put a hand over his heart after realizing that the light was attached to a camera.

There were no buttons to press inside the elevator. He didn't have to wait long before the elevator went down.

"King Black Uhuru Jones," Brandon greeted his older brother before the elevator doors opened all the way.

He shook his head from left to right. Brandon had gone from being tall and flagpole thin to a young black Hercules. "Bay bruh, what you been eating? Pancakes and steroids?"

"Can't get the mind right without doing the same to the body," Brandon said before the two brothers embraced.

"I'm sorry you had to...."

As if reading his older brother's mind, Brandon whispered, "I didn't have to do anything. You my brother, I love you and ain't no way I was going to lose you to that draconian Three Strikes law."

King Black pulled back from his now bigger brother. King Black smiled. "Last night, I took care of G-Swag."

Brandon shook his head. "Same old self-righteous hot head." Brandon looked up at King Black. "I know you're new to the Truth Commission, but come on, Black. You off on some cowboy-get-back shit when we trying to end a revolution before the powers that be figure out that they are even in a war. You all but fucked that up."

"Ho-ho-hold the hell on, bay bruh," King Black said, "I love you, but you need to back up off me with that."

Brandon took a step forward. "Back up off you. Big bruh, I ain't even begun to get up in yo' shit."

"H-Nic was my number one and ain't no way I was gon' let that slug ass nigga get away with what he did."

Brandon tapped a finger to the side of his own head. "You gotta think, Black. Think."

"I did. Bodying G-Swag consumed my thoughts from the time I found out he had H-Nic murked. Bitch made nigga stole my money, set me up on a phony drug beef, he had to leave this world."

"How'd that work out for you?"

"What you mean, Bran?"

"I'm sayin', now that G-Swag's a memory, is your bank account back on swole? Did H-Nic climb up from out the grave?"

"I don't like the way you comin' at me, bay bruh. I ain't feeling your tone," King Black said.

"You don't have a clue, Black!" Brandon said.

Both brothers stared at each other like two prize fighters about to square off for a fight.

"Black Uhuru," a familiar voice echoed. Tupac stepped through a steel door in the underground garage like open area, breaking up the tension between the two brothers.

"Pac," King Black said aloud, in awe of the man that walked across the gray concrete floor. Besides having a salt and pepper short beard and mustache, Tupac looked remarkably like he did eighteen years ago before he was supposed to have died.

"You got the gift, fam, but you on some Scarface shit," Tupac said standing beside King Black. "I know what type time you on, because I was livin' the same way back in the day. The way I was doing it, just gave ammunition to my critics and the media. My antics in the public entertained white folks, while they made my elders cringe in embarrassment. I was playin' get back games, letting my trigger finger go." The rap icon shook his head. "Fam, too many soldiers in the ground for bullshit, and ain't none of our dead soldiers perpetuated mass murder and rape of an entire people – black people, indigenous Hispanic and Native American people, the Chinese, Indian, the entire African peoples in the motherland." He looked at Brandon. "Li'l bruh here in his feelings because he see the shit we about to pull off, but now the game done changed after what you did to Swag," Tupac paused looking the young gun in the eyes, "Black, you went off on a Rambo mission that done drawn unwanted attention to what we doing."

"Yo, I fucked up, but I don't see how I jeopardized anything. I mean, I was in and out without no one seeing me. It was black-dark out when I did that slug."

"The CIA saw everything," Brandon interjected.

"What? How?" he asked.

"Amber Way," Brandon said.

"Fuck," King Black said putting a hand to his forehead. "Fuck! Fuck! Fuck!" He began to pace the floor. "Right before I did G-Swag, I heard him talking about how she was with CIA. Hold up." He turned to Brandon, just now realizing that Brandon had brought the CIA up and Amber's name. "Y'all knew she was CIA?"

"Of course," Brandon said.

King Black closed his eyes and breathed a sigh of relief. "How long?"

"Six years," Tupac said, "We got the intel right before you and Isis had the run in with Tarzan.

"Seriously? So, what the fuck. Y'all don't trust me? Y'all got me all up close and personal with the tramp." King Black was fuming. "Funky tramp coulda burned me. Y'all played me."

"Nah, fam it ain't even like that," Tupac said.

"So, tell me, playa, what's it like?"

"The Truth Commission's been around for damn near fifty years because information is only disseminated among the members on a need-to-know basis.

"Y'all didn't think I needed to know that Amber Way was CIA? I mean, we just spent the last few months together on a secluded fuckin' mountain."

"No, you didn't. We wanted everything to be natural. We wanted you to tell her whatever you felt comfortable sharing. The information you had was exactly what we wanted the CIA to know," Tupac said. "Amber is good fam—damn good—at reading people based on their behavior. Considering how much time you two have spent together over the last few months, if you knew who she was then, your behavior might have reflected your knowing, you might have held back, and as I said, Amber is a psychological profile specialist."

"Like the Behavioral Analyst unit on the TV show *Criminal Minds*?" King Black inquired.

"Yes, but she's better." Brandon said. "I think *Criminal Minds* calls it profiling. Well, we profiled Amber over the last five, six years and based on her past and her dissociative behavior, her loneliness, her always having to be a chameleon, we figured that given enough time, she would fall for you. After that, we'd be able to turn her and even if we didn't, we wanted the CIA to know who we are. And we wanted them to know about the compound in the mountains of Cuba. Don't worry, the compound has been evacuated. Isis is on the other side of the world."

"Shit, Amber knew!" King Black said.

"She knew what?" Tupac asked.

"That I was gunning for G-Swag."

"We figured as much," Brandon said.

"G-Swag's body disappeared shortly after you left the cemetery, "Tupac said, "And there hasn't been any news of Swag's death over the wire and you did him almost twenty-four hours ago."

"How'd you know the body disappeared?" King Black asked.

"The surveillance we had on you," Tupac said.

"Y'all watching me, too?" he asked.

"We watch everybody and everything. We even watch the watchers. How you think we've been able to stay under the radar for almost fifty years, fam?"

"I was well disguised and it was black-dark out, so whatever night vision cameras they used, still shouldn't be able to identify me."

"Black, the government got cameras in outer space that can take a high resolution picture of your fingerprint in the darkness. Besides, if they moved the body, they have no plans of bringing you into custody."

"So, where do we go from here?" King Black asked.

"All out," Brandon said.

"Huh?"

"Balls to the wall, baby," Tupac said. "Balls to the wall, ears to the beat, and mouth on the mike."

"The CIA has surveillance set up in the Sierra Maestra Mountains, thanks to Ms. Way. They know some of the players and we fed them the Barack Obama lifeline so they would panic and when people panic they make mistakes – even the government's alphabet boys. We got lucky when Amber came to kill you in the hospital."

"So, you knew G-Swag was plotting on H-Nic?" King Black asked Tupac.

"No," he lied, knowing that King Black wouldn't understand that in war even the good guys sometimes had to make the supreme sacrifice by giving up their lives. "We didn't know until Amber told you all that first day in Cuba."

VERSE 33

"Got damn son of a bitch is still alive." His west Texas Southern drawl was clearly evident as the director of the CIA frantically addressed the top assassins and covert specialists in the world. "You sons of bitches are supposed to be the best of the best, so how in the Sam damn hell could he still be alive?" Barack Obama's body had been dug up and a DNA sample had been taken from the dry bones in the casket.

In a calmer tone, the director asked, "So, what do we know about this Truth Commission?"

Bernie Schwartz, Amber's mentor and handler began. "Sir, at first we thought they were a spin-off of South Africa's Truth and Retaliation Commission, but now we know that one has nothing to do with the other."

"Son, do you think I give a good got damn about what the hell thoughts run through that tiny little pea brain of yours?" The director stared at the agent who had just spoken. "Well, do you?"

"Uhmm, no," Bernie said, unsure of what to say.

"How about you?" The director pointed to another agent sitting in the strategy room at CIA headquarters in Langley, Virginia. "How about you?" He pointed to a different agent this time.

"We know Fidel Castro is at the helm of the organization. We also know that they have a compound in the Sierra Maestra Mountains. We know that." The middle-aged bald handler looked to the paper in front of him, "Fidel and Raul Castro, Dr. Raena Harwell, Bo Jack Jones AKA King Black Uhuru Jones, Venezuelan president Hugo Chavez –

"The sixty-something-year-old director slammed a phone book thick file of papers on the huge conference table. "Son, are you going to frigging tell us something we don't frigging already know or are you going to continue wasting our frigging time with what the fuck we already frigging know?"

The director looked around at the twelve men in the room. "Secret Service is so busy fucking Columbian whores they let that bitch slip right through their hands," he mumbled.

"Excuse me, sir, but are you referring to Michelle Obama?"

The director looked over at the agent who'd just asked the last question. "No, I'm referring to Elizabeth frigging Taylor," he said before addressing all of the men in the room. "A black woman and two little girls just dissa-frigging-pere. I will take out that whole friggin' island before I allow that Muslim-change-we-can-believe-in-mud monkey to reappear and make us look like complete idiots. Charlie," he addressed the chief weapons expert in the room, "how quickly can you deploy a Cuban drone missile to the Florida peninsula?"

"You want a Cuban missile fired on Florida?" Charlie asked.

"I ask the frigging questions," the director barked. "Now how friggin' long?"

"Let's see." Charlie paused to collect his thoughts. "The USS Destroyer battle ship is currently about eighty miles north of Cuba, near the Florida Keys." He put a hand under his chin as he continued to contemplate. "I guess we could disguise one of our drones to look like a Cuban Missile in a few hours, let the paint set, put in the coordinates, load the missile." The chief weapons expert looked up. "Twenty-four hours, sir." Much louder and more assured Charlie said, "Sir, we could be ready in twenty-four hours from the time we got the green light."

"Franklin," the director barked at the chief political strategist. "I'll have Judy prepare a dossier on George Reyes. He's the Cuban who used to be CFO of Google. Impressive fella. Very smart, and most important, we can control him." The director paced the hardwood floor, thinking as he spoke. "We've been looking at Reyes for a while. He'll make the perfect president for the new democratic Cuba we are about to put in place after we bomb the frigging hell out of the island and get rid of them friggin' Commie bastard Castros."

"Sir," the man named Frank spoke, "you want me to commit Reyes background to memory and use it to convince him to be the next president of Cuba?"

"You got it, Ace. Take one of the jets. Fly to wherever he is. As soon as the missile hits Florida, Romney will call me. I'll tell him that this Truth Commission is Cuban based and are a real immediate and imminent threat to the American people." The director looked toward the CIA's chief media liason. "Mike, when the missile strikes Florida, you take care of the media. I want Cuba and this Truth Commission to become enemy number one, pronto." Turning his attention back to the chief weapons expert, he said, "Charlie, I don't want one, but two Cuban missiles to hit Miami in twenty-four hours. After the missiles hit, I want an all-out assault on Cuba and the Sierra Maestra Mountains. Shoulda' wiped out Cuba long ago. Above and below ground."

"What about the thousands of American lives that will be lost?" BS asked.

"Collateral damage. This is war."

"Who gave the green light on this, Chief?" the weapons expert asked.

"I gave the frigging green light, got damn it. Do you have any frigging idea what will happen if Obama resurfaces?" the director asked.

"We are keeping close tabs on Ms. Robinson, Michelle Obama's mother," another agent said, "and as you know Bo Jack Jones resurfaced forty-eight hours ago."

"A frigging twenty-six-year old rapper, kills Gregory Reagan, *Time* magazine's next Man of the Year. Ten years. I took us twelve years to make Reagan into the biggest negative influence in music on the urban community. The sagging pants, the body art rave, all G-Swag. He had done so much to influence violence, drug use, and self-hate. Shit," the director said.

The man in charge of the team that removed G-Swag from the cemetery said, "We still have Reagan on ice at the safe house in Louisville. What do you want done with the body, sir?"

"Burn it," the director said. "I don't give a good got damn about Reagan or that Jones boy. Hell, he's the least of our worries. We'll terminate him after we take care of this friggin' Truth Commission."

*****

38 hours later Thursday: May 15, 2014

"We can't even begin to describe the devastation," CNN's, Wayne Hunter said.

In the background people were screaming. "Dead bodies and animals are everywhere. Miami has been virtually leveled by a terrorist attack. At this time, we have no details to why, or who bombed the Florida peninsula." The fifty-year-old black journalist paused. He nodded. "I've just received word that a terrorist cell led by Cuban president Raul Castro is responsible for the carnage and destruction. The missiles are Cuban missiles."

*****

21 hours later Friday: May 16, 2014

A barrage of missiles exploded in the Sierra Maestra Mountains of Cuba, several more exploded in the capital city of Havana. There was still a significant loss of life on the island, but the vast majority of people took shelter in the two hundred or so underground bomb shelters Castro had built all over the island. The Castros had long ago begun planning for this day. Of course, there were some who didn't believe that America would attack. Clearly, they were wrong.

Amber Way had no idea of America's plan, and the members of the Truth Commission didn't warn her of America's plot to bomb the island nation. The Truth Commission wanted to show her that the CIA had no allegiance to her.

And she knew who she worked for and how ruthless and deceptive they could be, but she never would have thought the CIA would have forsaken her. It wasn't until about two AM, a couple hours before the first drone hit that she and the Cuban people were warned by a series of NCES's—National Cuban Emergency Sirens.

She sat on one of the two hundred twin beds in the part of the bunker she was ushered into. She never would have imagined that Bernie would've left her in the dark. After all she'd sacrificed. It was ironic that the people she was plotting to destroy had just saved her from the people she had pledged her allegiance and life to.

VERSE 34

Seventy-two hours later

The eighty-seven-year-old former Cuban leader almost fell into Michelle's arms as she opened the door to the suite.

The former first lady and her two girls had been a guest in the Peking, China hotel like mansion for a couple weeks now.

"They murdered Mariela, Nilsa, and my great nieces," Fidel cried.

"Momma," Sasha, Michelle's youngest, ran into the front room to see who was crying.

"Go back to bed sweetie. Everything's all right," Michelle told her twelve-year-old.

"Here, sit down." Michelle helped Fidel over to the couch.

"Fidel," Barack walked into the front room. "What happened? What's wrong?"

"The Americans killed two of my nieces and their children. Raul had a heart attack when he saw his children's dead bodies paraded over the Internet. What type of people do this? And what type of people follow a system that does this to women and children?" Fidel shook his head in disgust. "I have to get to Sweden. My brother needs me. They killed his babies and their babies. How could a country that speaks of democracy kill innocent women and children just to hurt the parents?" he asked again.

"If it weren't for the top one to three percent of the American people, we would be a true democracy, but Fidel, you know that America is a business and the powerbrokers do not care about anything but money and power," Michelle said.

"I should have made them leave Cuba after the strikes. I shouldn't have given them a choice. They wanted to stay and begin rebuilding. I never would have thought... Raul and I shouldn't have given them a choice. And now they are dead, slaughtered like wild animals."

"Don't blame yourself, Fidel." Michelle held the tired old man. "It wasn't your fault."

Barack stood next to the white leather couch while Fidel cried into his wife's arms.

"What about Alejandro, and Raul's other children and grandchildren – your children and grandchildren?" Michelle asked.

"They are safe. The Commission got them out."

"Does the family know of Raul's condition?" Barack asked.

"Picasso offered to fly down to Ghana, where the Truth Commission had sent my *familia*. He offered to inform them in person, but I asked him to wait until I see Raul. My *familia* is suffering enough already having to leave their homeland."

"What is the latest on Raul's condition?" Barack asked.

"Critical."

The former US president picked up the house phone and dialed Li Ki Shing's private cell number. He had the wealthiest man in Asia on the other line in seconds. Next, Barack went down the hall to Picasso's room.

Within the hour, Fidel and Picasso were on a helicopter on their way to a private airfield in Hong Kong, about a hundred miles from the Truth Commission's hotel sized Asian safe house where Michelle, Barak, Picasso, and other American Commission members were working.

After getting off of the helicopter Picasso helped the eighty-seven year old tired former leader board a private jet to be flown to Sweden where Raul was being looked after.

"Fifty-three years, it took me to make Cuba what it was. Fifty-five years of progress destroyed in less than a month's time." The former Cuban leader sighed.

"I know," Picasso said. He empathized with Fidel. His mother had been Cuban. When he was little, his mother often spoke of how Fidel liberated Cuba from the sadist American government pawn, Batiste. But, she also spoke of murder and other atrocities ordered by the former leader. But, Picasso knew that no government was perfect.

But, the merciless bombing campaign against Cuba, the sadistic murders of members of the Cuban Presidential family by the American government's alphabet boys was nothing short of evil. And, the bombing was a sign that the American power structure was panicking. "Change we can believe in," the slogan Picasso had wrote for the original Obama campaign was getting closer to being a reality. Barack Obama was truly a godsend. No other man in history could pull off what Barack had, influencing America into electing him, and giving it all up and disappearing.

For two years Barack's girls had thought their daddy was dead. Michelle had lived the life of the grieving widow and taking all of this into consideration, Picasso felt good about convincing Shing that the best place for Barack was in Peking with his family. Besides, Barack and Michelle had to finish revising the new United States Constitution and Bill of Rights that he, Barack, Gates, Picasso, Bill Clinton, Assata Shakur, and others helped to write. It had taken a year to do, but the new constitution and bill of rights were just about ready.

VERSE 35

In less than a month, the American media and the BBC had the world believing the Truth Commission was not only a national threat, but a world threat. The Truth Commission was said to have had ties with over twenty different terrorist groups around the world – Al-Qaeda, Shabab, Boko Haram, and even the Sudanese rebel slave traders to name a few. Every day, more negativity was spreading and the world got smaller for the world's new number one public enemy. It was only a matter of time before the world discovered all twelve of the Truth Commissions underground and above ground command centers around the world.

The underground compound in Basil, Sweden that sat under the sheep farm was the size of a small mall. It even had a state of the art hospital where Raul Castro had been recovering nicely for a week now.

While Fidel was at his brother's bedside, Picasso was in the underground state of the art recording studio listening to Tupac and King Black.

"I wasn't a killer until you smoked me. Now I'm back from the grave to tell the homies who you are, what you did," Tupac rapped with more passion than he did twenty years ago.

"As I walk through the valley of the shadow of death evil lurking everywhere that there's a breath," Bo Jack rapped.

A few minutes later, Picasso applauded. "Fellas," he pulled up his sleeve, "I've got goose bumps. What you just did? Those lyrics, Wow!"

"Preciate the love, fam. But yo, we need some things to really set this shit off. And word is bond, you get us what we need, we will have thirteen of the damnest tracks mixed down and ready in a couple weeks," Tupac said.

King Black smiled. "Straight up, Picasso, on everything I love, get us what we need and it's a wrap. Stick a fork in the U.S. government 'cause them faker lawmakers are done after we lay the shit down that Brandon and Pac been writing."

"Speaking of Brandon, where is li'l homie?" Picasso asked.

"He on the horn talkin' to moms," King Black said.

"Can you print out all the tracks? Let me read the lyrics. I'll send 'em up to the committee to read and if the rest is anything like what I just heard, than we will get you whatever you need," Picasso said.

Brandon opened the glass door and came into the studio.

"Bran-Bran, what up li'l homie?" Picasso asked.

Brandon lifted his head. "Kimani was taken into federal custody yesterday afternoon. This morning she was found dead in her cell."

"Noooo. No! No! No!" King Black shook his head.

Brandon continued in a monotone, "They say she hung herself with her belt."

"No! No! No!" King Black shouted, tears pouring down his face. King Black put his hands to his head and used the wall to brace his slide to the ground. "I never got the chance to tell her how I felt." He banged his head against the wall. "Why! She ain't have shit to do with none of this. I don't believe she took her own life." King Black looked up at Brandon. "What was she charged with?"

"Money laundering."

"That's bullshit and you know it, Bran. Kimani is straight as an arrow. And whose money was she suspected of laundering?"

"Yours," Brandon replied.

VERSE 36

Memorial Day weekend for black folks meant cooking out and spending time with friends and family. It didn't matter if you were paid or broke, if you were black you were at someone's cookout. Andre 'Dr. Dre' Young arguably the greatest DJ that ever put a beat to words had sponsored and hosted a quarter million-dollar cook out slash blockparty in his hood in Compton, California where he grew up. It was late. Dre' was on his way to his beach house in Malibu when flashing blue lights came out of nowhere. He pulled his million dollar Bugatti over. Two officers got out of the police cruiser, one walking up on each side of the white convertible. Dre' was reaching for his wallet when the officer at his door said, "Step out of the vehicle, Mr. Young."

Too familiar with the Gestapo like LAPD, the mega hip hop producer slowly stepped out with his hands in the air.

At the same time, across the country in Long Island, Nas and Mos Def were laying down tracks for Nas's upcoming *FREEDOM* album. Unfortunately for them, they were in Nas's soundproofed home studio when a half a dozen men in black with the word POLICE stenciled in white letters stretched vertically across the front of their black Tees, broke into the multi-million dollar home and drew down on the two rappers.

At the same time, fifteen hundred miles south of Nas's house, Michael Griffin AKA Rakim from Eric B. and Rakim was sound asleep in Miami when the police quietly came into the penthouse condo, and arrested the living rap legend. The woman with Rakim began to protest but the gun in her face stopped her.

Common and Erykah Badu were vacationing in the South of France when the police came into their bungalow late at night and arrested them.

All of the arrests were very discreet; no paparazzi, no witnesses.

Over the last month, the television broadcasted images of terroristic acts by the Cuban military on their own people. The actors that the NSA hired did an excellent job of convincing the American people that Raul Castro was perpetuating genocide, killing his own people. The actors portrayed themselves as Cuban refugees and other Cubans who spoke out on national and international TV against the terroristic fifty-five year reign of the Castro's.

*****

"Don't you think that's a little overkill," George Bush Sr. the former president asked the CIA director.

"Hell no. GB, this is all-out war. This shit storm was thrown at me overnight. The Truth Commission wasn't on any of our radars. None of our informants had heard of them. What the friggin' hell is this world coming to when assholes like these truth fuckers fly under our radar without us knowing who the hell they are? So, the actors we hired to protest Communism in Cuba and the short documentary we put together with Cubans denouncing Castro is priceless. If the American people didn't hate the Castros before, they sure as hell do now."

"I'm not talking about the Cuban people you hired to make Castro look like Genghis Khan. That was good. I'm talking about this nuclear threat. You know good and well Cuba doesn't have any nukes. I never sold to them," George Bush said.

"We have to do what we did after nine-eleven. We have to pull out all stops to scare the American people. When they fear, they follow. We blamed the Taliban for nine-eleven and days later we shifted our focus to Hussein and Iraq. The American people were too shocked and too scared to think. All they knew was the government had to protect them," the director said. "GB, our mistake with Vietnam was that we didn't put the fear of death in the American people."

"I have no problem with the fear factor. I created the fear campaign, but you can't create fear without knowing who the factor is," George said.

"In almost any other circumstance I would agree, but we don't know ape shit about them truth fuckers and we need to wipe them off the friggin' map. Hell, we bombed the fucker at the beginning of the month and now three weeks later we just now discovering a two square mile underground compound in the Cuban Mountains. You have any idea how long that would take to build, GB? That place was clean. No prints, no evidence. It's like these fuckers prepared for us to bomb them and it looks as if they planned for us to find their compound."

"This is exactly why I am thinking that we need to gather more information before you act any further."

The director gave the former CIA director and former president an incredulous look. "GB, you done gone soft in your old age. What we supposed to do, let these commie bastards destroy our way of life while we gather information?"

"I was trying to give you my expert advice, but now I'm ordering you to stand down until we find out more about this Truth Commission. Do you understand me?" George Bush Senior asked.

"Yes sir, loud and clear. Loud and frigging clear."

"I've spoken to the other families," the forty-first president said. "We've agreed to supply you with unlimited resources, pay whoever whatever you have to, but get us the information so we can effectively, quietly, and swiftly wipe them off of the face of the earth."

"Yes, sir."

Bush continued, "I need to speak with Agent Way alone, ASAP."

The director shook his head. "We didn't get her out."

"What did you just say?"

"I said, we didn't get her out, sir."

"So, you left her in the mountains to die?" the former president and head of the CIA asked.

"I had to make a decision and getting her out would've taken time, and time we don't have. I had to act while we had the element of surprise on our end."

"So," the former president closed his eyes and thought of ice cream and Oreo cookies for ten seconds, like his stress-relief coach had suggested. "You just left her there to divulge our secrets."

"We've had Amber since she was –"

"I know how long she's been with the agency. I knew her parents. I didn't ask for her bio."

"Nine times out of ten, she's dead," the director said, not believing what he was saying.

VERSE 37

Tuesday, September 2, 2014

At ten o'clock that morning *The Resurrection* was released on iTunes and any other medium where people downloaded music. Five hours later, every media outlet in the nation was talking about the album. At four o'clock, tickets went on sale for the Resurrection Revolution concert to be held at Giants stadium in eleven days on September 13. Within four hours of the sale, all eighty thousand plus seats were sold out.

It had been ninety-two days since the Truth Commission had kidnapped the hip-hop music icons and brought them and those in their households to Sweden. Of course, the six music icons and their families were fire hot mad at being kidnapped until they saw Tupac. And then they were bug-eyed, droop-jawed shocked into awe. Common, Rakim, Dre', Nas, Mos Def, Erykah Badu, none of them could believe their eyes.

It took a couple days before everyone understood what had been in the works for almost fifty years, and because of who they all were and what the six conscious brothers and sister had all gone through in their lives, they were immediately one hundred percent down to help emancipate the slaves as Tupac and Brandon referred to the Black, Hispanic, and poor peoples of America.

All of the music icons Tupac and King Black had selected were thinkers and readers. All of them knew their history and was adamant about teaching others through their lyrics as they had done for years.

Although the group had never seen the former president, they believed Barack Obama was alive as Tupac, Picasso, and King Black had said.

Fidel and Raul were in Ghana with their families while the eight music icons laid out thirteen tracks of conscious Hip Hop with an R&B flavor. Rakim and Erykah changed up some of their verses and some of the other lyrics for the better. It took almost eleven weeks, nine weeks longer than Pac and Black had initially thought, but by mid-August *The Resurrection* was a reality.

Within hours of its release today the album had gone viral like nothing ever seen in history. If anyone involved with the project and the Truth Commission ever questioned if God really existed, they got their answer that day. No one involved, not even the Truth Commissions top strategists came even close to anticipating the millions that were downloading the album around the world in record time.

Tupac's name was nowhere on any credits, although the rapper identified himself as Tupac Shakur and Makaveli throughout the album. On one of the albums tracks, "Soldier of Fortune," Tupac even explained how the CIA had tried to have him killed back in '96.

In less than ten days, the album had gone quadruple platinum, something that had never been done in such a short

336

time. Eight of the thirteen tracks were already on Billboard's top ten. King Black, Tupac, Nas, and Common held down the number one spot with the title track "National Anthem." This one song spoke of a New America, and how it would be run.

A huge part of the album's success was because of Tupac. When interviewed over the last few days since the album's unpublicized release, his mother, relatives and friends didn't know what to think or believe. Like everyone else in the world, they didn't even know the album was in the works. Besides, they had seen Tupac for themselves in his casket, but the rapper on "The Resurrection" album sounded just like the loved one they buried eighteen years ago. The world wanted to know who this guy was, rhyming on the album, claiming and sounding like the Tupac of old.

Not even the top nine families that controlled the hands of U.S. government could prevent the story from going viral like the "Resurrection" album had. *Conspiracy or Piracy* was the name of the *New York Times* front page story, replacing news about Cuba and how America was going to rebuild the war torn island nation and help stabilize its economy. America's new lead story was Tupac Shakur and the Super Eight as Erykah Badu had affectionately named the players performing on the album.

None of the Super Eight were under arrest, but the media were going crazy with the story and would stop at nothing to find out who the performer claiming to be Tupac was. And the Truth Commission knew that it was only a matter of time before the NSA, CIA, FBI and the other alphabet boys would be after the group.

What the Truth Commission or the albums players didn't know was that the NSA and CIA were coordinating all of their efforts to take the eight performers discreetly after their concert at Giants stadium in Jersey next Saturday. The government's number one covert killers, interrogation specialists, behavioral analysts, and historians knew that the

Truth Commission was much bigger and more organized than they initially thought and they didn't want the Truth Commission to see them coming or know that they were coming, so they decided to let the Truth Commission come to them.

The CIA director, President Romney, and the head of the NSA were in agreement that over 80,000 screaming fans would make the perfect cover to kidnap the group and literally bleed them for information until they had no blood left. And since none of the Super Eight had spoken to the media, then no one but them and the CIA knew that Tupac was really alive. The government had only known for a week. Digging up Tupac's body wasn't the problem, the DNA testing and retesting took time. But after the concert, no one would ever hear from the Super Eight again. The government's media propaganda machine would find a way to explain away the Tupac performance and the disappearance of the others.

"Gentlemen, I expect this problem to be handled by the time I speak at the United Nations week after next," President Romney said to the heads of the top American intelligence agencies.

VERSE 38

On September 2nd, the morning of the album release the Truth Commission flew the kidnapped recording artists back into the states. By September 3rd the Truth Commission realized they'd made a big mistake sending them back to the states. Media crews from all around the world smothered whatever area the recording artists were. Things became so crazy so fast, that the Truth Commission couldn't immediately get Nas, Mos Def, Common, Dre', Erykah, and Rakim back out of the country without attracting the attention of the alphabet boys. On top of that, the six that were stateside were being closely monitored by the alphabet boys too – but not close enough.

The Truth Commissions covert specialists had to tranquilize over eighty alphabet boy field agents before getting all six members to safety the second day after the release. For the next nine days leading up to the concert, the eight group members lived together and rehearsed in the underground compound Bill Gates had built in Idaho back in the early nineties not long after Microsoft went public.

On September 11th, two days before the concert, the Super Eight got onto a custom black titanium bulletproof bus and began their two day trek to the stadium. As to avoid any trouble by the alphabet boys, the Truth Commission leaked the bus trip to the media. And before the bus got out of Idaho, helicopters, vans, and thousands of fans followed and filmed the busses two day journey from Idaho to New York Giants Met Life Stadium in East Rutherford, New Jersey.

The morning of the concert P. Diddy had a ten-man crew prepare the stadium for the concert. P. Diddy promised each man a thousand dollar bonus the day after the concert if nothing about the stage setup was in the media before the concert began.

Twenty-four hours ago, you could hear your voice echo in the empty stadium as the Giants played their last preseason game of the year. Giants fans had a hard time getting out of the stadium, so many cars and people were already there, camping out for the sold-out concert.

*****

The Truth Commission players had everything and everyone in place, as tonight was the beginning of a new era. And the Truth Commission had no doubt that the fireworks would be set all the way off tonight. All eight hip-hop icons new of the dangers that they would be facing by performing that evening, and not one wavered from wanting to do the show.

*****

It was a breezy seventy degrees at ten o'clock that night in East Rutherford. Over 80,000 fans were screaming as King Black's intro to "Trick Ass Nigga's" began playing to the capacity sell-out audience.

The stadium football field began to shake as if an earthquake were in progress. Moments later, the grass and dirt began to move. *"Trick ass niggas can get it for free. You got the right one fuckin' with me,"* King Black's voice echoed around the stadium as eighty thousand fans sang, passed out and hollered while eight black coffins came out of the earth.

Over seventy five percent of the world's multimedia websites had the concert streaming live, thanks to Microsoft founder and Truth Commission member, Bill Gates.

Millions, possibly a billion people around the world saw the eight black caskets sitting upright. They heard the bass dropping. They heard the 80,000 screaming fans chanting the hook to King Black's megahit when the casket doors opened and one by one each member emerged through a cloud of thick white smoke wearing white linen suits and dark glasses. The internet zoomed in on the eighth casket where Tupac Amaru Shakur stepped out of.

Suddenly the music stopped. Everything went quiet. People all over the world thought it was a trick. Like what Dr. Dre' did back in 2012 at the Coachella fest when he and Snoop Dogg performed with a holographic image of Tupac. But this definitely wasn't an image as thousands, millions of fans and viewers saw for themselves.

If the *Guinness Book of World Records* had a category for the longest and loudest collective sigh, then the 80,000 plus capacity crowd now held that record as they looked at Tupac.

Internet viewers around the world thought this was an advanced image until the forty-three-year old legend stepped forward, put the mic to his lips, held a fist in the air and sang,
"Makaveli in this killuminati, all through your body.
This shit is real fam, feel me!

And God said he should send his son to lead the wild into the ways of man.
Out of the forest and off the desert sand
before I had the chance to lead a nation to the promised land
they tried to cut me off at the knee
sent the CIA for me,
had to get MIA to stay free
so I could be me
eighteen years later to the day
400 years work with no pay,
with my lyrical sword, the alphabet boys,
one by one I'll slay,
so follow me into a new day and a new way
as we decree a New America out of the rubble of racism
and any other ism that interferes with the schism
of the new nation rhythm we about to throw down for the lay down."

The other seven sang the chorus as the music blasted from the stadium speakers.

"Come with me
as we fight
the powers that be
Now do you want to ride or die.
Da-dadada daaadada."

King Black stepped forward reciting a verse from Tupac's 1996 hit Hail Mary,

"I ain't a killer but don't push me."

Tupac sang,

"Revenge is like the sweetest joy next to getting pussy."

People were fainting in the stands. The music was so loud, the stadium was so electric that the two back up agents didn't see the straw or the poisonous darts.

Now that all of the CIA field agents where incapacitated, Amber could get to the Super Eight before it was too late.

VERSE 39

"I don't give a coon's ass what you got on him. This is a matter of national friggin' security, son. I said to have your men stand down, Captain. Do not, and I repeat do not arrest Bo Jack Jones. And if you have a problem with that I can have the friggin' president call you. And son, you don't want Romney to call. He'll chew you a new ass as sure as shit stinks," the sixty something year old, CIA director spoke into the phone's receiver. "Do we have a problem, Captain?"

"No sir," the East Rutherford, New Jersey police chief said.

Hell, the chief could care less about the rapper. He was doing a favor for his old golfing buddy, Chief Dobbins down in Atlanta. Yeah, the arrest would make him look good in a couple years when he'd run for mayor, but he couldn't win a seat on the school board if he defied a direct order from the president.

So, when one of his men had radioed in about seeing a suspicious black woman with dreadlocks coming from under a black Chevy Tahoe with government tags on it, he told his man to watch her since they weren't going to arrest the rapper.

*****

No sooner than the gray haired CIA director had hung up the phone another call came in. "Yeah," he barked into the phone.

"Huey is at the bottom of the Hudson," the voice on the other end said.

"Survivors?" the director barked.

"Zero," the voice shot back.

Huey was the code name for the large helicopter that was going to land inside the stadium and whisk the Super Eight away after the concert.

The Truth Commission was efficient, damn efficient the director thought, but no one was more thorough than the CIA. The way the workers prepared the stage this morning, the metal ropes, the helicopter handles on the caskets, it was almost perfect. The only logical way out was through the sky. The rappers had to know we were coming, but they didn't know from which direction the director thought as he waited in the situation room at CIA headquarters in Virginia.

*****

Back in East Rutherford, the Super Eight were ending the concert. There was no sign of the helicopter, but there wouldn't be, everything was timed right down to the minute.

"Fam, we wanna thank you all for coming out supporting, but we still have a lot of work to do. Tonight is the end to oppression. Tonight is the end of institutional slavery. Tonight is the end of laws that only work for the haves and not the have nots," Tupac said. "Tonight is the end of the old constitution, the old branches of government. Tomorrow we will all be free." Tupac said to overwhelming applause.

All of a sudden a huge plume of white smoke surrounded the stage. Visibility was zero within seconds.

Amber Way appeared out of nowhere, she had a gun to Tupac's head. "Come with me or he definitely won't come back from the dead again," she said referring to Tupac.

The group followed her through a tunnel. While they were leaving through the smoke, eight high powered magnetic clamps locked onto each closed empty casket. In less than five minutes, the caskets were being lifted out of the stadium while the Super Eight, plus Amber climbed down something that looked like a manhole in the back of the stadium.

"Look, I am CIA, I mean I was CIA until," she looked at King Black, "until I discovered who I really was."

"You sure your change of heart didn't have nothing to do with them alphabet boys leaving you in Cuba when they set them bombs off?" King Black asked.

"My change of heart and why I'm here has a lot to do with them fuckers leaving me to die in Cuba." She looked into King Black's dark brown eyes. "But, it was you, King, who taught me how to think, how to see what was real."

"So why do you have a gun to my man's head and why'd you drag us down here?" King Black asked.

"Because I'm your best and only shot at waking up next time you sleep."

The others were silent.

She let Tupac go and threw Black her gun. "Shoot me."

He took seven steps forward until he was face to face with Amber. He checked to make sure a bullet was in the chamber. He put it to her head. "You hired the men who killed my best friend. You lied to me about everything. You stole from me."

"I didn't lie about everything." Her voice didn't waver as she spoke with the barrel of a loaded .45 pressed against her forehead. "And, I never stole anything from you, King."

"What didn't you lie about?" King Black asked.

"My smile. My laughter, they were genuine. And you can't name one thing that I ever stole from you."

"Wrong. What you stole from me is the only reason that you are still breathing."

"Bullshit," she said. "Stop running your mouth and pull the trigger, you need every second, because when the CIA and NSA discover those empty caskets, they will shut down the city and trust me King, they can do it and do it fast. So pull it!"

If he put a bullet in her head and she was telling the truth, then they'd all die. But if he let her live they still might all die, but something in her voice told him that she wasn't lying. He lowered the gun. He decided to play the game, see what happened. "I can't kill you until you return my heart." He smiled hoping she would buy the lame line he had just thrown out. They embraced.

"Ain't no time for that now," Rakim said. "We need to get as far away from here as fast as we can.

Minutes later, one by one, each music icon came out of a manhole that was located right under a black Tahoe SUV with government issued plates. The eight hip-hop stars piled into the Black SUV and before they were out of the stadium parking lot they were surrounded by East Rutherford, New Jersey police.

*****

While the Super Eight were being arrested for stealing government vehicles, six MX-65 jet plane-nuclear missiles were headed toward the United States. The six flying bombs could take out the entire eastern seaboard and most of the Midwest.

VERSE 40

The director was just about to call George Bush Senior and tell him that the CIA lost eight world-renowned hip-hoppers. Not KGB spies, not Special forces gone rogue, not Islamic fundamentalists, but friggin' song and dance men and women. It was definitely time for him to trade his service revolver in for a fishing pole. Forty-three years with the agency and he had never lost a man once they were in his grasp.

Right as he picked up the phone to call the former republican president, his other line rang.

"Yeah," he answered.

"Sir, this is Captain –"

"I got caller ID, I know who this is."

"Just calling to give you heads up. My guys just arrested King Black."

"I told you to stand down!"

"Yes you did sir, but earlier one of my guys saw a black girl disappear under a black Tahoe with government plates. When she didn't come from under the truck –"

"Cut to the chase, son. I ain't got all night," the director said.

"My boys arrested them for car theft."

"Them?" the director inquired.

"All of the performers, eight, well nine including the girl."

"Where are they now?" the director asked.

"On their way to the station."

"I'll send some of my guys down there," the director said before thinking of something else, "What was the girl's name?"

"Erykah Badu."

"No, idi... I mean Captain. I'm talking about the other girl."

"Angel Simone," the captain replied.

The director didn't know why he asked about a name. If it was Amber, she'd be using a different name. The director continued, "She wouldn't by chance have a heart shaped birth mark on her right forearm?"

"I don't know. Like I said, sir, they haven't reached me at the station."

"Got damn it, call 'em on the radio, I need to know about that tattoo now. You have no friggin' clue who you might have in the back of one of your cruisers."

"They should be here in say five, ten minutes, tops," the Captain said.

"That could be five, ten minutes too friggin' late. Now radio your men, Captain and get back with me pronto!" The director slammed the phone down.

*****

348

There were nine people packed into three Dodge Charger police cruiser back seats. Amber sat between Tupac and King Black in the last of the three car procession.

"My hair, twelfth dread from the dark brown one right above the end of my left eyebrow. Use your teeth," she whispered to Tupac.

"Get all that in now," the nosy officer in the passenger seat said looking at Tupac who looked to be playing in Amber's hair with his mouth, "'cause you'll be in lock up until at the earliest Monday morning. That's if you make the judge's docket. We've had a busy weekend with you folks bringing the world to town."

In no time, Tupac removed the nail-sized pick. A few blocks later, the three cars paused at a traffic light. Amber watched the cops in the front seat while she used the curved straight pin to unlock her cuffs. She waited until the cops were engaged in conversation with each other before reaching up and removing two darts and a straw from her dreads. In the blink of an eye, she loaded a dart in the straw and put it to her lips.

"Hey," was all the cop in the passenger seat said. His last vision was of a heart shaped birthmark on Amber's forearm. And the driver never saw the dart or the straw.

The light turned green, thank God, King Black thought. Because the cruiser was moving slow. The driver's foot relaxed and the car was still in drive. The two cruisers with the others in it were getting further and further ahead.

"Feet up," Amber shouted.

Tupac and King Black followed Amber as she kicked at the metal cage that separated them from the cops up front. The third kick dislodged the cage just enough for Amber to squeeze her body through. She was able to jam the gearshift in park before they ran into a light post.

The other cars had stopped a couple blocks ahead.

"What's going on back there? Smitty? Marty?" the police radio cackled. "Smitty? Marty? Pick up. Over."

The two cruisers ahead were turning around by the time Amber had squeezed her small frame all the way through the metal screen and was now sitting on a laptop between the unconscious driver and his sleeping partner.

She reached over the driver and opened the door, before pushing him out onto the side of the street next to the light post they almost collided with.

"Duck," Tupac shouted right before the cop that was riding shotgun in the fast approaching Dodge police cruiser, fired five shots in succession at the cruiser they were in. Amber didn't have time to duck; besides, the new police cruisers had bulletproof windows. She was in the driver's seat, her foot on the gas, her hand on the gearshift.

The first cruiser skidded to a stop in front of Amber, Tupac and King Black.

"Get out of the car, slowly," a cop in the car in front bellowed over a loudspeaker.

Amber's response was rubber burning and then the cruiser sped off in reverse.

"Shit, that fool has a shotgun," King Black said, right before the front window cracked behind the force of the shotgun bullet.

Amber was unfazed. She slammed on brakes while whipping the steering wheel to the right causing the car to fishtail one hundred and eighty degrees. She slammed the gearshift in low and hit the gas. She drove right past the police who had just tried to shoot them with a shotgun.

"Shit!" Tupac and King Black cursed at the same time as Amber jumped across the median and was doing a hundred down the wrong side of the expressway. Only one cruiser was in sight as Amber expertly dodged sparse cars in two AM New Jersey traffic.

VERSE 41

Leaders from all over the world where in Geneva for the World Energy Conservation conference. All one hundred and ninety UN member countries had leaders and state representatives there. This conference was extremely high priority and the security at the UN building in the Swedish capital city was better than in an American maximum security prison, at least that's what the media had reported.

French socialist president Francois Hollande was speaking when the three Jumbotrons in the theatre like conference room came to life. The UN delegates stared at themselves and the conference hall on the Jumbotrons before the massive sixteen-foot high, dark wood double doors electronically opened.

The two hundred plus faces looked as if they'd seen a ghost. Most thought they were looking at one as Barack Obama was followed by Bill Gates, Assata Shakur, former joint chief of staff Colin Powell, and former president Bill Clinton – all members of the Truth Commission.

"Ladies and gentlemen," Barack held his hands in the air, "as you can see I am not dead. No thanks to the CIA and NSA and those pulling their strings. As you all know, America is the land of the deceitful, and the home of the thieves," he said with calm. "My words today will draw anger. But what you will see on the Jumbotrons, on Facebook, Twitter, and almost anywhere you go on the web should disgust and anger you to no end. Many of you in this room will call me traitor, but how can I be a traitor when the only thing I have to trade is my life. I own nothing. At any time what I think I own can be taken and probably will be taken. If you will all turn your attention to the Jumbotrons." He turned and pointed to the huge screens behind him.

The director of the CIA appeared on the screen. His face was red as he spoke to several middle aged men. "No, I'm referring to Elizabeth frigging Taylor," he said before addressing all of the men in the room. "A black woman and two little girls just dissa-frigging-pere. I will take out that whole friggin' island before I allow that Muslim-change-we-can-believe-in-mud monkey to reappear and make us look like complete idiots. Charlie," he addressed the chief weapons expert in the room, "how quickly can you deploy a Cuban drone missile to the Florida Peninsula?"

The entire U.N. body of representatives gasped at what they had just heard.

"You want a Cuban missile fired on Florida?" the weapons expert asked.

"I ask the frigging questions," the director barked. "Now how friggin' long?"

"Let's see... the USS Destroyer battle ship is currently about eighty miles north of Cuba, near the Florida Keys." He put a hand under his chin. "I guess we could disguise one of our drones to look like a Cuban Missile in a few hours, let the paint set, put in the coordinates, load the missile," the chief weapons expert looked up, "twenty-four hours, sir. Sir, we could be ready in twenty-four hours from the time we got the green light."

"Franklin," the director barked at the chief political strategist. "I'll have Judy prepare a dossier on George Reyes. He's the Cuban who used to be CFO of Google. Impressive fella. Smart, and most important, we can control him."

The Jumbotrons went black. Barack continued, "Do you really want to be a patriot to a country like that? A country that destroys another nation, mass murders that nations people in hopes of killing one man, me. A country with military bases in everyone else's backyard because she's afraid that the world will one day retaliate for all of the suffering she has caused? Do you wanna be a patriot to a country that has 4.5 percent of the world population but has 25% of the world's prison inmate population? Or how about a country that cares more about killing for oil than it does about healing its own sick?"

Mitt Romney stood, but the two delegates beside him pulled him back down in his seat. Barack continued, "When I was in the oval office I couldn't help the poor for the rich getting in the way. I promised jobs, but if big business didn't benefit exponentially, my plans were killed in the House, the Senate or both."

The former president turned to the screen above him. "Take another look at America," he said. The huge screens came back to life. Again, the director of the CIA, and others appeared.

Everyone watched the scene play out....

"The detonators have been put in place, sir. Once the first plane makes impact, I'll use a remote to begin detonating the explosives," the unidentified man said to the CIA director.

"Timing is everything. Are you sure that the World Trade Center will come down and no one will see the small explosions?"

"No, sir. The explosions will not be seen as the C4 will only impact the buildings foundation. But I must warn you gentlemen, that any civil engineer with a set of blueprints will know that it is impossible for the World Trade Center building to crumble as a result of the two jet planes that will crash into the building from up high."

"And your point is," then-vice president Dick Cheney asked.

The weapons expert continued, "I don't see how you are going to convince the world that two jet planes made the World Trade Center crumble."

The director of the NSA spoke. "We turn the people's attention from *how* the building came down to *who* made it come down. We'll use the media to create mass fear. The American people will be terrified. Passenger airliners hijacked and driven into the World Trade Center, lives lost, we use the media to make the American people feel vulnerable."

"But, why blame Osama Bin Laden when Iraqi and Kuwait oil is what we are after?"

Collective gasps were heard throughout the room from the two hundred world leaders in the assembly. No one could believe what they were seeing and hearing. The video was time and date stamped. The world viewing clearly saw the February, 2001 date at the bottom left of the screen – eight months before the horrific World Trade Center disaster.

The picture on the Jumbotrons and on the internet changed.

"I don't have to explain what you just witnessed," Barack Obama said, "and there is so much more that will be streaming over the net all day today, but now what you are looking at is an MX-65. It is made out of a special material that can't be detected on radar. There are six of these planes in the

United States. If this one plane detonates, millions of lives will be lost from South Carolina to New York. Over the next few hours, the next few days, and months, a new government, a new constitution, a new bill of rights, will be put in place. After meeting with the heads of China, France, Venezuela, and several other countries upon seeing the evidence against America they have agreed to aid in America's rehabilitation."

Hugo Chavez stood and led the applause from the U.N. delegates.

After the applause died, the former president continued, "A few things, since the world is watching on computers all over the globe. Let me say to all of the non-violent drug offenders, rotting in prisons all over America, to the political prisoners, such as Sundiata Accoli, Mutulu Shakur, and Mumia Abu Jamal pack your things, you're coming home."

The former president changed directions. "To the oil companies, the pharmaceutical companies, Wal-Marts, and even my good friend," he put a hand on Bill Gates's shoulder, "the one to three percent who have and control more the ninety-five percent of America's wealth will be marginalized. They will pay off the American national debt. They will pay for the reparations start up fees for over 400 years of African-American suffering. They will provide monies to help us clean up the American streets and the ozone. And there will be no vote, no discussion, you will do what we have set in place."

*****

Back in the U.S. The CIA, NSA, and all of the government's alphabet boys scrambled to track down these missiles, while some were preparing a team to go to Richmond, Virginia where one of the missiles hid in a huge tobacco field.

*****

Back in Geneva, Barack Obama pointed a finger straight ahead before continuing, "CIA director Charles James, you will be brought up on war crimes, Dick Cheney, George Bush Senior and Junior. You too will both be brought up on war crimes and tried by a special tribunal and jury made up of Iraqis, Iranians, Libyans, and African-Americans. Until we have a new government in place, it has been agreed upon by a council of world leaders that I will resume the position as president of the United States, and all of America will be united and equally free. Now, as for the plane in Virginia ," Barack pointed at the Jumbotrons. "We will allow U.S. inspectors to search the plane and its contents, so you can see that we are for real. If any attempt is made to disarm or remove any of the plane's contents, you will be responsible for the millions of lives that will be lost from the detonation of the missile you attempted to tamper with."

"Mr. President," Venezuelan president Hugo Chavez raised his hand.

"Mr. President," President Obama conceded.

"What do you plan to do about Cuba?"

"Thanks to these new sanctions on big business, we will not only rebuild Cuba better than it was before. We are also lifting all the sanctions on Cuba and those responsible for the bombings will be brought to justice and judged by a special tribunal and jury of Cubans." The president put a hand over his heart. "My heart goes out to the Castro family and to President Raul Castro who can now come out of exile and go home."

"Mr. President," Felipe Calderon, the Mexican president raised his hand.

"Mr. President," President Obama conceded.

"What if America does not give in to your demands?" the Mexican president asked.

"I, *we* are not asking for anyone to give in to anything. We are taking what we demand. As America has taken so much from so many, it is her time to pay up."

THE FINAL CHORUS

Thirteen Months later: October 16, 2015

"Good morning, my name is Wayne Hunter with CNN. On the twentieth anniversary of the Million Man March, I'm reporting to you live from outside of the Richard Russell Federal building and courthouse in downtown Atlanta," CNN's top correspondent said. "As you can see, a steady procession of men and women, mostly black are being released from prison. Over there across the street you can see the police barricades."

Mostly white men held signs protesting the mass release of non-violent drug offenders.

Turning his attention back to the procession, the Pulitzer Prize winning journalist stopped one young black man. "Sir, can you tell us your name and how you feel to be free?"

Tears were in the young man's eyes. "My name is Trayvon Davis. I never thought I'd see the streets again. President Obama and the Truth Commission finished the job

Moses and Jesus started a few thousand years ago," the young man said.

The journalist stopped another young black man. "Sir, what are you going to do now that you have another chance at life?" Hunter asked before putting the microphone in the young man's face.

"First, I'm going to church. If I don't give it all the way up to God, I might as well go back to where I came from. And I after I go to church, I'm going to take advantage of the reparations college plan. I gotta get me some of this knowledge so I can help President Obama build a New America."

The fifty-two-year-old black male journalist stopped another. "Sir, what was your first thought after walking out of prison a free man?"

The man thought a second before saying, "My first thought was how hard I was going to have to work on staying free."

THE BEGINNING